# The Way, the Truth and the Dead

Francis Pryor



Unbound

**Unbound**

This edition first published in 2017

Unbound
6th Floor Mutual House, 70 Conduit Street, London W1S 2GF
www.unbound.com



Text Design by Ellipsis Digital Limited, Glasgow

A CIP record for this book is available from the British Library

ISBN 978-1-78352-326-9 (trade hbk)
ISBN 978-1-78352-327-6 (ebook)
ISBN 978-1-78352-328-3 (limited edition)

Printed in Great Britain by Clays Ltd, St Ives Plc

1 3 5 7 9 8 6 4 2

Dear Reader,

The book you are holding came about in a rather different way to most others. It was funded directly by readers through a new website: Unbound. Unbound is the creation of three writers. We started the company because we believed there had to be a better deal for both writers and readers. On the Unbound website, authors share the ideas for the books they want to write directly with readers. If enough of you support the book by pledging for it in advance, we produce a beautifully bound special subscribers' edition and distribute a regular edition and e-book wherever books are sold, in shops and online.

This new way of publishing is actually a very old idea (Samuel Johnson funded his dictionary this way). We're just using the internet to build each writer a network of patrons. At the back of this book, you'll find the names of all the people who made it happen.

Publishing in this way means readers are no longer just passive consumers of the books they buy, and authors are free to write the books they really want. They get a much fairer return too – half the profits their books generate, rather than a tiny percentage of the cover price.

If you're not yet a subscriber, we hope that you'll want to join our publishing revolution and have your name listed in one of our books in the future. To get you started, here is a £5 discount on your first pledge. Just visit unbound.com, make your pledge and type **theway** in the promo code box when you check out.

Thank you for your support,

Dan, Justin and John
Founders, Unbound

# The Way, the Truth and the Dead

# Prologue

Bert Hickson had seen many mutilated corpses, but few as bad as this. When he was young he would have felt sick, but not now; not after ten years on the streets of Belfast. In the 1970s, the army had taught him to master his body, but only later did they realise it was at the expense of his mind. As he looked down on the shattered limbs and shreds of skin and cloth caught up in barbed wire at the river's edge, instinctively he did what they'd told him back then: deep breaths; head back; eyes closed; clear the brain. Relax. Thirty years ago, it used to work. But now his mind wasn't so easily fooled. He could sense the panic rising. He felt in his pocket: no pills. He'd left them at home. His shaking hands grabbed at his phone. It took a huge effort, but somehow he dialled 999 and spoke. Then oblivion. He never heard the reply.

* * *

It was Detective Chief Inspector Richard Lane's first call-out since his transfer back to Cambridgeshire and Fenland CID. That had been back at the start of the week, but it could have been years ago. All evening he'd been kicking his heels in his office in Ely, supposedly familiarising himself with his new GDMPs (Grievance and District Management Procedures), when the desk sergeant downstairs got the call. By four o'clock Lane had waded through enough management jargon and his head was reeling. So he decided to go home: a bad case of migraine, or so he muttered as he returned his key at the desk. The sergeant was putting the phone down and Lane could see the shock on his face.

'Control said the caller reported he'd found a body by the river . . .'

'Which river?'

'The caller didn't say, sir, but the phone co-ordinates put it near Fursey.'

'That's Littleport way, isn't it?' Lane asked.

The sergeant, who was still reading his screen, nodded.

'Well, it's on my way home. I might as well call in.'

'I've got some more information here, sir. They say the phone belongs to a Mr Bert Hickson, who didn't hang up. He just said he'd found a body. Then silence.'

Lane frowned. 'That's all?'

'So it seems. But he didn't hang up, and they've just sent through a better fix. It says here it's lying just downstream of Smiley's Mill in the Mill Cut at Fursey.'

'That's off the Padnal Delph, isn't it?'

'Yes, sir, and I don't need to remind you that the rivers are very swollen after all the recent rain. So do please be careful.'

'I'll be OK – it's the poor bloke by the river who worries me. He could be in trouble. I'll let you know immediately if I need help.'

Lane strode rapidly across the car park, and as he put the

magnetic flashing blue light on his car's roof he caught a glimpse of his face in the mirror. He was smiling.

* * *

The main rush hour out of Cambridge had yet to build up as Lane approached Fursey, so he dropped his speed as he passed through the little Victorian country estate village. Smiley's Mill lay just outside, to the north. He drew up in the mill car park and crossed the Mill Cut by the little iron footbridge through the tall willows. Several elderly people were taking their dogs for their late-afternoon walks. He headed rapidly along the cut bank, beside the partially flooded meadow until he came to a barbed wire fence and a small gate with a large, neatly lettered, and quite recently erected, sign: *Fursey Estates: NO ADMITTANCE Except by Prior Appointment.* Ignoring this, Lane passed through the gate and headed along the now thickly wooded path beside the cut. Around the first and only bend he came across a very distressed elderly man, covered in mud up one side, from head to toe, kneeling on the wet ground. Lane glanced down at the water, and there below him was the body, semi-floating and snagged on rusty barbed wire. Part of the face was missing, but Lane could see it was a man, possibly in his thirties, and of medium height and build. Although his skin had been bleached in the cold water, he could see from the colour on his forehead, neck and hands that he worked outside. He was plainly very dead. Lane looked up: the living man was now his immediate concern.

* * *

The sun was setting and the first few drops of an evening shower were falling, as two paramedics helped Bert Hickson back to the ambulance in the mill car park. Lane had been joined by a sergeant and constable and all three policemen were wearing the hi-vis waterproof overalls that were standard issue on such assignments. Although it was only early October, Lane was grateful for the extra warmth, as the water was cold and the dead body, if anything, was colder. Before they tried to detach the corpse from the barbed wire the constable removed any loose clothing, which included one steel-capped rigger boot. They didn't want anything important to be lost during the body's removal from the water, so Lane began to search it. He handed a couple of coins from a trouser pocket to the sergeant who bagged them. One of the outside pockets of his waterproof Gore-Tex jacket produced a 6H pencil and a draughtman's eraser, plus the lid of an insulated plastic mug. The sergeant took them. Then he gently rolled the body over and put his hand inside the jacket. There were two inner pockets. One was empty, but he could feel the other was full of something. Carefully he unzipped it, then he cupped his right hand over the object and drew it out very slowly. The dead man's wallet. Even better, the zipped pocket had remained waterproof. Quickly they bagged it up, protecting it against the now persistent rain.

Lane stood aside as two wetsuited assistants arrived to help unhook the body from the barbed wire. He walked back along the cut to the mill car park, and as he stepped off the footbridge he was dazzled by the headlights of a car which had just drawn up. The lights went out and the driver got out and came across to him. He was a slightly overweight man in his early fifties, wearing a jacket and tie.

'Hello, I'm Derek Smiley, mill manager here. Your people

phoned me about ten minutes ago. Said a body had been found in the cut and that you were using our car park.'

'Yes, I'm Chief Inspector Richard Lane.' They shook hands. 'I could think of nowhere closer. Hope that's all right?'

'Of course it is. I mean it's terrible. Is there anything else I – we – can do: toilets, that sort of thing?'

'Possibly. I'll ask the sergeant to speak to you, if that's OK; but there are a couple of things you might be able to help me with.'

'Ask away.'

'First of all, did you spot anything unusual as you drove here? Anything at all?'

'What, on the drive? Or in the car park . . . ?'

There was a pause while Smiley thought. Lane looked at him hard. No, he wasn't acting a part. This was real. That came as a relief.

Smiley exhaled heavily, before slowly replying, 'I can't think of anything off-hand, no. But it might help if we turned on the car park lights.'

They walked across to a small side entrance in the Victorian brick-and-timber-clad mill building, which was quickly unlocked. Once inside, Smiley punched a code into a touch-pad. Suddenly the whole area was bathed in light.

'Anything strike you?' asked Lane.

'Hmm, there's nothing obvious . . .' He was hesitating.

'There rarely is. Such things are usually quite subtle.'

There was another, shorter pause. Slowly Smiley replied, 'There.' He was pointing towards the footbridge. 'The bike over there. Did one of your people come on that?'

'If only.' Lane sounded rueful. 'No,' he continued, 'we closed the Fursey station in '98, shortly after I joined Fenland.

So all our people are now based in Ely; the paramedics come from Cambridge. Could it belong to a dog walker?'

'Perhaps, but they usually use the sheltered racks over there by the toilets.' He paused, thoughtfully. 'And one other thing.'

'Yes?'

'It's not chained up. It's a smart bike too. And that's very unusual . . .'

'Why?' Lane broke in. 'Are they usually a bit old and battered?'

'You know what it's like, some of the older dog walkers can't be bothered with padlocks, keys or new bikes. But that one over there's a smart bit of kit. If it's not an actual racing bike, it's a very good sports machine. It could even be a Klansmann; I've got a cheap copy of something similar myself, which I take out at weekends and I wouldn't even leave *that* unchained, especially round here, so close to Cambridge.'

Lane smiled. For decades Cambridge had been notorious for cycle crime.

They walked back to the footbridge. As they approached the bike, Smiley couldn't conceal his enthusiasm.

'Oh yes.' He was lost in admiration. 'A Klansmann Fell Flyer . . .'

As Lane had anticipated, in his enthusiasm Smiley was about to take hold of the handlebars. Quickly the policeman placed a restraining hand on his shoulder.

'I think that would be unwise, sir. We may need fingerprints.'

Even under the sodium lights' glare it was clear that the manager was blushing deeply.

'Oh, my God,' he almost whispered. 'I hadn't thought.

That's terrible. You don't think it's a . . .' He couldn't bring himself to say the word 'murder'. 'A crime, do you?'

'Anything's possible at this early stage, sir. Which is why we have to be so careful.'

They walked back together. Smiley had opened the side door and was about to turn the lights off. Lane called across, 'Would you mind leaving the lights on, Mr Smiley?'

'I'm sorry, Inspector, force of habit. You know what electric bills are like. But of course, you still have people down here, don't you?'

'Yes, and here comes the body, so we won't be detaining you here for long.' As he spoke, Lane could see a small group of people, led by an officer with a powerful flashlight, who was followed by two men carrying a stretcher and two others behind them, both with bright lights. They were making their way slowly along the cut. They'd be at least ten minutes. Time to ask another question.

'There was one other thing I meant to ask you, sir. The body was in a very poor state.'

'What, decayed, that sort of thing?'

'No, far from it. In fact, I don't think it had been in the water for long at all. Maybe a day, but not much longer, although the post-mortem will be more precise. No, it looked like it had been chopped up or bashed. A foot was missing, as was most of the face and lower jaw. The clothes were torn and shredded. Frankly, it looked like it had passed through a huge mincer. D'you have any thoughts on how this might have happened?'

There was a long pause. Eventually Smiley replied, 'Oh dear, I feared something of the sort. The day before yesterday, during those terrible thunderstorms in the afternoon, one of the large willows that surround the mill pool was struck by lightning. It split from stem to stern and the trunk crashed down onto the mill wheel's protective cage. You might have seen it on the local TV News. Anyhow, it's just over here.'

They started walking along the front face of the mill towards the sound of cascading water. Lane said, 'I remember seeing that. Wasn't one of your people hurt?'

'Yes, Sam Hibbs. It broke his collarbone and hurt his back. He spent last night in hospital. I collected him this morning and he's back at home now.'

'Will he be OK?'

'Yes, thank goodness. They're a tough lot the Hibbses.'

'That's good. But what about the protective cage?'

'It got completely smashed, so we rigged up something out of the bits and pieces we salvaged, which we lashed together. It's not perfect, but you've got to understand we can't do anything permanent, especially anything involving welding, until water levels drop – and that won't be for a few days as things stand. Still, we managed to measure everything up and the estate blacksmiths are fabricating new panels and grilles for us. In fact, Mr Sebastian himself came down when he saw the piece on TV . . .'

'Mr Sebastian?'

'Mr Sebastian Cripps, who owns the Fursey Estate and all the land hereabouts. We've always worked very closely with them. They still own some of the land and buildings around the mill itself. I've got a lot of time for both the brothers.'

Sebastian's name rang a bell with Lane.

'Sebastian Cripps is on the district council, isn't he?'

'Yes, Tory, of course.'

'I wasn't aware he had a brother.'

'Name's John. Younger brother by a couple of years. Their parents – he's the third baronet – live over at Abbey Farmhouse, along with John and Candice, who run the Abbey Farm Shop and restaurant. You've probably seen it on the Littleport Road, as you head out of the village.'

Lane nodded. The family was well known in the area. But as much as he'd like to learn more about the local landowners, he still had a job to do.

'So you reckon the body passed through the mill wheel?'

'Yes, it's perfectly possible. I just hope the poor bloke was dead when he went through.'

By now they were looking down at the mill race: there was blue rope everywhere and a living person could certainly have grabbed hold of it and pulled themselves round to a steel access ladder by the main chute. The mesh of rope would probably have caught a dead sheep or cow; a human could just have passed through. But only just.

'It looks to me like you did the best you could, under difficult circumstances.' Lane could see that Smiley was very upset: his hands clasped and unclasped; his eyes were moist. He placed a comforting hand on Smiley's arm and continued quietly, 'Having seen this, I'm sure the man was either dead or unconscious when he passed through the mill wheel. You must try not to let it worry you too much.'

Smiley nodded silently. 'Thanks, Inspector, it's a relief to hear you say that.'

Behind them they could hear voices over by the footbridge. The police party had returned with their gruesome cargo. Smiley's body language was clear to Lane: he didn't want to look. He remained facing the mill.

'I know it's stupid, Inspector, but this whole business is

more than just upsetting. It's not just that a young man has died.' Lane could see that he wasn't finding this easy. He drew breath. 'You should know, there have been others, over the years.'

'Yes,' Lane replied gently. 'I was aware of that.'

'In fact, round here we talk of a curse . . .'

'Oh, yes?'

'They say it's the family, the Crippses, who are cursed.'

'And do you believe that?'

'Before today I'd have laughed at the idea.' He paused. 'But now . . .'

The mood was broken by the sound of ambulance doors opening in the car park behind them. Lane glanced across.

'You'll forgive me, Mr Smiley, but I need to have a closer look.'

They shook hands and Smiley departed. Lane arrived at the ambulance and the sheet covering the corpse was pulled back. He had noticed it before, but people lost their humanity, their dignity, when their bodies were removed from their scene of death. And it wasn't just the intrusion of the modern world – the bright lights, shiny aprons, the smell of disinfectants – either. Sure, human remains were always treated with respect: removed carefully; eyelids closed; limbs arranged with restraint. Maybe that was it, he thought: they hadn't flexed their arms, or closed their eyes themselves. It had been done for them. Like dolls or shop mannequins. Objects, not people.

But as he looked down, Lane became aware that this body was strangely interesting. Most of his face had gone, but somehow he could imagine his voice. A youngish man. And fit, too. He'd obviously worked outside, but he was no workman. Hands rough, but not calloused. Bit his nails.

'Seen enough, sir?'

The voice broke into his thoughts. Lane nodded and turned, lost in thought.

A double click. The back doors had closed. The ambulance drew away.

* * *

Back in his car, Lane put on rubber gloves and took the wallet from its police plastic bag. The driving licence identified the owner as a Mr Stanley Beaton, born 18 July, 1972. Current residence: 21 Priory Lane, Peterborough. Lane knew the road and the area well; it was to the west of the railway station, in the Longthorpe direction. Very nice middle-class residential district. Slowly and very carefully he looked through the various cards, searching for clues. He left the usual ones in place – Visa, MasterCard, National Trust, English Heritage – but two caught his eye in passing. The dead man had been a member of the Council for British Archaeology and of the Chartered Institute for Archaeologists. Suddenly the clothes and the few other items found in his pockets began to make sense.

In the last fold of the wallet were the cards he was looking for; these were from people, not corporations. In among them was a name he immediately recognised. Lane smiled – that was more like it. This time he carefully pulled the card from the wallet. It was corporate-style, quite well-designed and issued by Paul Flynn Consulting Ltd. Gingerly he turned it over. There were traces of a smeared muddy finger-mark, not a print, and a scrawled message: 'Great visit, Stan. Many thanks, AC'. This was followed by a clearly written mobile number. Just to be sure, Lane pulled out his own phone and checked it against what he had for Alan Cadbury. They were identical.

The next step was easy: he pressed the call button.

# Part 1

## Finding the Way

# One

Alan Cadbury was driving across flat, open fenland, broken only by leaning telegraph poles and isolated farmhouses. Each farm was accompanied by a bonfire, piled high with tyres, old pallets and the sort of farmyard rubbish that would cost a fortune to drop into a skip. It was going to be an explosive evening. It was 5 November, Guy Fawkes Night. Ever since he'd been a boy, growing up on a similar fenland farm, Alan had been made aware that Guy Fawkes had been a traitor and he was reminded that 'the Fens were for Cromwell'. He remembered, too, how life-like the effigies had been and how neighbours, well-oiled with local ale, had cheered when the flames eventually reached them. But today the symbolism had gone. Now Bonfire Night was merely an excuse for fireworks. Alan sighed. Maybe it was for the best. History is sometimes best forgotten.

It was a dry Friday evening, after one of the wettest autumns on record. Already the night-time frosts were starting to enlarge the thousands of potholes that had become such a feature of the ridged and tilting local roads. He was in the peat fens, a few miles north of Ely. Briefly Alan had considered exchanging his diesel-guzzling old grey Fourtrak for a smaller, more economic car, but it would never have coped with these conditions.

Lane's words were still echoing in Alan's mind: River. Body. Stan. Although a mere 38 years old, Alan was no stranger to death. Just over 18 months ago, his work colleague Steve Allen had been killed in a tragic event when a brick-built cistern collapsed beneath his feet. It had taken Alan six months to get over the worst of it. And he still had flashbacks to that terrible scene in the old cow shed. He shuddered at the memory. But Stan Beaton is, no, *was* different. Very different.

They had been very close at university – but away from halls of residence and lectures. They were both more Town than Gown. For a brief moment Alan smiled. In their first year at Leicester their fellow students had dubbed them Fish and Chips, partly because that's where they always ate, but also because they went so well together. Alan always claimed to be Fish.

'And you've the eyes to go with it,' Stan once said.

Alan shrugged, he wasn't bothered. 'You're just jealous.'

There were times they didn't need words. Alan felt his eyes reddening. He took a deep breath.

Stan decided to do the Romano–British option in their third year. Alan had focused on the Bronze Age, but they both shared a passion for fieldwork. They both believed that archaeology was over-obsessed with the study of objects and that you would never get to the truth about the past if you ignored site, landscape and setting. People don't live in a vacuum: their surroundings shaped them. Objects – artefacts – helped humans react to each other and the physical world around them. But that was all. It was the wider stage, the setting, that concealed the real insights.

As time passed, they kept in contact, even though their careers had started to take them in slightly different directions. Alan became more and more interested in the later prehistory of the Fens, while Stan was fascinated by what happened to the rural population when the Romans invaded Britain. Maybe, Alan wondered, that was why they had remained so close: Stan valued Alan's approach to landscape prehistory, which he himself was applying, but in his own way, to the slightly later period. In his heart of hearts Alan had envied Stan's new project at Fursey: it had *so* much potential.

And that was what had been keeping Alan awake for the past few weeks, ever since Lane had phoned him that night. After his two visits to Stan at Fursey the previous summer and autumn, Alan had realised that his friend had stumbled across the ideal site for context. Because everything was still there, buried and preserved beneath thick accumulations of flood-clay. Everyone knew about the volcanic ash at Pompeii and Herculaneum, but this was really no different: just wetter. And at Fursey it had happened towards the end of the Iron Age and into Roman times – precisely the period Stan had been researching for 15 years. A wave of sadness hit Alan as he remembered the last time he had seen his friend alive – and that was the word for it: alive. Fursey meant that his career had taken off. And it was an opportunity that his friend was grasping with both hands. They both knew it would be the making of him. And Alan had been glad: very, very glad.

He pulled into a field gateway and allowed the emotion to wash over him. No point in fighting it. He didn't know how long it was before he lifted his head from his arms folded over the steering wheel. He looked in the mirror: no tears. Even as a child he rarely wept. But he noticed his hands were shaking. Three deep breaths: time to get going. Ignition. Back on the road.

* * *

As he bounced across a particularly rough stretch of potholes, Alan recalled some emotional evenings when Stan had admitted he had a drink problem. Although Alan liked a few drinks himself, he realised that Stan's problems were altogether different. After talking things over with a medical friend, Alan became convinced that moderation would never be the answer. It was a case of all or nothing. Eventually Stan agreed. Then he'd landed a good excavation project in the Trent Valley and booze became a thing of the past. Or that's what Alan had believed.

Up ahead he could see the ruins of Fursey Abbey, which seemed far more spectacular than when he'd visited them first, the summer before last when the tall lime trees in the park had shaded and seemed to dwarf the monastic remains. That was over a year ago, but now, after several sharp October frosts, the leaves were mostly gone and the ruins seemed to have doubled in size against the infinite fens to the north.

Back then, his world had just been turned on its head: he'd had a terminal row with the only woman he ever felt any real affection for and his nice, secure job had blown up in his face.

He had first met Dr Harriet Webb on his previous case, which involved a death in Leicester and the excavation of the remote churchyard of St Guthlic's in the Lincolnshire Fens. Harriet had been the human bones specialist and his co-director of excavations. Their relationship had been entirely professional at first. Then it had grown into something very, very special, which Alan had screwed up – entirely, he now recognised, because he was obsessed with a mystery and unable to control his own feelings. So she had left.

As he approached the abbey ruins, memories of that previous November's visit came flooding back. It had been his first chance to examine one of the Ely islands closely and he'd been astonished by the steepness of everything: dry land islands seemed to dive into the black fen, and hills really were hills. It was so different from the north-western Fens, which he and Stan were more familiar with, where wet and dry blended together, almost imperceptibly, and where islands protruded at most a metre or two. They had laughed together after the tour: it was such a simple landscape to read. Stan, however, was worried that the wet fringes around the dry landscapes would be too narrow, because the ground was sloping so steeply. And it was these wet fringes that held the greatest archaeological potential. But Alan wasn't so sure. Yes, in theory, Alan acknowledged, his friend was probably right. But in life and archaeology the truth is rarely that simple: glaciers and water can do the strangest of things; narrow fringes can become extended borderlands of seemingly infinite potential.

He slowed down and glanced at his watch. He knew from his two previous visits that Fursey Abbey was owned by the Cripps family who were aristocrats and substantial local landowners. They ran the Fursey Abbey project that had employed Stan to oversee the archaeological survey; so they were bound to have given him a big send-off – the invitation he'd received had been properly engraved; left to him, he'd have done them on his computer.

The family wouldn't be back from the crematorium until

noon and he didn't want to stand around chatting to the local great and good, who were bound to be there, sipping cups of tea while glancing around to check who else was there. He detested that sort of thing; networking, they called it: all fake smiles and hypocritical 'darlings'. He pulled over to the verge and turned the engine off. He thought back to that last time he'd seen Stan. Almost exactly a year ago, but then it had been foggy and wet. Stan showed him a couple of trenches that he was having trouble understanding, but together they had worked the sequence out. It was quite tricky: two episodes of back-filling, with an off-centre recut. Then they went down to the pub. He smiled at the memory: the Cripps Arms.

As they'd walked down to the pub, Stan spoke a lot about his not drinking anymore. Alan even offered to drive them both to a coffee shop in Ely. But Stan would have none of it; he wanted to demonstrate his willpower. He kept mentioning the project's archaeological consultant, Dr Peter Flower of Fisher College, Cambridge, who, it seemed, had done a lot to help him. Stan had become a huge admirer of Flower – 'such a kind and helpful man' – a view that Alan most definitely didn't share. The two of them had an unfortunate shared history. Flower had been the external advisor for his PhD at Leicester. The thesis had been on *Bronze Age farming practices in Eastern England, in their European contexts, with special reference to the Fenland Basin.* Everyone who had read it thought it superb, but not Peter Flower. That gilded Cambridge academic had other, more trendy, ideas. At the time, he was heavily into post-structuralist general theory and wanted the thesis raised above 'the merely descriptive'. Alan had tried to argue that he had explained how the regional economies might have articulated, but no, that wasn't enough for Flower, who wanted him to suggest 'higher level resolutions' – whatever they were. One evening, after a few too many beers, Alan phoned him at Cambridge and told him where he might want to shove his higher level resolutions. He still didn't regret it, but that was the last time they had spoken. And thanks to Dr Flower, Alan was still *Mr* Cadbury.

Alan still detested the man, even after 14 years. Meanwhile, there was Stan, walking alongside him, singing Flower's praises: how he had encouraged him to apply for the job and had found him a place in a rehab clinic. All Alan could think was that he must have had some nasty ulterior motive.

Once inside the pub, Alan had ordered a beer and then felt bad as he drank it. Stan was pointedly enjoying his long Virgin Mary with lots of Tabasco, Worcestershire sauce and tomato juice. Stan had spoken warmly not just about Flower, but Candice, too. Alan clearly remembered him saying how he liked the set-up at Fursey: the staff on the estate, the pub, the locals; it still had the feel of a traditional rural village. How they gave him time to set up his work.

'I like to start things slowly,' his friend had said. 'No point in running before you can walk.'

Alan had smiled. It was like old times; his friend's caution had returned. Booze had clouded his judgement, but now Alan could see he was thinking more lucidly.

'So we're following the drainage board diggers, recording sections and levelling them in. I did a crash course at the old tech in GPS. Turned out to be very useful.'

This was the Stan of Fish and Chips days. He was always going on 'useful' courses. And Alan was quite happy to pick his brains. Another wave of sadness hit him, as he remembered the rest of that afternoon in the pub.

Stan had described how he was about to start surveying in the deeply buried floodplain soils, just off the slopes of the abbey island. Alan knew all about river flood-clay – alluvium – and what it could conceal, especially around the fringes of those slightly higher areas of land. This raised ground would have seemed like seasonally flooded islands in the pre-drainage era. He was able to offer Stan a few useful practical tips. Towards the end of their lunch break, Alan realised that he had stopped worrying about Stan's drinking and had begun to relax. He even bought a second round of drinks. Yes, he thought, it had been good. Very good.

His memories of Stan were suddenly interrupted by activity further down the road towards the village. It was the cortège of black undertaker's limousines returning from the crematorium. He took a deep breath; time to make a move.

* * *

As Alan turned off the road into the short, tree-lined drive leading up to the buildings of what had once been a working farm, he was struck by the amount that had been done since he was there last. A large and very elaborate marquee had been positioned to obscure most of the building site, but Alan could see that work on converting the two barns was well advanced. The old restaurant and visitor centre, which had been squeezed into some 1950s prefabricated, concrete-floored piggeries, had been abandoned and partially demolished, although the old kitchen block still seemed to be in use. Stan had told him that the next year was going to see some major changes, and he hadn't been exaggerating.

He walked into the marquee, feeling strangely confident. Normally such occasions were to be dreaded. But not this one.

He knew exactly why he was here: to find out the truth about Stan's death and this was where he was going to meet everyone who could have played a part in it. If real life had been a murder mystery, then he'd been given the final scene-in-the-library at the very beginning. It was a golden opportunity and he was determined to make the most of it.

He paused and looked around him. He was impressed. The Cripps family had gone to a lot of trouble to give their ex-employee a fitting send-off. Alan stood at the back of the small line of people who had arrived in the two limos, at the front of which, being greeted very warmly by Candice Cripps, who Alan had met on both his previous visits to Fursey, were, Alan assumed, Stan's parents – there was certainly a strong family resemblance. Alan was struck by the contrast between Candice and the older couple. She was standing tall and upright, her shoulders back, very much the relaxed host at the big event. And she had the looks to pull it off: luxuriant long dark hair and a close-fitting mourning dress that could have graced a catwalk. Behind them, came a few other younger relatives. Alan stood back; he liked being a fly-on-the-wall and he enjoyed working out how human gatherings were organised. In fact, it was what had attracted him to anthropology and archaeology in the first place. And it was clear that Candice Cripps was running this show. Every so often somebody would whisper something to her and she would nod or tell them to delay; messages were also coming through on her phone. The outside caterers, who had clearly worked for her before, had a person standing permanently beside her. It put Alan in mind of a television crew, and she was very much the director.

When she had finished greeting the last of Stan's relatives, a man in a dark suit and black tie handed her a cup of tea. He was about to leave when she took hold of his arm and to Alan's surprise, then horror, they both walked towards him. Instinctively Alan looked over his shoulder, but there was nobody more important standing behind him. He had been the last guest to arrive.

'Alan,' she almost but not quite gushed. 'Stop shrinking into the shadows. I want you to meet my husband, John.'

John was in his forties with the tiniest hint of middle-aged spread. He had an educated, but not over-precise, way of talking. Alan detected tradition, but tinged with modernity; his clothes and bearing gave the same impression. Alan also detected a privileged background, but not necessarily an easy life. There was something slightly tired about his manner.

'This has been a tragic time for all of us.' They shook hands as John spoke. 'Stan was such a nice man, and although most of it was well over my head, Peter Flower assures me that his research was truly groundbreaking – if you'll forgive the rather weak pun.'

'And do you agree, Alan?' Candice asked, almost imploring. 'It matters so much to us here.'

Candice's eyes were wide when she finished the question. Yes, Alan thought, it does matter to you, doesn't it? The cynic in him detected self-interest – she and her husband were, after all, running the Fursey Abbey Visitor Experience – but he also thought he detected something else, something he at least could identify with: a love of the past and the people who inhabited it.

'Yes, Stan told me quite a lot about his work. I was intrigued by some sherds of Iron Age pottery he showed me the last time we met. This wasn't run-of-the-mill stuff. It included high-quality cordoned jars dating to the late BC, early AD, I even thought that one sherd might have been from an imported vessel. It looked quite similar to stuff I'd seen from Barry Cunliffe's excavations at Hengistbury Head . . .'

'But that's in Dorset, isn't it?' John was now fascinated.

'Yes, and it's a very high- profile site indeed. In fact, it was a major port in early pre-Roman times, before Caesar's two visits. Now, I'm not saying that Fursey is another Hengistbury, as that would be ridiculous – we're too far inland here – but it's perfectly possible that the top people living at Fursey had contacts with very high status communities elsewhere in Britain.'

'Like Hengistbury?' John suggested.

Alan was determined that the archaeological project should continue after Stan's death. The site was potentially so important, he had to encourage their enthusiasm.

'Or more probably Welwyn or Colchester, which were the main regional tribal centres in the late Iron Age. Colchester was, of course, the precursor to Roman London. So, yes, I think the site is potentially very important indeed. I'd have thought it was just the sort of project that people like English Heritage ought to be supporting . . .'

At this point a large man in a sober tweed suit quietly materialised alongside them. He smiled at Alan. 'I'm so sorry to interrupt, but I thought it would be a good idea if we started to get things moving.' He looked significantly at Candice. 'The contractors will be here at six and I think Stan's parents are looking very tired.'

'Of course,' Candice replied. 'I'll be right over.' She turned to Alan. 'Before you leave, Alan, I must have a quick word with you, is that OK?' Her look suggested it was important.

John said quietly, 'I think Candice wants your advice about the archaeological project. She's a huge fan of yours, you know, she loves *Test Pit Challenge.* You can't drag her away from the TV on Sunday evenings.'

Alan smiled, he was slowly getting used to the fact that he was becoming something of a very minor TV celebrity. The viewing figures for *Test Pit Challenge* had been steadily climbing year on year, and he was a regular member of the team. But John hadn't finished.

'That big man earlier was my brother Sebastian. Sorry about the interruption, but I think he's a bit anxious about the wedding reception tomorrow. The groom's a very important contact for the estate and the shoot: a major property developer from London, and *everything*'s got to go smoothly. We can't afford any slip-ups.'

Things were beginning to make sense for Alan.

'That's a relief, for one moment I thought you'd hired this smart marquee specially for Stan's wake.'

John smiled. 'No, but it seemed a terrible shame not to use it. And I have to admit, Candice was right; it's ideal, isn't it?'

Alan was forced merely to nod his assent, because Candice had just asked everyone to be quiet to allow Stan's father to say a few words of thanks. It was time for the formal speeches.

* * *

Stan's father described a young man who was rather different from the Stan Alan had known at Leicester. He'd toyed with joining the Church at the time of his confirmation and had even contemplated taking up medicine, but was daunted by the science. He was a boy who was also good at sports, but one who never seemed to enjoy winning. Beating somebody else gave him no satisfaction. Was this a strength or a weakness? Alan was in little doubt: it was why they had become so close. Fish and Chips. All those years and some grim sites together. Typical bloody men, Alan thought, we never discussed ourselves. And was he regretting it now? Did he wish that they'd both shown more of their more sensitive, 'feminine' sides? No. Absolutely not. He was certain of that; some things are best left unsaid.

When Stan's father had finished, Candice stepped forward. 'And finally, my friends, my husband John would like to say something about how we plan to remember dear Stan.'

John Cripps rose and explained that the new restaurant and shop would be in the Victorian cow barn and the Stan Beaton Museum and Archaeological Research Centre would occupy the much larger 17th-century reed barn. Both buildings were on schedule to open at Easter. The entrance lobby to the museum would include a plaque in Stan's memory, together with a picture – he held it up of Stan smiling slightly shyly – taken during last summer's excavations.

At this point waiters appeared with glasses of Champagne.

After the toast to Stan's memory, Alan looked around at the throng. His eyes narrowed: there was Peter Flower. He had barely aged since they had confronted each other across the table at his PhD interview. His paper-thin smile concealed a cold man, certain of his own infallible authority. He was in deep discussion with John and Lew Weinstein, executive producer of *Test Pit Challenge.* Small world. Alan hadn't expected to see him here, although he knew he had been at Cambridge with Peter Flower. He noticed Candice pointing across to him and his heart sank as someone tapped his shoulder. He looked round and found he was staring into a green tweed waistcoat. The very large man was, of course, Sebastian Cripps, John's brother, who currently ran the estate.

'We meet again, Alan.' The voice was slower, calmer now. 'I'm Sebastian, as John no doubt told you. And this is Sarah, who manages me, my life and the estate.'

'No, Bas, you exaggerate,' she broke in. 'I merely oversee the shoot and make the tea.'

The lady who stood before Alan, was in her mid-forties and, despite being smaller than her husband by some six inches, now dominated the conversation. Her smile was judiciously broad, but her well-made-up eyes had a steely stare. She had a neat figure and Alan reckoned she was very fit. Her hair was fashionably blonde, but grey-brown eyes and darker eyebrows suggested she was naturally brunette. Her voice could best be described as unpretentious Sloane: a few 'OK, yahs', but certainly not gushy. To Alan, her way of talking suggested private education, tempered by the reality of running the shoot: essentially a small business in the early 21st century. Privileged, but realistic – possibly even ambitious.

'I'm so sorry I interrupted you just now. I hope you didn't take it amiss, but it's essential that we keep to schedule, and dear John and Candice do so love history. I was worried when I saw they had started talking to you, that they'd never stop.' Sebastian spoke quite fast. It was as if he was used to saying a few well-chosen words to many different people at gatherings such as this. But Alan also detected just a hint of shyness or reticence. Despite his size, this was not an over-confident man.

Alan was keen to put him at his ease. 'Think nothing of it. I fully understand: you had to get things going. And I should warn you, we archaeologists love to talk, so you may well have to throw some of us out when the time comes.'

'No, I'm sure it won't come to that.' He paused, obviously trying to work out how to steer the discussion in a slightly different direction. He clearly wasn't a very comfortable conversationalist. 'The thing is,' he continued, 'I didn't want you to think that somehow I wasn't interested in history. Like Candice, I'm a keen follower of *Test Pit Challenge* and I firmly believe that a society only holds together if it shares a common past.'

'So what aspect of history interests you?'

His reply was not what Alan had expected. 'I know that the goings-on at Court were always very exciting and I understand why television costume dramas love them so much, but I could never identify with what was happening far away in London. Somehow it all seems – no seemed – so remote.'

'Rather like today?'

'In fact, if anything, things are getting worse, not better. Westminster is more haughty and remote than it has ever been.' This was certainly not what Alan had expected to hear from a tweed-suited country gent. 'So I'm far more interested in landscape history . . .'

'W.G. Hoskins?' Alan broke in.

'Absolutely.' Sebastian's eyes came alight. 'Wonderful book. I must have read it a dozen times. No modern authors can touch it. And a few have tried.'

'Yes, sadly – and at enormous length. And of course your family comes from the one English landscape that has changed more than any other.'

Rather to his own surprise, Alan found he was enjoying their conversation. He always liked meeting people who had discovered history for themselves. Their take on the past was always far more creative and unusual – if not always academically kosher or PC.

'I know, and I do get fed up when people dismiss the Fens as flat and boring. Those old dykes out there have witnessed more history, drama and excitement than many a town or city.'

Alan could forgive the slight hyperbole. He shared Sebastian's enthusiasm.

'So although I'm a staunch Royalist, I'm also a huge admirer of Cromwell.' Again, this was unexpected from a fully paid-up member of the landed gentry. 'Without Cromwell's reforms and the release of capital tied up in the useless, self-indulgent and thoroughly corrupt monasteries, the Fens would never have been drained. Were you aware, for example, that the Duke of Bedford made use of funds derived from the Dissolution of Thorney Abbey to . . .'

His flow was broken by Peter Flower, who, together with Lew Weinstein and John, had just joined them. Weinstein looked slightly embarrassed, but Flower, as ever, was master of the situation. He adopted a school-masterly tone.

'Oh, come now, Sebastian, you know the history's not as simple as that. We've discussed it over and again, but you won't listen to reason.' He was smiling hugely, as he refreshed both their glasses. 'When you climb onto your hobby horse, there's no holding you back, is there?'

This annoyed Alan. He hated academics who patronised. But to his surprise, Sebastian was only slightly embarrassed.

He turned to Alan as he began to withdraw. 'Peter's quite correct. I love the Fens and their history and I'm inclined to get a bit carried away. Now, I think you all have more pressing matters to discuss.'

And with that he left and, as if choreographed, Candice materialised, joining their small group.

Slightly at a loss, Alan started the conversation. 'I hadn't expected to see you here, Lew – I didn't know you knew Stan?'

'Sadly I didn't, and it does seem a real tragedy that he died. But I'd been seeing my friend Peter in Cambridge' – he turned towards Flower – 'and he suggested I come along here . . .'

There was the briefest of hesitations before Flower finished the sentence. 'To see you, Alan.'

Alan was aware they were all looking at him. 'Bloody hell, what have I done?'

That lightened the mood, and they all chuckled before Flower resumed. 'Alan, we four fully appreciate that you have every reason to dislike me and I wouldn't be at all surprised if at the end you told me to get lost. But I would very much like to say that I regret what happened. At the time I was completely convinced that my suggestions were reasonable, but now I have to confess I have become less certain about many things in life; and your subsequent work has shown that you are the most able prehistorian currently working in the Fens. So I intend to do my very best to make up for what happened fourteen years ago.'

Alan was taken aback. And, yes, it had been 14 years ago. He was astonished that Flower remembered with such accuracy something that Alan had expected he would simply have shrugged off.

John seemed to have taken on the role of chairman. 'Thank you, Peter. That was well said.' Then he turned to Alan. 'I know this might seem a little strange, given that Stan was taken from us barely a month ago, but we all agreed that he would have wanted us to approach you, Alan. The thing is, he spoke very highly of you indeed, and your two visits here a year ago did a great deal to raise Stan's morale.'

'That's right,' Flower cut in. 'As he said to me, you were the only person currently working in the Fens who had any experience of the huge complexities of the sort of deeply buried deposits he was just starting to encounter. As you know, I worked with him on the first draft of the Fursey project Survey, which I also helped him edit.' Alan smiled, he was aware of Stan's dyslexia. 'And I'm sure it's going to make a big impact when it reaches English Heritage.'

'When do you plan to do that?' Alan was genuinely interested.

'With luck, before Christmas. But I need someone to write a general overview of prehistoric research in the region. I'm very aware that at present the project sits in splendid isolation. It desperately needs archaeological context.' As he said this he fixed Alan with what might be called a significant stare. Alan pretended not to notice. Flower continued, 'Anyhow, I slipped an early draft to Lew here, who was, I think it's fair to say, rather excited.'

Weinstein smiled broadly. 'No, Peter,' he said. 'That's not right. I was *wildly*, not *rather*, excited. We media folks are less restrained than the residents of Second Court.' He turned to Alan. 'Peter's still in Second Court and we had rooms opposite one another in . . .'

'K Staircase,' Flower broke in to remind him.

'That's right. Also in Second Court, at Fisher . . .'

'But back in the Bronze Age,' Flower interjected, smiling broadly.

'The thing is, Alan.' It was Candice's turn to speak. 'I have long thought that the story of the abbey would make a good topic for a television programme and I tried to persuade Stan to have a word with you. But he seemed reluctant. I mentioned it one day to Peter, who you should know has been the Fursey project's historical consultant . . .'

'And this includes archaeology, Alan,' Flower interjected, and they both smiled. Archaeology and history have not always been very comfortable bedfellows.

But Candice would not be diverted. '. . . Since Fursey Heritage Development's first board meeting back in June, 2006. He co-ordinated all the early surveys and a year later it was he who suggested we hire Stan, after, that is, we'd received our first English Heritage grant.'

'Yes,' Flower added, 'that was three years ago. And I've never had any reason to regret the decision. I concede it would have been nice to have had mainstream television involvement, but that was not to be. I think we all respected Stan's decision.'

'Indeed,' John added. 'The important thing was the research, and Stan was doing a superb job. Our visitor enterprise . . .'

'You mean the restaurant and the farm shop?' Alan wasn't quite clear.

'Yes.' John continued, 'They were doing quite nicely thank you, largely due to the top- quality produce from the farm and, of course, Candice's magic in the kitchen.'

She ignored her husband's flattery and added, 'But even so darling, we both knew we weren't making enough of those magnificent abbey ruins, so the archaeological project came along at precisely the right time.' She turned to address Alan. 'You see, somehow we've got to build up our local trade.'

Weinstein glanced down at his watch, then said to Alan, 'I've got a big meeting at T2 tonight, so if you'll forgive me I must, er, cut to the chase. Peter has completely sold me on the project, but it was immediately clear to me that it's far, far bigger than one of our normal fifty minute shows. So I've been thinking about other formats; in fact, that's what I'll be discussing with our commissioning editor at T2.'

'So what sort of format are you thinking about, Lew? Something live, or maybe a longer doc or mini-series?'

'All of those things, Alan, but the channel have made it crystal clear that whatever we negotiate with them, we have *got* to retain the successful dynamism of the TPC brand.'

Whenever Weinstein used the acronym, Alan knew he was getting serious. 'Do you mean the logo, the sig tune, the theme music – that sort of thing?' Alan queried. He had doubts. He didn't like the corporate world and this sounded too heavily branded and marketed.

Weinstein could see he had misgivings. 'Obviously all those things, but they stressed that the programme is as much about the people doing the research as the research itself. We must retain archaeological credibility. So obviously Craig will continue as presenter, but we also need regulars from the current series and, of course, you are one of them. In fact, your shows in series three consistently rated above average with the viewers. You may not be aware of it, but you've become quite a big name on Twitter . . .'

'Oh, no . . .' Alan couldn't conceal a groan.

'Yes, Alan, there's even a person out there who tweets as @AlanFrown.'

Alan was aware that he had a 'trademark' frown when he was confronted with an archaeological problem on camera.

From time to time he'd tried to get rid of it. But it always returned.

Weinstein continued, 'Last time I looked, he had 4,000 followers.'

'I don't believe it!'

'So we want you to be the *Test Pit Challenge* archaeologist . . .'

Alan had to interrupt. 'Lew, that's very flattering. But archaeology isn't like that. I've got nothing official to do with the project here; I can't just swan in and pretend I'm a dig director, when there's somebody else doing the job. That would be phoney; and anyhow, I wouldn't do it.' He paused for effect. 'Either I'm in charge, or I'm not.'

John and Flower both started to reply, then Flower gave way. 'No, Alan,' John said. 'We all agree with Lew. Peter thinks you're the right man for the archaeology, Candice and I think you'd fit in very well here at Fursey. And that's why we'd like to offer you the job of archaeological director.' All eyes were now on Alan. He knew it was quite straightforward: archaeologically Fursey was extraordinary. Unique. In a class of its own. If their offer was just a simple proposition without any extraneous complications, Alan would have grabbed the chance with both hands. Plus, he needed the work. But, though the job appealed to him archaeologically, despite Flower's earlier kind words, Alan deeply distrusted him, and that aside, emotionally there were huge problems: he felt uncomfortable about stepping into a close friend's shoes – and so soon after his death. Then he thought of a simple practical problem, which avoided the need for any emotional discussion. 'What about the new English Heritage grant, won't they insist you advertise the position?'

'No, they won't,' Flower replied. 'They agree the most important thing is experience of deep Fenland stratigraphy. Stan had it, but not as much as you. I've already spoken to the EH inspector and the regional scientific advisor and mentioned your name in confidence, and they both approved heartily.'

John Cripps stepped forward and shook Alan's hand. 'Look, Alan, you don't have to make your mind up this minute. Here's my card. Give me a ring in the next week or so. Then we can meet and discuss practical details. We'd like to see the project started in the New Year, if possible. And now I must take Lew to the station and Peter back to his ivory tower in Cambridge.'

* * *

Alan was lost in thought as he watched the three men hasten towards the exit. Instinctively he glanced down at his watch. He hadn't noticed Candice was still there, so her voice close by his left shoulder came as a surprise. 'Don't worry, Alan, they'll make it. In all our years together, I've never known John miss a train yet.'

There was a short pause while they both surveyed the people around them. Alan was still feeling rather dazed by what he had just been told.

Candice continued. 'I know you knew Stan quite well at uni, but did you ever meet his parents?'

'No.' Alan smiled ruefully. 'Things in those days weren't like they are now. We were students in the late '80s and early '90s, and in those days nobody admitted to having a family. Somehow it wasn't cool.'

'Same here.' She smiled, looking around her. 'Look,

they're over there, just beyond the buffet, talking to the Head Keeper, Bert Hickson. He was the poor man who found Stan's body. And he's with John's father, Barty. Follow me, I'll introduce you.'

As they drew nearer to the buffet another large man, although not quite as massive as Sebastian, was pretending to wring out an empty bottle of Champagne into his wine glass. He was wearing a freshly-pressed Norfolk jacket with matching tweed knee-breeches. He looked every inch the Victorian gamekeeper. With him were two other tweed-clad keepers and several estate workers.

'Hey, Mrs Cripps. Do you have a mangle we could put this bottle through?' he called across to Candice as they passed.

It wasn't funny, especially given the occasion, but the people around him smiled, and Alan could see he had quite a following.

'Thank you, Joe. I get the hint, but I'd remind you, this is a wake, not a party.' Alan could see she was having trouble concealing her irritation, so she changed the subject. 'Have you met Alan Cadbury?'

'No, missus, us folks wants drink, not chocolate.' This was delivered in a terrible Somersetshire accent, complete with forelock tugging. His audience had gone quite quiet. Even they couldn't believe what they were hearing.

If that had been me, Alan thought, I'd have hit him. But Candice handled it well. She put on the voice of an irritated primary school teacher.

'Mr Joe Thorey, you are a disgrace. Now I want you to be serious for a moment.' She turned to Alan. 'Alan here is an archaeologist who knows a great deal about the Fens, and was a good friend of dear Stan.' Alan could see Joe was about to attempt another stupid remark, but Candice was too quick for him. 'You may have seen him on *Test Pit Challenge.*'

The mood of the group changed.

'Yes, I thought his face was familiar . . .' someone said.

'So did I,' another replied. 'Couldn't think where I'd met him.'

Joe stared at Alan. Alan stared back.

'Can't stand silent broody types. I hope you're a bit more talkative than Stan.'

Alan bristled. Candice put her hand on his arm.

'Joe, that was unnecessary. I think it's time you went home.'

By now his audience was wide-eyed. Two of the young women covered their mouths with their hands. One man muttered, 'You asked for that, Joe.'

But Candice had already turned away. As they walked across to Stan's parents she whispered to Alan, 'That man always goes too far. If it were up to me, I'd have sacked him long ago, but Sarah and Sebastian say he's a superb head keeper and the estate shoot has never done better. But even so . . .' She was clearly very angry. As they approached the group by the buffet, she said quietly, 'If you don't mind, I'll introduce you and then leave. I've got to start getting things ready for the reception. Anyhow, it's been great meeting you, Alan, and I'm sure we'll be hearing from you soon.'

* * *

After Candice had left them, the atmosphere in the small group with Stan's parents became less formal, despite the fact that her father-in-law, the 3rd Baronet Arthur Cripps of Fursey – generally referred to as Barty – was with them. Alan didn't know it then, but it was typical that the elderly aristocrat should choose to look after the three people most affected by Stan's death: the deceased man's parents and the ex-soldier, who found the corpse. Hickson had clearly been much affected physically and mentally by the shock, but Alan detected strong self-discipline: he was determined to get better.

'Can I get you a chair, Mr Hickson?' Alan asked. He was genuinely concerned.

'No, that's all right, thank you very much, Mr Cadbury. I've got to relearn how to stand on my own two feet.'

'And you hope to throw away that stick in a month or two, don't you, Bert?' It was the kindly baronet.

'Yes, I do, sir.' He paused, then added, 'With a bit of help.'

'It must have been a horrible shock for you.' Alan said. 'I'm so sorry. I know dear old Stan would not have wanted it. He was a lovely bloke.'

'So you knew him well?' The baronet enquired.

'We were at university together and were old friends.' By now Alan was unable to contain his curiosity. He might never again get the chance to question the man who actually discovered his friend's body. 'But tell me, were there any obvious major injuries that could have caused the death: a blow to the head, that sort of thing?'

It was a bold question. Hickson stared back at him, open-mouthed. Stan's mother grabbed her husband's arm and looked away. Stan's father looked appalled. Then Baronet Cripps intervened. 'I fear grief has affected your judgement, Mr Cadbury. You must forgive us, but we, too, are having problems coming to terms with Stan's accident. I think such direct questions are probably best left to the authorities at this early stage.'

Alan felt mortified. He had behaved like a complete idiot.

'I'm so sorry, Mr Hickson, that was unforgivably insensitive. It's just that . . . I want to do the right thing by Stan.'

The older man looked up and attempted a smile. But it was Barty who stepped into the breach. 'Alan,' he said, 'Jack and Dorothy have been very worried about what is going to happen to Stan's notes and papers. As you may know, he was a great deal more than just a working archaeologist. Archaeology was his entire life.'

'Yes,' continued Jack Beaton. 'He was always out tramping the fields on weekends and his room at home is quite literally stuffed with notebooks and boxes.'

Alan tried to conceal it, but he'd had more than his fair share of notebooks and boxes recently, having just finished writing-up his two previous projects at St Guthlic's Church and the DMV (deserted medieval village) at Impingham. Admittedly, he'd been paid by English Heritage to finish off these two projects, one of which had ended unexpectedly, but even so, he was now keen to get out of the office and back into an excavation. The last thing he needed was what sounded like a rather routine literary executor task.

The baronet seemed to detect Alan's hesitation. 'No, don't worry, it isn't urgent at all, and will probably keep until next autumn. You see, Stan and Peter Flower have completed writing the report on earlier research at Fursey and we've decided to publish it ourselves. We'll be able to sell it in the museum and farm shop here and the money it raises can then go straight back into the research. I've discussed it at length with John and Candice and both are agreed on that.'

'That sounds very generous.' Alan was genuinely impressed.

'It's a wonderful idea,' a familiar voice said from just behind him. Alan turned to catch the smiling face of Clare Hughes, the county council archaeologist. 'And I'm sure the county can do something to help. Maybe with publication?'

'Thank you, my dear.' The baronet was clearly a fan of hers. 'That would be splendid. Most welcome.' He paused, frowning, then turned his full gaze on Alan. 'So the three – no four – of us think this a wonderful opportunity to provide Stan with a lasting memorial, something that most archaeologists will have on their shelves.' He swallowed. 'In a very real way, Stan will continue to be among us.'

By now Dorothy was sobbing quietly on her husband's shoulder and Alan was feeling thoroughly ashamed of his earlier reluctance to help them out. He must make amends. He turned to Stan's parents. 'Look, why don't I come over to see the extent of Stan's archive? I've been confronted with stacks of notebooks and piles of boxes before, and very often they're not so hard to deal with, especially if the person who was responsible for them was methodical. And we all know that Stan was nothing if not methodical.'

Alan glanced at Clare, who was looking serious, but nodding in approval.

Dorothy wiped her eyes and pulled out a pale-green diary from her handbag. 'How about this Sunday – for lunch?'

Alan pretended to look at a non-existent calendar on his phone. 'Yes, that's fine.'

As Alan finished speaking, the gathering was called to order. It was John Cripps. Candice was standing beside him, her hands clasped in front of her, her head slightly bowed. Her pose told Alan what was likely to come next. And he was right. Instinctively he felt resentful: he detested the Church and churchiness, but almost immediately he felt ashamed of himself; on this, of all occasions, surely religion could play a part? He found that his head, too, had bowed.

'My friends,' John Cripps's voice declared. 'We could not meet together to celebrate Stan Beaton's life without also praying for his immortal soul.'

To his left Alan could sense Stan's parents were both weeping freely. He detested the phrase, but he hoped the grieving process would eventually bring them relief, if not closure.

Then the Vicar started to read from the Book of Common Prayer. Her voice was clear and firm.

'*Lord, now lettest thou thy servant depart in peace, according to thy word.*
*For mine eyes have seen thy salvation.*'

Salvation? What salvation? The familiar words of the *Nunc Dimittis* were having an unexpected effect. Alan could feel Stan standing alongside him. Had Stan been seeking some kind of salvation through drink or suicide? The idea was so ludicrous that Alan almost cried out at the sheer injustice. Stan was, above all else, rational. He was sensitive, too, and wouldn't knowingly have put his parents through the hell they were now experiencing. Suddenly, deep, deep inside him, he realised that Stan's death wasn't suicide, nor an accident. He had never 'departed in peace'.

Alan was angry. But he was also at last weeping – freely.

* * *

It was getting late and the afternoon light was starting to fail as Alan crossed the car park, still occasionally wiping his eyes with his sleeve. He climbed aboard the Fourtrak and glanced at his watch: 3.30. He was running 15 minutes late and he knew Detective Chief Inspector Richard Lane hated being kept waiting. He put his foot down and swore under his breath as the rear wheels skidded on the loose gravel. Several people looked up at him, startled. Oh shit, he thought, that was not the way to be seen leaving a close friend's funeral. He could imagine Stan up there, staring down at him, grinning hugely. He'd always loved a good cock-up.

# Two

The weather had changed while Alan had been in the marquee and what had promised to be a nice clear Bonfire Night was shaping up to be fairly typical of late autumn so far: drizzle, patches of fog and low cloud. Put another way, Alan thought, bloody miserable. The wake had left him feeling very low: both tired and fed up. He wanted to be out and about; get the blood circulating. He sighed heavily. An oncoming car swerved slightly and sounded its horn. Suddenly Alan realised he was driving a grey vehicle on a grey foggy day and the light was starting to fade. Quickly he flicked on the headlights.

Although it was only a short distance away, it was getting quite murky as he drove into the car park at Smiley's Mill. Lane's car was parked close to the footbridge and Alan could see he was drumming his fingers on the steering wheel. Not a good sign. He glanced at his watch. Twenty minutes late. He sighed heavily: too bad.

Lane and Alan went back a long time together and Alan had helped him untangle at least a couple of difficult cases after their first meeting on what was the very beginning of Forensic Archaeology, the now famous Saltaire Forensics MSc. course of 1996–8. Alan had been a part-time tutor on it, following his failure to complete his PhD. It had been a two-way process for them: Lane raised Alan's spirits after his doctorate debacle and Alan taught Lane the basic skills of archaeological excavation. They'd been very close for those two years, then their lives had gone their separate ways. But last year they had come together again to sort out a difficult investigation in Leicester. In his heart of hearts, Lane was very keen to work on another case with his old friend.

He looked over towards the four-storey stone mill with the central arch leading to the internal waterwheel. A couple of fallen branches were snagged against the mill race's heavy iron protective grill.

Lane got out of his car, as Alan drew up alongside him.

There was no small talk, just a perfunctory handshake, before Lane said, 'Let's get along to where we found the body while the light's still with us.'

For a moment Alan hesitated. He had very little dress sense, but he was slightly worried that the thin, black Oxford lace-up shoes that he'd bought the previous day to go with the only smartish pair of trousers he possessed, might not be ideal footwear for a muddy walk. Should he slip on some wellies? But Lane was already halfway across the footbridge and rapidly heading north. Sod it, he thought, it's only money.

They strode along the path, through the gate and into the woodland, where it was now very much darker. In the reduced light of the wood, Alan realised why Lane had been in such a hurry. After a further short walk they arrived at the spot and Lane indicated where the body had snagged against the wire.

'Which suggests it floated downstream from the mill, because the tail-race bypass channel rejoins the main cut down there.' He pointed to a gap in the opposite bank of the cut, about 50 yards downstream of where they were standing.

'Yes, that makes sense, especially as even the mill race was in spate after all that rain in September and October.'

Alan tried to make this sound conversational, but in his mind he could see Stan being washed into the mill wheel. A hand reached out weakly to grab at a railing – his last effort to hang onto life –but it failed. Alan didn't want to think about what happened next. To his relief, Lane distracted him from his thoughts by showing him press pictures of the collapsed willow tree and the smashed grill.

'That's what it looked like the day before the body was found.'

Alan's reply of 'Horrible' was feeble.

Thankfully, Lane spoke again. 'Yes, the Fursey Estate fixed it for them double quick. That new grille was up just two days after the accident.'

'Ah, so that's why it looks so freshly painted.' Alan was glad they were discussing screens and paint. It was reality. He must keep a clear head. Still, it was hard, so hard, when a close friend was involved.

'And I've just had the results of the post-mortem: his blood alcohol count was massively up. About three times the legal limit for driving.'

For a sad moment Alan recalled Stan proudly sipping his Virgin Mary. No, he sighed, it didn't add up. 'And they're certain of that, are they? It's just that the body starts to produce alcohol as part of decomposition . . .'

Lane smiled. 'You've got a good memory, Alan. But this

doesn't happen when the body's in the water for such a short time. And it was cold water, too.'

'So you're in no doubt, Richard?'

'No, none. And neither are forensics.'

Alan was shocked. So he really had been back on the booze again, poor sod. 'Bloody hell. Poor old Stan. What on earth was he thinking of? Why come to a mill when the rivers are all in spate? It's madness.'

Lane could see Alan was upset, and paused before saying gently. 'Unless, of course, he wanted to put an end to his misery.'

'What – suicide?'

Alan still found this impossible to accept. It was so unlike Stan. And not at this stage in his career when everything was starting to look so good. But then, he thought, what if he couldn't shake the booze? He'd never do the site or its report justice. And he must have known that.

Lane gave Alan some time to think before continuing. 'It's not uncommon to drink a lot first, just before you jump. Dutch courage.'

'Well . . .' Alan hesitated; such a simple explanation still didn't feel right. 'I suppose you might be right. But even so . . .' He trailed off.

Alan couldn't think of an alternative. But he knew Stan well and he had never seen him as the sort of person likely to kill himself. When he was drinking he was usually fairly cheerful, and often outrageous. He was never one of those self-focused, introspective, maudlin drunks. But on the other hand, Alan knew he had been under a lot of pressure from Flower and the Fursey people to produce his report on the Fursey surveys for English Heritage. He must also have known that the future of the project depended on it. But even so, suicide? He shook his head. No, Stan would never have done it. Not in a thousand years.

'I don't know, Richard.' Alan sighed heavily. 'You're right, it's the explanation that fits the facts best. But I still can't believe it. It's just not like the Stan I knew.' He thought for some time, then took a deep breath. 'Well, you'll probably be proved correct, but right now I can't see it. I honestly can't.'

They were crossing the footbridge. Lane, who was walking in front, stopped and turned to his friend. 'Alan, if you only knew the number of times I've heard that from grieving friends and relations. The worst thing about suicide is the terrible effect it has on those left behind.'

'I know he was close to his parents, too, and he must have known how it would have affected them.' He paused, before finishing. 'No, I just can't see him doing such a thing. *Ever.*'

They were looking towards the cut, with the sound of water in the background. Eventually Lane spoke. 'I know this has been difficult for you, Alan, but I'm afraid there's another unfortunate factor, too. Stan worked for the Crippses, and the family have a terrible reputation locally. I haven't checked any of it out, but according to local gossip it seems that over the years people who have close connections with them often end up dead in the river . . .'

'Sounds a bit Hollywood. D'you think there's truth in any of it?'

'Again, it's only a guess, but I've come across similar tales and long-running feuds when I first worked here over ten years ago, and so far as I could see, in those cases the roots of the rumours and the hostilities seemed to lie back in the drainage schemes of the eighteenth and nineteenth centuries, when different landowners and engineers sometimes had to be very ruthless, or else their entire fen would have flooded.'

'Yes.' Alan nodded. 'It really was a case of co-operate or drown in those days. Of course, the history books stress the co-operation, but we also know the feuding could be fierce.'

There was a short pause while they both considered this unpleasant aspect of Fen history. Then Alan continued, 'So you reckon Stan's death will set the rumour mills grinding again?'

'Oh, yes. In fact, my desk sergeant told me that a couple of people had already said that "the Cripps Curse" had been revived, and that was only a day after we'd pulled your friend from the water. Word travels fast round here. And of course there was that terrible case of the drowned banker.'

'What, around here?'

'I suspect so. The man was called Hansworth. He was found at Denver Sluice back in 2004 – early summer, May, I think it was – but he was a tenant of the Crippses and we suspect he fell in the river. It was probably an accident when fishing. Then his body drifted downstream. It was quite a big case when I first worked for the Fenland force.'

'You said "probably an accident". Did you mean that?'

Lane drew a deep breath. 'I don't know, Alan. The body was very decomposed, so it was hard to do any useful forensics.' There was a pause. 'Well, anyhow, I'll certainly take another look through the Hansworth files when I return to the station.'

In the Lincolnshire Fens where Alan grew up, the folk memories were all about feuding abbeys and priories, fighting to extend their estates by building ever-larger flood banks.

King John's treasure may well have vanished as a long-term consequence of one of those feuds. Down here, in the Black Fens of the south, it was more a story of individual entrepreneurial landowners and family rivalries. The great estates of the higher land reaching out into the richness of the unclaimed, newly drained peats. Usually it was the poor owner-occupier who suffered at their hands. For these people, drainage meant a slow, impoverished death. At the time of the English Civil War the Black Fen was the landscape with the richest potential of any in England. No wonder, Alan thought, that resentments were so deep – and long-lasting. Alan was also aware that each feud was different. They were all closely linked to the landscape and the people who lived in it. Quite literally, the devil lurked in the detail – and he knew exactly where he could uncover his telltale traces.

* * *

They were sitting in Lane's car in the mill car park, sharing a flask of warmish tea. The late afternoon had given way to a misty twilight and in the distance they could already hear the first few pops and cracks as bonfires were lit. Lane was the first to speak, as he handed the mug to Alan.

'Personally, I think the coroner will enter a verdict of death by misadventure. For some reason he got drunk and decided to take a dip . . .'

'In a swollen stream? With his rigger boots on?'

'I agree, but people do strange things when they're so drunk.'

Suddenly Alan had a thought: that broken grille. It was so coincidental, or was it? 'Could it have been murder?'

Lane thought for a moment. 'That had crossed my mind.

Of course we can't rule anything out entirely. But who on earth would have had a motive? Did anyone hate him in archaeology?'

'Hate Stan?' Alan laughed. 'Absolutely not. He was one of those people who everyone liked. Sure, he could be irritating sometimes – can't we all? But no, I think he was one of the most popular people around. We all liked old Stan.' Alan reflected for a moment. 'But what about the family, those "Cursed Cripps", would any of them want to get rid of him?'

'No, absolutely not. It was in *none* of their interests to raise that old myth. In fact, I can assure you that the baronet . . .'

'Barty?'

'So you've met him?'

'Yes, I could see he was looking after – assisting even – Stan's parents at the wake. I must admit, he struck me as a quiet, no-nonsense, intelligent man.'

'Oh, yes,' Lane replied. 'He's all of those things and a very good businessman, besides. I didn't know it when I worked here before, but it was he and his wife Molly who established the restaurant and farm shop. It was all part of raising the money to pay off his father's death duties.' He paused. 'Funny thing, Mary and I often went to the restaurant. They did proper vegetables that tasted of something – unlike that supermarket rubbish you get everywhere now. All grown on the estate.'

'So did you know him when you were here before?'

'Not as a personal friend, no. But he was a magistrate on the Ely bench and I got to know him then. He always struck me as scrupulously honest. And open. But at the same time, he was nobody's fool. He could cut through slimy solicitors and crooked witnesses like a hot knife through butter. His pet hate was those whiplash cases. He *loathed* them!'

'Do you think he was aware of the family's local reputation?' Alan asked.

'Interesting you should ask that. But, yes, he was. I first met him at a grand official reception in the cathedral.'

'When was that?' Alan asked.

'It was my first year with Cambridgeshire, so it must have been Christmas 1997. Actually, I remember that conversation quite well. Barty was talking to an earnest schoolboy, who was doing research into Fenland drainage. It's a standard topic in these parts, as you might imagine. Anyhow, to my amazement, he described how his family had changed from Royalist to Roundhead in the Civil War and then something about drainage disputes in the eighteen century. I can't remember all the details, but he said that people in the Fens have very long memories and that the Cripps had never been very popular locally. I remember he said something like "We're the Campbells of the Fens".'

'Do you think there was ever a Glen – a Fen – Coe?'

'No, I'm sure there wasn't. Although I would image that people weren't too polite to each other during the Civil War.'

No, Alan thought, they most certainly weren't. It was a bloody conflict with high casualties. Much worse than it was portrayed at school – if, that is, it was taught at all.

'Do you think these myths, these stories, had any effects on the Cripps's businesses locally?'

'It crossed my mind, too. Of course, Barty couldn't produce any good solid proof, but he said that John – that's his younger son—'

'Married to Candice, right?'

Lane nodded. 'Anyhow, John had access to the White Delphs shop receipts, which he said were growing very much faster than Fursey's. Worse than that, most of the Delphs's visitors were locals and they weren't known as far away as Cambridge, even – where the real money lay.'

Alan was looking puzzled. 'Sorry, Richard, but White Delphs?'

'I thought you'd have known about it. It's that Second World War visitor attraction on the old railway line, by the bank just off the Littleport Road.'

Alan thought for a moment. Then nodded. Yes, he knew where it was.

'Anyhow,' Lane continued, 'Cambridge, especially the university, was where most of the Fursey restaurant's customers came from. Barty said that John was sure of that because they could often be found sipping a pre-dinner G and T while they strolled round the abbey ruins. He laughed – said that was where he did most of his customer research.'

Alan could picture the scene. 'So despite attracting richer people from Cambridge . . .'

'They were doing less well than White Delphs who were mostly attracting locals.'

'And presumably lots of them.'

'Yes. That's what he seemed to be saying. He reckoned the local market *had* to be cracked if Fursey was ever to be sustainable.'

'Tell me more about White Delphs? Its fame certainly hasn't spread as far north as Lincolnshire.'

'I took a stroll round there last week. It's a strange place, obviously run by volunteers, who were everywhere. But in essence it's part of an old marshalling yard that includes about a mile of the old Ely-Bedford line . . .'

'Which was axed by Beeching in the early 1960s, wasn't it?'

'That's right, but like many railway lines and larger dykes in the Fens, it was used in early wartime defences. It became part of what they called the Fenland Command Line, which was established in the summer of 1940.'

'A defensive line, not a railway line?' Alan wasn't too clear.

'A bit of each . . .'

'So it's got pillboxes, that sort of thing?' Unlike some of his colleagues, Alan didn't consider himself a 'concrete anorak', but he had to admit that wartime remains did have a strong appeal to him. His last case with Lane had involved a huge hangar where Lancasters had once prepared for bombing missions over Germany. In many ways its dark interior put him in mind of echoing cathedrals. And as for those myths about wartime airfields being haunted by the spirits of long-dead airmen: they weren't so strange to him now. Everyone said that place was haunted, too. But one thing he did know: ghosts don't exist in the past. They're all around us, in the actions and minds of the living.

'Yes,' Lane continued. 'There are several pillboxes and two very much larger field-gun emplacements, plus several spigot-mortars and a jumbled mass of anti-tank cubes that had been bulldozed to one side after the war. But I was struck by one thing: they weren't quite as amateur as I'd imagined.'

'In what way: their displays? Their facilities?'

'Both actually. They had quite a smart coffee shop with a souvenir and small bookshop alongside it. Both were housed in what looked like pre-fab wartime barracks. And the display panels were new and well-done; professionally, I reckoned. No, I was quite impressed.'

It was now almost night-time and as the temperature dropped, the mists cleared. Suddenly the evening sky was ripped apart by a dozen large rockets. As if synchronised, they arched gracefully high above their heads. There was half a second's pause, then simultaneously they exploded into showers of glittering celestial confetti. Briefly Alan caught sight of Lane's face staring up. In the fireworks' light, he seemed far happier, more confident and at ease now that he was back in the Fens.

As Alan drove away his resolve strengthened even more. Lane was only doing his job, following the most obvious leads. But Alan knew Stan, and Lane didn't. He had to do the right thing by his friend. And to do that, he needed to use Stan's own methods. Begin with the research. Find out about the place and the history. Take it step by step. The devil would be in the detail.

* * *

The financial crisis, bankers' bubble, call it what you bloody like, Alan was thinking as he drove into Cambridge, happened two years ago, but you wouldn't know it here; this is as prosperous as London – maybe even more so. And very, very different from the small towns and scattered villages around his brother's house in south Lincolnshire. He'd been in Grantham the other day and was shocked to see how many shops were closed, with 'For Sale' or 'Lease' boards in their windows. One glance at the local paper's property pages told the same tale: prices were falling and quite a few places had been put up for auction by the building society or bank. Alan sighed, it was depressing: a foolish investment for a banker was a ruined life, shattered dreams, for an ordinary family. But not here, not in Britain's fastest-growing city. He was driving through the northern industrial suburbs, known by locals as Silicon Fen, and already the road was packed with Lycra-clad executives cycling their way to their offices. For a moment he wondered how they displayed their wealth to their peers. Was it fancy helmets (wired for sound and vision), high-tech shoes, or just flashy suits and bicycles? He didn't know, these were other worlds, but on the whole he preferred them to the old ways of Rolls Royces and vast SUVs.

Slowly he drove his way through the rush-hour traffic to the Downing Street site at the heart of the city. He left his Fourtrak in the multi-storey car park that had been built over the remains of the Saxon city. Alan was fascinated by place names. The fact that he was saying words that he knew people a thousand years ago would probably have understood fired his imagination. So Cambridge or *Grontabricc*, to give it its eighth-century Saxon name, meant the bridge over the River Granta. The 'bridge' part of the name was Early English, or Saxon, but the name of the river was very much older: Celtic, with roots going back to prehistoric times. It was so old, in fact, that it had lost its original meaning. His interest in place names had taught him that rivers run very deep in people's consciousness: the Thames, or Tamesis, had been named for centuries before London was founded by the Romans. It probably meant 'Dark River' in Celtic, the Iron Age tongue. Dark River. How different from the foaming torrents of the hill country: slower, deeper, darker and more deadly. For an instant he saw Stan's face beneath the swirling brown waters. Then it sunk away.

He crossed Downing Street and joined the throng of students heading towards the large courtyard which housed the department of archaeology, where he turned sharp right and made his way to the Haddon Library. Just inside the door were pictures of past Disney Professors of Archaeology; among these distinguished, serious faces, his eye was caught by the warm smile of Dr Glyn Daniel. As a boy, his father had been a fan of Glyn Daniel who chaired the very popular TV show, *Animal, Vegetable, Mineral.* Alan frowned ruefully, *Test Pit Challenge* still had a very long way to go before it matched their viewing figures, but never mind, TPC was a much better programme. Then he remembered that Daniel had written the standard history of Fisher College. He made a mental note to check it out.

First, Alan enlisted the help of the assistant librarian to assemble as much information as he could find about the Cripps family. The sun was just starting to shine through the Haddon's tall windows when Alan looked at the books around him on the table. When he'd discussed the Cripps family with Lane in the mill car park he'd determined to reveal the devil in the detail of their family history. And this was the place to do it. But he'd need to keep his wits about him. Such research wasn't just about reading words in a book; it was about using reason to get at what the author was originally thinking. And that took imagination. But now he had the motivation for the task and, as if to give him a further boost, he remembered working closely with Stan the previous autumn, sorting out levels in the site notebooks. They'd made a good team.

He began reading, every so often stopping to tap on the Notes app and jot something down. In the past he would have taken notes in longhand, but recently he had been persuaded to try a tablet and now he swore by them. By one o'clock his tummy had started making loud gurgling sounds. People were even turning to look. Time for a beer, pie and chips. But before that, he read through what he'd written that morning:

> *1650: Cripps family acquire the lands that previously (pre-1538) belonged to Fursey Abbey (Benedictine). During the Civil War, the main family under Colonel Crowson Cripps began by supporting the Royalists, but then switched to Parliament when they started to rise after Naseby. For his loyalty, Cromwell gave him a grant of land at 'Fursbea, near Eley'. This was seen by many locals as the 'Devil's Due'. Crowson was known to have played an active part in the 'Fursey Massacre', when the (Royalist) vicar, a local squire and the congregation of the parish church was locked in and the timber building set alight. The squire who, like everyone else, died in the fire, was Edward Cripps, Crowson's first cousin. Local legend (see Powis ('49)* Cambridgeshire Folklore and Legends, *pp. 78–81) reported that Crowson's men stopped townspeople from taking water from the river to quench the blaze. Powis (p. 80): 'This inhumane act, if true, probably explains the persistent local myth of the 'Cursed Cripps' and the associated, and possibly equally ancient, link of that family to the river.*

Alan set the tablet aside and stared up at the ceiling. He was beginning to understand why the Crippses had been hated so much. And it wasn't as if they were outsiders, the equivalent of rich London second-homers today. No, they were Fen folk, born and bred. That must have made it ten times worse. His brain was now working at double speed. No time to go to the pub, he'd grab a quick bite instead. The pie and pint could wait.

Fifteen minutes later he returned, still licking the grease of a doner kebab from his mouth. He sat down again and resumed reading, but now his fingers were working overtime.

*c. 1695: Surface of the ground in Fens around Ely lowered as result of earlier drainage. Celia Feinnes, riding through England 'on a side-saddle' noted that Ely was 'ye dirtiest place I ever saw, not a bitt of pitching in ye streetes'. Cripps family established six-horse gin scoop wheels, which discharged their waters onto the common land of the parish, or so it was suggested by the villagers. This was disputed by David Cripps, Crowson's son who had inherited the estate by then. Thereafter, this common reverted to summer grazing. D. Cripps was the magistrate who judged the case.*
*1720: Horse gins replaced by windmills, Further complaints from locals.*
*1781: Act of Parliament enclosing all land within the Parish of Fursey. The Cripps family acquire Fursey Common, which they drain first with windmills, then (1813) with steam. They establish the Fursey Main Engine and its Engine Drain. Most village landholders now confined to poorly drained grazing on edges of Parish.*

Blimey, Alan thought, little wonder they weren't loved locally. But he also had to concede they could get things done – just like today. And if there's one thing that local people resent, it's the success of others when, that is, they achieve things they should be doing themselves. That's pure poison – and it lasts. Boy, Alan sighed, does it last . . . But how did this all fit in with Stan's work on the site? Was there someone out there who resented the work that he was doing? Alan realised he was in danger of getting ahead of himself. Step by step. He returned to his notes.

*C18–19: The Cripps family estate grew steadily. By WW1 it amounted to 3,000+ acres.*
*1922: 1st Baronet Cripps created. Close friend of Lloyd George.*
*1949: 1st Baronet RIP.*
*1949: 2nd Baronet takes over running of the Fursey Estate.*

Hmm, Alan mused, the 2nd Bart could have claimed that Lloyd George knew my father. By now the family history had become very predictable and typical of Britain in the post-war decades.

*1949–1960: 2nd Bart sells off land and Smiley's Mill to pay death duties and maintain the hall and farm buildings. Sells Isle Farm and its land. Fursey Abbey Farm is now too small to be profitable as an agricultural enterprise alone. The Fursey Abbey Farm is 250 acres and Woolpit Farm, 400 acres.*
*1971: 2nd Bart RIP.*

Alan looked up from the tablet. Reading between the lines, it seemed that Barty, now the head of the family, came to his senses after the 2nd baronet's death. Barty realised that the Cripps had come down in the world, but he didn't panic. Instead, he set about joining the late 20th century; making practical choices and connecting with the people around him. But what about his offspring, Alan mused? Had Sebastian and John made their father's journey, or had he shielded them from the new reality? And what about Candice? Was she shielding John by taking on the practicalities of the Fursey project, while he swanned around in the elite circles of tourism consultancy? The longer he thought about it, Alan realised that it takes more to change whole families than just one progressive individual. He sat back in his chair and sighed: there were so many devils in these details.

*1971: 3rd Baronet (Barty) takes over much reduced (2 farms and the park) estate. Estate much reduced by successive deaths and payments of death duties. The hall is very run down, so they get bank loan to do it up and convert into apartments. Bart and Molly move in to Abbey Farm.*
*1977: With the estate slowly recovering, 3rd Bart becomes a Magistrate on Ely Bench.*
*1978: 3rd Bart and Molly set up successful farm shop and restaurant at Fursey Home Farm, which they rename (probably as part of local marketing?) Abbey Farm.*

Alan could never spend much more than about two hours reading in libraries before his concentration began to flag. And now he was feeling distinctly drowsy. So he got out of his chair and took a stroll to the shelves where the books on Cambridge colleges were held. To his surprise there weren't very many, then he paused. Of course, this was Cambridge and each college would still hold the best material themselves. Nonetheless, there was quite a lot on Fisher, most of it written by Professor Daniel. He went straight to what he knew was the definitive volume, Professor Daniel's *A Short History of Fisher College*. It weighed fully 10 kilos. Thank God, he thought, he never wrote an extended version. As he lifted it off the shelf, his eye was caught by another, slimmer volume, *The Cambridge Murders*, by Dilwyn Rees, Daniel's pseudonym.

He scanned the pages by the learned professor. The college had been founded, like St John's alongside it, by Lady Margaret Beaufort, Henry VII's mother, and John Fisher, senior proctor of the university, whom she 'admired' hugely. By all accounts the college buildings had been completed by 1595, apart, that is, from the fine, delicate, Wren bridge over the river Cam, which still provided such a slender foil to the same architect's magnificent library for the much richer Trinity College, a few yards upstream. The college's history in post-Tudor times was undistinguished and overshadowed by the two larger colleges, St John's and Trinity, on either side. Daniel even quoted an example of undergraduate humour, then current in St John's and Trinity: 'Undergraduates at Fisher are truly unique; unlike everyone else, they have chips on both shoulders.' Alan winced: it would be cruel, even today.

But he was getting diverted. College history was one thing, but the Cripps family was another. How had they become involved with Fisher? More to the point, was drainage or land involved? He checked Daniel's index for references to Cripps, and found several. The first referred to David Cripps, Crowson's son, who was a student at Fisher in the very early 18th century. In 1720 he gave his old college £2,000 in cash and almost double that in 'bonds and promissory notes' – in other words, stocks and shares. Alan guessed his bequest was probably worth half a million in today's money. Needless to state, his son and all future descendants would be welcomed by the college with open arms. In those days the extensive old-boy networks that went with a Cambridge college would have given the Cripps family a big advantage over their less privileged neighbours.

There were further, smaller, bequests to Fisher in the 18th and 19th centuries, but one in particular caught his attention. It was made in 1753, by David's son Harry, and it consisted of a grant of land with rights of access onto Fursey Common. Daniel published a map of the holding, which was still in the college's possession when he wrote the book in the mid-1950s. Although hardly a major landowner (unlike its two neighbours), Fisher, in common with many other Cambridge colleges, had accumulated quite a substantial portfolio of holdings, which successive bursars had built up in subsequent years. As a result, the college was a significant landlord and Daniel's map showed their estate, of about 5,000 acres, covering large areas of what is today rural Lincolnshire. Alan could see at a glance that this was excellent agricultural land, which was doubtless why the college had bought it. There were one or two, generally smaller, holdings elsewhere, including Fursey. All were listed in an appendix.

Quickly Alan turned to the final chapter of the book, which described more recent transactions. Here he confirmed that the 2nd Baronet Cripps (Barty's father) had sold off Isle Farm in 1953 to pay the second death duty assessment. There were two pictures of it: a medium-sized unpretentious Italianate house built about 1850 with an attached farmyard and a walled garden. It looked delightful, even in the monochrome picture in which an elderly lady, with two children playing at her feet, stood in the sunlit orchard of gnarled apple and pear trees.

Alan put his head in his hands and closed his eyes: he could see the house out in the less open fen to the north of the pumping station and its Engine Drain that ran up to the very edge of Fursey Abbey. The fields towards Isle Farm were smaller and less regularly shaped and the landscape was less bleak, with more trees and even the occasional hedge. This would suggest it was drier land; probably a low-lying extension of Fursey island – as indeed its name suggested.

By the end of the 1950s, the Cripps's Fursey Estate amounted to just over 400 acres, centred immediately north of Woolpit Farm, which in turn was adjacent to Fursey Hall, the large ancestral seat of the Cripps family. Alan checked his notes to confirm that the hall had been sub-divided into apartments in 1971; these included the residence of Sebastian and Sarah Cripps, who now managed what was left of the estate. Alan smiled. He could imagine that the huge Sebastian was inwardly cursing the generosity of his long-dead forebear. An extra 400 acres could come in very handy today. Alan Googled Sebastian to see if he, too, had attended Fisher. But no, although his younger brother John had. Instead, Sebastian had gained a degree (1982–84) in agriculture from Nettlesham College, just north of Sleaford. Funny, Alan thought, that's where Dad wanted me to go. Indeed, his own brother Grahame had gone there; it was still widely regarded as one of the best agricultural colleges in Britain.

Alan leant back in his chair and looked out at the institutional roofs of Downing Street – and the sunshine. He was starting to feel cooped up.

Time for a pint. He went to a quiet pub he knew in a residential area the other side of the Downing Street complex, where he sat down and opened the local paper. His eye was caught by a story on page two about a big new academy school which was being proposed for Ely. The chairman of the district council, Councillor Sebastian Cripps, was quoted as being strongly in favour of it: 'It would enhance the life chances of new residents in the neighbourhood and would greatly improve their prospects in the future.'

He reached out for his pint, but his hand stopped in mid-air. His mind was racing. Was Sebastian's concern for the good citizens of the Cathedral city entirely altruistic?

Or was there more to it than that?

# Three

Alan was woken from a deep, dreamless sleep by the sound of men and machines in the farmyard below his window. He glanced across at his radio alarm: 5.43am. Then he remembered that his brother Grahame had arranged for the potato harvesting contractors to come today. He only had a couple of acres of Piper to lift, but after all the recent wet weather he was very concerned about slugs. So they'd very kindly agreed to fit the job in on a Sunday.

Below him in the kitchen he could hear the radio tuned into *Farming Today* which was giving an outline forecast for the week ahead: more rain, but not quite as much as last week. The pipes, which passed through his bedroom from the tanks in the attic above, hissed briefly as Grahame did something in the sink downstairs. Then Alan heard the door to the back porch open and close. A brief pause, while his brother slipped on his wellies, then the outside door slammed shut. Alan knew there was nothing he could usefully do to help, but he was now wide awake and he wouldn't be going back to sleep.

His mind was going over what he had learnt: first at Stan's wake, then down at the Mill Cut, and finally yesterday, in the Haddon Library. One question kept returning: where was the truth? Who could be believed in a family where self-interest and greed were a part of their identity, their DNA? Alan thought about the family members he had met: each with their own histories and conflicting motives. But at the heart of it all was Stan's death – and the river. Despite much evidence to the contrary, Alan was still convinced it wasn't suicide. But doubts were starting to gnaw at his confidence: he knew to his cost that he could sometimes get things wrong. Could he be mistaken again? But on the other hand, he thought, Lane seemed as reluctant as him to quit the case. Alan had huge respect for his old friend: after all, last year he had stood by him through a long and difficult case. So did Lane know something he didn't? And what about his new job in Fenland? He wouldn't reveal anything about it to Alan, yet he seemed to have time to hang around Fursey. Surely that wasn't on a whim? DCI Lane didn't act on mere whims. So what was going on? Where was the truth?

Another door opened and shut below him, but this was at the foot of the backstairs into the kitchen from Grahame and Liz's bedroom. The house had tipped over in the late 19th century and although more-or-less stable now, those backstairs were still dreadfully steep and uneven. Alan was convinced that sooner or later there'd be a nasty accident. He could hear the sound of his brother's wife emptying the dishwasher and stacking things in the appropriate places (which he always managed to get wrong when he did that job). Alan liked Liz. In the family she had the reputation of being a bit distant, of not engaging, but Alan had always respected her private nature.

When Alan emerged into the kitchen, she smiled, brought two mugs over to the table and sat down beside him.

'So, Alan, what's happening with you these days? We never seem to get the chance to chat. You're either out with Grahame on the land or stuck up there in your room surrounded by a pile of notes, plans and maps.'

'I'm sorry, Liz, I know my room's a bit of a tip, but you'll be glad to learn that I've just finished writing up two old sites. So that'll let me clear loads of stuff.'

'Oh, for God's sake, Alan, stop behaving like a naughty schoolboy!' She was laughing, despite her exasperation. 'I'm not worried about your room. That's your affair. No, I'm more concerned with *you*, with your life; you've been deeply hurt by Stan's death.' She reached across the table and laid a hand on his arm.

Alan knew the sort of things she meant him to talk about, but he'd never been much good at discussing his own problems. So he took the easy way out and mentioned his writing up jobs, his desk work. 'As it happens, I've been asked to pull together all Stan's papers.'

'Yes, but it's not exactly full-time work, is it?' she cut in. 'I mean, seriously, do you have anything else in mind?'

'Why?' Alan was smiling. 'Do you plan to double the rent?'

This was a long-standing joke between them. He'd agreed with his brother, after their father's death 20 years before, that he should treat Cruden's Farm as his second home. And for his part, he liked working on the farm, and helped Grahame wherever and whenever he could. His conscience was clear.

'Don't be silly, Alan, I'm being serious.'

Maybe this would be a good opportunity to get an objective opinion about Fursey. Liz was no fool and he knew Grahame relied on her heavily. Theirs was very much a partnership of equals.

'OK,' he said with slight trepidation. 'But it might take some time.'

She smiled, rose to her feet and put a tin of home-made biscuits on the table between them.

'Fire away.'

Alan sketched-in how he had found himself involved with Fursey: his two visits the previous year, then Stan's death and Lane's phone call to him that night.

'Do you normally find yourself so heavily involved with another person's project in this way?'

'How d'you mean, "normally"?'

'It just seems rather strange that you should have been very heavily involved at those two places you've just finished writing up.'

'Guthlic's and Impingham,' Alan added.

'Yes. And with the added complications that Richard helped you sort out.'

'Or not.' Alan still felt bad about his role in what came to be known as the Flax Hole Case.

'No, don't give me that, Alan. You two saw that justice was done. That's what matters. But yet you still found time to wander down Ely way. I'd have thought you'd have had other things on your mind?'

'Not really. My first visit was at the end of July and life had been very stressful.' Alan thought for a moment, then continued more slowly. 'If you must know, I desperately wanted to get back to normal. I didn't like my situation; I'd lost control of the events in my life. Seeing Stan and talking about work helped.'

'Yes?' Liz was listening closely.

'It was simple. I needed, quite literally, to get grounded.'

'But was it just a return to some sort of normality, or was there something deeper, too?'

'Since you ask, Liz, yes, there was something else.' He took a final sip from his now tepid tea. 'Most of the sites I'd been working on had been relatively shallow. In other words, the archaeology lay quite close to the ground surface, but over the years I've been lucky enough to work on one or two where the old land surface dipped below the plough-soil.'

'Sorry, Alan, what exactly do you mean by "old land surface"?' It was a question he'd often been asked by students and diggers.

'The old land surface, or OLS, is the ground on which people walked about at various times in the past. Now on most sites the OLS is also the ground on which we move today. In other words, it's directly below our feet, but mixed up within the topsoil by millennia of burrowing moles, earthworms and the like. Which is why if you take a walk across most fields in Britain after they've been ploughed, you'll discover pieces of Roman pottery, alongside Bronze Age flints or indeed fragments of Victorian clay tobacco pipes.'

'But whenever we've visited any of your sites, everything seems to be nice and distinctive. You point at Bronze Age post holes or Roman walls. How come?'

'That's because we've removed the topsoil and with it the OLS. So what we reveal below it is only a small part of the story. It would be like trying to establish how you and

Grahame lived your lives here, but only once we'd bulldozed the house and garden down to foundation level. So we'd find a few drain pipes, Scruffy's remains and Grahame's carp pond liner. Not much to go on, you must admit.'

'So all the really informative stuff is in the OLS?'

'You've got it. In fact, it's so informative that people have excavated below barrows, below hillfort banks, just to recover samples from the OLS that might be preserved there. And then they can use the seeds and pollen grains from the buried topsoil to recreate precisely what the environment would have looked like in the past.'

'So is it just about environment?'

'Oh no, far from it. In certain places – the Fens for example – old land surfaces can be buried in successive layers, separated by sterile deposits of, say, peat or river-borne flood-clay.'

'That's the alluvium I've heard you and Grahame talk about, isn't it?'

'Yes, usually it's alluvium, because peat takes so long to grow, whereas alluvium can be laid down overnight – certainly in a few days, during a bad flood.'

'So there were good bits of OLS at Stan's site, were there?'

Suddenly Alan's face lit into a big smile. 'Oh yes, Fursey was superb. Big build-ups of alluvium – and peat, too.'

'And that's what got you interested?'

'Yes, it was. Plus the fact that Stan was a bit at sea. He'd worked on alluviated sites, but as he said, the people in charge didn't know what they were doing, either. Usually they just machined everything off. Problem solved. But he didn't want to do that – which was why he asked me back for my second visit last November.'

Alan's explanation was ended abruptly as the external movement sensor turned on the powerful yard light. Grahame's Land Rover was back.

* * *

Alan was helping Liz clear up the breakfast things while Grahame sat back and watched. They could both see Grahame was tired out: it had been a long, wet and demanding autumn. For a short time they worked in silence; then the espresso pot on the Aga suddenly started spluttering and Alan took it across to his brother. A few minutes later Liz came to join them, carrying a fresh jug of milk. She sat next to her husband and looked into his eyes.

'Darling,' she said quietly, 'you look all in. Try to get some rest during the day.'

Grahame smiled and patted her arm. 'Don't worry. I'll be able to take things easier today, now the last spuds are nearly in.'

As if to emphasise his point, one of the contractor's three 10-ton trailers, pulled by a mud-spattered JCB Fastrac, roared into the yard and backed up to the potato store.

'Good crop?' Alan asked.

'Yes,' his brother replied. 'We should manage eighteen tons an acre, but much will depend on slug damage. We lifted a few roots first thing and they didn't look too bad. So fingers crossed.'

Alan could see that Liz wasn't about to allow him to change the subject by having a farming conversation, no doubt a tactic that his brother used as much as he did.

'Darling,' she broke in. 'While you were out, Alan was telling me about how he's going to be writing up Stan's researches.

And it does sound an extraordinary site. Do you think there's any chance you yourself might be able to do any work there, Alan?'

'Well yes, actually. I was going to tell you about it, but got diverted into alluvium.'

'Don't talk to me about bloody alluvium. Hate the stuff,' Grahame growled into his coffee.

'Yes, Grahame.' Liz had put on her schoolmistressy voice. 'I'm sure you do. But you're a farmer and your brother here's an archaeologist. And as it turns out, he quite likes "the stuff".' She turned to Alan and this time she was not going to be diverted. 'Be all that as it may, Alan, you were about to tell us something important, weren't you?'

Alan then told her about Stan's wake and his discussions with John, Candice, Peter Flower and Lew Weinstein: how they'd offered him a job, plus what amounted to a television mini-series. When he'd finished, Grahame was wide awake and Liz was wide-eyed.

There was a pause before Grahame spoke. 'Please don't say you told them to get knotted. Did you?'

'No, I didn't, but I still can't make up my mind.'

'Why's that, Alan?' It was Liz's turn to speak. 'Surely that has to be a good offer?'

'Oh, that's simple. It's Peter bloody Flower. I can't stand the man.'

'Yes, Alan, but that was a very long time ago. Surely you can put it behind you now. I mean, did he seem in favour of you?' said Liz, ever the voice of reason.

'Well, yes, he did.' Alan sighed. 'Almost too much. In fact, I found it rather creepy. He talked about making amends. Trouble is, I don't trust him further than I can spit.'

'I have to say, Alan,' Grahame said. 'I think you're in danger of making a very big mistake here. This job sounds like the break you've been waiting for. Everything about it, except Dr Flower, is perfect: the people running it are reliable, local worthies, English Heritage is closely involved, and *Test Pit Challenge* is filming the whole operation. And who knows, if Flower doesn't turn out to be the villain you suppose, he could even point you in the direction of academic appointments at Cambridge.' There was something very measured about his voice. It reminded Alan of their father, whom they both still missed.

'And like the loyal wife I am.' Liz turned smiling to her husband. 'I agree with Grahame one hundred per cent. You *must* take it, Alan. In fact, if I had my way, I'd insist you called them here and now.'

* * *

Alan's phone alarm rang. Eleven o'clock: time to be heading south to see Stan's parents in Peterborough. He threw his copy of *Current Archaeology* across to the bed and stood up. He'd been reading their news section and, sandwiched between a piece about a Bronze Age boat in Wales and a carved walrus-ivory phallus from the City of London, was a short item about job prospects in archaeology two years on from the bankers' bubble of 2007–8. It made grim reading: staff levels were down to a third of what they had been in the boom years and dozens of small firms, partnerships and consultancies had folded. So, in the grand scheme of things, would he even be able to scratch the surface of Stan's work? Or was it all pointless, he wondered, as he looked out of the window at the fields beyond, where the frost still persisted in a few shady places. That glimpse into the real world seemed to stiffen his resolution. No, he thought, this isn't pointless. It's the least I can do for Stan, for his parents. He should have added, 'And for myself, too.' But he didn't.

He put a couple of notebooks, his diary, a compact camera and folding monopod, plus a pack of spare batteries in his knapsack, then headed for the door. He looked back at his bedroom. It wasn't quite such a mess. He'd made an effort. The last thing he wanted was to upset Liz. Right now she was the only woman who seemed to care about him.

* * *

The drive south towards Peterborough was interminable. Other farmers had been lifting potatoes too and the rural roads were spattered with mud. Things were made even worse by contractors hauling sugar beet across to the big Norfolk factory, now that the Peterborough one had closed. But once in Peterborough, things were very different: the traffic moved briskly, roads were clean and as he headed south towards the city centre, he could see that the big multi-storey car parks were filling up. Even in the depths of a recession, people had to go Christmas shopping. For a moment he wondered what it must have been like here in the slump of 1929. Probably very different. That was before the New Town, when the city was more of a market town with a vast and improbable cathedral at its heart – a bit like Ely today, Alan mused.

He went all the way round the big roundabout, then crossed the main East Coast line and headed west along Thorpe Road. At another roundabout he turned right. Here the houses were smart and affluent; this was Ernie Wise country – like the comedian, smart but not too showy.

Alan was greeted warmly at the front door by Dorothy and Jack, who immediately pressed a small glass of medium sherry into his hand. Jack then escorted him upstairs to Stan's room, while Dorothy bustled in the kitchen, preparing lunch. They stood rather awkwardly at the door. A bunch of flowers, probably picked in the garden to judge by their slightly faded blooms and patchy autumnal leaves, had been placed on the bedspread that covered Stan's pillow. Suddenly Alan realised there were tears in his eyes. He took a deep breath and looked at Jack beside him. His eyes were red, too. Somehow they found themselves shaking hands. Englishmen still don't do emotion very well, Alan thought. Then, very quietly, almost whispering, Jack said, 'Lunch is at one. I'll be downstairs if you need anything.' Then he closed the door.

Alan had decided to approach Stan's room and the archive it contained as if it were an archaeological project; he would work from the known to the unknown and always leave a clear record behind him of all the stages he had gone through. So the first step was to take a couple of pictures of the room as he had first found it. He also took a close-up of the flowers: 'That one's for me,' he thought.

Then he approached Stan's desk. He had feared that it might be like his: a vaguely structured chaos, with books, papers and notes in various stages of being assembled, worked on or tidied away. But, no, it was impeccably organised. For a moment Alan was gripped by a thought: does this suggest he knew what he was doing? That he had tidied everything up to make life simpler for those who would have to clear up after his suicide? He opened the wide, shallow drawer above the desk's knee-space. This, if anywhere, was where he would have expected to find a suicide note. It was filled with old ballpoints, pencils, sharpeners, erasers, little 35mm film pots, paper clips, sticky labels, parcel tape, an empty tin of Altoids, a mobile phone charger and two dead mobile phones, both with cracked screens. Alan smiled; he'd got at least two wrecked mobiles at home – both with identical shattered screens, broken on-site. The early ones were designed for office, not site work. But there was no sign at all of a suicide note.

He was about to jot down the contents of the desk drawer, then decided he didn't have the time, so he took a picture instead and recorded that it was *Desk drawer above knee-hole.* Two items on the top of Stan's desk grabbed his attention. The first was a very battered double-box of index cards, each one of which had details of individual finds and layers Stan had discovered while doing his surveys. Alan knew he'd be using it a lot in the next few weeks. The second item was Stan's original (1955) hardback copy of W.G. Hoskins's classic, *The Making of the English Landscape.* Protruding from the back was a postcard printed with the Fursey Hall address and the message: *Many thanks, Stan. You were right. It's a masterpiece. Have ordered a copy from Heffer's. So grateful. Sebastian Cripps.*

Half an hour later he had carefully searched the whole desk, and had placed anything that might come in useful later to one side, along with the card index and Stan's copy of Hoskins's book. He put all of this into two large shopping bags to take home. He was about to turn his attention to a row of notebooks on the lowest of two shelves on the wall above the desk when Dorothy called from downstairs. 'Lunch is ready if you are, Alan.'

He glanced at the time: 1.10. He grabbed the two bulging bags and hurried downstairs.

* * *

Over lunch they chatted mostly about Stan and it was as if he'd just popped out to buy a newspaper or fetch another book from the library and would be back soon. Still, Alan thought, that's better than being maudlin. Life has to go on, but deep down he wondered if Jack and Dorothy would ever be able to find peace. Stan had been all they had. Now he was gone, and what Alan had to do meant so much to them.

As if reading his thoughts, Jack said, 'We're both determined that Stan's research, his work, should live on, and of course we're very grateful to the Cripps family for the memorial and naming the new museum after him, but things like that are somehow more about death than life.'

At this Dorothy rose and went through to the kitchen. They could both hear her quiet sobbing. Jack lowered his voice. 'We'd originally thought about asking you to edit together a special commemorative volume for Stan, but now we're not so certain. Such things appear – and then are soon forgotten. I've got several sad books of that sort on my shelves here. But we want something more . . .' He paused, searching for the right word.

'Relevant?' Alan suggested.

'Yes, that's it. Something more relevant and long-lasting. So we thought it would be a good idea if we put the money we had set aside for the memorial volume into the big final report on Fursey. Do you think you could write something on Stan for that?'

'Yes, I do. In fact, the more I think about it, the more I'm convinced it's a good idea. And I plan to incorporate all his survey results into the bigger picture our excavations . . .' As the words left his mouth, Alan realised that somewhere, deep in the back of his mind, he had decided to take the job.

Stan's father was quick to respond. 'Ah.' He smiled for the first time that day. 'That means so much to us.' He raised his voice, 'Alan's decided to take the Fursey job, Dorothy!'

Dorothy hurried in, ran up to Alan and hugged him warmly. 'Oh, Alan,' she said through her tears, 'we're so pleased. So very, very pleased . . .'

Alan felt humbled at this. Now, however, he knew for sure that he had made the right decision – and as for Peter Flower, he could go hang. But he was also a realist and he knew he couldn't quit till it was all over and done with. Not just with regard to applying Stan's research to the site, but also finding the truth about his death – and whether the Cripps family were accountable. It wouldn't be simple: their history told him that the Cripps clan didn't do simple. One way or another, he thought to himself, I've got to get to the truth, the whole truth.

And nothing but the truth.

# Four

The following week the coroner's court entered a verdict of Death by Misadventure on Stan Beaton. It was not unexpected, and for Stan's parents it was far better than suicide. After that, time had flown for Alan. There was so much to get done by Christmas, and he'd spent December working on the design for the second stage of the Fursey project, sending it off to English Heritage recorded delivery just before the holiday. In fact, they were probably opening the envelope right now, he thought, on his first day back in his Portakabin office at Fursey after the long Christmas/New Year break. He was starting to get frustrated writing endlessly about what they *might* discover in the future. Plans were all well and good, but Alan preferred action.

He got out of his chair and exhaled loudly. His limbs felt stiff as he straightened out. He needed fresh air. Once outside the Portakabin, Alan looked around him: work was progressing on the conversion of the old reed barn into the new museum and archaeology centre and across the old farmyard, the Victorian small barn was still covered in scaffolding as it required extensive alterations to turn it into the new farm shop and restaurant. Despite all the work, one or two stray visitors were still being admitted to the abbey ruins, and two small caravans, one a tea stall, the other a gift shop, were intended for them – although the young couple who ran the tea stall said that most of their trade came from the people involved with the two barn conversions.

And they make an excellent cuppa, Alan thought, as he stirred his insulated plastic mug – an exact replica of a Nikon 20–70mm lens – that had mysteriously arrived in his mail on Christmas Eve. Alan set it on the counter. It looked amazing, just like the real lens in his camera case, and it worked perfectly: kept the tea warm and never leaked. But he had no idea who had given it to him. He was just about to take another sip, when his phone rang. The voice at the other end – it was a man's – started to break up. Then the line went down. Alan held up the phone. As usual: no signal. Sod it. He hurried back to his Portakabin.

The landline phone on his desk rang as soon as he'd closed the door behind him. As he had half suspected, it was Lew Weinstein.

'Great news, Alan. I've just been phoned by Charles Carnwath.'

Carnwath was the commissioning editor at Terrestrial 2. This could only be about one thing and Alan was starting to have doubts. He was suspicious of Peter Flower's role as historical advisor, he had no idea who would be chosen to be his on-screen advisors and, most important of all, he wasn't entirely convinced that he wanted to be a much bigger TV personality. He didn't really enjoy being recognised. He could see what it had done to other people. OK, they were minor and personal worries, but they were still there.

'And?'

'And it's commissioned! They've accepted it, without any major alterations. Just a few tweaks here and there, which we can discuss when next we meet.'

'And the budget?'

'Charles hinted strongly that it could be increased quite dramatically.'

Alan couldn't decide whether a big budget was good or bad. But he feared the worst: big budgets brought more pressure from the broadcasters to increase viewers, come what may. And that was how standards slipped. Inevitably, the story would be over-dramatized and the true subtlety revealed by the archaeology would be lost. That's what Alan hated most – and of course the high-ups, the media luvvies, wouldn't take the rap, because they were safely hidden behind the scenes. So it was the people on-camera who were made to look like idiots, both to the world at large and, worse, to their peers.

'So when do we meet?' Alan asked.

'It'll have to be quite soon.' Weinstein paused. 'I've got a great young director in mind, and I mentioned it to him when I was in the States just before Christmas. It would be good if you two could get together.'

'What, an American?' From experience, Alan knew they often found it hard to grasp the intimate scale of the British landscape.

'No, he's a Brit, Frank Jones, but he's been working over there for a couple of years. Got lots of new ideas. I dropped his name to Charles some time ago and he was dead impressed.

Probably helped us land the contract. What say we all meet up here on Friday?'

'Fine.'

Despite his new job, Alan's diary was still depressingly empty. And a trip to London would certainly liven things up.

* * *

Lew Weinstein and Arthur Hall had set up New Ideas Productions in 1989. Weinstein had been a keen cinema-goer since his childhood and he had directed several small documentary films while at Fisher College, where he had been reading English. His friend and business partner Arthur Hall had read Law, but had no wish to stay in the profession. He was an entrepreneur to his fingertips. At first the company was run from their shared flat in Paddington, but soon it was successful enough to rent an office in Balham. Much later, and following the rapid success of *Test Pit Challenge*, they were able to move to larger premises in central London, where they were to this day.

Arthur Hall had good contacts in the then developing world of satellite television and they had made several successful documentary series for these clients in the sky. In mid-2005, Arthur Hall raised the money to make a short pilot programme, which they offered to Terrestrial 2, where Charles Carnwath was commissioning editor for history and the environment. Carnwath, who knew and trusted Weinstein from their Cambridge days, saw the show's potential and, although the pilot was never broadcast, he commissioned an initial series of five programmes, which were screened in the winter of 2006–7. The strand was a big success from the outset and by the end of series two, they were regularly being seen by upwards of four million people. By then, however, the number of episodes in each series had increased to ten, which is what was planned for the current, fifth, series, being filmed this spring and summer. The Fursey programme was to be additional to the main set of ten: a one-off *Test Pit Challenge Special*.

Despite their name, New Ideas Productions were located in a somewhat ramshackle Victorian two-storey workshop, complete with countless alterations and additions. The original building was constructed, Alan reckoned, around 1850 and used the same grey London stock brick as its distinguished neighbour, King's Cross Station, on the other side of the Euston Road. Like most of the houses, pubs and shops in the area, it almost certainly owed its existence to the nearby railway and may well have been built by one of the many sub-contractors who provided parts and services not just to the railway companies, but to the many service industries – the hotels, the caterers, the bus and cab companies – that sprung up when what was now known as the East Coast Main Line came into existence.

The workshop was reached through a short cul-de-sac, which gave onto a rather moth-eaten park, where the grass never really thrived because the sycamores and surrounding buildings effectively screened out most of the sunlight. But it was pleasant enough, if, that is, you didn't mind being regaled by the two semi-resident drunks who occupied its two benches.

Alan had had to get up early to be in London for a ten o'clock meeting and the wet streets of Camden did not seem particularly welcoming. But at least it wasn't snowing, he thought, as he crossed the Euston Road and walked through a waft of oriental aromas issuing from the extractor fans of

Chip Chop Noodle Bar's kitchens. His guts rumbled – he'd forgotten to have breakfast.

Once inside the New Ideas building he signed in at the desk, climbed the stairs to the upper floor and made his way along the corridor that served the individual editing suites. At the end was the meeting room. He paused to look through the glass panel in the door before entering. He was the last person to arrive. At the head of the table was Weinstein and alongside him was Carol, his PA. Next to her were two people he didn't recognise, a swarthy-looking man in his late thirties or early forties and a very attractive young woman with flaming red hair. Opposite them were Craig Larsson, the show's presenter, and Joe 'Speed' Talbot, Weinstein's favourite lighting cameraman.

He tried to enter with the minimum of fuss, but failed, as they were all waiting for him. Weinstein introduced him to the two people he didn't know, who turned out to be Frank Jones, the director who had recently returned from working in the States, and Dr Tricia Neave, who had just gained her PhD.

In the run-up to Christmas, Alan had been working on material from Stan's trial trenches of the previous summer, and had been struck by the amount of Roman pottery they'd revealed. It was all fairly usual stuff – NVGW (Nene Valley Grey Ware) and NVCC (Nene Valley Colour Coat), together with quite a few Samian sherds, which hinted at earlier origins – but Alan couldn't pretend to be any sort of a Roman expert and he needed a consultant to help him out. Peter Flower had suggested they should approach one of his post-doctoral research students, so presumably, Alan thought, this was her.

Being Alan, he asked the question outright. 'Forgive me

asking, Tricia, but Peter Flower said he knew of a Romanist who could advise us about pottery, small finds and that sort of thing. Am I right in thinking that's you?'

She gave him what could only be described as a winning smile.

'My dissertation,' she said, almost apologetically, 'was on the small towns of Roman Britain, with special attention to *Durobrivae* and its region. So I do think I ought to be able to bring something to the project.' She paused and gave Alan a shy smile. 'If that's OK by you, of course.'

Alan was now beginning to regret jumping in feet first. And, yes, her work on *Durobrivae*, just west of modern Peterborough and one of the most successful and prosperous smaller towns of Roman Britannia, was highly relevant. Grudgingly, he had to admit that Flower's choice had been excellent. And one glance at her beautiful face with its sparkling brown eyes was enough to see why Weinstein had taken to her so readily. Indeed, he thought, looking at their body language together, she already seems to be getting on well with the new director, too. Or was it him more than her? Hard to say.

Weinstein cleared his throat loudly, drawing the meeting to order. 'Great to have you with us, Alan.' Then he very slightly raised his voice and turned to the rest of the table. 'It's nearly 10.15 and we've a lot to discuss.' He glanced down at a print-out. 'Charles Carnwath has told me that in-depth analysis of the ratings for *Test Pit Challenge*, series three, shows two important trends. First, an increase in the A and B social components, that's the better-off and more professional classes. You may have noticed that the commercial breaks have featured more SUVs, finance houses and the like. But at the same time, and this is what makes TPC so special in T2's eyes, we seem to be appealing more and more to the 18–35 demographic.'

'Wow.' Frank Jones was certainly impressed. 'Seems like I'm joining a winning team.'

'Thanks, Frank. But our success might prove a mixed blessing, so we've got to handle things very carefully.'

'Do you mean the split between the two growing components of our audience?' Tricia asked. 'Is that going to cause us problems?'

'It could, if it isn't handled very sensitively.' He turned to Frank Jones. 'And you and I, Frank, will be the ones who'll have to do the balancing act.' He looked back to the table. 'We're not so worried about the main series of ten episodes. They have a quite a rigid format, which is tried-and-tested. And I'll be quite frank with you all, T2 will be using the Fursey programmes to test new markets and, crucially, to increase their audience share. Currently they are averaging about sixteen per cent and we are aiming for around twenty.'

'Sounds a bit optimistic?' Alan couldn't help asking.

'It is, Alan, but Charles and the top people at T2 have some ambitious plans as well. I won't say they're going to throw money at us, but I don't think we should have many problems raising any necessary expenses.'

This was greeted with an impressed silence. Alan suppressed the urge to demand a pay rise. He looked across at Craig Larsson. I bet he isn't appearing for £300 a day plus travel, he thought.

Unexpectedly, Speed was the first to speak. 'If we're going to be so all-singing and all-dancing, isn't it time we moved to HD?'

'You're right, Speed,' Weinstein replied. 'High Definition was the first thing I insisted on when Charles outlined their plans. And he agreed. They're coming up with some technical specs right now. They'll be emailed to you shortly.'

Speed nodded. He was obviously well pleased.

'But first things first,' Weinstein said. 'T2 can plan what they like, but nothing will happen if we've got nothing to film. And that, of course, is why Alan's here.' All eyes were now on Alan. 'So, Alan, could you give us a brief outline of what has been found so far and how you intend to discover more? Timetabling is going to be essential here.'

While Weinstein was introducing him, Alan reached into his knapsack and pulled out a manila folder containing his notes and a draft of the report to English Heritage that Peter Flower and Stan had been working on immediately prior to Stan's death. He had added a more up-to-date summary of recent discoveries, plus a few references, but essentially it was their work.

'Thanks, Lew,' Alan began. 'There's so much . . .' He paused, assembling his notes and his thoughts. 'So where do I start?'

'Try the beginning?'

'Thank you, Craig, that's very helpful. But it flags up how hard it will be to run the archaeology to a strict timetable.'

'No, I appreciate that, Alan,' Weinstein broke in. 'But I think we must try to be very disciplined about when and where we do things. It won't be like one of our regular shows where there are cameras everywhere and nearly all conversations are recorded.'

'Or re-recorded in hindsight.' Alan couldn't resist replying.

'I know, but what I'm trying to say is that you mustn't come up with new plans without telling us. And on our side, we mustn't suddenly decide to run a live episode, say, on a day that you've scheduled to move the site huts.'

Speed and Craig had suddenly looked up at the word 'live'. They looked happy. Alan wasn't. As in real life, film gave you time to change your mind and modify your views. Live TV forced rapid decisions – which were often either wrong or misguided.

'So you're planning to go live?' Craig asked.

'Possibly, but that will depend on what Alan thinks we might find. So over to you, Alan – and everyone else, please give him a chance to say his piece.'

At that, the people around the table sat back in their seats.

Alan began by describing Fursey's location on a small natural island of drier land, just off the northern shores of the main Isle of Ely. Briefly he explained that in medieval times and earlier the islands and shores of the modern landscape would have been real islands and shores in a reedy wetland, especially during the dampest months of winter. The flood-free land of the islands and fringes of the fens were usually thickly populated from prehistoric times. That population grew in the Roman period and there was no reason to believe there was a decline during the subsequent Dark Ages, either. Apart from being flood-free, the main reason why people settled along the edges of the wetlands was the fens themselves, where in the drier months of the summer and autumn, huge flocks of sheep and herds of cattle could be grazed; while in winter, the watery landscape provided something that was always scarce in ancient times, namely, a reliable and plentiful source of meat, in the form of fish, eels (hence the name Ely: 'rich in eels'), and wildfowl, such as geese and ducks. The wetland was also a rich source of wood and peat for fuel, reeds for thatching and flooring; and finally, salt could be extracted from the tidal creeks a few miles to the north. All in all, it was utopian. When Alan used that word, Weinstein smiled broadly and jotted it down.

Alan gave him time to make a note. As he did so he could picture the T2 trails in his mind: 'Join us in the ancient Fens near the beautiful cathedral city of Ely. In this utopian landscape our Celtic ancestors were cruelly butchered by incoming Roman—'

Alan realised that the room had gone silent. Weinstein had finished writing. Everyone was looking at him and waiting.

He mumbled an apology and went on to outline how Stan's work had revealed extensive evidence of a later prehistoric, Iron Age, settlement in the Fursey area, mostly dating to the final four centuries BC and the half century or so AD leading up to the Roman invasion of AD43. Some of the pottery was of exceptional quality and suggested a very high-status community: maybe even a tribal capital or regional centre of some kind. There was some evidence that these settlements, or this settlement (it still wasn't clear which), continued into Roman times, possibly as late as the start of the fourth century AD, but probably no later. Next came the monastic settlement at Fursey. The origins of the name are still not entirely clear. The last two letters, '-by', referred to the Viking word for a farm or settlement. Normally the first part of the word would be the name of the person who owned that farm, so Grimsby was once a Viking-period farm that belonged to a man called Grimr, but they knew of no name that could become 'Furs'; so the best idea yet suggested was that it referred to a rump-shaped island, 'furth', as in Barrow-in-*Fur*ness.

At this point Tricia asked if Fursey was indeed rump-shaped.

Alan smiled. 'If it is, she had a very slender figure.' This earned him a mild titter.

Although not a place-name specialist himself, Alan was not at all convinced of the accepted explanation, but it was all he had to go on. He went on to describe what was known about the monastic site, mostly from documents in the library at Ely Cathedral. Essentially, it was a Benedictine sister house to Ely itself, but possibly not quite as early, perhaps even post-1066. It was always a smaller institution and towards the end of its life in the years leading up to the Dissolution of 1538, it had almost reverted to being a grange, in other words, a farm that was wholly owned by its larger and wealthier close neighbour.

At this point, Weinstein intervened to ask Alan what he thought would be the main questions they needed to answer. Alan had expected this, and produced from his folder copies of a short list which he handed round.

*1.* Are there earlier origins, before the Iron Age?
*2.* The high status of the late Iron Age: did it happen gradually, or was it introduced from outside?
*3.* Why did the high status not continue into Roman times, as happened so often elsewhere? Normally we would have expected a small villa in the fourth century.
*4.* Why on earth found another Benedictine house so close to Ely?

When he had finished, Tricia was the first to speak.

'Alan, could you bring us up to date about the English Heritage research grant. How's that looking? Peter said he'd handed everything over to you, and that's all he knew . . .'

'Yes, I'm so sorry. I should have contacted Dr Flower, so do please give him my apologies.' In truth he still didn't like communicating with the man and didn't think the nuts and bolts of his, Alan's, job should be any concern of his. He, Alan, had said he'd submit the report to EH before Christmas, and that surely was enough. Tricia's response was, however, slightly surprising.

'I would, but I don't see him very often. I'm no longer at the university. In fact, to be honest, I'm quite keen to make my own way in the real world outside it, but that said, I was glad of the tip-off from Peter: this job came at precisely the right time for me.'

'Don't tell me you were about to start stacking supermarket shelves?' Craig Larsson could be quite mischievous when he chose.

'No, worse. They wanted me to supervise the second years' annual field trip around Dorset.'

This merited a restrained laugh.

'Oh no.' Alan had to agree. But he hadn't forgotten her original question. 'I sent the report on Stan's previous research, plus a detailed proposal and project design to English Heritage and heard from one of the regional team's inspectors just after the New Year.'

'Can I ask who it was?' Tricia asked.

'Yes,' Alan replied. 'Her name didn't mean anything to me: Shelley Walters. I think she must be new there.'

'Oh, Shelley!' Tricia was delighted. 'I'd heard she'd applied for the job.'

'She any good?' Immediately Alan wished he'd rephrased that.

'Yes, she's great. You'll love her, Alan. Everyone loves Shelley.'

Tricia was trying not to sound gushing, but not succeeding, Alan thought.

Weinstein intervened to bring them back to the point. 'And what did Shelley think, Alan?'

'At the time she hadn't read it, but she phoned me yesterday, as it happens. Had some queries about specialists and some of our pay rates, which I pointed out were IFA recommended. So she seemed quite happy with that. But, yes, she sounded very optimistic.' He tapped the tabletop. 'Touch wood, I think we'll probably get it – the grant, that is. I also gather on the grapevine that the current year's money from the treasury is underspent. And between you and me, that's what really matters.'

'Yes,' Weinstein intervened. 'I agree, up to a point, Alan – the money does matter, as we're not exactly millionaires at New Ideas, either. But the key and most important thing is to get the English Heritage name behind us. That will add huge credibility to our show. I can't tell you how much it matters to our viewers that we're absolutely authentic. With all the weird celebrity reality television now being screened, the discerning public are losing trust in what they see. It's a real worry.'

'I'm so pleased to hear you say that, Lew.' Alan really meant what he was saying. 'All the fans tell me that it's the way we argue among ourselves that gives *Test Pit Challenge* its credibility. It's as if they were there in the site pit alongside us. It's a glimpse of *real* reality, not some media luvvie's glitzy TV creation.' He stopped abruptly. Had he gone too far?

But he needn't have worried. Weinstein was grinning broadly.

'Thanks, Alan.' He turned to the rest of the table. 'So that's what we've got to show the world. The next question is simple: how do we do it? But we'll need coffee to decide that one.'

* * *

After a short coffee break downstairs, the group reconvened in the meeting room. Everyone returned to their original places around the table. There was a short pause while people waited for Weinstein to rejoin them. Then they heard his office door down the corridor close and his approaching footsteps. He sat down at the table and opened the discussion.

'Right, we've heard from Alan what the project has to offer archaeologically and I think it's fair to say we're all very excited at its potential. Now, as you may know, T2 has been flatlining in its audience share . . .'

He was interrupted by Speed Talbot. 'Ah, so that's what we call decline, these days . . .'

'Well, yes,' Weinstein admitted. 'Speed's right, their audience share has actually been dropping very slowly, and they're planning what their PR people are describing as a multi-stranded offensive, where two new celeb-focused reality shows will appeal to the 18–35 demographic while we take the message to the more upwardly mobile As and Bs, and of course the over-35s. The emphasis of the new approach, which they're styling "Come Alive with T2", will be on live coverage wherever possible. It launches with the new season, not in

September, but at Easter. Again T2 are trying to outwit the opposition.'

'And do you think it'll work?' Alan was sceptical.

'What the moving of the start of the new season, or the new initiative?'

'Both.'

'To be honest, I don't know. But they've got to try something radical or they'll be going out of business in five years.'

Something was worrying Alan. 'But surely, I thought they were supposed to be a public service broadcaster. Don't they have at least some obligation to produce good programmes?'

'They do, Alan, which is why they're putting so much faith in us. We provide their credibility, not just with the public, but with the government too.'

'So all these bright new ideas won't affect the quality of our output. You're not planning for us to dumb down?'

Alan was aware that the words 'dumb down' were like a red rag to a bull as far as media executives were concerned. But what he was hearing was worrying him a lot.

'I think it might help if I explained what we've been discussing together, Lew.' It was Frank Jones. Everyone turned to him and Weinstein nodded for him to continue. 'I think there is a widely held misconception that live television is somehow less intelligent than more conventional documentary shows. And, sure, that can sometimes be the case. I've seen some live TV that made me cringe, but I've also seen some docs that were frankly stupid: they were either misleading or else told you nothing. I call them "wallpaper docs" in a film I made for *US World View*.'

Weinstein, Speed, Craig and Tricia exchanged significant glances. Alan had never heard of it.

But Frank was still speaking. 'The way I was taught to see things in the States, the live element in a show was the means whereby you linked the show's content to the audience. It was a way of providing relevance for the here and now, because people at home are aware that during a live broadcast the people on the screen are just as vulnerable as them. So when you make, say, an archaeological discovery, even quite minor finds become more important.' Alan could see he was warming to his subject. 'More to the point,' he continued, 'they immediately identify with the new discovery, even though they hadn't actually revealed it. That doesn't matter. What matters is that they were there when it was found. I've even heard members of focus group audiences taking ownership of certain things, describing them as "my" dog jaw or jug handle after they had seen one of our live digs on TV. And I think that sense of individual proprietorship is very important. In effect, it's giving people back their own past.'

This was stirring stuff. Frank had captivated the small group around the table. Even Alan felt moved and not a little fed up that he hadn't delivered his earlier summary with more passion. He realised that he would have to up his game, if, that is, he wanted to compete with Frank – and probably with Tricia too.

'That is so inspirational, Frank,' Tricia was plainly very moved. 'So you don't see any possible live element as an end in its own right – as something put there to boost ratings?'

'No, I most certainly don't,' he replied, his face a picture of serious concentration. 'In fact, I wouldn't work for anyone who suggested such a thing. No, if we *do* go live—'

Weinstein interrupted. 'Forgive me breaking in, Frank, but the reason I was a few minutes late after coffee was that

Charles phoned me. He told me that the programme director at T2 had given him the go-ahead to commission six half-hour live shows to be screened during March, with additional and near-continuous coverage on 2-Much.'

2-Much was the digital and Internet channel owned and operated by T2.

'So forgive me, Lew,' Alan asked, 'but will the live shows go out first, because if they do, surely we'll need to have some sort of initial scene-setting, won't we?'

Weinstein was smiling. 'No, don't worry Alan, it won't be like that at all. The mini-series will start with two standard fifty minute documentaries, which will be screened at peak viewing times, probably in late February or March.'

'Phew,' Speed interjected. 'That'll keep the Avid Suites red hot.'

The Avid Suites were the digital equivalent of the cutting rooms of celluloid film studios.

'Guess I'd better sharpen my trowel – and my wits.' Alan was stunned. There was *so* much to think about.

* * *

As he made his way back to King's Cross Station, Alan couldn't help wondering whether that huge amount of televised scrutiny would merely produce platitudes about the distant past – whereas he was after truthful insight. He'd only been working at Fursey for a few weeks, but already he was growing suspicious. Too many people with widely differing motives were involved. And the all-pervading culture of respect for the Cripps family did nothing to encourage free communication, either at Fursey Abbey or indeed in the village, among the estate workforce or local tenants. He was becoming increasingly convinced that when the cameras arrived and media pressure began to increase, other things would soon become apparent. People's motives would become clearer. Ambitions would be harder to conceal. Maybe the veneer of upper-class politeness that concealed so much of Cripps family life would begin to crack. But he also knew it wouldn't happen without help. Without his constant prodding – and alert observation. Ideas were tumbling around in his head. He found he had stopped walking and was standing, stock still, in the middle of the pavement, staring up into the dripping branches of a young plane tree.

He'd got it.

He now understood his role. It would be simple. Whatever he might think about what was happening in front of the cameras, his job was to stay there, come what may: to stir the waters and observe the scum that floated to the surface. Eventually some of it would probably be relevant to Stan's death. If his experience of television had taught him anything, it was that the cameras hastened change: events that would normally have taken years to evolve happened in a few hours. His task was to stay and note down and observe everything that took place around him. It was something that Stan was so good at – as those meticulously observant card index boxes demonstrated. He now realised he was in a uniquely privileged position – and he mustn't blow it. He mustn't let his old friend down.

He thought for a moment about Stan sitting at his desk, with everything sorted and in order around him. What had been going through his mind? Was it all routine work, or was he on the verge of something much bigger? A major discovery? If he was going to do his friend justice, Alan was now acutely aware that he had to up his game. He couldn't muddle through this case as he had done in the past. Things were going to be far more complex: more people, more events, more public attention, more motives and more opportunities to conceal or commit evil. Big productions bring big facilities: helicopters, hydraulic towers, powerful diggers, drones. And all of these could be abused. He would have to be focused and disciplined. And persistent, too: like a Jack Russell terrier with a live rat, he must hang on – regardless. There was so much at stake and it seemed to Alan inevitable that someone would reveal his, or her, hand. His task now was to make sure he was there when it happened.

Survival, he realised with a growing chill, would now be the name of his game.

# Five

It had been a long, wet winter and even January, which Alan knew from his childhood on his family's small farm in Lincolnshire, could often be dry, if cold, was starting with rain. The previous week the contractors working on the new Fursey farm shop and restaurant had got a forklift, carrying a pallet-load of roof tiles, stuck when it dropped a wheel off the concrete floor of the old pig yard. To make matters worse, building inspectors, on one of their routine site visits, had parked on the environmentally friendly cellular plastic car park surface, which covered most of the open space between the old reed barn, the pig yard and Abbey Farmhouse, where John, Candice and Barty lived. The cellular car park surface had been the last word in what today would be called eco-friendly car park solutions when Barty had had it installed in the late '80s.

Alan had been preparing to leave for a bite of lunch at the pub when the large, low-slung car from County Hall arrived on-site. It had been raining hard all week and Alan had thought it wisest to leave his Fourtrak on a corner of the pig yard, well out of the way. But not so these important officials, who drove straight onto the cellular matting – which promptly gave way. And hence today's meeting. After the incident, which involved several pairs of shiny black shoes getting covered with sticky alluvial mud, all visitors to the site, petting farm and abbey were being accommodated on the concrete surface of the old pig yard, which now sported some rather narrow, but freshly-painted parking spaces.

The site office was housed in a Victorian implement store attached to the reed barn, which Barty had converted in the late '70s when he and Molly were setting up the original Abbey Farm Shop. Now it had to be reached by a duckboard walkway from the reed barn. As so often seemed to be the case, Alan was the last to arrive. Once inside the office, Candice introduced him to the two officials from County Hall, a planner and Clare Hughes from development control, who had offered to help Alan publish Stan's papers at the wake. Alan knew she was no fool. Although still quite young, and unlike most of her contemporaries, Clare had actually worked in a contracting unit, so was able to appreciate their problems. But on the downside, it also meant she could see through most of their bullshit.

Candice began the meeting. 'First, let me apologise for John not being here, but he had a prior engagement with the bank in London.'

This sounded very impressive, but Alan was surprised that she felt it necessary to apologise at all: she was, after all, a partner in the Fursey enterprise.

'I would also like to apologise for that unfortunate business last week. I do hope your people weren't too badly affected. We had no idea the cellular car park would be so wet. It's never, ever, been like that before. I'm sure it's just the rain.'

Far from being made to look a fool by her collapsing car park, Alan admired the way she had used it to keep control. Her poise was remarkable.

'I wouldn't be so sure, Mrs Cripps,' the planner interjected. 'We've come across this sort of thing before. Those cellular surfaces are wonderful and generally very effective, especially on well-drained surfaces such as sand and gravel. But they often encounter problems on heavy clay soils and particularly when patterns of use intensify, as is happening here. I'm pleased to hear that your visitor numbers are doing well.'

'Thank you, yes they are.' Candice was suitably gracious. 'So it would seem we've no alternative but to put down a more durable—'

'And drainable,' the planner added. Unnecessarily, Alan thought.

'Indeed, and drainable, surface,' Candice continued, undaunted. 'But we've had contractors visit the site and they are most insistent that we remove all the surface clay, right down to the gravel subsoil. They don't think we need go any further, provided we lay a geo . . . a geo . . .'

'A permeable geotextile sheet.' This time the planner's intervention was welcomed.

Next she turned Clare. 'And what are the archaeological implications of doing that?'

Clare pulled a face. She had no idea. 'I think Alan here, is the best person to ask.'

'Well, yes,' Alan began, 'if Stan's survey is correct, the clay alluvium is pretty even across the area of the cellular surface, but perhaps a little thicker to the north, towards the old pig sheds – but not much, maybe three inches. Then below that is the buried soil that was in existence prior to the widespread flooding of the third century AD. So that's going to be very important and will require close attention, although there shouldn't be any need to excavate down into features below it, unless, of course, they're filled with alluvium, too. But then you'd want to get rid of that anyhow.'

'So how long will that take you?' Candice asked.

'That depends on the team I can assemble at such short notice, but I can't see it being finished in under six weeks. Maybe ten. It just depends on what we find.'

'The thing is,' Candice said with a hint of anxiety, 'we've got a big opening ceremony planned for the Easter holiday.' She paused to check the date on her phone. 'Which is the weekend of 22 to 25 April. The contractors reckon it'll take two weeks to do the job and they'd like to allow another week for line-painting and consolidation. So your deadline is the end of March. Can you do it?'

The question was posed to Alan, but to everyone's surprise Clare answered. 'I don't think that's up to Alan, Mrs Cripps. We at County Hall decide when and if the car park can be built, and Alan has to satisfy us that the archaeology has been properly dealt with.'

Blimey, Alan thought, that was a bit strong. Even for a county mounty. But still, he had to concede, it did need saying.

* * *

The car from the county council was heading down the drive, when Candice turned to Alan. 'Are all the county people like her?'

'I wouldn't worry, Candice. I think her bark is worse than

her bite. I've worked with her on several jobs and never had a problem.'

'Oh, well,' she sighed. 'Let's hope it was a one-off. So tell me what you honestly think: can we meet the deadline?'

Alan shrugged. 'I'll be frank. Normally I'd say yes. In fact, six to ten weeks would easily be enough on most sites, but we're on an island here, plus there's a known Iron Age presence and just over there' – he nodded towards the abbey ruins – 'is an important Benedictine monastery. So I honestly don't know. But as we don't have to excavate any features below the palaeosol—'

'The what?'

'Sorry, the ancient pre-flooding topsoil layer. If we had to dig them as well, I'd say that six months wouldn't be long enough for a site of this size.'

By now Candice was looking very anxious. Outside the office the watery sun had retreated behind cloud and light rain was beginning to fall. Alan looked across at Candice. She was obviously determined to make a go of the Fursey enterprise, although Alan wasn't altogether certain how much real help her husband John was actually providing. But he could see she was determined, and that worried him. A determined woman was not what you wanted when you were trying to prise open a tightly-knit family. Increasingly he realised that poor, gentle Stan would have been no match for her.

'You may well have guessed, Alan,' she had now adopted a quieter, more confidential tone, 'that John and I have invested a substantial sum of borrowed money and a lot of ourselves in this project. But I think we knew more or less what we were doing, until, that is, we came across archaeology. Neither of us really understand anything about it, which is why, of course, we invited Peter Flower to join the board of our company back in 2006.'

Hmm, Alan thought, I'd have chosen someone with some practical experience. But instead, he asked about their company. 'That's Fursey Heritage Developments Ltd?'

'That's right, FHD.' She paused briefly. 'John, Barty and I set it up the previous year, when John was starting to become more closely involved in the estate and realised that the farm shop and restaurant were not very tax efficient and the petting farm was potentially missing out on huge tourism grants. So, using the abbey ruins as an excuse, he was able to convince the Charity Commission that part of the organisation – the Fursey Heritage Trust – should be registered as an official charity. As a result, FHD now pays a proportion of its gross profits to the charity, tax-free.'

'That's quite a complex arrangement.' Alan had come across similar set-ups elsewhere, and they didn't always operate very efficiently. 'And does it work well?'

'Yes, very well. But you've got to understand that setting up companies like ours was meat and drink to John. He did it, indeed, he still does it, for a living. He has a large practice with offices in London and Cambridge.'

Alan didn't want her to think he was prying unnecessarily, but he had good reasons to find out more. Very often the organisation of family companies reflects the power structure of the people behind them.

'So did he do his consultancies for all sorts of companies, or just ones like yours, in the heritage sector?'

'Perhaps heritage is defining it a bit closely. No . . .' She thought for a moment. 'He's interested in projects and companies that involve the public directly. So his firm advises several large theme parks, including Belton Towers and Madame Gaspard's in London, not to mention Mrs Lipton's Cave. But they also provide management services to at least one chain of pubs, a group of specialised cinemas and two franchises of high street betting shops.'

'Gosh, that's quite a portfolio. How does he find the time to do all that and still work here?'

'Well, I suppose I do most of the day-to-day running of Fursey. Like this morning.' She smiled. 'The thing is, he has always enjoyed working in the corporate world and he's very good at it. Ever since he was at Cambridge he has been closely involved with tourist attractions and that sort of thing. He enjoys the public side, too. In fact, strictly between ourselves, I was quite worried when he started to look into the running of betting shops and then found he was actually rather good at it.'

Alan was intrigued. Betting shops? Not at all what he'd have expected. 'At what? Running the companies, or betting?'

It was meant as a slightly risqué joke. But to Alan's surprise, Candice took it at face value.

'Betting. Believe it or not, he made quite a lot of money for himself that way. In fact, I had to make him promise he'd stop. It was starting to worry me. They always say you never win in the long run . . .' She trailed off.

'And did you succeed?'

'Oh yes, of course I did. And I don't think he has the sort of addictive personality that gets sucked ever deeper into gambling. I'm fairly sure he did it with his eyes wide open. And as I said, he was very good at it. So he still goes racing—'

'Really? I'm surprised he finds the time?'

And I wonder what else he gets up to when he's away? Alan was starting to wonder whether the John/Candice marriage was quite as Made in Heaven as it first seemed.

'And I used to accompany him. But now it's purely and simply for the horses, which he loves. In fact, we'd have a race horse if we had the money.' She paused, frowning slightly. 'The thing is, Alan, it's not like he's got the sort of personality that enjoys taking unnecessary risks. Far from it. But he can spot opportunities and has got a very sound business head, too. And that's why for several years he's been very keen to get involved with White Delphs down the road.'

Alan didn't quite get the connection. 'Sorry, I don't follow you.'

'Well you know White Delphs?'

'Only vaguely. It's over towards Outwell, isn't it? Something to do with wartime remains. Pillboxes. That sort of thing.'

This was slightly untrue, as Lane had told him quite a lot. But he needed to discover what Candice thought of John's idea. And what were his motives? Maybe she could give him the Cripps family line on what might be seen as local opposition? Or was there such a thing as a Cripps family line at all? If ever a family was composed of individuals, Alan mused, this surely was one.

'That's right. Up until recently it was being run by a group of local enthusiasts, but then it was taken over by Historic Projects Management in 1996. They run it very successfully. In fact, even now, their visitor numbers put ours in the shade. I tell myself they've got more popular appeal, being wartime – *Dad's Army* and all that – but even so, I can't help wondering how much of it is down to the family's bad local reputation.'

Her husband's familiarity with their operation suggested something to Alan. Was this John's way of getting away from the Cripps Curse? And did he tell Stan? Alan knew Stan's views about recent, especially wartime, archaeology – and they weren't printable. The kindest thing he ever said was: 'They'll do the archaeology of *The Archers* next.'

'And was John anything to do with that takeover?'

Candice was amazed. 'How did you guess? Well, actually he was. And still is. He's their principal projects consultant and between you and me he is very keen that HPM become partners here. They seem to have unlimited access to capital and all the people at White Delphs speak very highly of them.'

'So they've had no trouble at White Delphs?'

'I think there were a few problems when they took over. You can image the sort of things: health and safety issues, insurance etcetera, but once the people there realised their work could be properly financed, they shut up. And there's never been any more trouble since.'

Now he had been told that John Cripps was involved with them, Alan needed to know more about the company that ran White Delphs. From what Candice had said, he guessed they'd soon be getting more closely involved with Fursey. He was beginning to suspect that John had agendas of his own. But first he needed to discover more about the way Fursey was managed – and by whom.

'So is Fursey Heritage Developments still run by the two of you?'

'Yes, plus Peter Flower,' she reminded him. 'And then two years later we had to ask Sebastian to join us.'

'Had to?' Alan wasn't sure if he dared ask, but he did. And she didn't seem to mind.

'Yes, had to. He felt it ridiculous that the manager of the estate should be excluded. In fairness, John and I thought he'd be too busy, what with running Woolpit Farm, the hall and his district council work, but of course we invited him to join the board that autumn.'

Alan had some sympathy with Sebastian: they were wrong not to have invited him from the outset.

Candice continued. 'Then he wanted his wife, Sarah, to join, but we drew the line at that.'

'Why was that?'

He asked that question in a casual and unconcerned voice. He feared it wouldn't work and she'd ask him to mind his own business. But instead she smiled, and replied, 'She had never run a company of any sort and had no business background at all. At least I ran quite a successful restaurant in London before I joined John at Fursey.'

'So what made you change your minds?'

She sighed heavily. 'I know it sounds odd, but quite suddenly she seemed to grow up. She wasn't the rather brain-dead county bimbo we thought Sebastian had married. I don't know, but then in March 2004 there was that tragic accident.' She trailed off and lifted up her handbag, probably for her phone, Alan thought. He knew he mustn't let her stop. This was crucial.

'An accident? What, here, on the estate?'

'Yes, in the river.' She put down her bag and looked Alan in the eye. 'You'll find out sooner or later; everyone who stays here seems to. One of the tenants at the hall was a London banker called Hansworth. He was a keen fisherman . . .' She trailed off, unsure of how to phrase the next bit. 'And he drowned.'

Alan decided not to reveal that Lane had already told him about it. There was a short pause, while Candice again contemplated her handbag. She was frowning heavily.

'That's terrible,' Alan said as gently as he could. 'And was he well liked?'

'Yes, that's what made it worse. He was. And of course it revived all that rubbish about the family curse. It was so sad, because Sarah and he had worked closely on improving the hall's gardens, which were then very run-down.' She paused. Alan could see that the memories were still very fresh and painful. With a sigh she continued. 'No, it's hard to find anything positive from such a horrible event, but I often think it was Hansworth's death that made Sarah change. She seemed to become more serious and focused overnight. It was shortly afterwards that she began to make a big effort with the social side of the shoot – doing lots of catering and organising house parties. That sort of thing.'

'But commercially?'

'Oh yes, her enterprises were making money for the estate. And remember, they've barely got 400 acres at Woolpit Farm, so they need every penny they can earn.'

Alan was smiling. This wasn't at all what he'd expected. Sarah hadn't impressed him with her business acumen. Alan began to imagine Fursey Heritage board meetings, with the huge bulk of Sebastian dominating the table.

'And what does Sebastian think about John's plans to collaborate more closely with HPM and White Delphs?'

'Oh, he's dead against them. Thinks it'll bring in the wrong sort of people – whoever they are. And so far he's managed to convince his father, too, which is rather more worrying, although John thinks he'll come round in time.'

Alan was nervous about asking any more questions and thought he'd pushed his luck as it was. He needn't have worried.

Candice glanced up at the clock on the wall. 'Heavens, is that the time? I must be off. And don't forget, Alan, *do* try to squeeze in a visit to White Delphs. I think you'll be impressed.'

And with that, she walked briskly to the farm office and shut the door.

Alan turned around and looked across to the car park. He couldn't just shut the door on that one. How on earth were they going to get it dug in time? It would be bad enough if that was all he had to worry about. But it wasn't. It certainly wasn't. He felt very low.

* * *

Alan strolled across the car park into the wintry shadows cast by the lime trees lining the avenue. He moved behind a large tree, pulled out his phone and dialled Richard Lane.

'Richard, I've just had a very long conversation with Candice Cripps.'

'I'm sure that must have been interesting.'

Lane was being drily inscrutable. He did it sometimes for effect. But Alan needed to get to the point. 'She gave me lots of interesting details about the management companies at both Fursey and White Delphs. Anyhow, it's clear that her husband John, is the driving force behind them both, although I suspect it's she who does the lion's share of the real work.'

'Yes,' Lane broke in. 'I've suspected as much myself. But I think their relationship is straightforward compared with Sebastian and Sarah. They're the strange ones . . .' He trailed off, deep in thought.

Alan was thinking about Sarah and the banker Hansworth working in the garden together. How did Sebastian see that? But this was getting nowhere. Time to focus on the current problem. 'But what I want to know, Richard, is what did John do for a living after he left Cambridge?'

There was a short pause, before Lane replied: 'Yes, that's something I've been meaning to look into myself. Leave it with me; I'll get back to you ASAP.'

* * *

The next two days were hectic. Contractors arrived to lift the cellular car park reinforcement, which they took away, but it left a very rough surface behind. Alan's heart sank. He phoned Clare, the county mounty to tell her it was far too uneven for a geophysical survey. He suggested that instead they should very carefully remove all the alluvium and then do the survey on the surface of the exposed palaeosol beneath. He wasn't at all sure she'd agree to this, but to his surprise she did. He also told her he wasn't planning to lay out any trial trenches until they'd got all the field walking and geophys results in front of them. And again, she thought this an excellent idea. Alan still felt very pessimistic about meeting the deadline but at least things were starting to move. With the survey done, they'd be able to start digging. And time was pressing.

Once Alan's plans had been agreed with County Hall, he set about his next and most important task: to find a good digger driver. As any experienced field archaeologist is well aware, a skilled machine driver is at the heart of a good excavation. So he needed some advice on who to hire. Alan knew that his old friend Jake Williamson was working on a watching brief at White Delphs, so he decided to give him a call. It had been far too long since they'd spoken and Alan felt bad about the fact that he'd called Jake in to supervise at Impingham after that terrible accident when the cistern collapsed and Steve had been killed. It had been a very difficult time for both of them. With hindsight Alan realised that Jake had treated him with kid gloves. He had always avoided any rows or major disagreements and Alan was still grateful for that. In fact, he had a very soft spot for Jake and he was acutely aware that he had never thanked him adequately.

He phoned Jake who, as chance would have it, was busy machine watching as he spoke, so was able to ask his driver, Davey Hibbs, whether he'd be available to do another archaeological job the day after tomorrow. He was. Jake handed Davey the phone and Alan asked him a few questions about the machines he could get hold of and ordered a long-reach 20-ton 360 on bog-crawler tracks: the sort of digger that the internal drainage boards used to clean the dykes. Then Davey returned the phone to Jake, who spoke very highly indeed of Davey. He said the county mounties approved of him, too, which was always comforting. Before he rang off Alan mentioned that he was planning a visit to White Delphs.

'Why not come on Saturday?' Jake suggested. 'The trench will still be open and I could give you a quick site tour. We finish on Sunday.'

'Who's we?' Alan asked.

'Jon and Kaylee, my two oppos. They're great. You'd like them.'

'So you're all going to be available after the weekend?'

'Yes, at least I don't think any of us have work planned. There's not a lot around as it is – and seeing as how it's early

January, we're dead grateful to have this. It wasn't very big, but it was work.'

Alan knew only too well how hard things still were in commercial archaeology.

'Would you be interested in coming across to Fursey? There's a bit of a panic here. I've got nobody on my books and I desperately need help. Any chance you three could join me here Monday morning? I don't know what you're all getting now, but I promise we'll match it. How does that sound?'

'That's brilliant, Alan. I'll speak to the others, but we'll meet up on Saturday and can discuss any problems then. Cheers.'

And with that he rang off. All of a sudden, Alan could see a glimmer of light at the end of the tunnel. Was he starting to feel a bit more optimistic?

* * *

The digger was delivered on a low-loader late on Wednesday afternoon. Davey Hibbs followed the lorry in a small and very muddy white van. By now it was getting dark. After Davey had unloaded the digger, which he did very expertly but in the non-approved way, straight over the side, using the long-reach digging arm as a huge mechanical crutch. The lorry driver, grateful that he hadn't had to lower the rear wheels and go through all that performance, gave Davey a big thumbs up and headed back down the drive. As the driver eased the low-loader out into the road behind them, Alan introduced himself to Davey Hibbs.

Davey was a good-looking, fair young man in his early thirties. When Alan asked where he was based, he explained that he had been born and brought up in the village and that he owned this slightly ageing JCB 360 plus another standard, smaller digger. The lorry driver was a mate of his. When Jake had mentioned his name on the phone it rang bells with Alan.

'Davey, I'm sure I've come across the name Hibbs before. It rings loud bells.'

Davey laughed. 'Yes. We were in the news. It was my little brother Sam who got hit by that willow tree at Smiley's Mill.'

'That's right. It smashed through the grille. And is he OK?'

'Yes, much better, thanks. Dad said he did it to get the time off.'

Alan smiled at this. Fen humour: dry, unlike the landscape. Yes, he thought, he seems a nice bloke. When Alan returned to his Portakabin, he left Davey starting to grease the machine for the next day. A good sign that. Some drivers left it to the following morning, when they could add it to their time sheets.

* * *

Alan drove the Fourtrak onto the old pig yard and drew up. When he turned off the headlights he could see that, far away on the south-eastern horizon, the sky was just starting to lighten up. He peered out of the window. Not too bad. Light cloud cover, a slight breeze. The farmers' forecast had said the next three days would be dry with just the occasional shower along the east coast. Ely was well inland, so they should be OK.

He got out, walked round to the back, opened the big single door and took out his steel-capped rigger boots. Then he started to pull them on. As he was finishing, his eye was caught by three sets of headlights turning into the drive off the Ely-March road. That must be the crew. It didn't make him feel particularly good. In fact, for a brief moment he wished they weren't coming. The site was starting to get into his blood and he wanted to give it all his attention, but he knew that would be impossible once the filming started. It was so frustrating: they were off to a good start, with an experienced young digger driver, and Alan would have liked nothing better than to spend a day with him alone, watching how he worked, without all the distractions of the film crew. He sighed heavily; it was not to be.

He reached deep into the back of the Fourtrak and dragged out a large and very dirty hi-vis topcoat which he struggled into. It always felt cold – he much preferred good old-fashioned donkey jackets, but they'd long gone. He returned to the front and reached onto the sill, where he kept his trowel. Instinctively he thumbed it clean. Nothing worse than a dirty trowel.

By now the three vehicles had drawn up alongside him. Two VW vans and a very clean Citroen hire car. The car was closest and both passenger side windows wound down as it drew alongside him. Through the half-light Alan could discern two faces. In the front was a lady in her mid-forties; in the back a younger woman.

The older woman was the first to speak. 'You must be Alan Cadbury?'

Alan nodded and stepped closer.

'I'm Sonia Hawkes, the production manager. I always like to visit any major new locations so I know what I'm dealing with. Offices and screens can be so impersonal.' Then she turned towards the back seat. 'And this is Trudy Hills, our PA on this shoot.'

It had been several months since Alan had last filmed and

for a moment he couldn't remember the difference between an AP and a PA. Then Trudy stepped out of the car and he could see she was very young.

'This is only my second shoot, Alan, so you must be patient with me.'

Alan couldn't think of anything to say that didn't sound hopelessly patronising. So he smiled benignly. Then the driver's side door opened and Frank Jones, the director, got out. He gave a huge stretch, his arms straight out, and yawned widely.

'Ah, that's much better. Morning, young man. I trust you're feeling alert. Lively and well-informed. We've got to get this film off to a good start, you know.'

Alan could see these words were just a long way of saying hello. Frank opened the boot and hunted around for his wellies.

'Alan, be a treasure and show young Trudy here where you keep the tea-making stuff. I think we're all desperate for a cuppa,' said Sonia Hawkes.

Trudy produced two large bags from the boot. Alan took one and escorted her around the perimeter duckboard walk, past the reed barn, to his Portakabin office, where he had a small fridge and an electric kettle. He told Trudy, who was looking rather anxiously at the tiny shelf, that over the weekend contractors would be delivering two more Portakabins for the dig, and one would have a larger sink and more power points. Meanwhile they would just have to make do.

As he walked back, this time taking the direct route across the disturbed surface left by the removal of the cellular paving grid, he was in time to see Davey's small van arrive. By now the two other members of the film crew had got out of their rather larger vans and were preparing their equipment. Speed Talbot was frowning as he wrestled with the settings of the HD camera he had had to hire for the shoot. His sound recordist and long-time sidekick was Dave Edwards, known to everyone in the business as 'Grump'. In fact, Grump and Speed had become something of a legend, a few younger people even referring to them as 'G and S'. When Alan first heard this, he assumed it was a pun on Gilbert and Sullivan. But it wasn't.

Alan stood by his Fourtrak and watched. He liked to see how directors handled their subjects and crews; it told you so much about them. He'd seen Frank having a few words with Speed as he was walking back from his Portakabin, but now he was nowhere to be seen. That was odd. Then he noticed that Speed had stopped fiddling with his camera settings and was filming, while sitting on the tailboard of his van. His camera was pointing at Davey who was pulling on his boots. He continued to film as Davey extracted two heavy jerricans of diesel from the back of the van and carried them the few paces to his digger. He was still filming as Davey collected a third can, plus a large yellow plastic funnel and began to fill up. He only stopped when Frank, who had appeared from nowhere, tapped him lightly on the shoulder. Alan was very surprised. This was the first time he'd worked on a shoot where the subject didn't know he was being filmed. He decided to have a word with Frank, as he was blowed if anyone was going to treat *him* like that; but then he paused. Would that be entirely wise? No, he reminded himself, he was here for the long haul. Best put up with it for now.

His thoughts were interrupted by the sound of the digger engine starting up. This time Alan noticed that Speed had the camera on a tripod and Grump was recording on a boom. Alan had to confess it looked quite spectacular with the machine against the clear sky and the abbey ruins looming in the background. As Davey pushed on the throttle the smoke from the exhaust briefly turned dark and they could all smell the diesel, but soon the engine warmed up and the fumes ceased. Alan walked over to the cab, this time wearing hi-vis and a hard hat. He pointed towards a rather battered red-and-white range pole where he wanted Davey to start stripping. Slowly the great machine began to move off, then it slewed hard right. By now Speed was on his knees, the camera focused on the single turning track as it churned its way through the sticky clay.

The crew and Alan walked rapidly towards the range pole, in time to film the digger arrive and stop. Slowly Davey extended the boom and dipper, then it froze: the bucket about an inch off the ground. He looked towards Alan, who beckoned him forward. Then he raised a hand and the digger again stopped more abruptly this time, rocking slightly under the weight of the long-reach digging arm. Again Davey looked towards Alan, who was aware that Speed was now pointing the camera directly at him. He held one hand about six inches above the other, a signal that Davey immediately understood. The bucket was about two-and-a-half metres wide and had a sharp, toothless cutting edge, which bit into the ground, then pulled back gently to remove a smooth slice of clay, almost exactly six inches thick. Alan was impressed. Jake had been right: Davey was a superb driver. Alan was a useful digger driver himself, but he recognised Davey was in a different class. The machine vibrated as Davey shook the bucket to get the sticky clay to detach. Then he was back.

Normally Alan would have taken a whole area down one spit at a time, but as this was the first trench of the day he decided to go right through the clay to the surface beneath, to see what was there and how deep they'd have to go. He jumped as Frank tapped him on the shoulder.

'Can you get the digger to do that again, to one side. Speed needs another shot of the first scoop. It's always better from several angles.'

Alan shook his head. 'Sorry, that'll have to wait. We need to go down now.'

'But the light may have changed!' Frank shouted against the digger's engine. Davey had boosted the revs.

Alan pretended not to hear. It was important to establish who was boss, and he also knew that they'd have many more opportunities to film close-ups of buckets cutting into virgin ground. What mattered now was to establish the depth of clay to be removed. Again he signed six inches with his hands. And Davey repeated the manoeuvre. They did this five times before Alan held up his arm. Instantly the digger stopped. Alan jumped into the trench, pulling his trowel from his back pocket. He scraped down and started to feel a slight grittiness. That was what he wanted. He stood back, this time indicating two inches.

Most drivers would have slackened off the revs to do something delicate, but Davey was more experienced; the higher revs gave him greater control – it was just a matter of working the hydraulic levers with immense finesse. And that took skill. Slowly he drew the bucket back and lifted it out of the slot. This time he didn't slew round to the spoil heap, but gently lowered the curled bucket to the ground. Alan went over to it. He was very impressed indeed; Davey had lightly tickled the buried land surface, but no more. He went over to the cab and asked Davey to empty this bucket on the nearside of the spoil heap. Davey did as he was bid, lightly spreading the loose earth at the same time. This would make it easier for Alan or the metal detectorists to search later.

Meanwhile Alan was back in the trench. Should he go down any further to get colours to define better, or should he stay at this level, right at the top? Generally speaking, he liked to go down to where everything was a bit clearer, but that was also the way to scrape off original floors and surfaces. The best way to decide was to get down on his hands and knees and have a good trowel-scrape. He signalled to Davey to cut his engine, then walked over to the cab and told him to take a break for five minutes. At this point the PA Trudy appeared with a tray of tea and biscuits. He grabbed one and had jumped back into the trench, when again Frank stopped him. This time he was being more circumspect.

'Alan, I don't suppose you could get back in the trench again. Speed missed it. And what are you doing now?'

'I need five minutes to have a close look at the surface that's just been exposed and then I'll be able to decide if we go down further, or else we go sideways at this level and open up a wider area.'

'OK, Alan, that's fine.' He looked towards Speed who made a churning motion with his free hand to show the camera was turning over. 'And action . . .'

Alan jumped back into the trench, crouched down and began trowelling the surface. Speed and Grump recorded this from every conceivable angle and were about to return to their cups of tea when Alan instinctively gave a little 'Hmm' and leant back into the daylight, holding something in his hand. As an old pro he tilted his hand towards the camera which zoomed in on something resembling a large broad bean. Alan put it by his teacup at the side of the trench and then resumed trowelling. After a few scrapes, he came up with another piece, this time a bit larger than the first.

Davey wasn't in the cab, but for Speed's benefit Alan looked towards it and shouted, 'Davey, I think we've got something interesting here!'

Out of the corner of his eye Alan had noticed that Frank was back with the others supping tea. As he shouted to the non-existent Davey in the cab, he caught a glimpse of Frank's reaction. He sprayed tea everywhere. Wonderful.

A few moments later Frank hurried across to rejoin them.

'OK, everyone, we'll go from Davey's reaction in the cab, to Alan in the trench.' Frank looked at Speed, who muttered.

'Turning over . . . Speed!'

Frank turned to Alan, nodded twice, and said, 'In your own time, Alan.'

Alan took a deep breath and shouted, 'Davey, I think we've got something interesting here!' He'd been doing television long enough to make the words sound reasonably fresh and original.

Davey, now back in his cab, looked up, seemingly slightly startled, yet inquisitive. Hmm, Alan thought, he can act too. After a few seconds on Davey, Speed panned back to Alan.

Then Frank said, 'And cut.'

Alan breathed a sigh of relief. That was the first scene out of the way.

* * *

The two small fragments of pottery were instantly recognisable to anyone who has ever dug on a Romano-British site in eastern England. There was a huge industrial complex of Roman pottery kilns in the suburbs of the small town of *Durobrivae.* Earlier in the Roman period they produced Nene Valley Grey Ware (NVGW) which was later replaced by Nene Valley Colour Coated Ware (NVCC) and both were traded widely across the province of Britannia. The two sherds in Alan's hands, which Speed was filming in ultra-close-up, were undoubtedly of the distinctive Grey Ware, which has a slightly darker exterior and a paler grey interior. The second of the two sherds had been chipped by the digger bucket to expose the lighter core. So Alan was in absolutely no doubt whatsoever about what they had found. The other thing that interested him was the small size and rounded shape of the fragments, which Alan was fairly certain showed they had been lying around on the surface for some time before they got incorporated into the soil. On Frank's suggestion Alan found himself explaining these things to Davey, as neither Tricia nor Craig Larsson could be with them until Monday. Nobody had expected this much action so early in the dig.

But as Alan had already noticed, Davey proved to be a TV natural – and in more ways than one. Somehow he managed to be enthusiastic, but without going too far. He was the perfect representative of the viewing public and instinctively posed the questions they wanted him to ask. As Frank said to Alan at the end of the day, 'Blimey, that Davey's good. Craig had better look out!'

As they cleared a larger and larger area, they found a lot of pottery lying on the old land surface and Alan marked the position of each potsherd with a white gardener's tag. By lunchtime they had stripped an area the size of a small bungalow and Alan's bag of 50 garden labels had shrunk to close-on half its original size. Again, the pottery was quite consistent with an early Roman date: first or second century AD, with some hand-made sherds, but mostly NVGW. Then after lunch they began to find a few small sherds of Samian Ware. This was top-quality table pottery made in a distinctive clay that fired to a vivid reddish-orange. Today, of course, it would be glazed, but in Roman times it was given a hard, bright polish known as a burnish. Samian was made in the south of France and was not what Alan expected to find on a small rural settlement in the Fens. And again there were several worn sherds and from more than one vessel. By the end of the day, Alan was in absolutely no doubt: they had stumbled across a higher status Romano–British site that had developed out of the rich Iron Age settlement that Stan had discovered the previous summer.

As he explained to Davey on camera, in the final interview of the day: 'The people who imported this fine pottery from the south of France would have been the children and grandchildren of families who had been living in the area for generations. What we're witnessing here is the process of people becoming Romanised. They basically bought Roman things and then used them. And that was the way the period began for most ordinary folk in Roman Britain.'

It sounded splendid and Frank was delighted when a few moments later he declared to the crew and a couple of bystanders who had wandered over from the building site, 'Thank you, Alan. And that's it, folks. Well done. A great first day. That's a wrap.'

Alan sighed. He was exhausted. Filming was much harder work than just digging – and doing both was knackering. He had contemplated going to the pub for a quick beer with Davey, but now found he couldn't face it. He needed to plan for tomorrow. He climbed into the Fourtrak, his legs stiff from so much standing. Then he thought about what they had found: so much Roman material and some of it very upmarket. As sometimes happened, he found himself thinking about the present, through the past. Were the Iron Age Brits who lived here at Fursey like the Cripps family in the 17th century? Did they take ruthless advantage of new circumstances? And then what happened? Did they hang onto their wealth and status, or did they lose it, through indolence and the Roman equivalent of death duties?

Alan turned on the ignition and headed slowly along the drive. He smiled as he remembered Frank's efforts to call the shots. But he had to concede, Frank had been dead right about one thing: it had been one hell of a good first day. Stan wasn't a great fan of TV but he would have been over the moon about the high-status Roman finds, which had to be a development from his original Iron Age settlement.

When he got back home he went straight over to the fridge, opened a beer and raised the bottle to his old friend. That felt better.

# Six

The next day was Friday and to Alan it did indeed feel like the end of the week. Still, he thought, while he walked behind the digger as it tracked its way back to the trench, the pressure's off this morning. The crew had had to return to London to collect more lighting gear but they all planned to be back on-site to do an end-of-day scene, where Craig would introduce Tricia. Alan wasn't looking forward to that much. But on the plus side, he thought, I've a full day of uninterrupted archaeology ahead of me. And it isn't raining. So things could be a lot worse.

As it turned out, his optimism proved short-lived. Alan's heart sank as he saw the huge frame of Sebastian Cripps climb out of his mud-spattered Land Rover and stride across the site. Alan took a couple of paces back from the digger's slewing arm, as a nod towards health and safety, and handed his visitor a hard hat.

Sebastian was the first to speak. 'Frank Jones phoned last night. It would seem you've found a lot of Roman pottery. Is that right?'

Alan pointed to the two dozen or so white plastic labels on the ground. 'Yes, it's proving very rich. These are what we've exposed already this morning and we've barely been working half an hour.'

As he spoke he kept an eye on the digger. Then he lifted a hand, as if requesting silence. Both could see that Davey was taking the final cut that would expose the clean, pre-flood clay surface. Alan pulled a small bag of labels from the back pocket of his jeans and walked closer to the bucket, which Davey was slowly pulling back with a look of intense concentration on his face. Sebastian joined him. Nobody said a word. By this point Alan's eye had become very good at spotting the distinctive colour of Nene Valley Grey Ware, which only contrasted slightly with the darker grey-brown colour of the Roman land surface. The bright pinkish-orange of Samian was much easier to pick out.

Towards the end of the first pull-back, as Davey was starting to curl the bucket up, Alan stepped forward and picked something off the surface. As he did so he poked a label into the ground. Davey stopped the bucket and Alan went round and briefly looked inside it, turning the loose lumps over with his trowel. He picked another small piece out, then stood back, giving Davey the thumbs up. This was the sign they'd agreed that it was OK to empty the bucket, which Davey did, but this time on the smaller heap directly alongside the trench. This would be the spoil heap that the detectorists would search first when they arrived on-site in a couple of hours' time.

'More Grey Ware,' Alan half-muttered to a fascinated Sebastian.

'So what date are these?' Sebastian asked, as he held the two sherds gingerly in the palm of his right hand.

'Hard to say from body sherds, but probably second century.'

'Aren't they wonderful. So much history here, in my hand.'

Alan said nothing. He could see Sebastian was lost in thought. Then he looked up. 'I do envy you, Alan.' He was smiling now. 'I'm sure people say this all the time, but you do have a superb job.' He paused for a moment, considering his words. Alan could detect that a confidence was coming. 'I wish I'd been born more academic, like John.' Again, he paused. 'John went to Cambridge, of course, where he read archaeology, then history. That's where he met Peter Flower, you know?'

'Yes.' Alan nodded. 'I did know that.'

'But I'd never have got in. I was always more hands-on, so I went to Nettlesham College and studied agriculture. Don't get me wrong, I had a great time there. No regrets at all. But even so, I wish sometimes we could have done more about the history of farming and the landscape.'

Suddenly Alan remembered their conversation at Stan's wake. 'That's right, you told me you enjoyed reading Hoskins.'

'Oh, what a book. Stan loved it, too.' He paused to draw breath. Alan could hear pheasant calls echoing in the woods beyond the abbey ruins. 'In fact, it was that book that got me talking to Stan about his work here. He lent me his copy.'

And you returned it, too, Alan thought. He remembered seeing it on Stan's desk.

'I thought it was just about walls and ruins, but he showed me all sorts of other things, especially how landscapes changed and how people changed with them. And it wasn't just a one-way process. You could influence outcomes if you were on the ball. It's all about understanding what's going on – and not just in the landscape, but with people, too.'

'You're right,' Alan agreed, although he wasn't entirely clear what Sebastian was referring to in his slightly incoherent fashion. Or was he simply trying to be friendly, as he was with Stan? And if so, why? But he knew he needed to keep him on side, so it was safest just to agree. 'Especially out here in the Fens. You can't mess with rising water levels.' As he spoke, Alan could see his words had gone down well.

'No, you're right about that, Alan. I think that's why the second baronet, my grandfather, was so annoyed he had to sell Isle Farm to pay death duties.'

'Oh, really?'

Alan pretended he knew nothing about it. It might persuade him to say more. He suspected Sebastian might be a man of rapid mood swings, but he still couldn't understand what motivated him.

'Yes, it's that cluster of buildings over towards the pumping station. It's not a very large holding – maybe the same size as Woolpit Farm, about four hundred acres, but none of the land's as wet as Woolpit. Dad always said he was gutted when they sold it. He thought they'd somehow betrayed the family—'

'But his father had no option. The Inland Revenue wouldn't go away, would they?'

'No, he didn't. But it was such a shame. And it's a fabulous house. I know it's not huge, like the hall, but it's well built and warm.'

'Who lives there now?'

'My father sold it to the Greatfords in the '70s. Anyhow, they retired to Spain in 2003 and it came back on the market early in 2004: the second week in January, to be more precise.'

He shook his head. 'I remember it well.' He sighed, he was gazing out across the fen. 'Yes, very well.'

Alan didn't rush the next question. 'And who owns it now?'

'It didn't sell – at least not at the price they were looking for. So the Greatfords still own the land, which is run by their agents. The house was rented until recently by distant cousins of ours who eventually retired to somewhere smaller in the south. Now it's taken by a series of rich entrepreneurs from Cambridge. I can't keep up with them. Sarah usually invites them along to the hall for a meal, but to be honest I can't understand what any of them actually *do* for a living.'

There was a loud bell. Sebastian's phone had received a text. He glanced down at the screen and frowned. The mood had been broken. 'It's my agent: wheat futures down again.' He sighed again, heavily. 'Still, I must be going. It was good to chat, and I hope you won't mind if I take quite a close interest in your work here, will you?'

'Of course not. I'd be delighted.'

They shook hands.

'And if I do become a nuisance, you'll just have to blame Stan. He shouldn't have been such an inspiring teacher.'

As if that last remark wasn't enough, Alan was beginning to warm to the man. Unlike many visitors, he chose his questions carefully and listened closely to what Alan had to say. He was clearly fascinated not just by the results of their research, but by the way they achieved them. In the past Alan had found some landowners could be very patronising, as if they were the ones doing the 'real' work, while Alan and his like were indulging in a pet hobby. It could be very frustrating.

Without being asked, Sebastian carefully placed the two small sherds back on the ground alongside their white marker label. As he was straightening up Alan took another rapid step towards the bucket, which was halfway through its pull-back. This time he picked-up a ten-pence-sized green-coloured coin, which he showed to Sebastian.

'Gosh. I suppose that's Roman, too. But it's incredibly heavily worn. I'm surprised they could see what it was. If I were given a coin like that in a shop, I'd hand it back.'

'Yes,' Alan agreed. 'It's almost smooth, isn't it? But from its size I'd guess it was a sestertius . . .' He trailed off as he carefully cleaned damp soil off the coin's underside. By now Davey had joined them. Suddenly Alan went rigid and stared intently at the coin. The others craned forward as Alan deftly removed a few more crumbs of soil to reveal that the worn surface of the coin had been cut into by a rectangular punch, which had been inscribed with five letters: the first three weren't very easy to read, but the last two were a clear 'PR'.

'*Is* it a coin, Alan?' Sebastian asked. 'It looks like somebody has stamped it. Isn't that the sort of thing that happened to tokens very much later? It's a way of claiming ownership, isn't it?'

Alan smiled. It was a very intelligent suggestion. 'Yes, you're right, but I'm also quite sure this is a fairly standard Roman coin and not anything later. I'd expect something like an eighteen century token to be far thinner, lighter weight and with sharper edges. Also, if you look here' – Alan held the coin in the slowly growing morning light – 'you can see the letters AESAR behind and above the very worn profile of a man's head.'

Sebastian peered closely. 'Presumably that's CAESAR, but

they've gone and put the stamp right across the emperor's name . . .' He trailed off.

'I wouldn't worry about that, Sebastian,' Alan said. 'We learnt about these coins as students. They're *countermarked.* That's the word. I can't remember the precise details, but for various political reasons the Roman mints didn't produce many new coins during the mid–first century AD.'

'But that was the time of the Roman Conquest?'

'Precisely. So the authorities stamped older, worn-down coins with these official countermarks. They're very distinctive and can't be anything else.'

'So what does the stamp say?'

'I honestly can't remember, but it's an abbreviation. In essence it's official approval of old coins, giving them an extended life. Anyhow, I'm sure Tricia will know.'

'Tricia?'

'Yes,' Alan replied, slightly surprised he hadn't been told. 'Dr Tricia Neave, the expert on Roman small towns.'

'Oh, really, I didn't know. Is she part of the TV show, or does she come with you, as it were?'

'She's part of the programme, but she's also somebody I'd have chosen myself . . .'

'Good-looking, you mean?'

Sebastian was indulging, slightly awkwardly, in man-to-man banter. Alan tried to keep his reply factual.

'I've only met her once and, yes, she was very pleasant. More importantly, she obviously knew her stuff, as she hasn't long finished her PhD at Cambridge.'

'Presumably one of that man what's-his-name's students?'

'Peter Flower?' Alan suggested.

'Yes, Flower. Can't say I took to him myself. A bit

Cambridgey, a bit know-it-all, if you get my drift. Still, John and Candice seem to think very highly of him.'

'Yes,' Alan replied. 'He can be a bit . . . A bit remote.'

Sebastian handed the coin back to Alan. 'I'll never get the hang of history. We learnt at school that the Romans were damn near perfect. They had everything organised. And yet they couldn't arrange for a few extra coins to be minted when they needed them.'

Then Alan remembered. It had been a long time ago when he attended Dr Cartwright's introductory lectures on life in Roman Britain, but he had been a good lecturer and a lot of what he said had stuck. He had used the example of the Romans' ability to improvise when the need arose – and that's what the countermarked coins were all about. For various reasons new coins were in short supply, so the authorities issued the countermarked ones to the army in the legionaries' pay packets. That way, it was all official and above board. But it set Alan thinking: maybe this site wasn't quite as straightforward as he had believed yesterday afternoon. You don't expect to find countermarked coins on a simple domestic site, no matter how high its status. No, he thought, something else was also going on. Nothing about Fursey, ancient or modern, was ever quite what it seemed.

* * *

The pale-blue sunlight of mid-January lit the scene. To Alan's relief, Davey had turned off Radio 1 and he could concentrate. The machine scraped away and Alan focused on the bucket. As it pulled back, he spotted another sherd of NVGW and close by it some fragments of shell-tempered Iron Age or 'native' Roman period pots. Damn and hell, Alan thought, why isn't Stan here now? He'd have loved this: he was red hot when it came to late Iron Age/RB coarse pottery. Knew more about the local stuff than anyone else – even in Cambridge. He had been building up a card-based archive, complete with hundreds of pencil sketches of pot rims and profiles that he had been in the process of digitising when he died. Alan had been working through that same card index before the car park excavation got going so unexpectedly. Well, he thought, if ever there was a time to put Stan's work to good use . . .

For an instant Alan went very still. It was weird, almost as if his old friend was standing beside him. Stan had put a lot of work into that pottery archive – in fact, far more research than a collection of fairly ordinary, if upmarket, Roman pottery would normally require. So what was going on? It can't have been the finds themselves, but what they meant – what they signified. Would that news have been welcome to everyone? Archaeologists and history buffs would be delighted, but sadly they were a minority. Things were getting more complex. Alan straightened up, his eyes were staring towards the abbey, but they saw nothing. The present had intruded on the past again.

But this time it wasn't the fault of a film crew.

* * *

Midday. Davey was taking his lunch break and two local metal detectorists were doing their regular sweep of the spoil heaps. Alan had set up the GPS while Candice, who had volunteered to help out until the three people from White Delphs arrived on Monday, stood holding the staff over one of the white labels that marked the pottery find spots. Candice called out finds numbers, which Alan entered into the machine as he recorded each level and co-ordinates. It was boring work, but essential, and Alan was amazed that Candice had chosen to do it herself. She could easily have nominated somebody junior from the farm office, but she didn't. Although he was aware that he was using her to learn more about the internal workings of the Cripps family, he found himself warming to her. She seemed different from the others: less remote, more engaged. He realised that she possessed great PR skills, but do people always have to act by the book? Maybe she was genuinely intrigued by what Alan was doing – and the way he did it? It had occurred to him that she might be interested in him as a person. But he had his doubts about her: what was her agenda – specifically with him, Alan Cadbury? He wasn't aware, as he tweaked the GPS, but he was showing his trademark frown. But she could see it – and she smiled.

After half an hour they had finished, and by now Davey was checking the main bearings of the slightly elderly digger, which needed plenty of grease to work smoothly. He was just climbing back into his cab when John Cripps appeared from behind the spoil heaps. He obviously knew enough about archaeology to hesitate before stepping into the trench. As soon as Alan beckoned him across, he joined them. At the same time Reg, one of the metal detectorists, appeared at Alan's side with the morning's haul.

Alan gave John and Candice the coin they'd found earlier to look at, while he quickly sorted through the detectorists' finds. Quickly he rejected a few scraps of modern rubbish – rusty nails, a tin milk bottle top, that sort of thing – that had fallen down the wide cracks through the alluvium, which are such a feature of modern, hot, dry summers. Aside from those, it was quite an interesting set of metalwork. Several rings and strange bronze fittings that Alan didn't recognise immediately. Again, he wished that Stan could have been there to help him. He was keen to see if any of the coins could have been Iron Age, so he looked at them more closely. One in particular caught his attention, made of copper alloy and a bit smaller than the sestertius they'd found earlier.

John had noticed his interest and was looking at the coin in Alan's left hand.

'That's quite well preserved. I can read BRITANNIA quite clearly and the seated figure is just like the one we used to see on old pennies . . .' He paused in some doubt. 'Except that she isn't *quite* like her. A bit fat and sloppy, if you know what I mean.'

'John, you're being impossible,' Candice interjected with cod seriousness. 'Yes, she is a little generously proportioned, but it's . . . it's . . . it's very old.'

'Yes,' Alan agreed. 'And you're both right. To be frank, it's a terrible likeness of Britannia. That left leg is ludicrous and her right arm appears to have two elbows. I'd have said it was inept.'

'But does that matter?' John asked

'I think it might. Let me explain,' Alan took a swig from his water bottle, while he frantically thought back to those fact-filled lectures by Dr Cartwright. 'The Romans were very methodical . . .' Slowly the facts were swimming into his memory. 'They rarely did things by chance, or without good cause, so there was probably a reason why the drawing of Britannia is so ham-fisted.'

'Which was?'

'I'm fairly sure this coin is an *as*.'

'A what?' Candice asked.

'An *as*, sometimes known as an *assarius*. As I remember, they were an early form of cast coin. And I think you'd have got two, maybe three of these for that sestertius we found earlier. Anyhow, pictures of Britannia are generally rare on coins, with the exception of this particular issue, which is found quite widely across Roman Britain, but not on the continent. I'm no expert, but most numismatists seem to think it was a one-off coin made, and made rapidly, to be distributed to the garrison troops in Britain.'

Both John and Candice were listening closely. 'And the date?' John asked.

'I *think* it was issued by Antoninus Pius in the mid-second century – I'd guess around AD150.'

'Forgive me, Alan.' John was puzzled. 'I still don't get it. That story is very interesting, but it's still just a coin, isn't it?'

'I'm sorry, neither of you were around when we found that countermarked sestertius I just showed you.'

He retrieved the earlier coin, showed them the countermark and explained the story. When Alan finished John was still looking puzzled.

'So, the connection seems to be the Roman Army, am I right?'

'I think you might be. I'd expect to find both these coins on military sites.'

'D'you think there was a battle here?' Candice asked, clearly quite excited.

'Oh no. You don't find coins and pottery on battle sites. No, I suspect the military presence here – if there was one – was longer-lived and more permanent. After all, soldiers were spending money and eating and drinking – if the pottery is any guide.'

'So a barracks, or something like that?' John suggested.

'Possibly. Or, more likely, a fort.'

'But shouldn't that have stone walls?' John said. 'Like the one at Brancaster on the Norfolk coast. I used to go there in the summer as a child.'

'Not necessarily, and not if there isn't good stone in the area. But we mustn't count our chickens.' Alan paused to put the sestertius back in its bag. 'Having said that, I'm quite suspicious about some of these other bits and pieces of bronze. They do look a bit military to me.'

'How do you mean?' Candice asked.

'I haven't seen things like these on any of the domestic sites I've dug, and the Roman legionaries wore armour and uniforms that were made from various strips of leather with numerous belts and straps. And they were very effective, too, but they also required a variety of links, clips and buckles to hold them together. I could probably identify some of them with a text book, but there's no need, as Tricia's arriving later this afternoon.'

Alan wondered whether she would come to the same conclusion as him. He hoped so, as he was growing increasingly certain he was right. And if his suspicions were to prove correct, then this would be a major discovery. National news, even. He looked up. Candice was standing wide-eyed with excitement. John's face betrayed no emotion whatsoever.

What, Alan wondered, is he thinking about: the Roman Army or the Fursey Estate?

* * *

The afternoon session went well, but by half past three the cloud cover had grown, and Alan decided the mid-January light was too poor to continue. He knew from experience that headlights and floodlights were no use for seeing subtle changes in soil colour; you could spot stone and brick walls, that sort of thing, but not the slight tone and texture differences he was interested in. Frank had just phoned from the car to say they were approaching Royston and should be with them by four. He'd suggested to Alan that there should still be just enough light to film a quick scene outdoors, before moving into the Portakabin to shoot a discussion about the finds. When he'd finished talking, Alan pocketed his phone and headed for the temporary abbey offices where he knew Candice would be working. Five minutes later she was out on-site helping him set up the GPS to plot the afternoon's finds.

He had to admire her discipline: she had been deeply immersed in the intricacies of a detailed stock-take – all part of the setting-up process for the new farm shop and restaurant – when he called in. She didn't hesitate. He'd have finished the column, or whatever it was, but not her. She just got up, slipped on a pair of wellies and abandoned the computer. It was as if the archaeology was more important than the book-keeping. Or was there more to it than that? Had he become the new Stan? That thought sent a slight chill through him.

Hiding his suspicion, Alan thanked her profusely.

'Well,' she said, as they removed the GPS from its case, 'it's the least I can do. I know you're short-staffed till Monday. No, Alan, don't be silly, I can always add up figures and you can't leave these finds out here to be damaged by the frost.'

'Yes,' Alan replied. 'And there's talk of a sharp one tonight, although the way the cloud cover is building up makes me think they might have got it wrong.'

Candice smiled. 'You are funny, Alan. You're always talking about the weather. You and Sebastian should get together one day. Have a trip to the Met Office for a boys' day out. He's always talking about the weather, too.'

'Well he's a farmer so it's hardly surprising. You don't start making hay when there's a cold front approaching from off the Atlantic. And that's where I got interested in the weather.'

By now the GPS was set up and ready to go. Candice watched while Alan rapidly sorted out his notes and finds bags.

'That was one thing I noticed about Stan,' she said.

'Oh yes, what's that?'

'He had no eye whatsoever for the weather. I'm not much good, but John has always been interested – I guess because he was also brought up in the country – and he could never understand why Stan was always being surprised by rain. It was as if he never looked at a forecast.'

Alan smiled. 'Come to think of it, dear old Stan wasn't unusual. Most archaeologists are hopeless when it comes to the weather. It must cost the profession thousands every year. If I had my way, I'd make meteorology a minor option in degree courses.'

'So Stan came from an urban background?'

'Yes, his father was an engineer on the railways.'

For a moment Alan could remember Stan telling him tales of how his father coped with various problems of the steam age: collapsed coaling towers, decrepit turntables etc. Some of his dad's gift for practicality had brushed off on him, too.

A visit to one of Stan's dig tool-sheds was always a treat: spades, mattocks and shovels neatly hanging up, cleaned and sometimes even oiled.

Candice was looking at him. 'You were very close to him, weren't you, Alan?'

'Yes, I was.'

'And is that the real reason you're here?'

Alan was quiet for a moment. That was a leading question – which required a very careful answer. Truth was now irrelevant; her perception of him was all that mattered. Time to play up the archaeological importance of Fursey. Its forensic significance could come later – and hopefully from DCI Richard Lane.

'Probably.' He paused to make it look like he was examining his innermost thoughts. 'Yes,' he continued slowly, 'I suppose it might be.' She was listening intently. He knew he mustn't give his true motives away. 'But, on the other hand, it's a stunning project, as you know only too well. Frankly, it's a once-in-a-lifetime opportunity.'

Thank God for clichés, he thought. He looked at her closely; he knew he wasn't a very good actor, but she seemed convinced.

'And the television – has that influenced your decision to come here?'

Alan shook his head. 'I won't deny that their money helps, but . . .'

'Oh yes.' She laughed. 'It certainly does.'

'But if you must know, filming can be very distracting, too. There are times, like now, when I'd like to get finished, then go back to my room and do some work on the finds – or whatever.'

'Well, what's to stop you?'

Alan looked down at his watch in the fading light.

'Frank and the crew will be back in less than half an hour.'

'Oh, I didn't realise that. Sorry, Alan, I'd better stop jabbering.'

And that's exactly what she did. For 25 minutes they worked in silence and had got everything lifted and levelled-in by the time the two vans and Frank's hire car drove onto site.

* * *

Frank and the crew had obviously been on the phone to each other while they headed north out of London, as they went into action immediately they arrived. Frank strode across the site towards Alan who was carefully clipping the Trimble GPS back into its case. Candice had taken the surveying staff back to the dig Portakabin en route to her own office. Instead of greeting him with small talk, Frank paused and looked around.

'Well, the light's not ideal, but it'll do. Add a bit of atmos. But you'll need to be brief, and I mean that Alan. Don't go into discussions. Just show Tricia the extent of the site and range of things you've found. That's all we need.'

Alan nodded. 'OK, that's clear.'

Frank was still looking towards the west. 'I'm worried about that cloud over there,' he said, half under his breath.

Alan looked up. 'Don't worry about that. It's miles away; it'll never reach us.'

'No, Alan, it's not rain I'm worried about. If that cloud covers what little sunlight there is, we're sunk.' He looked towards the parked vehicles. 'Hurry up, folks, we've only got a very short time!'

Tricia broke into a run, and the camera crew quickened their pace. Slightly ahead of them was a woman Alan did not recognise, but she carried a clipboard and pink manila file, so was probably an Assistant Producer. Right behind them all, Trudy was closing up the hire car.

Frank turned towards Speed and showed him how and where he wanted the sequence shot. Speed shook his head and pointed towards the now quite red, but still very direct, sunlight. He suggested a more sideways-on set-up. Alan loved this sort of discussion, even though he couldn't hear precisely what they were saying. It was a glimpse into other specialised worlds. His thoughts were interrupted by a light tap on his shoulder.

'Alan, I'm Terri, Terri Griffiths. I'll be the AP on this shoot.'

They shook hands. Terri was about 35 with auburn hair, made flaming crimson by the setting sun. She was slightly shorter than average, fairly thick-set and had a very pleasant, smiley face. Alan knew they'd get on well. Sometimes Assistant Producers could be hard work, but not, he thought, this one.

By now Tricia had joined them and she greeted Alan warmly with kisses on both cheeks. She was dressed more or less for a dig in a dark-blue Barbour waxed coat, the regulation skin-tight jeans and bright-pink children's wellies, decorated with intertwined smiley baboons. The outfit said 'I am serious; I understand what fieldwork is all about, but I also have a lighter side'. Alan couldn't help wondering whether it was Tricia who was sending the message, or some image consultant behind the scenes. Or was he being unfair?

'Can we get going please? Light's failing fast.' Frank was getting anxious and wasn't concealing it very well.

Tricia and Terri ran across to where he was standing with

the cameraman and sound recordist. Alan walked briskly. He was frowning, as if thinking about important archaeological concerns. In fact, he was blowed if he'd run, and the frown made it look like he had more important problems to address.

'Tricia, there.' Frank pointed to one of two small lens bags lying on the ground, 'And Alan, there.' They stood facing each other while Frank and Speed checked how it looked.

'Do you come here often?' Alan thought he might lighten the mood. It worked, Tricia giggled.

Frank was holding a monitor screen showing what Speed's camera would be filming.

'A gnat's to the right, Tricia!' he called out, still staring closely at the monitor.

She took a small sidestep.

'No! Too much, half that!'

She did as she was bid.

'Thanks, love, hold it there. Now, Alan, move closer to Tricia, but angle towards us.' He moved in a way that let the low light illuminate Tricia's face. She blinked as his shadow moved off. 'That's better, much better.'

Speed then said something to Frank who looked up sharply.

'Terri, there's something white and shiny back there. Could you move it, please?'

Alan swivelled round. It was the old fertiliser bag they used for pegs, nails and string.

Terri shouted, 'Can I move this, Alan?'

Out of the corner of his eye Alan could see that Frank thought this question unnecessary, but Alan was impressed. It could have been important. He could tell she had worked on excavations before.

Frank called, 'Hurry up please!'

That irritated Alan. 'Hold it, Terri,' Alan called out. 'That's important, it's marking the spot where the detectorists finished this afternoon.' It was a fib, but what the hell. 'Put a nail and a label there. Then we can replace it afterwards.'

Alan watched while she did that, carefully avoiding Frank's stare, which he could feel on the back of his neck. By now the light was failing fast. Terri ran back.

As soon as she was out of shot, Frank called out, 'OK, turn over.'

Speed said quietly, 'Speed.'

'And *action* . . .'

Nothing happened. Alan looked at Tricia. Tricia looked at Alan. Before either of them could say a word, Frank called out, 'And cut!'

Alan thought he'd better speak first. 'I'm sorry, Frank, but who's interviewing who? And what are we talking about? The site or the finds?'

'I don't mind. I want you to talk about what's going through your head at this moment in time – at the end of the first week of the excavation.'

'Oh, OK,' Alan said doubtfully.

He'd never worked with a director who didn't direct before. He looked at Tricia. She was looking mystified, even slightly anxious.

'We'll do it again,' Frank announced, then quieter, to Speed, 'Start on the horizon, pull back to a two-shot, then swinging singles, OK?'

Speed nodded, then after a few seconds said, 'Speed.'

'And action.'

Although he hadn't been told to, Alan counted to three to

give Speed time to pull back from the horizon and compose his two-shot. Then he spoke.

'It's been a fantastic first week, Tricia. We've removed a thick layer of flood-clay and have found an intact ancient surface beneath it. Before we started digging I thought it would be Iron Age, but the finds we've been discovering in the past two days make me think we might have been wrong.'

'Oh, really? What sort of things have you been finding?'

'Coins, strange shaped pieces of bronze and lots of pottery.'

'And you're quite sure that everything you've found is earlier than the flooding?'

'Oh yes, we're absolutely certain about that.'

'And when did the flooding begin?'

'Sometime late in the second century AD.'

'So we're talking Roman?'

'Yes, we are, and Iron Age, too.'

'Wow! That *is* exciting!'

That was a good up-beat note to end the scene on, Alan thought. There was a longer than usual pause while Speed pulled back to reveal the setting sun dip below the horizon.

'And cut,' Frank called out, quietly. Then much louder. '*Excellent!* Well done everyone and a great shot of the setting sun, Speed. I loved it.'

Grump was standing directly behind Alan who heard him mutter under his breath, 'And the bloody sound was shit-hot, too . . .'

* * *

The scene in the Portakabin with the finds went well. Tricia confirmed what Alan thought about the two unusual coins and revealed that the countermarked inscription read 'NCAPR', which she checked against the BM website and was short for *Nero Caesar Augustus PRobavit*, or Nero Caesar Augustus approves – of the revalidation of the coins. She also pointed out that the original coin had been issued by the Emperor Claudius, who reigned from AD41–64. Nero followed directly on from Claudius and reigned until AD64. So the extended-life coins would have played an essential part in paying for the army during the crucially important decades of military conquest and consolidation that followed the invasion of AD43.

Tricia also agreed that the *as* coin, with the rather inept representation of Britannia, would have been issued to Roman troops, and was able to date it to the Emperor Antoninus Pius, around 154BC. Alan was relieved: his near-guess on-camera had been correct. The other coins were fairly routine, but she got very much more excited about some of the smaller pieces of metalwork, which she identified as the bronze or iron fittings of Roman military armour, known as *lorica segmentata*. They looked a bit like brooches or old cupboard hinge fittings, but often with hooks or tabs with holes. At least one of the small hooks had been worn down and had broken – which suggested that the armour in question was being worn locally. Towards the end of the interview, she spotted what she thought might be a bronze harness fitting, which hinted at the presence of cavalry, too.

The final moments of the scene were memorable. Tricia was summing up the finds she had just described. 'Well, Alan, that's an extraordinary collection. And quite unexpected. If I didn't know otherwise, I'd say you have a military fortress here.'

'But we don't know otherwise.'

'What?' Tricia was genuinely wide-eyed with astonishment.

Her questions were uncontrived. 'But why would it be here? What's it defending? And besides, there's no hint of it on air photos, is there?'

'As for defence, it ultimately provides control over access from the major southern fen rivers towards the hinterland of Cambridge, and as to the air photos, they're largely irrelevant as the entire site has been buried and concealed beneath flood-clay. No' – he slowed down to give his words added emphasis and Speed zoomed in to an ultra-close-up – 'I think we may have stumbled upon something new, something truly remarkable. But only time will tell.'

'And, cut!'

Frank gave Alan a pat on the back. He had delivered. To give her credit, Tricia was delighted, too. Alan had been worried that she'd turn out to be egotistical and jealous.

She gave him a small hug. 'You were great, Alan. That's got the film off to a cracking start.'

* * *

It had been a hard afternoon's filming and Alan was dog-tired as he walked up to his Portakabin and let himself in. He'd forgotten that he'd told Speed and Grump they could use it as somewhere clean and dry to store their equipment until their own cabin was delivered, so the floor was littered with boxes, stands and cables. He picked his way over to his back-up flask and poured himself a mug of coffee. There was a knock on the door and Speed entered. Alan offered him his mug, but Speed shook his head. Alan stood back and watched. He loved the technical side of television and was a keen digital photographer himself.

As Speed checked over the big camera's settings, Alan

asked, 'I know you're keen on HD, Speed, but is it really *that* good?'

Speed smiled as he turned round. 'Well only if your television at home is HD, too. Otherwise there's no point in having it. You can get a bit more depth of field and the colours can be more true to life. You can sometimes see that on an ordinary set, but you won't get the full benefit.'

Alan laughed. 'I don't think I'll be getting a new set any time soon. Not on an archaeologist's salary.'

'Well, you might if I showed you some footage on the High Def. monitor.'

He put the camera down on the bench and opened a stainless steel case on the floor from which he pulled a shiny new monitor, which he plugged into the wall. Then he connected the camera and turned the set on. The screen flickered into life.

Instantly Alan could see that this was indeed an improvement. Everything was so crisp and sharp from foreground to background. Of course it helped that the cameraman was a Speed Talbot, but Alan could see he had made full use of the camera's potential. Then Alan found his attention being grabbed by the action rather than the picture. It was filmed at the very start of the dig yesterday morning. But it felt like a week ago. Davey was filling the digger with diesel. Alan could tell that the shot was handheld. The scene cut to a longer shot of the digger, this time taken on a tripod. There was a puff of smoke as the engine came to life and the camera panned left towards the horizon. Alan spotted something. He put a hand on Speed's shoulder.

'Hold it there, Speed.'

The picture froze.

Alan pointed at the screen and Speed zoomed in. There, standing in the shrubs beyond the abbey wall was a figure observing the dig. It was Sebastian Cripps. Why was he there? Was he trying to keep an eye on them unseen? Or was he interested in the archaeology? Maybe he was just looking at the view, or wildlife, or Isle Farm behind them all?

'Someone you know, Alan?'

Rapidly Alan pulled himself together. 'No, just somebody gawping. But that HD is amazing, isn't it? You wouldn't have seen him at all on regular digi film, would you?'

Speed grinned. He liked to make converts to HD.

Meanwhile Alan was looking down at the edge of the abbey lands. He was still thinking about that figure standing among the shrubs.

* * *

That evening Frank and the crew went back to their hotel in Ely. They asked Alan to join them, but he didn't feel up to it. It had been a hard week and he just wanted to get back to his rented house on the outskirts of the village, open a cold beer and chill-out. Alan had been commuting to Fursey from his brother's farmhouse near Crowland while the Fursey Estate did a bit of decorating and carried out essential repairs to his current home, a medium-sized bungalow, built for an assistant keeper by the 2nd Baronet Cripps in 1958. Alan couldn't understand why the estate would have built a bungalow for a member of their staff, as at the time bungalows were seen as very lower-class by the landed gentry. Soon, however, he realised that the land it had been built on was soft and peaty – and the single-storey suddenly made practical sense.

Still, it was convenient for the site and, better, the pub, and to his surprise, the rent was very cheap, too.

Two hours later, he woke up at eight, feeling refreshed, the half-drunk bottle of beer warm beside him. He realised that he was very, very hungry. He looked in his small fridge and the cupboard that passed for a larder – nothing whatsoever, except for several packets of plain chocolate digestives, his usual breakfast blast of sugar and energy. No, he thought, I've got to eat something substantial, preferably with added chips. And more chips on the side.

It took him ten minutes to walk to the Cripps Arms. The night air was cold, frosting already, Alan reckoned, looking at the long grass of the verges when it was caught by the headlights of passing cars. Soon he'd come to the first of three streetlights that ran along Fore Street to the east of the pub; to the west were five more lights, linking the pub to the village hall, but the former centre of village life, the Church of St John, stood on the south side, remote and unlit.

Alan reckoned the village had shifted east after the Black Death in the later Middle Ages, a process that was speeded-up in the 18th century by the construction of Fursey Hall and the then squire's desire to have a view of the nave and tower uncluttered by untidy, ramshackle cottages. Alan smiled; in those days a country gentleman had the power to alter the shape of villages. After the last war, though, a small housing estate had been built by the Rural District Council, bang in the middle of that view. Alan was secretly rather fond of what that little estate of council houses represented, although, of course, he would never have said as much to any member of the Cripps family. But it was a sign that the old order had started to change. Absolute power was no longer in the hands of local gentry. He always reckoned that the war had defeated more than just the Nazis.

Some things had changed for the better. For a moment he paused. Or had they? His study of the Cripps family history in the library at Cambridge had set him thinking – and what he had observed since, hadn't made him change his mind at all.

Alan pushed open the back door into what had formerly been the Public Bar, but was now the Ploughman's Rest. Being a Friday night, the place was well filled, although not quite as crowded as he would have expected ten or fifteen years ago. The landlord, Cyril, was a local who had run a much larger pub in Ely as a younger man and had moved back to Fursey when he retired. He genuinely ran the pub as a social enterprise: yes, he did earn a modest living from it, but he also knew the Cripps was the main focus of village social life. Alan reflected that it wasn't just doctors, nurses and vicars who had a sense of vocation.

His arrival was greeted by a cry of 'Look who's just arrived!' from Davey Hibbs, who rapidly drained, then held up his empty glass. He tried to persuade the two men he was with to do the same, but they shook their heads.

At the bar Cyril had seen the exchange and had already poured a foaming pint of Old Slodger by the time Alan reached him. Cyril looked up for confirmation as he was about to pull the second pint. Alan nodded. 'Might as well, Cyril, he's earned it.'

'You had a good week, then?'

Cyril made no secret of the fact that he was a big fan of *Test Pit Challenge* and had started a 'Dig News' section on the pub noticeboard.

'Unbelievably good, Cyril.' He took a long pull from his pint. Then ordered ham, eggs and double chips.

Cyril scribbled a note to the kitchen and Alan paid for his beer and the meal. As he waited for his change, Davey came alongside. Alan pushed the pint towards him.

'Cheers, Alan,' he said as he took a long draught. 'We've had a good week. And I've enjoyed working with you. Come and meet my brother Sam.'

Alan remembered Sam Hibbs had been the man who had been hit by the falling willow tree during that storm shortly before Stan's death. He'd obviously been hurt quite badly, as he was sitting down and two walking sticks leant against the table beside him. Next to him sat Bert Hickson, the Fursey Shoot's ex-soldier and Davey Hibbs's uncle, whom he'd met briefly with Stan's parents and Barty at the wake. It was Hickson who had found Stan's body and Alan winced as he remembered his insensitive comments to him, but Bert appeared not to remember. He seemed more at ease, enjoying his pint of Slodger.

Alan asked Sam how he felt. 'Nothing permanent and I'm seeing a physio—'

'But you know what Thorey said at the time, Sam: take the buggers to court. That's what he'd have done,' said Bert.

'Yes, Bert, that's fine for him to say, but I've no complaints with the Smiley's. They've been good to me, and they've given me all the time off I need. And as for Joe Thorey, he's plain greedy, that's all. And you know as well as anyone, he'd no more take his own employers to court than fly.'

'Well, he doesn't need to, does he? He's got it made. He wouldn't sue the goose that lays the golden eggs, now, would he?'

They all nodded. He was dead right. Meanwhile Alan's head was racing. The Thorey they were talking about so disparagingly was presumably Joe Thorey, Bert Hickson's replacement as head keeper. Alan remembered his rude behaviour at Stan's wake. He had not made a good impression.

Bert stood up. He nodded at their glasses. They gave thumbs ups and he headed towards the bar. Alan joined him ostensibly to help carry the glasses, but actually to re-introduce himself. It was Bert Hickson who had phoned the police about Stan's body and there was much Alan needed to learn.

'I am impressed, Mr Hickson, you look even fitter than when I saw you last. You been taking exercise?'

'I've been swimming and doing a bit of cycling, too.'

'Well, it certainly seems to have worked.'

The older man smiled. 'Well, you can't sit at home all day. I'm better off being out and about.'

'Do you ever do any work on the estate? I'd imagine Joe Thorey would welcome the help of a fit man like you.'

'In your dreams, young man. He wouldn't let me back into Fursey Park if I offered to work for free. And I'm damned if I'll do that. I know Barty wouldn't object, nor would Mr Sebastian, come to that. Trouble is, neither of them are running the shoot. That's strictly between Thorey and Mrs Sarah.' He paused. 'And what they say *goes*.'

This was very interesting. The more he learnt about the Cripps family, the more complex they seemed. Wheels within wheels; different people, differing ambitions, yet no external cracks. To the outside world they were as solid as rock – or maybe as thick ice.

Cyril had been pouring their pints and obviously listening in to the conversation.

'Talking of Thorey, he never turned up last night. I'd got his evening meal ready as usual.'

'Prompt at seven?'

'That's right. As he likes it.' He lifted two full pints up onto the bar. 'So I had to eat it myself.'

Alan felt it was time he said something. 'That must have been a chore for you, Cyril.'

'That's enough lip from you, young whippersnapper.'

The two older men smiled.

'But it's not like him, is it?' Bert asked.

'No, it isn't,' Cyril replied. 'As you know, he always eats here. That's how he puts his teams of beaters together every weekend. Everyone knows he's here at seven. Grace says we should pay him a commission.'

As Alan and Bert picked up their pints and started to move away, the young man who had been standing at the bar next to Alan received a text. Alan glanced back at him. The man's face looked puzzled.

'Cyril, I've just got a text.' Bert and Alan stopped on their way back to the table. There was something about the way he said it. 'It says here that Joe didn't report to the office all day. And I was waiting for him down at the pens all morning. Gave up in the end and helped clean out the game larder.'

By now the bar had gone quiet. Then somebody asked, 'Has anyone checked out his house?'

'Yes, Dan,' a lady sitting on the settle by the fire called back. 'I did the cleaning all morning. Come to think of it, he hadn't used the electric kettle, which was cold. I remember thinking that at the time.'

'That's you all over, Dolly,' another lady called out. 'Tea first, cleaning second.'

Normally that might have raised a small laugh. But not now.

Slowly, conversation resumed. After all, Alan reflected, people are allowed to take a day off from time to time. But everyone he spoke to was agreed: it was odd that he hadn't told anyone he was leaving – not even the estate's cleaning lady.

Just before closing time, Alan's sense of foreboding increased when another elderly man, who he could hear discussing Thorey's disappearance with Bert Hickson, called cheerily over his shoulder, by way of goodnight, 'Oh well, Cyril, here we go again. Curse of the Cripps – call in the police divers!'

Alan put a bunch of empty glasses on the bar and turned to leave. Those parting words were echoing through his befuddled brain. When was it, 2004? That's right: the gardening banker at the hall. What was his name: Hambledon? Hampton? No, Hansworth. That's it: Hansworth. Hansworth. And then poor Stan.

But now his blood was running cold. Cold as the swollen waters of the Mill Cut.

# Part 2

## Seeking the Truth

# Seven

Alan detected a glint of black ice on the village street as he stood at his kitchen window sipping tea from his Nikon mug. On the table beside him was a packet of chocolate digestives. Two women who helped out at the village shop walked gingerly by on their way to work. Alan glanced down at his watch: 6.45. The weekend starts early for some, he thought. Still, the tea was working its magic, dissipating the after-effects of the night before. He'd got up promptly to resume work on Stan's notebooks, which had been starting to slip behind schedule. But now he found he was thinking not so much about levels in dykes, as the river into which they drained. And from there it was a short step to Hansworth, fishing and to Joe Thorey. Would he be walking to work today? He very much doubted it.

Across the fields he could faintly hear the sound of an ambulance siren. He started to imagine who might have fallen ill at that hour when his musings were suddenly interrupted by the bright-yellow reflective jackets of two police community support officers who were caught in the headlights of a passing car. Alan guessed they must have walked out of Fursey Hall's drive, to the right of his cottage, and were heading back into the village.

He took a large bite from a biscuit. Police. So, he thought grimly, maybe the loud-mouthed Joe Thorey hasn't reappeared.

* * *

The sun was just starting to appear above the open, peaty fields of Padnal Fen away to the south-east, as Alan took the right fork onto the Littleport Road. In the mirror, the ruins of Fursey Abbey Church looked superb in the clean light of morning. Normally he'd have pulled over and taken a photo, but not today, as he'd agreed to meet Jake and the team for a cup of tea and a chat before they began their last full day's work at White Delphs.

After fifteen minutes the road rose steeply to ascend the huge man-made banks of the River Great Ouse. He remembered driving here with his dad who explained that in the 1950s and '60s that slope had been the only place where learner drivers taking their test in Littleport could practise handbrake hill starts. For a few hundred yards the road ran parallel to the Kings Lynn–Cambridge railway line, then it came off the bank and veered west, towards yet another riverbank. He slowed down. He knew the turning was around here somewhere. A huge tractor with a load of sugar beet thundered past him, heading towards Norfolk.

*Welcome to White Delphs Wartime Experience and Adventure Playground* proclaimed a large notice, which Alan thought had been designed with some care. The khaki and brown camouflage shouldn't have been eye-catching at all, but it was. Maybe it was the raised, brightly painted lettering plus a zigzag line of cod-machine-gun bullet holes that did it. But whatever it was, it worked – and had been professionally executed. 'And it wasn't cheap, either,' Alan muttered under his breath as he turned into the visitors' car park.

The car park proclaimed that it was free and welcomed people to come and use it, even if they were not planning to visit the attraction 'on this occasion'. Smart marketing again, Alan conceded. There was even a picnic area, complete with benches and tables. Another, smaller, painted 'camouflage' notice proclaimed that 'The White Delphs Wartime Experience and Adventure Playground was owned and operated by Historic Projects Management ltd., a registered charity'. The brief terms and conditions were signed off by Blake Lonsdale, Chief Executive, at the HPM Registered Offices in Stratford, east London – of all places. Alan wondered what on earth the connection might be.

Jake was waiting for him and they walked across the car park to a Portakabin behind a screen of tall black poplars, which Alan reckoned had probably been planted during the war. People rarely think of plants being historic monuments, but those trees almost certainly were. Around them were several massive concrete anti-tank cubes, the base of a spigot mortar, another more active anti-tank weapon and pieces of old railway tracks which had been cut into short lengths and set deep into the ground, again against incoming armour. Alan was impressed. It was nice to come across a small corner of the fens that hadn't been flattened out in the interests of intensive agriculture.

Although it wasn't the summer tourist season, the car park was by no means empty and Alan's eye was immediately caught by a gleaming dark-blue Bentley. As they approached the side entrance to the visitor centre, a door a few yards away opened and a man in a smart suit emerged. He pointed the keys at the Bentley, whose lights dutifully blinked. Alan was fascinated: the man's suit and the Bentley's paintwork were a perfect match.

Jake touched Alan on the shoulder and semi-whispered, 'That's Blake Lonsdale, he's chief executive of the company that runs this place.'

Their hesitation had caught Lonsdale's attention. He looked up and strode towards them. 'So one of you gentlemen must be Jake Williamson?'

'That's me.'

They shook hands. Close up Lonsdale was strikingly handsome. Fit, fifties. Film star good looks. Slightly greying temples.

'And I'm Alan Cadbury. I'm an archaeologist at Fursey Abbey just down the road.'

'Indeed, I know it well. My friend John Cripps has told me all about your project. Sounds most interesting.'

Blimey, Alan thought, word gets around quickly.

'I was just going to show Alan what we've been up to here,' Jake added.

'Excellent. Be our guest. And please be polite about the company, Jake.' This was said with a broad smile. They then chatted about the perils and pleasures of running a historic visitor attraction, and Alan was impressed not just by his obvious business ability, but by his interest in archaeology. Then a phone rang in the Bentley. 'I do apologise, that might be quite important. I'd better answer it. So nice to have met you both.'

Jake closed the door of the side entrance behind them.

'So, will you be "polite about the company", Jake?'

Jake smiled. 'To be quite honest, I will. They've treated us very well indeed. They've given us everything we've asked for and never quibbled over contingencies.'

Clients of excavation contractors always quibbled over contingency clauses in project specifications. It was part of life in commercial archaeology. But not, it seemed, at White Delphs.

Once inside the Portakabin, Alan felt immediately at home; this was familiar territory for him. The place had that early morning feel to it: the chill of night-time was still there, but pushed into the background by the steam of kettles and the ubiquitous portable gas stove. This Portakabin also smelled good because Jake's finds assistant, Henrietta 'Hen' Clancy, couldn't stand instant coffee and had brought a filter coffee maker with her.

She greeted Alan with a warm kiss on both cheeks. She was a little shorter than Jake, but about the same age – late twenties/early thirties – and as Alan looked at them standing together, it was clear that their relationship went beyond the professional. As Alan knew only too well, such things often happened on digs. He thought back to Harriet on the Guthlic's graveyard job. The memory of her was still fresh, and still, he had to admit, warm. But then he'd blown everything – and pointlessly. It had shaken – in fact it still shook – his confidence. He found his mind returning to those days made dark in high summer, when he knew his obsession was driving the only woman he had really cared for away. But he couldn't help himself. He'd gone over and over those times, trying to learn lessons from them. And had he? Would he handle things any better now, more than a year on? He hoped he would, but doubted it. His introspection was abruptly broken by Hen who was trying to stack a finds tray on the trestle table behind him.

He stepped aside with a muttered apology. Hen had acquired her nickname because she was a punctilious finds assistant and had a reputation for clucking around people when they handed in their finds trays at the end of a day's digging. Once Alan had put a rubber egg in her tray. He smiled as he recalled her reaction, which was to return it to Alan, to store in a place 'where the sun don't shine', much to the delight of some tired, mud-spattered diggers.

Jake introduced him to the two professional diggers, Jon and Kaylee, both of whom had graduated the previous summer from the Field School at Westbourne. Alan had a high opinion of Westbourne graduates, who were often motivated and hard-working.

Hen asked about the people behind the Fursey project, as she was becoming increasingly aware that during the current depression some potential employers were a bit financially unreliable, and that the White Delphs company, Heritage Projects Management, had been excellent. Jake added that they also paid promptly, and didn't quibble over budget changes. By way of response, Alan explained that Fursey was both a long-term visitor attraction and a publicly-funded research project. He told them that so far he'd also found them very good to work for.

Both Hen and Jake already knew Alan and they were glad of the work. The two others were slightly hesitant at first, but once Alan had explained what they were finding and the potential of the Fursey site, they rapidly became more enthusiastic. Soon they agreed to come along, too.

At this, Alan smiled broadly. 'Thanks for that. It's good to know I'll have an experienced team to start the new project. It's always difficult, when you don't get much notice. So you've helped get me off the hook. Thanks a lot. I appreciate it.'

After their short chat, Jake took Alan across to the site. Digging had finished, but it still looked neat and business-like. Alan smiled: for all the world it could have been a Roman villa or a Benedictine monastery for the care and attention they had given the remains. The fact that most of the structures dated to the autumn of 1940 was entirely irrelevant. Everything was there: sunken cable ducts, exposed and displayed as if they had been the flues leading into a Roman bath house hypocaust; rough-cast wartime concrete, brushed and cleaned like the finest Norman masonry.

'You'll have to find your own way around, Alan, as I've got loads of things to get cleared up before the end of the day.' Alan nodded; he fully understood. 'But just to put you in the picture, at the start of the dig I was asked to investigate what they thought might be the accommodation area—'

'What, for the troops?' Alan broke in.

'Yes, but also civilians.' Jake couldn't conceal his enthusiasm for the site and the period. 'Remember, only a few of the specialist gunners were regulars. The rest were Home Guard and some were veterans of the First World War. These chaps would have needed support of some sort.'

'And did you find it?'

'Yes, very much so. Over here we've got the block-work stub walls for Nissan-hut-type buildings and you can see over here' – they walked a few paces towards the poplar trees – 'the remains of tiles and slabs for the floor. We also found spoons, forks and broken glass salt and pepper pots, some with Bakelite tops still in place. We reckon it was the canteen.'

'So this seems an important site – maybe a regional centre?'

'Very much so. As you may know, the idea of defensive stop lines was dropped towards the end of 1940.'

'That was after the collapse of the Maginot Line?'

'That's right, and there was a change in the army command back here in Britain. As a result, early in 1941 they went over to a system based on what they called nodal points, which were intended to resist for much longer than the thinly-manned stop lines.'

'And this is one of them?'

'Yes, but on a previously existing stop line, the Fenland Command Line, which links into the country's primary defence, the GHQ Line, over towards Huntingdon. If you climb the Delph bank you can see two spigot mortars, three pillboxes for machine guns and a large shell-proof field gun shelter, which our volunteers have restored to its original wartime condition.'

Alan couldn't help pulling a face at this. 'What, gas masks and tea flasks?'

'I know, Alan,' Jake continued. 'I'm not too fond of restorations or re-enactment myself, but I must say, they've done a great job, and were advised by an old boy who was actually stationed here, during the war. So it's 100 hundred per cent genuine. More to the point, they haven't altered anything structural.'

Alan smiled. He had deserved that.

He said goodbye to Jake and the others, then headed up onto the Delph bank, first pausing to read one of the many information panels, which were concise, well-illustrated and carefully positioned to be unobtrusive, yet avoid the bleaching effect of direct sunlight. Again, Alan detected a professional hand behind it all. No doubt that was why John was so keen on closer co-operation with White Delphs. But how would that go down with other members of the Cripps family? He could clearly imagine how Sebastian would feel.

He was standing on the top of the bank, admiring the view, when his mobile rang. He glanced down at the screen: four missed calls, all from the same unknown Peterborough number, which was phoning him again, now.

'Alan!' It was DCI Lane's voice. 'At last I've managed to get through. Are you digging deep in a lead mine somewhere?'

'No, Richard, I'm out at White Delphs, as you suggested.'

'Oh well, then, it'll be the Delph bank. Seems to cut out signals from Norfolk. You on the top of it now?'

'How did you guess?'

But Lane had more important things on his mind. 'Alan, something has been drawn to my attention that I'd like to discuss with you face-to-face – and fairly soon, if that's possible.'

Alan could detect a note of urgency in Lane's voice, which was unusual. This had to be important. 'I've nothing on today, but I'm hoping to get to grips with Stan's notes and stuff tomorrow – but even so, I could do it.'

'No, let's make it tonight. Mary's keen to see you, too. It's been too long. And we'd like you to see our new place here in Whittlesey.'

Alan well remembered Richard had told him the previous summer that they were planning to move; but that was quick, even for Lane. Alan couldn't help wondering whether their previous exploits together at Blackfen Prison and Leicester hadn't made life too hot for the two of them back in the Midlands.

* * *

It was dark when Alan turned the Fourtrak into Straw Bear Close. Alan had smiled when Lane had told him the address: the Straw Bear was the name of the traditional mid-winter Molly Dance – a Fenland variant of Morris Dancing – that Whittlesey was locally famous for. Like other Fenland ceremonies, it was a great excuse to eat and drink too much.

Alan drew into the small gravel pull-in in front of Number 6. Richard Lane answered the bell and ushered Alan into a hallway. Mary emerged from the kitchen and gave Alan a kiss on the cheek.

'And how's life in the Fens suiting you both?' Alan asked her.

She looked across at her husband. 'We really like it here,' she replied. 'I can see my father's family, who I'd begun to lose contact with.' Mary had been born and raised in Peterborough. 'And Richard feels at home with the Fenland force.' She paused, before adding, 'So, we're happy.'

Something about the way she spoke decided Alan against asking whether she – they – were happier here than in Leicester. Some comparisons are best left unmade.

'Come and have a drink, Alan,' Lane said. 'And can I get you another, darling?'

Mary shook her head. 'No, I'm fine, thanks.' She looked up at the grandfather clock that stood by the front door, as it had in their last house. 'Supper will be ready at eight.' Then she added, looking pointedly at Lane, 'And don't get too involved, you two. It's fish and it'll turn to rubber if it's stewed.'

'No, ma'am,' Alan replied, taking out his phone and setting the alarm. 'There, that should do it.'

* * *

Lane and Alan moved into the sitting room, both with glasses of locally-brewed beer. As they walked across to two chairs on either side of a coffee table, Alan couldn't contain his impatience. 'Joe Thorey has vanished, hasn't he?'

'You seem very certain,' Lane replied.

Alan explained about the comments in the village pub when the news first broke.

'So what do you make of that "here we go again"? Was that the banker, Hansworth, or Stan, they were talking about?'

Lane took a long drink from his glass. 'Oh, it has to be Hansworth. His death had a huge local impact. I was involved when I was with Fenland previously, and helped them sort out a few problems. So I was quite familiar with the case.'

Alan sat forward, listening intently.

'It all goes back to the 3rd Baronet Cripps, that's the man everyone calls "Barty".'

'Yes,' Alan broke in. 'I met him at Stan's wake. I have to say I liked him. Seemed down-to-earth – and he was the only person who paid any attention to Stan's parents.'

'Yes,' Lane smiled. 'Well, he was the man who rationalised what was left of the estate in the mid-1980s. A major source of income then, and now, was Fursey Hall, which Barty, with the help of a very good architect, converted into extremely upmarket apartments, which were let to rich Londoners as second homes.'

'A shrewd move.'

'On the face of it, yes. But it wasn't universally welcomed by the family, many of whom used to stay there themselves – for free.'

Alan smiled. 'Yes, I can imagine that.'

'Anyhow,' Lane continued, 'One of the first of these new

tenants was, predictably enough, a rich London banker named James Hansworth.'

As Lane knew, Alan had a visceral loathing of bankers and financiers in general. 'Yes, reptiles like rivers. He'd have been happy there.'

Lane decided not to rise to this. 'He actually leased the main, ground-floor apartment – not that it's an "apartment" in the sense we know it; it's more like the whole ground floor – in fact it's the place where Sebastian and Sarah now live. Anyhow, he was no ordinary banker. He didn't swagger around and was said to have taken the apartment following a sympathetic piece in the *Sunday Times* about Barty's efforts to rationalise the estate, which back then was in a pretty poor state. Apparently he genuinely admired people who turned enterprises around – who made successes out of failures.'

'So was that the area where he made his money?'

'Yes, he was one of the British hedge fund survivors, following some spectacular collapses overseas in the late '90s and early 2000s. It would appear he was much more cautious and would only put money in to businesses he had thoroughly researched.'

'And he approved of what Barty was doing?'

Lane shrugged. 'So it would appear, although local tongues did wag at the time.'

'Really?'

Lane smiled. 'No, Alan, I wouldn't get excited. The Met were later brought in and they did a detailed forensic check of his firm's accounts and there's no evidence whatsoever of any shady deals. It would seem he was absolutely straight – although perhaps that's not quite the right word—'

'You mean, he was gay? How did that go down in a rural spot like Fursey?'

'I think most people followed Barty's lead.'

'And he approved?'

'I don't know about that. But he was a pragmatist. So why rock the boat? And the local people knew their jobs depended on the estate being turned round; so they went along with his reforms, which included the Fursey Hall apartments. But, of course, one or two loudmouths weren't very happy. But that's inevitable.'

'So when did Hansworth move in?'

'Nineteen eighty-eight. By all accounts, Barty's architect had done a superb job on the conversion, which won some prestigious awards. The plaques are still there in the front hall.'

Alan was impressed. Barty rose even further in his estimation.

'OK, so what happened then?'

'Ten years passed. Then Sebastian and Sarah decide to get married. As you've probably already gathered, Sebastian can be a bit down-to-earth.'

Alan smiled. He secretly rather admired Sebastian's rural directness. Put him in mind of his own father. 'Don't tell me: he asked Hansworth to move out of the main apartment?'

'Almost. It would seem he did have a "conversation", but Hansworth, quite reasonably, as he'd been living there ten years, wanted to stay put. And besides, he'd bought a 99-year lease and in those days leases and rental agreements didn't favour the landlords.'

'So he didn't move out?'

'No, and more to the point, Sebastian accepted the fact

and moved into one of the other apartments which had just fallen vacant, and they lived there happily until March 2004.'

'But presumably they must have resented the fact that they couldn't move into the main apartment?'

'Apparently not. As you know, Sebastian has a pragmatic – I've heard you call it rural – approach to life and he seemed to have decided to let the matter drop. Sarah, on the other hand, was more proactive; she went out of her way to re-establish good relations with Hansworth.'

'How on earth did she do that?' Alan found the idea of a rather conventional, church-going, rural lady forming a friendship with a gay London banker interesting – to say the least.

Lane grinned. 'As you might know, the gardens at the Hall are quite famous and a few months after the parterre garden won its first award, Sarah told the press that she realised Hansworth was a potential gardener when she saw all the hanging baskets he had arranged in the grand entrance hall.'

'So that's how he got involved with the garden.' Things were starting to fall into place for Alan. 'Candice mentioned it earlier.'

Lane took a sip from his drink and continued, 'At the time some people said she had only approached him because of his money; but actually, it does appear he was a natural-born gardener and had always been interested in plants. As time passed, he spent longer and longer at Fursey.'

'What, days, weeks, months? How did he fit it all in?'

'In the early '90s he would only spend weekends there. He had a strict rule about being in the office for Monday morning. But slowly things began to change.'

'What, the Monday bit?'

'No, that never altered. Instead he'd return to Fursey earlier in the week – sometimes even on a Wednesday.'

'Does that mean he was getting bored of banking?' Alan asked.

'That's what I thought, too, but I was wrong. He was 45 when he died and would often say that he'd spent his life delegating and was now reaping the rewards. Again, the Met finance boys made enquiries and it would seem he was right. Apparently his office was very well run – and he was trusted and highly respected in the City.'

'It sounds like he was in control, not just of his office, but of life in general. So did he spend much time with Sarah in the garden?'

'Yes, a fair bit, but he also took up fishing. Whether by accident or design, the lease he'd negotiated back in 1988 included exclusive rights to two hundred yards of riverbank – in fact, the same stretch of water where we found Stan's body.'

'And what about his gay partners? How did they fit in with the gardening fisherman?'

'For the last eight or nine years of his life, his only partner was a man called Andrew Fellows. He was an estate agent in Northampton. There's nothing about him to make us suspicious. But it was Fellows, I think, who got him interested in fishing.'

'Game fishing, presumably?'

'No,' Lane replied. 'That's the surprising thing. They both enjoyed coarse fishing, especially for eels, which are still quite plentiful hereabouts. Sarah also told me that Fellows was a good cook and she would sometimes be invited to their apartment to share an eel with them.'

There was a pause while both men thought through what had been said. Alan was the first to speak. 'Right, so that takes us, I think, to 2004.' Lane nodded. Alan drained the last of his beer before speaking again. 'Although I think I can guess from what you've already said, but I've got to ask: what happened next?'

Lane was about to reply when the phone in Alan's shirt pocket sounded the alarm. Time for supper – and they both knew it would be a fatal error to continue their conversation away from the table.

* * *

Mary was standing at the stove putting the finishing touches to the parsley sauce, while Lane and Alan were piling their plates high. She took off her apron and put the steaming sauce boat on the table.

'There,' she said. 'Help yourselves, boys.'

Eating in the Lane household had always been more about enjoying the food hot, than the usual, rather prim, English social niceties. The sauce jug came to ground near Alan, so he immediately helped himself, then handed it on to Lane.

'It's great to be back with you both,' Alan said. 'And I do like the house. You must have a good view from the upstairs rooms at the back.'

'Yes, we do,' Mary replied, helping herself to a buttery spoonful of Savoy cabbage. 'You can see right along the King's Dyke and over across to the old knot holes which are teeming with wildlife: buzzards, hares – even the occasional deer.'

The 'knot holes' were what local people called the pits dug deep into the Oxford clay by the London Brick Company before the war. These vast holes were the raw material of

Victorian and Edwardian London. But half a century of abandonment had changed them dramatically – for the better.

'Anyhow, Alan, Richard has been telling me all about what has been going on at Fursey. You do lead an exciting life, don't you?'

'Well, I hope this time it all blows over. I think I'd rather be an archaeologist than a bad amateur sleuth. And believe me, Mary, the site is extraordinary. It's already producing loads of Roman military stuff. All completely unexpected.'

'So you don't reckon anything strange is going on there. You'll simply be able to do your dig without any distractions?'

Alan hadn't meant to imply that. And she knew it.

'Obviously Stan's death will need to be sorted out, but that's more Richard's affair than mine—'

'And Hansworth?' she broke in. 'Is that linked in any way?'

'I honestly don't know.' Alan was feeling very wrong-footed and he couldn't decide if Lane was enjoying his predicament. 'But, obviously,' he continued without much conviction, 'I'm keeping my eyes open for any possible clues.'

Mary pressed home the point. 'What about that curse business. You think it might be relevant?'

'Oh, I wouldn't worry too much about that,' Lane said. 'I think a lot of the Curse of the Cripps stuff is rubbish; mostly gossip by jealous locals.'

'Yes, I'm sure you're right,' Alan replied, keen now to clarify what he actually thought. 'But I think two, and now possibly three, unexplained deaths in the stretch of river that passes through the estate do need to be explained – if only to silence the rumour-mongers.'

'Of course, we were very sad indeed about your poor friend Stan,' Mary said. 'And we were around when Hansworth vanished. But that was rather strange. I remember thinking at the time there was something not quite right about it.'

'How do you mean?' Alan asked.

'I don't know. It all seemed "managed" in a sort of PR fashion: information came out in dribs and drabs. Put me in mind of the way the Blair government "managed" the official enquiry into the lead-up to the Iraq War. It was all about "spin" and cover-up – not truth. Don't you agree, Richard?'

Lane was smiling slightly anxiously. It was unusual for Mary to be quite so frank.

'I will admit that everyone's story held together and was consistent. But then that's what you'd expect in a well-run family team. I imagine people probably did consult together and yes, I think there was an element of damage limitation there, too. But again, given all that curse business, and the fact that the family were involved with a popular visitor attraction – which is what the farm shop and restaurant were, let alone the then new Abbey project – I don't think that's particularly surprising.'

Some of this was passing Alan by. He needed more precise information. He had stopped theorising and was now actively looking for clues.

'I'm sorry, Richard, but you'll have to tell me precisely what happened. All I have gathered is that a banker named Hansworth, who was a keen fisherman, died in the river, near to where Stan's body washed up, sometime in 2004.'

'It was mid-March, actually,' Lane said. 'We don't know for sure, but it seems most likely that the accident—'

'If that's what it was,' Mary interrupted.

'Yes, dear, if that's what it was. And remember the coroner's court passed a verdict of death by misadventure—'

'Like Stan.' It was Alan's turn to disrupt his friend's narrative.

'Indeed, like Stan – and just like Stan, I can't start rumours about murder. So I've got to be very, very careful. It's worth remembering that the Cripps family are very powerful. So we've got to be extra discreet. If they get so much as a whiff that you're looking into the case, Alan, you can kiss goodbye to your job and your precious archaeology.'

Alan nodded. He was only too well aware of that.

Lane took a deep breath and resumed. 'As I was saying, we reckon that the accident probably happened on the weekend of the thirteenth and fourteenth of March, the last two days of the coarse-fishing season. Normally, the riverbanks would have been crowded on the Monday, and maybe his body would have been spotted. But the place was deserted.'

'But you told me before supper that he usually went fishing with his partner?' Alan had to ask.

'He did,' Lane replied. 'But on that particular weekend, Fellows couldn't join him. So he was fishing alone. Then next morning, Joe Thorey had some business to attend to in Ely – something to do with the estate shotgun licences – so didn't get back to Fursey until after dinner. He found Hansworth's stool, rod and keepnet, which he took back to the apartment. Apparently he quite often left tackle on the bank if it needed to be repaired – which was something Thorey did for him—'

'Privately, "on the side"?' Alan broke in.

'Yes, from time to time. It was simpler than taking stuff over to Keeper's Cottage. And I gather Thorey did quite a lot of work of that sort. It seems he quite enjoyed it.'

'And did any of the kit need repairing?'

'Yes, all of it. Thorey described it as "end of season maintenance". So he cleaned it all up.'

'And in the process' – Alan was thinking aloud – 'he removed most of the evidence. Unfortunate, that?' The question was asked with a hint of irony.

'Yes,' Lane replied, also deep in thought. 'You're right, it was; but I think it's an understandable mistake for a keeper to have made. There had been very heavy rain over the previous week and the river was still rising. It might all have got washed away.'

'Hardly ideal fishing conditions, then?' Alan still wasn't altogether convinced.

'Yes, that's what we thought too, but apparently the stretch of water downstream of the mill is much calmer than the main river. In effect, it's a backwater and, according to Thorey, fish tend to gather there when the river's in spate.'

'OK,' Alan conceded. 'So did they find his fingerprints on the rod?'

'Yes, they did, along with Thorey's, of course. Anyhow, Hansworth's absence was noted the following morning when he failed to arrive back at work. His absence caused consternation, as the end of the financial year was approaching. And he didn't turn up at his smart flat in the Barbican, either. The next day the press got to hear about it and there were big headlines on all the financial pages – "Prominent banker disappears", that sort of thing. All were speculating that he'd "done a runner".'

'But then he never reappeared,' Alan added.

'Quite,' Lane replied. 'So the "done a runner" story died. Eventually his body turned up close to Denver Sluice, but that was in May and by then all useful forensic evidence had long rotted away. In fact, he was almost unrecognisable and was eventually identified by DNA.'

'Any broken bones?' Alan asked. He was thinking of Stan.

'No, none, but then there aren't any more mills downstream of Fursey.'

Alan had one last important question to ask. 'You mentioned that Joe Thorey found Hansworth's rod. As a matter of interest, what happened to him after that?'

'At the time he found the rod, he'd been employed, if that's the right term on a part-time basis; he used to help out when needed on shoots and during the fishing season, but Sarah Cripps had ambitious plans for the shoot, which soon became very much larger and better organised. I gather they charge over a thousand pounds a day for a gun. Joe Thorey got a full-time job as a keeper on the estate at the end of March. Eventually, the following summer, he was appointed head keeper on Bert Hickson's early retirement. Hickson moved out of Keeper's Cottage and Thorey moved in. That's the way things work on such estates.'

'And of course, it was Hickson,' Mary added quietly, 'who found your friend Stan.'

Yes, Alan thought, wheels within waterlogged wheels. Two 'accidents', both involving water and on land owned and controlled by the Cripps family.

In Stan's case, Alan could see at least two clear links already: to the Smileys and to Sebastian, both of whom had known about the storm damage to the mill before it appeared on the television news. And in the Hansworth case it was difficult to ignore Thorey's role, although Alan was also aware that his judgement might be clouded by his dislike of the man. And as for motives that linked the two deaths? That was much harder. The obvious one for Stan would be some archaeological discovery which adversely affected the Fursey Estate. But that couldn't possibly apply to Hansworth. But what about Candice and Sarah? At first glance they didn't appear very close, but life had taught Alan that women were far better at dissimulation than men. And they both had a strong interest in seeing that the Cripps family fortunes increased: Sarah, through the shoot and 'field sports'; and Candice through the abbey dig. Then his mind flicked forward: and of course poor old Stan didn't like doing television. Candice had told him that it didn't matter, but Alan had detected more than a hint of regret in her voice when she'd said it. Maybe she realised that Fursey would always be a second-division attraction without national publicity. So did she see Stan's refusal to do TV as damaging her career – her life? More to the point, she was now absolutely delighted that he, Alan, was leading the *Test Pit Challenge* project. So from both Candice and Sarah's point of view, things had worked out well. Very well indeed.

* * *

Alan didn't spend a very restful night; his mind was constantly working. There was nothing for it but to take charge. Look for the evidence, rather than speculate. He put on his black North Face jacket and rucksack, pulled up the hood, then clicked his phone on to silent: 4.03am. He stood still, took a few deep breaths, then turned out the house lights, opened the back door and slipped noiselessly out. He climbed out of his untended back garden and headed away from the few village streetlights, then he crossed to the unlit side of Fore Street, and a gap in the brick wall surrounding the park.

Everyone in the village knew that this led to a shortcut that younger people used if they needed somewhere away from prying eyes – which was exactly what Alan was after now.

The trees in Fursey Park were quite famous and included several massive old oaks, some of which had been pollarded in the Middle Ages. There were also the remains of an early medieval deer boundary ditch, which may well have been in active use when the monks took the site over in Norman times. Alan hurried from tree to tree as by now the wind had got up and occasionally moonlight lit the scene. He caught sight of roe deer and a tawny owl returning to its nest with a small rat clasped in its talons. The tree cover became thinner as he approached Abbey Farm and he waited for a large patch of cloud before he attempted to cross the open ground behind the 1950s pig sheds. Alan clearly remembered seeing Stan in what he called his 'cupboard', when he came for his second visit in early November, just over a year ago. But now things had changed and were about to change even more, Alan reckoned, as he looked at the teleporter parked on the edge of the yard, just outside the abandoned buildings. They belonged to a firm of demolition contractors. He knew it was now or never.

He climbed through an open window and found himself in what had been the main Fursey Abbey offices, until the end of last year. Alan had helped them transfer stuff into the current, but temporary, Portakabin office, three weeks previously. He glanced at a tattered Year Planner for 2009, which was still pinned to the wall. On the wall, too, were scraps of Christmas decorations, presumably the last office party in the old building, which somebody had attempted rather half-heartedly to remove.

The floor inside the broken window was damp and slippery, but once he'd got further into the building he even detected a hint of warmth, presumably left over from daytime sunshine on the single-storey flat roof. Everywhere there was the sad, musty smell of abandonment. Nobody cared about these buildings anymore and soon they would vanish forever.

Alan tried to picture that day when he visited Stan. They'd come in through the main door and someone, probably Candice he now realised, had spotted him through the half-open office door. He must have looked like an archaeologist, because she'd called out, 'If you want Stan, he's further down the corridor, third door on the right, just before the freezer room.'

When he'd first walked along the corridor he'd been passed several times by kitchen assistants in pale-blue overalls and white aprons heading towards the double kitchen doors at the end. Just out of interest he pushed them open and had a look: the place had been stripped clean of everything, except the worn linoleum floor. All that remained were several drain holes in the floor and walls and the larger openings for extractor fans in the ceiling. There was a strong smell of stale cooking oil.

Next he pushed at the door into Stan's 'cupboard', half expecting, for some reason, to find it locked. But it opened. He shut it quietly behind him. As he did so he pulled a small torch from his pocket and looked around. The desk had been moved to the centre of the room, as if they had planned to take it away, but had had second thoughts. And who could blame them? It was very tatty, with woodworm holes across the whole of the back. Alan flashed his torch at the wall where he remembered it had originally stood and, yes, woodworm was there, too.

He pulled open the large drawer at the centre of the desk. It was empty. The drawers on either side of the knee-space were empty too and the top one had been removed and was still lying on the floor. Then he walked across to the two-drawer filing cabinet close to the wall opposite the door. Stan's old and slightly warped drawing board was propped up against it. Alan pulled open the top drawer and looked in: a few disposable draftsman's pens and some elderly scale-rules, but nothing else. Alan looked carefully through the hanging-files in the lower drawer, but they were all empty. Then he stood back. He was certain there must be something else here too. But where?

Suddenly the early morning silence was shattered by a loud creaking rasp. All the hairs on the back of Alan's neck stood up. It was a strange, unearthly, sound. He looked around for a weapon of some sort, but the tiny room was absolutely bare. He opened the door and slipped into the corridor. Then the sound came again, quieter this time, and clearly from the old office. Alan took out his clasp knife. Hardly an offensive weapon, but much better than nothing. Then rapidly he threw open the office door and pulled it back. When he gingerly looked again, the place was empty. But he could feel a very slight breeze. Then the ungreased iron-framed window creaked. Bloody thing! Feeling a bit of a fool, Alan shut it.

As he returned to Stan's 'cupboard' Alan thought about the building's original use as a piggery. They'd had a smaller one on the farm at home, until his father had got fed up with the long hours and unstable prices for pork. At one end of each unit there used to be a small compartment where his father would keep food supplements, veterinary supplies and a card index of the current batch of sows and their litters. This is what Stan's little office had once been.

Half of the wall away from the door was angled at 45 degrees, which was where the 'clean cupboard' had been when the building was still part of the farm. Now the floor space in front of it was occupied by the filing cabinet. If it was anything like the piggeries back home, Alan thought, this angled wall still covered the place where they'd kept things that they didn't want to get dirty: wormer guns, spray cans etc. Alan tapped the wall with the butt of his torch. It was hollow, but had been neatly covered-over with a sheet of plaster-board, presumably during the original conversion in the late '70s. He moved the filing cabinet. And it paid off. Just above the floor was a small and very home-made sliding hatch of white cardboard.

Alan raised the little hatch and shone his torch inside. Propped against a quarter-full bottle of whisky in front of dozens of empties was a battered brown notebook. The cover bore the felt-tip legend, in Stan's handwriting: '*Fursey BH log: Nov 11–28, 2008.*' Why wasn't it in the desk? Why would Stan have kept a secret log, Alan wondered? Presumably he was keeping it secret from someone in the Cripps family, as there were no archaeologists with him at the time. John? Candice? Surely not Sebastian? He shook his head.

Outside it was that 'darkest hour just before dawn'. He knew he didn't have long, but he couldn't resist taking a closer look at the notebook's pages. They were full of little colum-nar stratigraphic sketches, complete with notes and levels above or below sea level, known in the trade as Ordnance Datum (OD). Typical of Stan, Alan thought, each sketch is dated and even timed: 'Completed 20.15'. He glanced at another: '20.25'; and another '21.00'. Alan had several notebooks of his own like this one, and he recognised it for what it was instantly: a set of auger, or borehole logs. He also knew they'd make no sense unless he could work out the levels and draw up a collated transverse section at 1:20, or smaller if needs be. And that would take time. He slipped the notebook inside his jacket and zipped the pocket.

Next he pulled out the lone bottle with whisky still in it. A small glass had been up-ended over the stopper. Alan sniffed it. He could just detect the faintest aroma of one of his friend's last drinks. Scents and smells had a powerfully evocative effect on Alan. Briefly Stan stood beside him. No need for words. The bottles said it all. How very sad and what a bloody awful waste of talent. Then the moment passed. He almost shouted at the injustice of life in his rage and frustration. Finally, a tired calm took over: what was the point?

He was about to put the bottle back in the wall recess, but then he paused. He was shining his torch on the small label on the back of the bottle. A 20-year-old Glen Hubris McTavish – probably the finest Speyside malt money could buy. He looked more closely and there, in tiny print at the very bottom of the back label, was the line: *Distillers by Appointment to Fisher College, Cambridge.* For a moment he hesitated, then he slipped the bottle in his rucksack.

He remembered what Stan had said about Peter Flower: 'Such a kind and helpful man'. Oh yeah? Somehow Alan choked back his anger, but the discovery of the bottle was important to his search for the truth. What would Flower have gained – what was his motive? Then it came to him. It was so bloody obvious. What would an academic gain from a shy, reticent but technically competent co-author who had started to drink? Control was the answer. Complete control of everything that mattered – everything that allowed him to enlarge his own reputation at the expense of Stan's. And to add to the irony, in the eyes of the world, it would be he, Peter Flower, who was trying to help Stan fight off his addiction. From now on, Alan knew his investigation would be more focused, and personal. Horribly personal.

# Eight

Alan arrived on-site early. It was a lovely, sunny Monday morning, the last day of February, and the main car park dig had been underway for six weeks. At this stage it had not been an excavation, so much as a scrape, with the whole area being carefully trowelled over at least twice. Davey and his digger had been gone for four weeks. The geophysics team, too, had finished a week ago. They'd revealed lots and lots of small features, but nothing very substantial – which was what Candice and John wanted if the new Fursey visitor centre and shop/restaurant project was not to be held up. But in his heart of hearts, Alan was a tiny bit disappointed. He'd have liked a bloody great fort ditch and gateway; something to have got his teeth into.

At the end of the previous week, Clare Hughes the county mounty from the local county council's development control department had visited the site, unannounced, as she didn't particularly want a load of developers breathing over their shoulders. She and Alan trusted each other and got on well together. They had looked at digital plans of the finds, which they placed over the newly arrived geophys plot, and it didn't take long before they'd isolated several areas of potential interest. Some time ago, Clare had phoned Alan and they had agreed that they couldn't simply abandon the site to the new car park completely unexamined. True, in theory it would be protected and preserved below the thick layer of tarmac, but you can't protect something if you don't know what it is. Maybe a heavy covering would be inappropriate; maybe water should be permitted to soak through? They just didn't know. So somehow they had to characterise the nature and extent of the more deeply buried remains together, of course, with their preservation. This would require a number of hand-excavated trial trenches. The Fursey management company had been co-operative and reasonable, so they didn't want these trenches to delay completion of the car park beyond the Easter deadline – and to Alan's huge relief, Easter was late that year (24 April). Alan had explained to Candice that if the worst came to the worst, there might be a delay, but if that did happen, the extra local TV coverage and added visitors would more than make up for the disruption.

After about an hour poring over plans, Alan and Clare had decided on two initial trial trenches to characterise contrasting areas. Both would be aligned east-west. Trench 1 would be placed over a seemingly blank area, where there were few finds or geophysical anomalies. But as Alan knew only too well, archaeological 'blanks' were often full of surprises. Trench 2 was intended to examine what looked like part of a large rectangular building.

While they had been deciding on the trial trench locations, they couldn't help noticing the activity outside. They both knew what was happening, in theory, at least. But the reality was very impressive. While they'd both been shut away in Alan's Portakabin discussing trial trenches, Jake and the digging team had been on-site with road spikes and hazard tape, marking out no-go areas as Frank and Weinstein had strongly advised them to mark clearly where people shouldn't walk. And they knew what they were talking about, Alan thought, as he watched four huge articulated trucks pull up in the park. Behind them were two mini buses full of men and women, some of them wearing new black overalls bearing the discreet dark-blue logo of New Ideas Productions. As Alan was aware, the black and the dark blue was to avoid unwanted reflection when the many lights, which were just starting to be unloaded from the trucks, were eventually turned on.

As they stepped out of the Portakabin, Alan handed a plan of the site with the two trial trenches to Jake Williamson, Hen Clancy and Jon and Kaylee, the two diggers from White Delphs, who had been at Fursey for six weeks. They were all very grateful for the money and the work, but there is a limit to how many finds one can trowel from an area of 50 by 120 metres, without going mad, and everyone, Alan included, was getting sick of the sight of tiny Grey Ware sherds. As Jake memorably announced in a tired voice one rainy afternoon tea break, 'Even bloody Samian seems a bit samey.' No, they were all itching to do some 'real' excavation. They'd had more than enough of trowelling. And if it had to be live on television, then so much the better. Because that was what Frank and Weinstein had decided – with, of course, Alan's agreement – but in reality, as they all knew, he had no option.

At first Alan had been very sceptical at the suggestion, which an over-excited Frank had proposed at the end of the first week of conventional filming. Alan didn't think that Weinstein or T2 would buy the idea. It was far too risky: what if they found nothing? What if the big building on the geophys plot turned out to be rabbit holes? What if the blank area did indeed prove to be empty? Did they really want to make idiots of themselves in front of 3 million people? 'I hope 5 million', was Weinstein's unexpected response. Oh well, Alan thought, on your own head be it. And he was still far from convinced, despite Weinstein explaining that modern television was all about calculated risks and taking the individual members of their audience out of their comfort zones. After all, *Big Brother* had done it with massive success – so why not them? Again, Alan had a terse reply in mind, but he decided not to use it.

Clare was impressed at the way Jake and the team were standing guard over the archaeological areas. Nobody would be taking any shortcuts with them around. Alan escorted her back to her car and when she had left, he returned to the roped-off dig, to find Jake and Hen measuring out for Trench 1.

Alan checked the plan against the site grid – just to be completely certain the trench was in the right place – and then told the team to move on to Trench 2. The actual work of laying out the trenches was being done by Jake and the two diggers he'd brought with him from White Delphs. Meanwhile Hen Clancy and two additional diggers, who Alan had taken on that morning to help with the trial trenches, were setting up the finds processing area. So although the site crew of a director, two supervisors and four diggers was quite small, Alan was satisfied. He liked to do things that way as he felt more in control and it also meant that he got to do some digging himself. Directors of large urban excavations, with dozens of staff and several layers of supervision usually contrived a daily site visit, but the rest of their time was spent in the office 'doing management', as Alan called it with ill-concealed contempt. He might have to take on an extra three or four diggers if they opened more trenches, but he was not keen to see the team rise much above a dozen, at most a dozen-and-a-half.

Lew Weinstein and the bosses at T2 had been very impressed by the viewing figures and audience share of the two introductory half-hour documentaries, which had gone out a week previously. John, Candice and the Fursey Abbey team had almost been overwhelmed by the upsurge in visitor numbers and had erected a small viewing stand alongside the newly-exposed area. The stand would hold around 200 people, and on some Sundays it was almost full.

It was one thing to have two good sets of viewing figures, but quite another to build on them. Audience loyalty was what the top brass at T2 were desperate to achieve.

After much discussion, T2 and Weinstein came up with a change to their original schedule. Shortly after the two introductory docs had been screened, they'd see how audiences reacted to five short live broadcasts, each one lasting thirty minutes, starting on Monday at 8.30pm – peak viewing. These would be followed by a final, one-hour episode on Saturday, Day 6. It was hoped the five run-up episodes would boost their Saturday evening audience, which had been slipping badly of late, due to strong sports output from satellite stations, both at home and, more importantly, on large screens in city-centre pubs. It was a very risky strategy indeed for T2 and would probably cost both the commissioning editor and the boss of the history and factual department their jobs if it failed.

The first live show would be a behind-the-scenes introduction to the dig. The presenter, Craig Larsson, would generally be on-site. From there he could interview Alan in the trenches and Tricia in the finds hut with Hen; he'd also be introducing clips from the earlier two shows, plus some new aerial shots they'd filmed a fortnight ago.

* * *

A few days later, shortly after midday, Alan returned from a quick visit to a hearing-aid shop in Ely, where he had been fitted with a small earpiece, after a visit the previous week when his outer earhole had been moulded in wax. The nice lady in the shop had advised him to wear it as often as he could over the next few days. 'Before you know it, you won't know you're wearing it', was what she had said. 'But right now,' Alan thought, 'It feels like somebody has shoved a concrete tank trap into the side of my head.'

After a hot lunch from the *Test Pit Challenge*'s excellent caterers, Alan and Tricia walked over to the two trial trenches, which were both being trowelled-down. Originally Weinstein and Charles Carnwath, the commissioning editor at T2, had insisted that the trowelling had to start live on-screen, but Alan had pointed out the stupidity of that idea: archaeology isn't a race; and besides, all you'd see would be dry soil. It would be much better if they started a few hours earlier, then at least they could point at any areas that were starting to look exciting.

They arrived at Trench 2 first. Both trenches had been covered with clear plastic rain shelters which acted a bit like greenhouses during the day, so the flaps at each end were folded back. Late February sunshine can be surprisingly hot. During the morning, various black-overalled technicians had been working away on the lighting, but now everyone was still away at lunch. Alan had advised the diggers to make the most of it: free meals are rare in archaeology, let alone ones with starters, a choice of three hot main courses, a pudding and cheese – not to mention limitless tea and coffee. Belching slightly, Alan pulled a trowel from his back pocket and stepped into the trench. It was still very shallow – barely two inches deep, but already colours were beginning to show up.

For a couple of minutes Alan trowelled, concentrating closely. Then Tricia broke the silence. 'It looks darker towards this end, Alan.'

Alan nodded, still deep in thought.

'Is that something important, or is it where they were trowelling last?' When there was no answer, she tried again. 'I mean is it fresher, damper here?'

That wasn't much better either, but Alan knew what she was trying to say.

'It's hard to say. A trowelled surface is best when it's fresh. What you're looking at has been messed around. It's been walked on and there are scuff marks left by toes and kneelers and finds trays by the edge of the trench there. But on the other hand, you may be right. I've been having a look at it and I think the colour change may well be real, but we're still very much in the OLS—'

He broke off. She was looking puzzled. He hadn't yet grasped the extent of her lack of field experience. She'd come to archaeology via an Art History BA, and was very much an artefacts person. For a moment his mind flicked back to Harriet, his co-director on his last dig. She too had been a specialist – in human bones – but she could also dig like an angel. The way she dug those tiny and *so* fragile baby bones . . . He sighed. Still, there's no going back. What's passed is gone. End of.

'Sorry, that's the Old Land Surface, or buried topsoil – so I wouldn't expect to see much at this level.' She was looking disappointed. 'But you're right,' he continued more brightly. 'It is darker and a fraction softer, too – and that may well prove significant.'

'Do you think we'll find out tonight?'

For a moment it was Alan's turn to be lost. Then he realised what she was getting at. 'Oh, you mean for the "live"?'

'Yes.'

She was looking genuinely concerned. Unlike Alan, she plainly cared about the broadcast's impact on viewers. He was more worried about what the trench had to reveal – and about not looking a complete idiot in front of millions of people.

'I doubt if we'll be able to define precisely what's there, but I think we should be able to say if it's man-made, or natural.'

They walked over to Trench 1. By now one or two people were beginning to drift over from the catering tent.

Again, Alan pulled out his trowel and started to scrape. He'd been at it for a minute or so when Jake Williamson joined him.

'Thought I'd find you here, Alan.'

He hadn't noticed Tricia who had been standing by some heavy-duty lighting stands. He knelt down beside Alan and also started trowelling.

After a bit, Alan leant back. 'Very different texture to Trench 2, isn't it?'

'Yes, very. More stones and much more sandy.'

'And I don't think we're much higher here?'

'No,' Jake replied. 'That was my first reaction. I checked the OD levels over lunch: Trench 1 is 1.57 and we're at 1.65. So no difference at all. Certainly not enough to cause that.'

Tricia had been paying close attention. But she didn't understand the technical speak.

'Sorry, Alan, I don't get the significance of all that.'

She'd stepped out of the shadows and Jake looked astonished at what met his eyes. Alan wondered briefly what it must be like to have such an effect on men. He shot Jake a look as if to say 'pull yourself together, man', which Jake did. Alan then introduced them. Instead of shaking hands, she smiled broadly, to which Jake responded with a hint of embarrassed flush. Alan decided it was time to resume her crash course in field archaeology:

'We noted a textural change in the two trenches. This one is more stony and sandy. Normally that particular change happens when the ground level rises, especially as here, where one is on the edge of an ancient island. But as Jake pointed out, the levels are virtually identical, so we don't think that very likely.'

'So what do you think it is?' She was leaning over the trench, listening intently.

'Well,' Alan shot Jake another rapid look, this time it said: please keep your mouth shut. 'I think we both have our suspicions, but again, we're still high in the OLS, so we'd better not speculate—'

'Not even for me, Alan?'

The broad smile she gave him was indeed winning. There could be no doubt about that. But Alan remained obdurate.

'Sorry, Tricia, but no,' he replied in a mock schoolmaster voice. 'It'll all come out in the wash. You've just got to be patient.' He turned briefly to Jake, smiling, and said, 'And if you say anything, Williamson, you're on a fizzer. Get it?'

Jake snapped a salute with his trowel. 'Yassir!'

* * *

The afternoon was frantic. The Call Sheet, essentially a detailed timetable that was prepared before every shoot, itemised what was supposed to happen. It was issued to everyone.

*15.30–16.00: Tea break (crews and contributors)*
*16.00–18.00: Rehearsal and run-through (contributors and camera crews)*
*18.00–19.00: Lighting, set preparation and sound check (camera and lighting crews)*
*19.00–19.30: Film 'as live' sequences (contributors and camera, lighting crews)*
*19.30–20.00: Break (sandwiches, on set)*
*20.00–20.30: Final run-through (contributors and crews)*
*20.30–21.00: Live TX*
*21.00: WRAP (contributors and camera crews)*
*21.00–21.30: De-rig (lighting crews)*

During the previous week the production people at New Ideas had tried to persuade Alan to leave the lighting equipment in place during the six days of the live run, but he pointed out that if they did that, then it would be impossible to extend or open new trial trenches and it would also massively slow down daytime digging, which would be essential if the excavation was to be seen to be advancing. Eventually, and after much discussion, they had reluctantly agreed – and that final half-hour for the lighting crews was the result. Over lunch he muttered something apologetic to one of the riggers who looked at him as if he was mad. 'Blimey, mate, I saw that and rubbed my hands. We'll be well into overtime by then. And that'll be a nice little earner. We owe you a pint.' Alan smiled at his own naivety; and as for the beer, he knew that would never happen.

Alan had found Call Sheets, like most modern paperwork, of limited use. They gave details of hotels, train times and that sort of thing – they even gave information on local real ale pubs, which some fortunate production assistant had had to prospect for on one of the recce days, but they also had pages of health and safety crap and the usual management disclaimers that nobody with even a slightly active mind could bring themselves to read. Alan found them useful for the names of crew members and the mobile numbers of visiting experts and suchlike, but mostly his Call Sheets remained, unread, in his house or hotel bedroom. But not now. He'd never done a 'live' before and the Call Sheet was proving very useful.

Things went more or less to the Call Sheet timetable, which had mostly been drawn up by Lew Weinstein himself. Like many people in television, Weinstein loved doing live shows, largely, Alan suspected, because of the massive injections of adrenalin, which he soon discovered were a feature of all such work.

Weinstein's job was in the T2 studios in London, where he mixed the various site sequences, together with contributions from a panel of three experts, including Peter Flower, and chaired by guest celebrity and retired gameshow host, Michael Smiley – who was also in the London studio. To cover the transition between the various live feeds, Weinstein had a small library of recorded clips, plus the 'as live' sequences, filmed earlier that evening. These were background shots of the dig and the diggers, intended to convey 'atmos' rather than anything specific.

The direction on-site was being done by Frank Jones, who Alan reckoned hadn't done that much live work. He was more a film director, but Alan could also see he was going to give it his best shot. He didn't think he'd ever seen anyone quite so wired. Tricia had noticed it too.

'I think Frank's going to explode. If he keeps this up he'll be a wet sponge by nine o'clock. Just listen to him!'

They both had their radio mikes turned off, but their earpieces, which Alan had now grown entirely used to, were positively crackling with Frank's voice. He was discussing Camera 4's move while Craig was doing his opening PTC (piece to camera). Alan couldn't follow everything he was saying, but he seemed to imply that if the camera didn't do precisely what he suggested the entire show would fall apart. They could tell that Weinstein was getting near the end of his tether:

'OK, Frank, that's great. Great. Yeah, I've got that . . . Yeah . . .'A pause, while Frank's voice doubled in speed. Then came Weinstein's final response: 'Great, yeah. We'll keep it in reserve.'

Then the line went dead.

Tricia and Alan were standing open-mouthed, each with a hand cupped over their left ear. Then simultaneously, when the jabbering was cut off, they fell about laughing.

* * *

The final rehearsal and run-through went as smoothly as could be expected, and Alan could see that the presenter, Craig Larsson's, stage fright was building. He was standing still, but fidgeting with his script, his earpiece, his radio mike – whatever came to hand. He was also growing quite pale. Then a studio voice came through on Alan's earpiece and through radio speakers that Grump Edwards had set up alongside Trenches 1 and 2 and in the dining tent (which had been converted into a temporary viewing theatre for the duration of the broadcast). The flap into the dig shelter was lifted to allow a cameraman to enter, dragging a long cable from the camera he carried on his shoulder.

Alan looked through the gap, across the stripped surface towards the wide entrance into the dining tent, where he could see quite a big group of people watching the large flat screen. At the back he could clearly see John and Candice Cripps standing together, their heads almost touching as they looked at the screen through a narrow gap in the crowd. Then John moved and Alan realised he'd been wrong: it was Sebastian. But their body language fooled me, Alan thought. As if to confirm his error he then spotted John running towards the tent, glancing anxiously from time to time at his wristwatch. He wasn't going to miss the start of the show. Then the flap on the trench shelter fell back in place.

That voice in Alan's earpiece was still making routine announcements – the usual sort of stuff: health and safety, insurance and the need for quiet on set – and then it said, 'Start positions everyone. And now it's over to London.'

Briefly the radio speakers crackled into life. It was Weinstein's voice. 'OK, folks, we're about to start countdown into the opening sequence . . .'

Alan looked across to the corner of the shelter where Craig was to start the walk into his opening PTC and to his horror he was vomiting into a plastic bag, which was hastily taken away by a long-suffering runner. Craig wiped his mouth with the back of his hand.

'I'll start the countdown on a five.' There was a brief pause. Then the speakers went off and Alan's earpiece suddenly crackled into life.

This time it was a different voice: 'Five . . . four . . . three . . . two . . . one.

Simultaneously on 'four' Weinstein's voice, now very calm and controlled, said, 'Cue Camera 1' and on 'one' the familiar, 'And *Action*!'

Craig took two steps out of the shadows and began his opening PTC. He was calm and smiling.

'Welcome to Fursey Abbey and *Test Pit Challenge*'s first live broadcast. We're all incredibly excited here because we just don't know what's waiting to be revealed. This is going to be a real-life voyage of discovery for everyone. We've got two trenches open this evening. The first one is being supervised by an old friend of *Test Pit Challenge,* Alan Cadbury—'

In his earpiece, Alan could hear another studio voice call out 'Run Astons'. Astons are the name-tags that are shown on the bottom of the screen when a new face appears. So he knew the camera was close-up on him. He tried to look serious and responsible as he trowelled, and in the process neatly sliced a small sherd of pottery in half.

'Evening, Alan!'

As rehearsed, Alan glanced into the lens of the camera beside the trench and gave a big smile – with just a hint of his trademark frown.

'Nice to have you back,' Craig's voice continued. 'And in Trench 2 it's a new friend to this programme, Dr Tricia Neave, who is also our resident expert on Roman finds.'

Alan could imagine Tricia's smile to the camera and the reaction of all men, old and young, everywhere. But Alan found he was starting to like her. True, she seemed to know nothing about excavation, but she was aware of it. And she did understand artefacts. He'd expected that she'd somehow dumb-down for television, which was something he detested, but to his surprise she didn't. No, he thought, she was OK.

'To discuss,' Craig was still speaking, 'the team's discoveries, if there are any . . .'

This was a transparent attempt to build tension, which Alan didn't think worked in rehearsal. And he was right. There was a miniscule pause, but no laughter from the audience in the studio. Craig rapidly carried on. 'The studio panel is chaired by a very familiar face who has come out of retirement to watch the village where he was born and brought up make its first live appearance on television. He needs no introduction . . .' By now the audience was applauding warmly. ' . . . Mr Michael Smiley!'

As the applause began to fade, and with the perfect timing born of experience, Michael delivered his familiar catchphrase. 'Take cover folks, it's Michael!'

But this time he said it with just the tiniest hint of irony, as if he was laughing ruefully at his past self; it was entirely appropriate to a man out of retirement. Alan was amazed at his professionalism and his powerful on-screen presence. Michael was a Smiley of the mill family and his presence had given a big boost to the show's ratings. Alan wondered whether his appearance on-screen out of retirement had been entirely voluntary. Maybe the Cripps family had called in a few favours? It was just a thought, which Alan filed away.

The studio panel was a device dreamed up by Lew Weinstein, partly on the advice of their commissioning editor, who wanted to make sure that the show had academic credibility – to fulfil the channel's public broadcaster remit. Alan had his doubts: it would adversely affect the programme's flow and besides, didn't they have a perfectly good artefacts person in Tricia?

He glanced up at the monitor being carried by an AP who was standing behind the fixed camera above the trench. She could see he was looking, and angled the set slightly downwards to give him a better view in the trench.

In his earpiece Michael Smiley was introducing Peter Flower and the two other members of the studio panel. Then Weinstein's voice cut in. 'Cue Camera 1. We're coming back to you, Alan.'

This was Alan's cue to resume trowelling. While he had been listening to his earpiece and musing about the past, Kaylee, who was trowelling alongside him and had started the broadcast level with him, was now a full metre further down the trench. This was embarrassing. He looked at where she was scraping and noticed that her trowel was just starting to cut into a deposit of blue-grey alluvial flood-clay. He frowned. That was unexpected.

He was still frowning, still trying to work out what the clay might mean, when Craig strode enthusiastically up to the edge of the trench. By now he should have been standing, ready to give the presenter, and viewers at home, a quick résumé of everything that had happened on-site: how they had removed a large area of flood-clay and found an intact

Iron Age and Roman occupation surface, etc. etc. Then in the next scene, Tricia would say a few words on the metal finds and pottery. But Alan hadn't heard Craig's question. He was still frowning. What on earth did Kaylee's alluvium mean?

'Alan, are you there? We're live on television, you know!' It was Craig.

Alan was brought to his senses by the sound of studio laughter which Weinstein had cleverly mixed into the broadcast feed. He sprung to his feet.

'I'm sorry, Craig, but I think we might be about to find something important. But I should first tell you something about what we've been doing here so far,' Alan continued; he knew he had to make amends.

Alan could see that Weinstein was instructing Craig, while he was appearing to listen to Alan. Before Alan could resume, Craig cut in, 'No, Alan, that can wait. We're far more interested in what you just found.'

Alan pointed down to where Kaylee was trowelling. Suddenly he realised that the explanation wasn't going to be simple. He wished they *had* let him do a brief introduction. Sod it. But he pressed on, frowning intensely. 'That bluish clay that Kaylee is revealing' – a second camera appeared on the other side of the trench and focused down on Kaylee's hands and her bright-purple nail varnish with glitter flashed across millions of British screens – 'was laid down by a succession of seasonal freshwater floods which began in the later third century AD—'

'So that's well into Roman times?' Craig added to help the viewer, but only succeeded in breaking Alan's tenuous flow.

'Er, yes. The mid-Roman period. It was probably due to the

introduction of winter wheat . . .' Oh, bloody hell, Alan thought as he listened to his own words coming back through the earpiece, I mustn't be diverted. 'Which meant that fields stood bare over winter, so topsoil got washed into the rivers—'

'And ended up here in the fens?' Again Craig was trying to be helpful, but Alan now had the bit between his teeth.

'That's right, as flood-clay. Alluvium we call it in the trade.'

'So that's Roman flood-clay is it?' Craig's question couldn't conceal the fact that he was underwhelmed.

'Probably not. If you look at the trench section here . . .' He waited a moment while the camera moved up from Kaylee's hands to the wall of the trench beside her. 'You can see that Kaylee's alluvium is slightly paler than the stuff around it and appears to be cutting down through it.'

'And what does that mean?'

'I don't know. But I'd guess it was early post-Roman. Maybe Dark Age or Saxon.'

Craig couldn't understand why Alan was getting so excited and was about to say something along the lines of 'So what?' when Weinstein's voice cut in. 'That's enough. Just give us the history of the site, Alan.'

It was as close as the ever-diplomatic Lew Weinstein ever got to a put-down.

* * *

Alan pulled the earpiece out and stuffed it in his shirt pocket. He was only too aware that his first live broadcast had not started well. That interview had been farcical. But all his instincts told him that Kaylee's sticky clay alluvium, which she was still doggedly exposing was important. There was something about the way it dipped down in section and had such a clean, sharp edge in both plan and section. That edge looked for all the world like a clear cut-line. He pulled out his trowel and began to scrape vigorously; he had to catch up with Kaylee.

Happily for the programme, Tricia's piece in Trench 2 about the Roman finds had gone very well and Weinstein had allowed it to run on for an extra three minutes.

'Put your earpiece back, Alan. Lew wants a word with you.'

Alan knew that Weinstein had seen people, even very experienced broadcasters, go to pieces on live television, so he was aware that he wasn't going to reprimand him. At least not now: encouragement would work better.

'That was great, Alan.'

'No it wasn't, Lew. It was crap. And you know it. But I think you'll find out why shortly. And this time, I promise I won't screw up.'

Viewers caught a glimpse of Craig hurrying through the now quite heavy rain into the shelter over Trench 1.

'So that patch of sticky clay has turned out to be something, Alan?'

'Yes, Craig.' A short pause. 'And just as I suspected.'

Most people would have been smiling, but not Alan. This was too serious. Next, and quite unconsciously, he heightened the tension further by wiping sweat from his face with the back of his right hand which he had just grazed on some gravel pebbles during his session of rapid trowelling. He'd done it so many times before, he hadn't noticed; grazed knuckles are part of a field archaeologist's life. But the swathe of yellow clay and dark bloodstains right across one side of his face could not have been bettered by Hollywood. 'Indiana Jones, eat your heart out' an admiring Weinstein couldn't help muttering through Alan's earpiece. Alan had no idea what he was on about.

Craig Larsson stepped closer to the edge of the trench and looked down. 'Alan. We're all on the edge of our seats.'

Alan couldn't help smiling. Craig was a master of the inappropriate metaphor and besides, neither of them had even the slightest desire to sit down.

'So, come on, tell us: what *have* you found, Alan?' This was said with breathless enthusiasm.

Alan paused. This reply would need to be succinct, but the explanation wasn't particularly straightforward. He frowned, while thumbing some clay from off his trowel blade. Of course, this built tension, but Alan was also giving two cameramen time to crawl along the trench side to get close-ups. And he knew his story would need good pictures.

As they got closer Alan resumed trowelling. 'Can you hear the sound of the gravel I'm scraping?'

Ever the professional, Grump lowered the long microphone boom. And it worked. People at home could clearly hear the distinctive scrapes, pings and clipping sounds against the now rather persistent background noise of rain.

'Yes, Alan, I can.'

Craig's reply wasn't very clear to Alan on his knees in the trench. But he pressed on. 'We're beginning to think that these gravel pebbles are the weathered upper part of a Roman track or roadway of some sort.'

'Wow, that *is* exciting!'

But Craig had missed the point. This was just the lead-up. Alan ignored him. He rose to his feet and took a couple of steps towards Kaylee who was now over half way along the trench and still trowelling.

'Craig, do you remember the clay that Kaylee had just revealed when you were here before?'

'Yes, I do.'

'Well, look at it now!'

The camera tilted down and pulled back to reveal Kaylee and Alan, who had just dropped down beside her. It also caught a glimpse of the two close-up cameramen who didn't have time to get out of the way. But it didn't matter. If anything, it was more real. Less managed.

Alan looked directly into the green bottle-glass of the camera lens. Before filming had begun, Frank had told him he could do certain very important replies straight to camera for added effect. Normally on *Test Pit Challenge* this would have been an absolute no-no. But not now. Not on a live show.

'See the sharp edges of the clay against the gravelly soil of the possible Roman road?'

The lead close-up camera followed Alan's trowel as he pointed this out. The third camera had pulled back, to give a more general view.

Craig was obviously admiring the way Alan was handling this. 'Yes, Alan, that's very clear.' This was said quieter, less breathless. More supportive.

'When you were here last I thought this might turn out to be a man-made pit, and I'm fairly sure it is.'

'Yes, Alan, I think you're right. It's far too straight-sided and regular to be anything natural.'

At that point Weinstein's voice came through their earpieces. 'Thirty seconds till we roll the credits.'

'Look at the width,' Alan continued, now gathering pace. 'Just over half a metre wide. We don't know how long it is yet, but Kaylee's already almost two metres from here—'

Alan's words were interrupted by an excited shout from Kaylee.

'I've just got to the end, Alan!' She was trowelling and pulling the loose earth back with her bare hands.

The third camera did a superb crash close-up. An experienced eye could see the exposed clay edge, but most viewers were happy to accept Kaylee's excited explanation.

Weinstein's voice was now starting the end credits countdown in Alan's earpiece. 'Ten . . . nine . . .'

'So what's over half a metre wide, two metres long, with straight sides and sharp, neat corners?' Alan's question was rhetorical.

He paused.

Craig was frozen. Tension was building.

Meanwhile the quiet voice in their earpieces continued. 'Three . . . two . . .'

Alan's final words were to guarantee massive audiences for the next five episodes.

'It's a grave!'

# Nine

Alan didn't get a lot of sleep as it took him a couple of hours and several whiskies to kill the adrenalin. But eventually he drifted off into a restless slumber. The next day, instead of walking to work as he usually did, he decided to take the Fourtrak and park it out of the way somewhere in the park, down by the dig. That way, if the chance arose, he could sneak off and grab a few minutes' sleep. But like so many of Alan's plans, this one didn't work out.

He pulled up at the village shop to buy milk and a newspaper.

'It's a grave!'

Last night's closing words greeted him as he opened the door. They were said, in unison, as if rehearsed, by three customers and by Kashmir, the proprietor's wife, who usually took the morning shift at the counter. Alan was amazed. He didn't think the show's out-line had been *that* memorable. A bit lame, if anything. But one of the laughing customers, a young man in a set of John Deere overalls, who was paying Kashmir for two pork pies, a packet of crisps and a bottle of

Coke, said he'd heard it twice on Radio 1 already this morning. Someone else said they'd just heard it on the television breakfast show. Alan smiled, but rather weakly: there was far more to last night than a catchphrase. Didn't people realise how extraordinary the preservation of everything on that site was going to be?

'Yes, Alan, my friend. You're now famous.' Kashmir was smiling broadly. 'And so is little Fursey. Sanjit and I are hoping shop trade will improve rapidly. In future we will have to call you Mr Cadbury!'

Trade was one thing, but Alan wondered what effect such publicity would have on the Cripps family. Instead, he replied. 'That's fine by me, if I don't have to pay in your shop, Kashmir.'

It wasn't Alan's best one-liner, but at least it got enough of a laugh for him to escape back to the Fourtrak, albeit empty-handed.

* * *

Alan first caught sight of the queue of people waiting to be admitted to the dig as he neared the end of the drive leading up to the old farmyard of what had once been Abbey Farm. It was quarter to nine, and already the temporary car park was almost a third full and he'd passed about a dozen visitors walking or cycling along the drive. He'd no idea that television could have such an immediate effect – and neither, it seemed had Candice, John or the Fursey Abbey staff who were all bustling around the yard getting ready for opening at ten. Candice and John seemed to be glued to their mobiles. Later Alan realised they were organising new and larger viewing platforms and hiring a marquee to be used as a temporary, and additional, shop and tea room. Alan could see they were going to make the most of the new trading opportunities.

He approached the end of the queue and slowed down to ease the Fourtrak over the ruined stub of a wall, which gave him access to the open parkland between the dig site and the imposing Georgian bulk of Fursey Hall in the middle distance. As he did so, some people in the queue managed to catch sight of him and although the windows were still firmly up and the noisy heater was on at full blast, he could still hear voices call out, 'It's a grave, Alan!'.

Out of the corner of his eye he could see that Candice had heard the noise and was observing him from behind the admissions booth. Whoops, he thought, I'd better do some PR for her. So he eased the Fourtrak into reverse and wound his window down. Immediately the people fell silent.

Then one little child called out excitedly, 'It's a gwave!'

This got a laugh from the crowd – and Alan. He leant out of the window.

'Sorry I can't stay longer, folks. But as I think you've all gathered, there's something that needs my attention in the dig. Enjoy your stay here – and don't forget to tell your friends. See you later!'

This little speech earned a ripple of applause and some further, but more muted, calls of 'It's a grave!'. Alan wondered how long it would be before he detested that little catchphrase.

Alan wound the window up and started to move off, when he spotted John Cripps heading towards him. Again he lowered the glass.

'Isn't this wonderful, Alan? I'd no idea visitor numbers would increase quite so rapidly.'

Alan smiled. No, John, he thought, nowadays people don't wait to read the review in *The Times* or *Telegraph.* They text, they tweet.

'I'm glad we've been of some use.' This was said slightly ironically, but it didn't work.

'And of course we're all hoping the rapid rise will continue. And then be sustained. That's the key thing.'

'Yes, I suppose it is.'

By now Alan was feeling more than a little irritated. And all because of a stupid catchphrase. He could see why Stan had been so suspicious of television. He felt slightly ashamed and could almost hear Stan say, 'I told you so.'

John Cripps's enthusiasm was undiminished by Alan's muted response. 'But we need to improve the visitor's on-site experience. I think that's crucial. In fact, absolutely key.'

'I'm sure you're right, but you mustn't forget that if you have more visitors they will need to be controlled. I don't want them damaging the archaeology.' Alan paused to let this sink in. 'I'm really worried about the stripped surface around Trenches 1 and 2. I don't think the folded tarpaulins we laid down are enough. There are simply too many people. We urgently need duckboards or a proper raised walkway.'

'Of course, Alan.' John had slipped into Dynamic Manager mode. 'I'll have it seen to right away.'

* * *

It was a clean, fresh early March morning. The previous day's rain had long gone and high in the sky Alan could see the parallel vapour trails of jets heading east towards Holland and northern Europe. The first days of spring in the Fens were like nowhere else. There were no hills or tall buildings to cast their chilling shadows; all was open – and somehow above board. Straightforward – like the people, or rather most of them, Alan mused as he headed towards the temporary tea and coffee stall. He was desperate for a brew before he went down to the dig. He was handing over his 40p when Candice hurried up. She was plainly very excited, almost overwhelmed, at the size of the crowds.

'Alan,' she gushed. 'You are a sweetie. Let me give you a kiss.' Which she did, twice, and on both cheeks, to the evident delight of Doris in the tea stall.

'Yes.' Alan was slightly at a loss for words. 'Yes, it did seem to go down quite well, didn't it?'

This rhetorical question earned a reply. 'Yes, it most certainly did. John's thinking of changing our name from Abbey Farm to Itsagrave Farm.'

Despite his misgivings, Alan had to smile. Not at all bad for so early in the morning. But Candice hadn't finished.

'Obviously you were the star with that last appearance . . .'

Alan remembered ruefully that the first one hadn't been too hot.

'But John and I thought Tricia's stuff on the Roman finds was first rate, too. In fact, you both made quite a double act. It really came off well. And of course the audience loved it.'

Alan was genuinely pleased, and was beginning to cheer up. He'd come to like Tricia. She certainly wasn't the usual sort of young woman he met on the digging circuit, but he didn't find her as self-centred and stuck-up as he'd feared. Yes, she obviously had an eye on a career in the media, but so what? They both knew that academia was becoming less attractive, with far too much focus on publication quantity rather than quality, and endless teaching and student 'contact time'. The students, too, were now so bloody middle class, as archaeology fees were often quite high. To his surprise, Tricia was fairly left of centre in her political views and she, like he, was very worried about the widening gap in modern Britain between rich and poor.

'John and I discussed it last night. We feel you've made such a big contribution to Fursey, we really do. And we'd like to say thank you in some way. So we wondered whether you'd both like to come to dinner next Sunday, when all the fuss has died down. We'll invite a few close friends along. I think when this is finished we'll all need a little celebration. Are you free?'

Alan was impressed. More to the point, this would be a superb chance to view the Crippses at home, off-guard, maybe even as a short-term member of the family.

'And d'you want me to approach Tricia?' he asked.

'I've spoken to her already and she's free that night. So I do hope you can come?'

'Yes,' he replied, 'I'd be delighted. That's very kind. Very kind indeed.'

She was turning to leave, when she suddenly remembered something else. She looked back. 'Oh yes, one other thing, Alan.'

Alan stopped and turned. 'Yes?'

'When I got back last night there was a message on the phone from Peter Flower. You won't believe it, but on Friday, his selection as bursar by the master was confirmed by the college council. So it's official.'

She seemed to think that Alan knew of Flower's selection. But he didn't. And anyhow, he was distinctly underwhelmed. He couldn't sound enthusiastic, but he did his best.

'So I imagine he'll be with us on Sunday?'

'Oh, you bet: Peter's always up for a celebration.'

'I bet he is.'

Alan made this sound genial and was smiling at Candice broadly, but all he could think of were those bottles in the hidden cupboard. Sure, they'd once held the finest malt whisky money could buy, but in reality it was a slow poison that had been deliberately and callously administered. Flower had become far more than just a nasty irritant from his past. Far, far more. Suddenly Alan's anger abated. He knew he mustn't let his loathing of Flower disrupt his hunt for Stan's killer, or killers. And that dinner would in effect be a line-up of the principal suspects, who would all be off-guard, relaxed and feeling secure. He must find a way to disrupt their complacency and shake their security and he was beginning to realise how he could do just that.

* * *

For the rest of the morning, Alan, Kaylee and Jon, were on their hands and knees trowelling vigorously. The excitement of the previous evening had caused both Alan and Kaylee to scrape a bit too vigorously. The surfaces they'd left were not as clean and flat as they'd both have liked. And there was also a lot of loose earth lying around. Jon had been helping out in Trench 2 during the 'live' and was a bit surprised by what he saw when he returned.

'Looks like a bomb's gone off in here, folks.'

'Yeah, I know it does, Jon,' Alan replied. 'But we both got a bit carried away. You know what it's like.'

Alan could see from Jon's expression that he didn't appreciate 'what it's like' at all. Although still in his late twenties he was very old school in his approach: methodical, tidy and fastidious. Which was fine for 95 per cent of the time, but it was that 5 per cent that made the difference between success and failure. The trick was to recognise when and where to use plodders like Jon – which was why Alan had moved him to Trench 2 the previous afternoon.

'Morning everyone and a huge thank you for last night. You were terrific. You honestly were. All of you.'

It was Frank Jones. Frank hadn't risen much in Alan's estimation after the first 'live', but at least he hadn't got in the way. Alan now realised that Frank owed much to Speed and Grump, who not only knew what they were doing inside out, but had also advised Weinstein on the best local stringers (self-employed cameramen and sound recordists) to employ. Sadly, it was not the first shoot he'd been on where the director was essentially a passenger. Between them, Weinstein, Speed and Alan took all the important decisions.

But then, somewhat to Alan's surprise, Frank began with an intelligent question.

'So did the people who dug that grave leave it open – otherwise how did it get to be filled with flood-clay?'

'Yes,' Alan replied. 'That's exactly what I wondered when I first came across one. Then we dug down and found that the alluvium – the flood-clay – was only in the uppermost part of the grave fill. The rest had been back-filled in the normal way.'

'But how did that happen?' Frank was still looking puzzled.

'You've got to imagine what happens today, when a grave's dug and a coffin is buried. The usual thing is to leave a low mound of soil for several months, a couple of years in some cases, before the gravestones or formal edgings to the grave are added. That interval gives the earth that's filling the grave time to compress. Worms will break down large lumps of soil and get rid of pockets of air.'

'So if you don't leave a small mound, the grave filling will compact and leave a small depression instead?' Frank asked.

'Precisely. And then the flooding happens and the growing hollow starts to accumulate alluvium – if the grave was placed in the river flood-plain, as seems to have happened here.'

Frank's interest had been aroused. 'So these would have been Roman graves, would they?'

Alan shook his head. 'No, I think they're a bit later. Look here.' He pointed at the section behind Kaylee that they'd filmed on that disastrous first visit to the trench the previous evening. 'You can see a distinct cut-line a few inches into the Roman flooding.'

'So what do you reckon?'

'I think it's got to be post-Roman, but probably not by very much. Maybe as early as seventh century? Even eighth. I don't know. But if it is a grave, it's most likely Christian, given its rough east-west orientation.'

'But it could be Roman, too, couldn't it?' Frank asked rather anxiously. For him, 'Roman' obviously sounded more precise, more interesting – and more glamorous – than the disappointing and ponderously academic 'post-Roman'.

Of course, Alan mused, I could have used the dreaded words Dark Ages, rather than post-Roman, but that would have sent Frank into orbit. Alan was only too aware that the post-Roman centuries of the supposed Dark Ages were crucially important to the emergence of what we now call England. It's when English emerged and formed a new national identity.

No, Alan thought, we couldn't have made a more exciting discovery. But Frank was waiting for a reply.

'No, that's impossible.' Alan indicated the section again. 'The stratigraphy doesn't work. It *has* to be post-Roman. There's no argument, I'm afraid.'

A deflated Frank then headed off to Trench 2.

* * *

The Call Sheet for Tuesday was pretty much as for day one. Alan looked at his watch. Three o'clock: just half an hour before tea break, then rehearsals and run-throughs. This would be their last chance to do any digging without being pestered by directors, cameras and microphones. Must make the most of it, he thought, trowelling hard, but taking more care this time not to remove the scabs on the knuckles of his right hand. Then he hit clay, just as he was starting to catch up with Kaylee who had been working on defining the end of her grave. He didn't even look up, but muttered loud enough for her to hear.

'Bloody hell, Kaylee, I think I've got another one.'

She looked up. 'You sure?'

Alan continued scraping for a minute, then straightened his back. 'I am now.'

Kaylee leant across for a closer look. 'Yes, I see what you mean. Edges very sharp' – she glanced at where she'd been working – 'and it seems on the same alignment as mine.'

* * *

During the run-through Alan told Frank about the new grave. He did so quietly, as he didn't want everyone to come crowding round his trench, especially now, when the trench shelter's sides were up to let a bit of air through after a sunny afternoon.

'Wow!' Frank exclaimed loudly. 'That's fantastic news, Alan! Another grave! Another "It's a grave" moment! I could hug you, Alan!'

And I could happily knife you, Alan thought, as visitors started to head towards Trench 1. He took a pace away from Frank. Time to take control.

'Stay where you are, everyone!'

When necessary, Alan could be authoritative.

'I'm sorry, everyone, but the ground near Trench 1 is getting quite soft and I don't want any more people around it until we've laid some duckboards and that won't be until tomorrow. So please stay where you are and don't come any closer.' Some people were looking puzzled and disappointed. Alan continued, slightly softer, more confidential. 'But I can tell you all now that we don't know for certain that either of the clay-filled pits are indeed graves. They probably are, both of them, but we can't confirm that until we find bones.' The place had gone quiet. He had their complete attention. 'Please bear in mind that if we have two graves, we may well find more, as graves tend to occur in graveyards. And that's why I don't want people trampling everywhere. Thank you so much for being so understanding.'

By now Alan was feeling quite annoyed, not just with Frank, but also with the Fursey management team, who seemed far more concerned with capitalising on the massively increased number of visitors, than in managing them. And John had promised to see to the duckboards 'right away', but nothing had happened. Then Alan spotted Candice. He ran across to her.

'Candice, we've got to do something about crowd control. I spoke to John about it this morning, but nothing has happened. The thing is, if they do cause damage, both English Heritage and the county mounties will go ballistic – and quite right too. It'll be all over the press and TV and I can guarantee visitor numbers will plummet.'

In reality, he thought, they'd probably rise, as people like to visit controversy. But the threat sounded ominous.

'Oh dear, John's over at White Delphs. A very important meeting. But where do you want the fences? I'll see what can be done, Alan.'

So, what's going on at White Delphs that's more important than a live TV show? thought Alan. But he had no time to dwell on it.

Alan showed her where he wanted them and 20 minutes later a temporary barrier of bright-red plastic construction site fencing, supported on steel road spikes, had been erected.

The walkie-talkie 'comms' hanging from his belt crackled into life.

'Frank for Alan.'

'Come in, Frank,' Alan replied.

'Switch to channel 5.'

Alan's heart sank. All ordinary conversations took place on channel 1. Channel 5 was reserved for more confidential matters. And right now Alan wasn't in the mood for a confidential chat with Frank. But he switched.

'Alan here, Frank.'

'I've just told Lew about the second grave. And he's very excited.'

'That's good.' Alan's heart was in his boots. He didn't like the sound of this at all.

'I suggested that we do a repeat of yesterday's success. We'll spend most of the show in Trench 2, then switch across to you for your killer pay-off line: "It's another grave!". But we'll need to work on the drama: maybe get you to jump to your feet.'

'Oh, for God's sake, Frank—'

'Don't be silly, Alan.' He brushed his objections aside. 'And we can involve Tricia, too. Maybe get her to "wander" into the scene.'

Alan hated the way Frank often called the programme the 'show', as if it was some brain-dead reality crap.

'And did Lew agree to this?'

'You bet. He loved it!'

Alan was incredulous. Weinstein had principles.

Before he could reply, Frank added, 'We'll see you in Trench 1 in fifteen minutes for a run-through of that scene. OK?'

'OK and out.'

Alan switched off the power to his comms, then headed rapidly across to his Portakabin office, where he dialled Weinstein's number.

He told Weinstein about the second grave and his subsequent conversation with Frank. When he had finished, there was a long pause at the other end.

'Ah,' eventually came the reply. 'That wasn't quite how Frank told it to me. So I gather you're not entirely happy with Frank's plans?'

'No, Lew, I'm not. I'm quite happy to delay the moment of discovery if we're doing a film and it takes a couple of minutes to find a crew, but not this. Frank's asking me to fake it. And I won't do that. It would undermine our credibility.'

'Yes, you're right, Alan, it would. But you must understand, Frank's been in the States and everything is much more contrived and Hollywood-style out there. Audiences have come to expect big drama; it's part of the "show".'

'I know, but I detest that word. But the thing is, Lew, we're about to do a run-through. Could you phone him and tell him you've changed your mind, as I can't guarantee not losing my rag?'

'We'll talk later, Alan, but try not to get too upset. Please. And remember, he's a fantastic editor: those two docs he cut earlier were brilliant and really impressed Charles Carnwath at T2. I'm sure that's why he voted through the money for the "lives". So please try not to fall out with him too much . . .'

'Sorry, Lew,' Alan replied, feeling a bit calmer now. 'But we've always steered clear of anything that even hinted at fakery – and this was going too far. So thanks. Now I'd better get off the phone.'

* * *

Alan was desperate for a coffee. After his phone call to Weinstein the adrenalin had worn off, and now he remembered he'd barely slept the night before. One of the lighting riggers standing in the short queue at the tea urns called across to him.

'Alan, Frank wants you on comms.'

Oh shit, Alan had forgotten to turn his handset back on. He did so, switched back to channel 1 and pressed the transmit button.

'Alan to Frank. Sorry, my comms were off.'

'Yes, I know. We're doing a run-through in three minutes.'

Even over the radio, Alan could detect the frostiness.

As he walked across the roped-off area, Tricia joined him. She was looking very anxious.

'Don't look so worried. I've spoken to Lew and Frank's "it's a grave two" is off.'

'Oh, well done, Alan. I'm so relieved. It was all so fake. And I'm no Keira Knightley: I'd never have pulled it off.'

Alan smiled. If anything her face was as beautiful. 'I don't think any of us would: we're diggers not actors.'

'At least you all are. Sadly, I don't think I am.'

She said this with genuine sadness. Alan wasn't sure what to say next. She was right: she didn't have the right temperament to be a full-time professional field archaeologist. But she was very good at what she did do. And she had a great screen presence, too. Alan was surprised by her insecurity.

'Oh, come on, Tricia, it's early days yet.'

'So you don't think I'm a complete fake: an imposter?' she asked quietly, standing very close and looking deep into his eyes.

* * *

When Alan arrived in the trench shelter, Craig Larsson came up to him.

'Well done, Alan,' he said confidentially. 'Lew phoned me and I was horrified. Frank seems to think you're all actors. It would never have worked.'

Alan didn't feel quite so angry. Craig did have a point: Frank had been working almost exclusively with actors, many of them out of work, on his so-called reality shows in the States. They'd do anything – and more – that he asked. And Craig should know, his background was in children's television, but he'd been to drama school and still appeared from time to time in films and dramas.

'I just hope I haven't upset him too much. It never does to have a row with the director.'

Craig smiled. 'Oh, I wouldn't worry about that, Alan, the show needs you far more than it needs him. And anyhow, you've got Lew behind you and he's the one who pulls the strings.'

Their conversation was interrupted by Terri Griffiths, the auburn-haired assistant producer. Alan was glad to see her smiley face back on set.

'Alan, Frank wants you to walk with Craig as he does the opening PTC.'

Ah, Alan thought, so that's what Lew must have suggested. 'Then he'll ask you about the new grave. OK?'

Alan could see Terri was listening to something on her earpiece. She scurried off.

Together Craig and Alan walked to the presenter's starting position. Alan wasn't entirely clear what was to happen next.

'So we'll have our chat, then what? I return to the trench?'

'Yes, you could. But why not take me over to see the new find. That's what you'd normally do, isn't it?'

'OK, that's fine.'

Alan always felt relaxed when working with Craig.

* * *

Despite the pre-shoot disagreement – row would be too strong a word – live Day 2 went very well and Alan had a trick up his sleeve, for when the camera came to Trench 1 for the second time. In the previous, opening, scene that followed their walk-up to camera, Alan had shown what he thought was going to be a second grave. Then for the ten or so minutes it took to film Trench 2 and the studio panel, he trowelled a band along the side of the grave down to the end, where it made a right-angled turn. Had a student done this, he'd have been furious with them – it was the worst sort of 'wall-chasing' and a common mistake made by first-year undergraduates. When you 'chase' something like a wall, you can easily remove it from its setting, for example by damaging its junction with other walls. But this was different. He had to show Frank that there are other ways of achieving what you need.

Craig arrived for the second interview. 'And how's it going, Alan?'

'I've taken a few naughty shortcuts, the sort of thing I wouldn't allow students to do, but look: can you see, I've scraped a band about a foot wide that follows the edge of the grave until here' – he scraped some more – 'where it ends in a neat right-angled corner.'

'So you're certain it's a grave?' Craig asked.

'Well,' Alan stood up. 'What d'you think?'

Before filming began, Frank had told them that he didn't want the interviews to be question-and-answer sessions. He was after a more conversational, informal feel to the show. That word again, Alan thought, but he had to concede, he did have a point.

'I agree, it's certainly the right size and shape.'

'And look, Craig, the two features are laid out on precisely the same alignment. And if I'm not mistaken . . .' Alan reached into the back pocket of his jeans and produced a folding compass, which the second camera focused down on. 'Yes, they're aligned a few degrees off east-west. And that, of course, suggests they are probably Christian – like churches, they're pointing towards Jerusalem.'

'Does it matter that they're not precisely east-west?'

'Not at all,' Alan replied. 'In medieval times rural grave-diggers, even architects and stonemasons, didn't routinely carry compasses, so the east-west alignment is never precise. In fact, the layout of tombs and graves in the Bronze Age was a lot more accurate.'

'You always stick up for prehistory, don't you, Alan?'

But instead of smiling, Alan was frowning. He needed to change the mood. In his ear, the countdown to the end credits had just begun.

'The thing is, Craig, there's still space for another grave in this trench and I wouldn't be at all surprised if we didn't find it tomorrow. Graves 1 and 2 are set quite close together and parallel. This suggests to me that we've found a graveyard. And that's exciting, because somewhere near here must lie the buried remains of a long-lost Saxon church.' He only just had time to draw breath. 'And if I'm right, we could have one of the earliest churches in England – and possibly, too, a direct link to Roman times.'

The *Test Pit Challenge* signature tune faded-up as soon as he delivered the last words.

Weinstein's voice cut in. 'That was fantastic, Alan. What a fabulous ending! Well done. But make sure you get some sleep tonight. We've still got four days to go and I thought you were looking a little weary on the run-throughs.'

'Thanks, Lew, and you're right, I'm knackered.' He lowered his voice and tried to direct his words at the mike pinned inside his shirt. 'I'll nip off now. Make my excuses to Frank, Tricia and the others.'

'Will do. And again, well done. Sleep well.'

Grump Edwards must have read his mind, or listened-in to their conversation, as he was standing alongside when Alan finished speaking to Weinstein. Quickly he unpinned the radio mike, while Alan unplugged the lead from the transmitter in his back pocket. Then he headed back to his Fourtrak, which he had left in the park nearby. It was a clear night and he had to scrape a light frost off the windscreen. As he waited for the de-mister to warm up he texted Jake to tell him that he'd be on-site at ten tomorrow. And when he got home, he didn't set his alarm and slept for a full eight, dreamless hours.

* * *

The next morning a refreshed Alan left the Fourtrak in the park and headed over to the coffee stall, while munching an aged cereal bar he'd just found in a long-forgotten pocket in his rucksack. The place was deserted. Alan asked the lady dispensing the coffee where everyone had gone and she pointed across to the large tent where people ate their meals. It was packed. Sipping his latte and wiping the last crumbs of cereal bar from his beard, he went round to the back of the crowd where there was still some space. At the front of the tent he could just catch glimpses of the Cripps family: Barty, Candice, John and Sebastian, with Frank standing beside them. They were sitting most graciously; very much the obliging county family. Alan tried hard to read their body language, but it was impenetrably rigid. Too rigid, perhaps. Did they realise?

Frank introduced them. 'Thank you all for coming here and I know you've all got a lot to do, so I'll cut to the chase, as we say in television.' That got a polite titter. 'The Cripps family would like to say a few words. And Candice, I think you're going first?'

Candice smiled and stepped forward. She was plainly used to speaking in public and her words were clear and confident. She thanked everyone for their collective efforts that had made the live shoot such a resounding success – so far. And as she said, she was being careful not to count chickens before they were hatched, but in the event that no disaster intervened, the estate was going to provide Champagne after the final shoot. This went down very well. Barty followed with a broad smile and very few words, but his presence made all the difference: he transformed a rather blatant PR exercise into something more like a genuine, old-fashioned, family gathering.

The two brothers spoke last. John apologised for the rather poor crowd control on Day 2, but everyone had been taken aback by the massive increase in visitor numbers following the success of 'the Itsagrave shoot'. Alan noted that he used the term casually. It was now part of the language, certainly locally, if not nationally. He went on to say that he hoped things would improve today. They had called on professional guidance from staff and colleagues at the nearby White Delphs visitor attraction, some of whom were already on-site. They would be bringing in new crowd-control barriers, improved walkway surfaces and better signage and supervision in the parking areas. With luck, they would not have to turn anyone away, as they had had to do on Tuesday. He finished by saying that if the closer co-operation with 'our friends' at White Delphs did indeed prove to be successful, the two attractions would be working more closely together in the future. He made this final announcement with some satisfaction.

Alan studied him closely: Sebastian must have conceded defeat. Yes, John was now in control.

Then Sebastian stepped to the front. His height should have given him a big advantage, but if anything, he made less of an impression than his far more confident and assured younger brother, who was completely at ease when surrounded by television crews and media types. By contrast, Sebastian seemed rather remote, as if he'd be far more comfortable out on a tractor, drilling spring barley. Alan could sympathise. On the other hand, Sebastian was also a local councillor, so he'd have thought he'd know a little bit about public speaking. And his first two sentences were reasonably clear.

Even though he was standing right at the back, for a brief moment, Alan thought he had met the big man's gaze, but it proved fleeting. Soon Sebastian was mumbling from a set of notes, towards the first two rows of his audience. So far as Alan could make out, Councillor Cripps was giving advance warning that he would be escorting an all-party group of county and district councillors around the site and the excavations on Saturday morning. Alan's heart sank: the last day of the shoot. That was all he needed.

Finally, John Cripps stood forward for a second time. There was a respectful hush.

'My friends,' he began. The tone of his voice was very distinctive, and Alan was immediately transported back to the final moments of Stan's wake. He couldn't help it, but he found his eyes were filling with tears.

John continued. 'This live shoot has been a very moving

occasion for all of us, and I firmly believe we must never forget the efforts of past generations who created this special place. So if I may, I would like us all to observe a few moments' silence, while we pray for the lives and souls not just of the monks of Fursey Abbey, but of the many ordinary people who looked after and protected them, and whose remains lie buried here.'

But no mention of Stan. Just the big-bellied bloody monks. Alan was livid. For him, at least, this glib piece of pious PR had gone badly wrong.

* * *

When the gathering had dispersed, Alan and Jake Williamson did a detailed feature-by-feature tour through the two trenches. They'd established a good working relationship and were both clear about what had to happen next. That done, Alan drove to Sybsey Airfield where the English Commission on Ancient Monuments (ECAM) housed their leased aircraft. Sybsey had been an aircrew training establishment during the war and there was a substantial War Memorial by the main gates with dozens and dozens of names. Alan always nodded respectfully towards it as he passed: there was something so sad about those many hopeful young men whose ambitions had come to nothing.

Alan knew Dennis, the ECAM eastern region archaeologist, well and they'd done many Lidar surveys together. Lidar was a remote sensing technology that essentially combined the principles of photography and radar through the use of a reflected laser beam. Lidar surveys couldn't capture the differences in vegetation growth that gave rise to the dark crop marks of conventional aerial photographs. Instead, the laser beam penetrated vegetation and was able to reveal the tiniest undulations in the ground surface. Lidar had proved a huge success in the Fens, where very often ancient features had been largely covered, or filled in, by peats or flood-clays. So the top few inches of once-huge Bronze Age burial mounds could clearly be detected. Alan knew of a group of five such barrows in the Nene Washes about half a mile away from Richard Lane's new house.

During the planning stage of the live project, Alan had insisted that they couldn't just dig. They had to put more into the project than that. Weinstein didn't need persuading, but Charles at T2 proved less enthusiastic and it took Alan a full two hours in the T2 offices at Southwark to persuade him. In the end it was the new technology of Lidar that proved irresistible. Alan was also aware that ECAM were doing a detailed survey of the southern Fens, so they welcomed the unexpected extra cash and were able to re-jig their schedule. As Frank so unmemorably described it later: 'a win-win for all concerned'.

The breeze at Sybsey Airfield was surprisingly chilly as Alan, Dennis and the pilot walked briskly towards the light aircraft that was waiting on the tarmac apron outside one of the wartime hangars. The pilot opened the door and the two archaeologists climbed aboard. Alan watched as he did a quick check of the plane's exterior, then he joined them. First he rapidly checked their seat belts, but he could see they'd both done this before, then he put on his headset and started the engine. Soon they were airborne and climbing to 500 metres.

Alan looked down from his window directly below the

wing. They were following a pre-arranged flight path. Sites and landscapes always look different from the air and Fursey was no exception. Somehow, in Alan's vivid imagination, the slight changes in level between the abbey on its low island and the surrounding, low-lying flat fields, seemed monumental – almost cliff-like. From the air you could see, quite literally, the wood from the trees: the smaller islands that fringed the main Isle of Ely were more thickly spread with trees, woodland and even hedges and there were fields with livestock. But out in the open, peaty landscape of the fens the hedges and trees vanished, as did grassland: the fields were much larger and the dykes deeper and straighter. Alan loved flying and not just for the view. Aircraft removed you from everything: from ambitious people and human frailty. Below him, down there, lay the truth.

* * *

At the end of the scheduled Lidar runs, the pilot asked if there was anything they'd like to look at more closely. Alan and Dennis knew this was his way of asking whether they'd like to be given a bit of a fairground ride: not exactly aerobatics, but a few swoops, dives and steep turns. In actual fact, Alan wanted to take a closer look at the orchard and copse along the northern side of the lime tree avenue leading up to Fursey Hall. If the pilot followed the line of trees to the west, they'd get a good transect out into the open fen. They all agreed this was an excellent idea.

Earlier, Alan had warned Frank that he planned to make a low pass or two along the avenue and he had positioned three cameramen between the trees. They were treated to a very low tree-top 'recce' fly-past, followed by others at increasing altitudes. The crowds, of course, loved it all and cheered and waved enthusiastically.

When they had landed, Alan arranged to see the initial Lidar results at Fursey on Saturday, around midday. It would be something they could film then and there, or maybe retain for the final 'live'. Either way, he thought, it would give me an excuse to get away from the massed ranks of councillors on their dreaded visit that Sebastian had just announced. He was also very aware that ECAM were going out of their way to help the project and he made a mental note to make sure he credited them live, on screen. Sadly, nobody these days looked at the end credits when they flashed by, drowned out by strident voice-overs proclaiming what's 'coming up later'.

* * *

Day 3 live kicked off with pre-recorded footage of Alan climbing into the plane and taking off. Then the screen cut to the low fly-past, while Craig's urgent voice-over proclaimed, 'The results of this survey could be very exciting indeed. The powerful lasers used in Lidar can reveal the earth's most closely held secrets and on Friday we will discover why this quiet corner of the Fens is capturing the imagination of people right across Britain . . .'

Or far more likely, Alan thought, it'll reveal sweet FA. He'd taken part in many aerial surveys around the Fens and he usually spotted some hint of what was to come when he looked out of the plane's window. Lidar wasn't magic: it didn't create; it had to work on something – and this time he'd spotted nothing. He'd said as much to Frank, but to no avail.

The live sequences began with the studio panel who

discussed what the Lidar might discover. Being clever academics they came up with wonderfully learned and unusual ideas which made them look and sound like imaginative pundits, but which Alan reckoned bore precious little resemblance to the sort of things that might actually turn up. Alan also reckoned that the members of the panel (aside from Michael Smiley their chairman) seemed somehow remote; none of them appeared to have been affected by what was increasingly becoming a wave of national enthusiasm for this previously obscure corner of Fenland.

Then Craig delivered his opening piece to camera in Trench 2 with Tricia and Jake Williamson. Although not a television natural, and a bit hesitant at first, Jake did very well and Tricia was good, too, Alan thought; she didn't try to overshadow Jake and was quietly encouraging.

It was when they'd finished the opening three-way discussion and Tricia and Craig were looking through the day's finds, that Jake, who had resumed trowelling for a few minutes, made his big discovery. He looked up.

'Trish,' he called out. 'I think I've got something here!'

Cameras 2 and 3 of the second unit hurried round to the other side of the trench to get close-ups. Camera 1 instantly tilted down, just in time to catch Jake's ' . . .something here!'.

'You know that small pit or large post hole we were working on this morning?' Jake continued.

Tricia was leaning forward, her excited eyes wide and catching gleams from the surrounding floodlights. 'Yes?'

'I think I've got a packing stone for a large post.'

'Are you sure?'

'Yes, quite certain. It's right up against the sides of the hole and the ghost of the post is much clearer at this level. It looks squared-off.'

The post 'ghost' was a dark stain, the final trace of organic matter left by a long-rotted timber.

'Oh really? And it's in that dark area, which we thought might be a ditch of some sort?'

'Yes, it is,' Jake replied. 'But don't you see, that means it can't be a ditch? The dark staining may have been left by rotted timbers. I think we've found the footing for the wall of a big building.'

'And can we tell what kind of building?'

'Most pre-Roman Iron Age buildings used roundwood or half-split timbers for posts and beams. A squared-off post suggests the use of heavy-duty saws, which were introduced to Britain by the Roman Army. So what we have here is . . .' He paused briefly, as if he could not believe his own discovery. 'A big Roman building.'

The discovery of what immediately came to be called Jake's Building was almost, but not quite, matched by the revelation of a third alluvium-filled grave in Trench 1. Alan had pointed to the spot during an interview on Day 2, and now, on camera, Craig accused him of being 'an archaeological prophet'. Alan frowned, deadpan, assuming an air of false modesty and announced that predictive archaeology was his current specialism. At best, it was an obscure piss-take, aimed at theoretical archaeologists, but it seemed to go down quite well with the audience – God knows why. He finished by stressing that there was now no doubt: all three graves were closely aligned. They had discovered part of a hitherto unknown Christian cemetery.

* * *

When Alan got back home he felt exhausted. He was discovering that live television made massive demands on those who took part. He had filled his flask with hot coffee on-site and now sat at his kitchen table drinking it. The naked light bulb overhead cast a harsh, unwelcoming light. He knew the fridge was empty, no milk even, as he couldn't face a repeat of that last visit to the village shop. Then he thought back on the previous three days: the discovery of the graves, Jake's building, not to mention lots more pottery and metalwork fragments. Stan would have been proud of them. That made Alan feel better. He was dog-tired, but not unhappy. It had all been worth it. So far. And the hot coffee felt good.

Alan glanced down at Stan's notebook which lay on the kitchen table alongside his laptop. Over the previous few evenings he'd just finished going through the levels, one by one, and they were all internally consistent. Stan's surveying had been spot on. But why hide them away? What were they telling him? Somehow he had to find the time to go down to the pumping station and take a reading off the Ordnance Survey benchmark on the wall there. Only then would he understand why Stan was so concerned to hide the notebook. But that must be done carefully, without telling the rest of the world – assuming, that is, that Stan's fears were indeed justified. Now, though, it was time for a well-earned nightcap.

Alan reached into the cupboard and pulled out a bottle of Islay malt he'd bought at Aldi two weeks ago. For a moment he considered sampling the remains of Stan's bottle of 20-year-old Glen Hubris McTavish that lay hidden in his chest of drawers among his socks and pants. But the time wasn't yet right. It would have to wait. He added a drop of water from the tap, then raised the glass of Islay to his dead friend. His brother Grahame had always sworn by coffee and whisky. And as usual, he was right.

Ten minutes later, Alan tipped the coffee dregs down the sink and rinsed the flask in cold water. As he turned to head upstairs, he wondered what on earth the dig was going to find on Days 4 and 5. Would the Lidar survey be the big anticlimax he feared? After all, nothing was apparent to the naked eye when they flew over. But he knew it was stupid to try to second-guess the future – not with landscape, nor with people. He smiled: predictive archaeology, my arse.

# Ten

Alan began Day 4 with a couple of phone calls to do with the dig, but he wasn't in the mood for any more admin. It could wait. He wanted to get outdoors. He glanced down at his phone: 9.17. Time to get going.

Clear, bright springtime mornings in the Fens were one of Alan's favourite times: shadows are banished; light is everywhere and by early March the birdsong is starting to build. As he closed the back door behind him, Alan was greeted by an angry wren with machine-gun-like alarm calls, while high in a lime tree overhead, a blackbird sang joyously. Alan had always liked birdsong and what the various sounds really meant; that blackbird, he smiled, wasn't proclaiming the joys of spring, but was telling all other blackbirds to get lost: this is my territory, so keep your distance. Even so, it was an uplifting sound, and as he headed down the path along the gable end of his cottage, he could hear the fierce call of the wren behind him easing off. Then another started close by the front door. Alan reckoned there were at least seven wren territories in his small garden.

It was far too nice a day to drive to the site and Alan was looking forward to the twenty-minute walk. A tractor thundered past, towing a trailer of round bales down to the cattle farm on the Littleport Road. It had been wet lately and they'd be needing the straw, Alan thought, ever the farmer's son. Behind the tractor was a mud-spattered Land Rover. Alan waited for it to pass, before he crossed the road. But instead it pulled up alongside him, and the front window slid back.

'D'you want a lift down to the dig, Alan?'

It was Sebastian Cripps. Alan hesitated: he could have used the village shop as an excuse. But he decided not to. He was starting to like Sebastian – and he needed to take his mind off work.

As he climbed aboard, Alan nodded towards the trailer of bales, now fast heading around the corner. 'They going to the cattle farm on the Littleport Road?'

'Yes,' Sebastian replied as they pulled away. 'It's wheat straw from our big barn down by the Delph there.'

'Oh, I know the one – just outside the village, on the Ely Road?'

'That's right. Ellis's have always taken their straw from us. And it's a good trade right now, what with all the rain. We're selling quite a lot to farms in the West Country who are crying out for it.'

'Yes, poor devils,' Alan replied. Everyone had heard about the recent floods. 'I'm glad I'm not in their shoes.'

'It's difficult. None of us want to profit from their misfortune, but the prices are rising fast. And of course the dealers are loving it.'

'I've heard some farmers hereabouts are actually giving straw away?'

'Yes,' Sebastian replied. 'I've agreed to give twenty per cent of our wheat straw to the NFU's hardship scheme. The first bales have already gone. I only wish we could do more.'

Alan was about to say something, then he stopped. Too much probing made people suspicious and he felt Sebastian was going to talk anyhow.

'The trouble is,' Sebastian continued, 'the estate isn't as large as it was after the war.'

'What, death duties and that sort of thing?'

'Yes, they were crippling after grandfather's death. He was very hands-on and didn't want to lose control of anything.'

'Which was natural, in a way, wasn't it?' Alan suggested.

'Oh yes, but it meant we couldn't claim anything under the seven-year rule. So we got hit for the full amount. And there were also some big bank debts that had to be repaid. So poor Barty had to sell off two small farms and Smiley's Mill. That just left him Fursey, which he renamed Abbey Farm, and us at Woolpit Farm.'

He had heard this before, but Alan was happy that Sebastian was now talking so freely.

'But there's a limit to what you can do with 400 hundred acres.'

'Yes, I can imagine,' Alan slowly replied. 'My brother Grahame also farms 400 hundred acres, mostly rented or leased, and he finds it hard, especially last year, when wheat prices were down – although not as low as this year.'

'It's certainly getting harder to make a medium-sized farm profitable, especially with the house and park to maintain – which is why I do the council work. Between you and me, I don't like it at all. I'd much, much rather be a farmer full-time. John and Candice love their diversification, which is what Barty called the Abbey Farm Shop when he set it up. And that's fine' – he slowed the Land Rover down to pass some early visitors – 'for them. They both like that sort of thing. But it's not for me. You know they say that farming's in your blood, and in my case I think they might be right.' He drew breath, then carried on, more reflectively. 'Of all the land the family has sold off since the war, the one I regret most is Isle Farm, over there towards the pumping station.' Sebastian nodded towards the middle distance to the right of the road.

Alan knew it: an attractive mid-19th-century house, still just Georgian without the later Victorian heaviness.

'Why's that? Is it the land?'

Sebastian sighed heavily. 'Yes, it's the best land for miles. It'll grow anything: spuds, salads, even caulis and sprouts. And up towards the yard there's good, dry pasture. So I could even run a proper, no-messing, mixed farm. And that's what I call *real* farming.'

'So you're not too keen on all this modern specialisation, then?'

'Absolutely not. It's food production, not farming. Some of those blokes never leave the farm office. They're always staring at their bloody screens. No, I'm never happier than when I'm out on the land. You become part of it, out there in the fen. That's why I like shooting, although to be quite honest, I don't enjoy the social side. That's more Sarah's country. I won't say she likes them much, but she can get on with those rich Londoners and they do seem to have bottomless pockets.' He shook his head. 'I mean, would you pay nearly a thousand quid for a day's shooting?'

'Not when I can go out and shoot pigeons for free.'

'Oh, I agree, Alan. I'd much rather shoot pigeons than French partridges and those Michigan Bluebacks that Joe was breeding for us last season. More like shooting poultry than pheasants. Still, the Londoners seem to like them.'

Alan was tempted to ask directly if there was any news about Joe Thorey, but he didn't want to arouse Sebastian's suspicions. Instead he spotted an opportunity to see how Sebastian would react to something that was also much on his mind. 'I would imagine Joe Thorey's down-to-earth attitude isn't much to their liking, is it?'

It was as if Alan had jabbed him with a pin.

'That man . . .' He gave Alan an intense glance, before looking back at the road. 'Sarah thinks he can do no wrong. She says the "clients" – as she insists on calling the guns on the shoot – love Thorey. They think he's *such* a character.'

'And do you?'

'To be quite frank, Alan, I can't stand the man. Still, we need him because the shoot's what's keeping the estate afloat right now. And Sarah's doing an amazing job. So I bite my tongue.'

He'd said what Alan needed to know. Time to end it. 'As a matter of interest, do the guns take many birds back with them to London?'

'They wouldn't do that, Alan. I doubt if they'd know which end to start plucking.'

'You're right: they're not pheasant pluckers!'

An ancient joke and hardly hilarious, but it made them both smile.

They were approaching the dig. There were people everywhere. Alan glanced across at Sebastian: he was looking at the visitors much in the way he'd be checking the ear-tags of his cattle as they filed into the yard. Alan paused for a moment before he got out. He'd phone Lane just as soon as he could.

* * *

Alan and Frank had another minor row during the day. Frank wanted him to do a scene with Tricia where she dressed him in replica Roman armour: 'It would lighten the mood.' Alan refused, point-blank. He detested re-enacting and hated coming across people dressed as monks in old monasteries, or as kitchen maids in country house kitchens. They always looked like what they were: 21st century office workers looking for something to liven up a boring weekend. He also knew his attitude was unfair and unreasonable – which of course made him even worse.

The Roman armour spat took the best part of an hour to resolve, and by that time Weinstein in London had been involved. And all the while, Alan was desperate to get back to the trenches. That alluvium in the three graves was just starting to dry out, and if they left it for very much longer, it would set like bricks.

Then at eleven, Clare Hughes arrived to discuss extending Trench 1 to reveal the three graves in their entirety. Normally this would have been a routine matter, and dealt with over the phone, but Clare, like everyone else, had been caught up by the 'live' and wanted to see things at Fursey for herself. And Alan was certainly not going to upset her, of all people. So that took another hour.

As soon as Clare had given the OK, Jake had gone across from Trench 2 to help Kaylee and Jon dig the extensions by hand. Shifting a thick layer of alluvium was very heavy work, but they couldn't use a mini-digger because of all the cables, the lighting stands and the rain shelter. By noon, when a rather weary Alan stepped into Trench 1, they'd already made good progress, so he and Kaylee began the smaller extension over Grave 2.

At lunchtime, a mud-spattered Land Rover, its front doors discreetly marked with the university arms and the label: *Sub-Department of Quaternary Geology*, arrived in the site car park. Hell, Alan thought, bang goes lunch. He'd almost forgotten, but first thing that morning he'd arranged for Dr Alan Scott to take micromorph samples from the deposits directly over Grave 2. Alan himself was a great fan of soil micromorphology. Essentially it's a technique that examines soils in very thin sections through high-power microscopes. A good soil micromorphologist – and Alan Scott was probably the best – could reveal all sorts of information in a soil's developmental history: when trees covering it had been cut down, when grassland became established, and, of course, when ploughing began. Alan reckoned a few carefully positioned *in situ* samples might throw light on when the grave had been dug, relative, that is, to the start of the later Roman alluvial episodes. In other words, he wasn't expecting the equivalent of a radiocarbon date, but it could provide them with other essential information.

Dr Scott was a busy man, and he had agreed to fit Alan's samples in between those of a much larger project he was doing for the ministry. An hour later, as people were returning from their lunch break, the two Alans were standing by the Cambridge Land Rover. Scott held a canvas bag with two full sample tins. He climbed into the driving seat and leant out of the window.

'I'll get straight down to these, Alan. Get them consolidated and ground down over the weekend. I might even be able to get back to you with some preliminary thoughts on Monday. But I'm not promising . . .'

Alan couldn't believe his ears. That was *so* fast.

'And make sure we get a mention!'

The power of television.

'Don't worry, I'll see you're given a knighthood!'

And with that, Alan roared away.

* * *

Kaylee had seen that Alan had missed his lunch, and had ordered two extra rounds of sandwiches for him. Alan thanked her profusely and fell on them as they walked across the car park back to the trench shelter. By two o'clock Jake and Jon had exposed all of Grave 1 and had started clearing Grave 3. After a further 15 minutes Alan and Kaylee had finished Grave 2 and then they all worked together on Grave 3, taking it in turns to do the heavy mattock-swinging. By three o'clock they had finished the job and were drinking mugs of tea. They'd shifted a lot of earth, and even though it was only early March they were all sweating, but their spirits were up: the graves looked very impressive indeed. A rather subdued Frank was standing behind, supposedly directing Speed, who was filming the graves from above. These clips would be used as cut-aways during the evening's 'live'.

When they'd finished their tea, Jake returned to Trench 2, leaving Alan, Jon and Kaylee to start removing the much thinner, capping layer of alluvium from each of the graves. They soon found that the stiff clay came away quite cleanly from the grave filling below, largely, Alan realised, because it hadn't stuck to the gritty, gravelly material they had been cut into and filled with.

About five minutes before they began the final run-throughs, the sound recordist Grump Edwards came into the shelter carrying a monitor screen, which he put on one of the lights' carrying cases, which sat just back from the trench edge. He showed Alan how to work it, then hurried off. Shortly before the dressing-up incident, earlier in the day, Alan had asked Frank for monitors to be set up in both trenches, because on Days 2 and 3 he'd found it very difficult to follow what had been going on in Trench 2 and the studio panel.

* * *

Craig began his opening PTC kneeling at the edge of Trench 1. 'Welcome to Day 4 of *Test Pit Challenge* live at Fursey. Today Alan Cadbury and the team enlarged Trench 1 to reveal the full extent of the graves. Here they are earlier in the day. You can see the outline of the graves quite clearly because of the paler flood-clay that fills them.'

Speed's footage was screened and the outline of the graves was highlighted by graphics, for the benefit, Alan thought, of the near-blind and partially-sighted.

As he waited for Craig to join him, Alan was air-trowelling a bit of the grave he had cleared of alluvium three hours previously.

'So how's it been going today, Alan?'

'It's been hard work, Craig,' Alan replied, wiping his brow. 'But well worth the effort.'

He then took viewers on a rapid tour of the trench. Thanks

to the new monitor, he knew they'd already screened Speed's earlier footage. He finished with, 'So we removed the flood-clay an hour or so ago – it was only three inches deep – and we're all now trowelling down through the upper filling of each grave.'

Craig's next question was only to be expected. 'So do you expect to find bodies?'

This was a bit blatant. Why does TV always have to be so explicit and unsubtle? Surely sometimes some things are best left to the imagination, unsaid? Alan could barely contain his exasperation: why did Craig always have to be so ridiculously sensationalist? What else do you expect to find in a bloody grave? Woodpeckers? Mince pies? Tea cups?

He took a deep breath before replying. 'Bones, d'you mean?'

'Yes, all right, bones.'

Craig gave him a secret look off-camera, which said: fuck off, please don't come the smart-arse with me; I'm only doing my job. Alan felt bad and tried to make amends.

'That depends on their depth. If the graves are deep, the lower filling may well prove to be waterlogged, in which case you may be right: some of the soft parts, even pieces of clothing, may be preserved.'

Craig smiled. Alan knew he had redeemed himself.

* * *

Before Alan rejoined the team in Trench 1 to resume trowelling down through the filling of Grave 3, he turned the monitor's sound up. For five minutes they all worked busily and Alan even had the time to fill and empty a bucket into the black barrow, which he'd moved back to the edge of the trench when the film crew had left. Nearer the centre of the trench, John wheeled their full barrow out of the shelter towards the spoil heap, where Reg and the other local metal detectorists would give it a good going-over. Then the monitor switched from the studio panel to Jake in Trench 2.

Alan looked up and smiled. On Day 1 Craig had conducted most of the interview with Tricia, as the trench supervisor, Jake, seemed far too nervous. But not now. He was still quiet, even reserved, but he was far more confident. Earlier in the day, the Trench 2 team had recovered several fragments of bronze from the old land surface around what was clearly now an emerging timber-built wall. They'd left a baulk untrowelled at right-angles to the wall, to preserve the succession of soil layers that were beginning to emerge. Normally such baulks are quite narrow – say a foot, or so, but some instinct made Alan decide on a wider one, which he knew they would need in order to maintain stability should the wall prove to have deep footings.

Jake explained to Tricia (who knew perfectly well already) where they'd found the various fragments of bronze. Then he made an excuse and resumed digging. This worked well and added to the sense of urgency.

Tricia acted as if she'd never seen the finds before and was very excited. Almost *too* excited, Alan thought. Alan could see from the look on Craig's face when the camera cut-away to him for listening – so-called 'noddy' – shots, that he was feeling the same. But somehow her enthusiasm about the finds won through. And they were most remarkable: more examples of *lorica segmentata*, Roman leather armour fittings, and for the first time some rather undistinguished-looking loops and strap-ends, which Tricia confidently identified as coming from military horse harnesses.

At this point Tricia produced one of the very new iPad tablets, which had only just been released in Britain. She'd been given it by her brother in the States and she was very pleased with it. Her fingers flashed across the face of the screen, rather like a magician at a children's party, Alan thought as he watched her, fascinated. Then she showed the screen to the camera to reveal a clear drawing of a Roman cavalry soldier on his horse. She spread her fingers on the screen, which miraculously enlarged the horse's head, to show slightly pixelated close-ups of the various harness fittings they'd found.

Meanwhile Jake had been cleaning back to the sharp edge of the baulk. He was working quite rapidly as he was keen to start going down to the next level. Suddenly he stopped. His trowel had just exposed a spread of green-coloured silty soil. He leant forward and started to probe very, very gently.

Jake hadn't said anything, but the sudden change in the way he was working caught Craig's attention. He broke in to Tricia's explanation of three-linked horse bits.

'Hold it, Tricia, I think Jake might have found something.'

The camera zoomed-in to see Jake's hands and the green silt. By now he had produced the small plastic ice cream spatula that he always kept in the change pocket of his jeans. He was carefully scraping.

'Yes, Craig,' he said, his voice had a strange booming quality as his words resounded off the ground just below him. 'It's definitely copper alloy and I'd guess it's about three or four millimetres thick. In remarkably good condition . . .' His voice trailed-off. He was concentrating.

By now Harry, the lighting engineer, or gaffer, had produced a small floodlight which he pointed down at Jake.

'Alan?' It was Weinstein's voice in Alan's earpiece. 'We may have to stay here. Could you drop everything and come through to Trench 2?'

When Alan arrived, he could see Jake had revealed a slightly curved oval or triangular piece of bronze about 5 or 6 inches long. He'd seen something like it before. He frowned, trying to remember. In a museum case somewhere. But locally or in London? He couldn't recall where. Then Tricia looked up at him. She mimed something with both hands on either side of her face. For a moment Alan was perplexed. Then suddenly he got it. He looked back at her, open-mouthed. She smiled. Gently he shook his head in amazement and looked down into the trench again, more closely this time. And yes, she was right.

* * *

Alan joined Jake in the trench. By now Jake had cleared all round it. The piece of metal was in remarkably good condition, largely, Alan suspected, because it had lain sealed beneath the clay, which had maintained it within a uniform environment – not too wet and not too dry – and without too much oxygen, either. Most of the surface was remarkably uncorroded, probably, Alan thought, because of a thin coating of a paler metal, possibly tin, but where the bronze had been exposed it had acquired a greenish tinge.

'Alan,' Craig's voice broke in to his thoughts. 'Can you tell us what Jake has discovered down there?'

This was not what Alan wanted or needed. He didn't have time for explanations right now.

His reply was not what Craig or the viewers at home expected, either. He pulled out his comms. 'Alan for Hen Clancy, finds supervisor. Come in, please.'

Her voice crackled back through the handset. 'Hi, Alan, Hen here.'

'We've got a piece of bronze about twenty centimetres long which may need rapid lifting. We'll need your emergency kit, ASAP, if that's OK'

'Will do, Alan. See you shortly.'

Next Alan turned to Jake. 'What about the surface oxidation? D'you think it's getting worse?'

Jake straightened his back to get a more distant view of the object. Then slowly he nodded. 'Hard to say for sure, but I'd be nervous about re-wetting it and it's certainly starting to dry. Some of that greenish colour around the sides might be getting worse, too . . .' He trailed off, leaning forward to resume clearing soil away from the last part of the edge.

Alan was also now leaning forward. Very gently he scraped a small patch of silt from near the apex of the most rounded side. As he suspected, the bronze sheet here had been reinforced with a stout iron rib beneath.

'There's iron beneath it,' Alan said quietly to Jake, but Grump had raised the mike levels and his words came across clearly to millions of viewers at home, now glued to their screens. This beat any of the orchestrated 'spontaneity' of the rubbish reality shows.

'Oh shit!' Jake muttered, he'd completely forgotten they were live on national television. 'Bi-metallic corrosion. That's all we bloody need.'

As if on rails, Hen slipped silently into the shelter carrying a substantial box, which she carefully placed on the edge of the trench.

Making no apology for not answering his first question, Alan looked over to Craig, who was now kneeling on the trenchside. Two cameras followed his movements.

'Sorry to keep everyone in suspense, Craig, but I think we've found a helmet cheek-piece.'

'What Roman?'

'Oh yes, Roman all right. It's made of sheet bronze, probably given a thin coating of tin. But what's important is that it has an iron reinforcing rod on the inside.'

'Yes?'

Alan didn't want to give away too much, too quickly. 'Well that means it was almost certainly intended to be used.'

'You mean in combat?'

Alan nodded. 'That's right. But Tricia will know more. I just dig these things up.'

Thanks to her tipping Alan off, Tricia had given herself time to go online and research Roman military helmets. Now she was standing by Craig's side.

'Alan's dead right. It's the left cheek-piece of a Roman cavalryman's combat helmet. But what's extraordinary is that there's one that's almost identical in the British Museum. It's got large bosses, just like this one—'

Alan broke in. 'And where did that come from?'

As she was speaking it had come to him. He could have answered his own question, but it was time to repay Trish for her tip-off earlier.

'That's the extraordinary bit . . .' She paused and was about to continue speaking, then rapidly changed her mind.

Alan thought he heard Weinstein in London whisper, 'Oh, this is bliss!' under his breath.

She pulled out her iPad, which she showed to Craig, but

being a professional she actually angled it towards the camera alongside him. Very gently she spread her fingers. The image grew larger. Craig was leaning forward to see the screen.

'Cavalry combat helmet,' he slowly read aloud. 'First century AD, from Witcham Gravel, Ely, Cambridgeshire.'

There was a long pause, while the camera homed-in on the screen. Tricia winced at the effort of holding the iPad dead still for the close-up. Alan sympathised. Across the back of the camera their eyes met. He smiled encouragement. She was doing a fabulous job; they made a great team.

For the last minute and a half, Hen had carefully covered the helmet with cling film, then gently started to apply the plaster of Paris bandages, which would provide the rigid framework they would need when they attempted to lift it the next day.

It was all too much for Jake, still kneeling in the trench. He was looking on, wide-eyed. 'That's fucking amazing . . .' he muttered under his breath.

But the highly sensitive mike had caught every breathy syllable.

As the end-credits rolled, a delighted Weinstein told Alan through his earpiece that Jake's naughty words had echoed what viewers were thinking everywhere. Alan was delighted, too. It was a great find, but now he would have to rethink the entire site, which had suddenly become hugely complex. The earlier settlement had somehow morphed into a major military installation, complete with helmet-wearing cavalrymen. For a moment, Alan imagined John and Sebastian Cripps charging at each other like jousting medieval knights. No, nothing was ever what it seemed, when you really started to dig.

# Eleven

It was Friday. Day 5, early in the morning. Alan leant across to the chair by his bed and looked at his watch: 6.30. Damn that, he thought to himself, I need more sleep. So he lay back and hoped for oblivion, but nothing happened, except in his head, which was full of last night: an excited Frank jabbering, 'Seven million, seven million!' to anyone who'd listen. And then there was that helmet. He had a lot of reading and thinking ahead of him.

A passing headlight threw a pale gleam across the bedroom ceiling. And then another. And another. He could hear the cars decelerate as they approached the Abbey Farm drive. Had he nodded off, as he'd hoped? He glanced across at his watch again: 6.35. He couldn't believe it: visitors were arriving *already*.

He had an important phone call to make, but it would be unfair to call anyone at this ungodly hour. So what to do? More cars passed in the road outside. He knew that reading a book wasn't going to send him to sleep. He was far too awake. Better get up. Then he had an idea. He dressed rapidly, took his phone off charge and climbed aboard the Fourtrak.

Alan was driving south-west towards Sutton and Mepal when his mobile rang. He pulled into a field gateway. Only one person would call him this early. And he was right: Richard Lane was the name on his screen.

'Bloody hell, Richard, how did you know I wouldn't be asleep? It was frantic last night.'

'Yes, I saw it. An amazing show. I thought Mary was going to pass out when you revealed the cheek-piece. Talk about tension!'

'I'd love to, Richard, but I don't suppose that's why you phoned. Are you angling for a site visit, because I'm sure I could find you a couple of site crew passes, if you'd like?'

'No, Alan, wrong on both counts. Of course we'd love to come, but I know you're crowded out and I'd hate to add to the crush. And Mary doesn't care for large crowds, either. She gets a bit claustrophobic.'

'So how can I help you?'

'It's simple, really. Yesterday I was checking through my desk diary and it's been just over six weeks since that man Joe Thorey vanished off the face of the earth. I know what country villages are like. Have you heard any rumours? Any gossip? Anything at all?'

'No, absolutely nothing. That's the odd thing. Trouble is, in the village everyone wants to discuss the dig. It's the sole topic of conversation. And I didn't hear anything before the shoot began, either. Remarkably quiet, come to think of it.'

'Have you had any conversations with members of the Cripps family since then?'

'Of course I have. I talk to Candice every day.'

'Yes, but you know what I mean, Alan: private, one-to-one chats. Anything like that?'

Alan thought for a moment. Then he remembered that drive in Sebastian's Land Rover. 'Oh, I did learn one interesting thing: Sebastian can't stand Joe Thorey. I think he'd sack him tomorrow if it wasn't for Sarah and the shoot. He told me the shoot was essentially keeping the estate afloat. Those rich London shooters pay a fortune.'

'That's fascinating. I'd always taken Sebastian and Sarah as a closely-knit team. That suggests there's tension between them.'

There was a pause. Alan was the first to break the silence. 'And if Thorey has disappeared, it also gives Sebastian a motive . . .' He trailed off.

'Quite, Alan,' came Lane's dry reply. 'My thoughts precisely.'

Suddenly there was silence. Irritated, Alan glanced at his phone. No signal. Bloody Hell! Alan put the phone down on the seat beside him and eased the Fourtrak back into motion and glanced in the mirror: the road behind was completely empty. Deliberately he put thoughts of Thorey and Sebastian out of his head. He had to focus on that helmet cheek-piece. Presumably the Roman cavalryman would have spent most of his time on the uplands of the Haddenham Ridge – one of the highest of the islands on the western approaches to Ely. During the 'live', Tricia had gone on to explain that the helmet might well have been made on the continent in the decades just prior to the Roman Conquest of AD43. But where would its wearer and his cohort have been based?

He could remember his university lecturer at Leicester stressing that the Roman Army of the conquest period was an extraordinarily flexible fighting machine and that cavalry, the *cohorts equites* as they were known, were distributed through the legions and their auxiliary camps and fortresses. It wasn't until much later that more specialised cavalry forts, such as The Lunt near Coventry, were built. So the men who wore the Witcham and now, Alan thought with some pride, the Fursey helmets would have been based locally. But where? That was the question that still needed answering.

He drove around for about 15 minutes refamiliarising himself with the landscape, then a passing shower hit. Like much early spring rain, it was quite heavy. Peering through the rapidly misting windscreen, Alan spotted a deeply rutted and very muddy farm track, which he entered rather too fast, sending up a huge spray of puddle water that covered much of the driver's side of the vehicle with a dark coat of peaty mud. He stopped, turned off the engine and looked around him. He was parked near an old, flooded gravel pit.

Presumably the track had been closed off when the gravel pits were dug, probably in the 1950s or '60s. In those days old gravel workings were just abandoned when they were quarried-out. There was no attempt at restoration. As a consequence, bits of rusty ironwork were protruding from the deep, cold water; grebes, moorhens and ducks swam busily through the industrial debris, among thick stands of reeds, flag irises and willows. Today, of course, Alan knew from personal experience, having excavated at numerous quarries, that the planners dictate how worked-out pits must now look, with trimly landscaped edges and nice, neat-looking platforms for individual fishermen. But as he gazed at the ducks and debris, he knew his sympathies lay in the older, unplanned days.

He wound down the window to let in the fresh spring air,

then picked the phone off the seat. He glanced at the handset, which now showed a strong signal. He scrolled down to the name Harry and looked out of the window again. This wasn't going to be easy. But this time it was going to be very different. Work would come first, second and third. He owed it to the loyal team at Fursey: to Jake, Hen, John, Kaylee and the diggers. And of course to Stan. He sighed at the memory. Time passed.

Then he pulled himself together, now more determined to do it. He had to call her: she had unique experience in the post-Roman period; in fact, she was the only person capable of revealing the site's full potential. But would she be willing to take part at all? Sadly, he had his doubts – serious doubts – about that.

He took a deep breath and pressed call.

It was some time before her irritable voice answered. 'Hello?'

'Hello,' he replied brightly. 'It's me.'

'I'm driving.'

'OK.' His heart sank. 'I'll be brief. I'm digging at a site near Ely and we've found three graves.'

'Yes, Alan, I'm well aware of that. I'd have to be brain-dead not to have heard of your exploits. Half Britain is watching you.'

Not a promising start.

'The thing is, I need somebody good to excavate the stiffs. And we've got the Home Office approval. I did all that weeks ago.'

'But surely you've got somebody there who's experienced?'

Alan knew that Hen Clancy dug a good stiff, but she had her hands more than full with the finds. And of course, if needs be, he or Jake could dig them, but neither could be spared. And besides, none of them had the specialised knowledge of palaeopathology that the very best skeleton excavators possess.

'Yes, there's me and Hen—'

'Do give her my love. It's been years since we dug together.'

'I will.' Alan was now getting worried. 'But couldn't you find the time? We've only got three graves. They shouldn't take you more than a week.'

'Alan, you're being ridiculous and you know it. Yes, I could probably dig three bodies in a week, providing there weren't any complications, but you've proudly announced to the world that you've almost certainly discovered a cemetery. And as you're no doubt aware, most cemeteries contain more than three graves.'

'I know, but think about it this way: the graves we've got are sealed beneath alluvium. Metalwork is superbly preserved—'

'But that won't matter if they're Christian, will it? There'll be no finds.'

Alan was getting desperate; he tried another approach.

'That's as may be. If this cemetery is as early as I think—'

'Meaning?'

'Judging by the stratigraphy it has to be very early post-Roman indeed, maybe even sixth, but more probably seventh century.'

'Hmm, so earlier than Guthlic's?'

Had that been a mistake? He didn't want to remind her of their last time together.

'Yes, by quite a lot.'

'I must admit that does sound very intriguing . . .' There

was a short pause. When she resumed, her tone, Alan thought, seemed brighter. 'You may not know it, but I've just been given a Moorhouse Fellowship to collate all the known sub-Roman and early Christian burials in Britain. It's a five-year project.'

Moorhouse Fellowships were very highly regarded indeed and Alan felt slightly deflated that he hadn't been told.

'It sounds right up your street, then.'

This was more hopeful. If all else had failed, he knew he could appeal to her enthusiasm for her specialism. Had it worked?

'Look, I'm nearly at the station, so I can't come over today. I'll watch the programme when I'm back from London tonight—'

'But we may not come down on the bones. They could be quite deep.'

'Yes, I'm well aware of that, Alan. So I'll be with you bright and early tomorrow morning. I'll see you at Fursey at nine.'

And with that, she rang off.

He put the phone down and leant back in his seat. That could have gone worse. A lot worse. Suddenly he started to feel elated, but then he got a grip of himself. No, that wasn't the way forward. This time everything about their relationship was going to be professional. Strictly professional.

* * *

If the live shoot could have been said to have had a quiet day, it was Day 5, Friday evening. The discovery of the Roman helmet cheek-piece had moved the programme from the centre to the front pages of all national newspapers and visitor numbers to Fursey had continued their relentless rise.

It was approaching 8am when Alan turned the Fourtrak into the staff car park at Fursey Abbey. He drew up alongside a familiar Land Rover. As he got out, Sebastian did the same. Both doors slammed in unison. Sebastian glanced across at the peaty mud, still wet on the Fourtrak.

'Been out surveying?' Sebastian asked cheerfully. He was in a good mood.

Alan was desperate for a coffee and couldn't face a long explanation.

'Yes, sort of. All this filming gets in the way of my normal work. You know what it's like.'

'Yes, I do. For me it's the council; for you it's the camera.' Sebastian was plainly very pleased with this.

'Yes, but they both have their pressures, don't they?'

'Could be worse. Could be worse.'

Sebastian reached into the Land Rover and rapidly pulled out a briefcase. 'Can't hang around,' he said as he locked the door. 'Got an FHD board meeting. All your fault, Alan. John says the place's crowded. Too many visitors to deal with properly. But I thought that's what we wanted, wasn't it?'

And with a cheery shrug he turned and headed rapidly towards the abbey office.

Despite the rain, Alan paused for a moment. Why would John want to call a full Fursey Heritage Developments board meeting so urgently? Surely it was just a simple management decision? Clearly Sebastian wasn't about to give anything away, but something was happening, and presumably it was quite important. But what? And more importantly: why? Try as he would, Alan couldn't get his head around it.

* * *

As he left the catering trailer holding a mug of coffee, Alan met Frank who was poring over a clipboard of papers. He looked up. For a brief moment Alan feared he was going to propose another strange idea, but he was wrong. Frank merely smiled and asked what he was planning to do today. Alan explained that as soon as they'd lifted the helmet cheek-piece, they must crack on with the three graves, if they were to have any hope of revealing bones on Day 5, let alone on Day 6. To his surprise, Frank agreed – he was very aware that what with the Lidar results, the developing building in Trench 2, not to mention all the military finds, the final day would be hectic verging on the impossible. Whereas today looked relatively quiet. So he promised to do everything possible to ensure they were not interrupted in Trench 1. Alan thanked him, but wasn't even slightly optimistic: someone, or something, was bound to turn up.

But he was wrong, and they got a good day's work done. The graves' fillings were quite soft and the ancient grave-diggers had back-filled them with the clean soil dug out of the grave. Unlike graves in later churchyards, the filling of these very early burials was not mixed with material disturbed from much older, completely decayed graves. They did find a few small and weathered pieces of Roman pottery in the top of the filling, but that was to be expected. But to Alan's great relief, the main graves' back-fill was sterile. He even contemplated being naughty and using a mattock, but decided against it, given the visitors and ubiquitous reporters. He could see the tabloid headline: *WHOOPS! Shock Horror! Clumsy Archaeologist Smashes Ancient Skull!!*

By the time Frank called everyone together for the final

rehearsal, the graves were now looking like graves: each one a foot to 18 inches deep and with nice steep, clean sides. Alan was clearing up pieces of loose earth from around 'his' grave, as he now unselfconsciously thought of it, when Charles Carnwath, T2's commissioning editor, arrived.

'I've only just got here, Alan. Just thought I'd let you know how well you've been doing.'

'Thanks, Charles, we've got a great team here—'

'No, Alan.' He crouched down by the edge of the trench, his tone more confidential. 'I'm not getting through, am I?'

Alan looked at him, his mind still largely on the live session that would start in five minutes. Carnwath continued more urgently, 'It's not just me, Alan, it's everyone at T2 from the controller of television downwards we all think you personally are doing a fantastic job.'

Alan still didn't know quite what to say. 'That's, er, very nice to—'

'All the feedback we're getting is about what everyone is calling the *real* reality of this show. And they all say it's down to you.' Alan tried to interrupt, but Carnwath wouldn't let him. 'Yes, Craig and Tricia are great, but they're not unusual. There are Craigs and Tricias right across television. But you're different. You're real. You're fresh and you're not seen as bland. We're wiping the floor with the opposition. On Day 2 our audience share topped twenty per cent, while that *Road Rage* spoiler slumped to eight per cent. Tonight with luck we might make twenty-five per cent. So keep it up – and stay yourself. Don't forget: Lew and I will back you, whatever you decide. And I mean that.'

He tried to take in what had been said as he watched Carnwath leave the shelter. Then he smiled. He wasn't even slightly sad that the *Road Rage* special – *Chelsea Tractors from Hell* – had flopped. But 'stay yourself' – what did that mean? Right now he wasn't entirely sure who he was. The old Alan Cadbury, Stan's close friend, had long gone. The straightforward man-of-the-trenches field archaeologist was being stifled by the 'Itsagrave' media star. The amateur sleuth couldn't decide who to follow: Thorey? John? Candice? Sebastian? – even Sarah? And then of course there was Harriet: what would she make of this character stew?

Carnwath's encouraging words had had the opposite effect.

* * *

Alan was back in Trench 1 trowelling away. Over the day he'd managed to catch up with Graves 2 and 3, not of course that they were being at all competitive – although they had agreed that the other two would buy the first one who hit bones all their drinks in the pub for one evening.

The monitor on the side of the trench had been turned on, but the three archaeologists all had their heads down and were scraping vigorously. Rather unusually, Weinstein had decided to start Day 5 with the studio panel discussing the significance of the helmet cheek-piece. They began with the more complete and better preserved example from Witcham, currently on display at the British Museum – and of course there were lingering shots of light glinting off its silvery surfaces. And yes, Alan had to concede, glancing up, it was very fine. Very fine indeed – if, that is, you liked that sort of thing. But was our – as he now thought of the Fursey cheek-piece – fragment *precisely* the same? Were they by the same maker, even? The only way they'd ever know would be to visit the hallowed display cases in the BM and do a close comparison. Ever since his student days, when he'd first heard the nation's premier museum referred to as the Bloomsbury Lubyanka, after the Soviet Union's most notorious prison, Alan had found it very daunting. He much preferred Portakabins.

Then the panel moved on to discuss why the Roman Army would have needed horses in an environment where the ground was so soft. Alan could hear the monitor jabbering away in the background. But the Fens aren't a quaking bog, you bloody halfwits! He sighed heavily and trowelled even harder to suppress his anger at such rubbish. As if reading his mind, Weinstein came over the earpiece and explained that this had been the main worry of the thousands of people who contacted T2 via Twitter and social media. Alan paused while Weinstein spoke and felt slightly mollified when he'd finished. Then he resumed trowelling. Hard. Even after years of such work, his wrist was beginning to feel the strain.

He stood up: he had to straighten his back. Instinctively he looked at the visitors over by the barrier and checked their faces. Was Harriet among them? But she wasn't there. Briefly he felt irrational disappointment. Then he pulled himself up short. Time to get a grip: the filming wasn't going to be easy and he needed his brain to be focused. He got back to his trowelling.

Weinstein's original plan had been to finish the studio piece, then Craig would kick off the live section in Trench 2 where viewers would see how the find spot of the cheek-piece related to the emerging timber wall. Towards the end of the middle of the programme they'd make just one visit to Trench 1, before returning to Trench 2 for a discussion of the day's finds, including some fine and quite large pieces of Samian ware with clear makers' marks on their bases, which had got Tricia very excited in the afternoon. One highly decorated bowl had been imported around AD140–175 from a particular maker, Cinnamus, who was based in Lezoux, in southern France. Alan could anticipate her holding forth at some length about that. And as he'd told Weinstein, they needed time to work their way through the graves' fillings or they wouldn't have a chance of reaching bones on the all-important Day 6. So just one visit to Trench 1 would be fine by them.

That, at least, was the plan.

The panel discussion was starting to wind down, but for some reason the sound-feed on the monitor had become rather crackly and Grump was approaching the trench to fix it when he was frozen in his tracks by a squeal from Kaylee. Alan immediately straightened up and looked into Grave 2. Kaylee was no longer kneeling forward. She was smiling hugely. But instead of anything memorable or broadcastable she announced to everyone in the shelter, 'You two boys owe me an evening's Bacardi and Coke!'

Her squeal had caused near-panic behind the scenes. Mercifully for Kaylee, nobody at home heard the Bacardi and Coke remark. Somehow, and in a very few seconds, Weinstein engineered a crash-cut from the studio to Trench 1. Luckily Speed was on stand-by and his camera was turning over in time to catch Alan's response, which was picked up on the camera mike alone at first, so was rather indistinct.

'Skull?'

'Yes,' Kaylee replied, her voice still faint. 'Lying prone, I think.'

By now Grump had twiddled his knobs and switches. Suddenly the sound improved as their mikes cut in.

'Let's have a look.'

Alan moved from Grave 1. As he did so, Weinstein came through the earpiece.

'Play for time, Alan. Craig'll be with you very soon.'

Alan knelt at the edge of Grave 2 and suddenly felt the silt beneath his knees start to shift. Immediately he knew the graveside was about to collapse. Very, very carefully he pulled back, then rapidly collected two short kneeling-boards from a heap behind the now dead monitor. Meanwhile Kaylee was continuing to clear soil away from the skull. Weinstein had told Speed to go in close, and people at home were able to see her expose the skull's left eye socket. It was a wonderful moment of live television.

Hundreds of thousands of children right across Britain shuddered in unison. Alan looked down at what Kaylee was revealing. The orbit, or eye socket, was sharp and well-defined which meant that the bone was well preserved. He knew that would please Harriet. And for some reason he found it pleased him too.

* * *

By the end of Day 5's filming, Kaylee had exposed the upper part of the skull and John had come across a toe bone in Grave 3. The skull was at the west end of its grave, the toe bone at the east: final confirmation of their Christian status.

It had been an interesting 'live', with much less chat and discussion and more focus on the actual archaeology. Alan preferred it that way and knew that Weinstein could see it provided contrast and further evidence, not that this was needed, that this was indeed real reality television.

Alan was aware that bone preservation was the main concern of the special human osteologist he wanted to join them.

'Alan,' Craig asked in the scene before the end credits. 'You seem more than usually excited by the bones.'

'You're right, Craig, I am. You see, I'd been a bit worried. There's a lot of peat around Ely and peat can be very acid. Bones, of course, are made from calcium which is easily attacked by acid soils. But when I examined the skull closely' – he didn't tell the world the truth: that he'd tapped it with the tip of his trowel – 'I could see it was hard and in exceptionally good condition. All the surfaces seem smooth and intact.'

'And is that important?'

'Yes, it is. Bone surfaces preserve muscle scars, so we can tell a lot about a person's build and even their lifestyle.'

'And disease?'

Clearly Craig knew that TV audiences relished anything about disease, the nastier the better.

'Absolutely. It's been said that there was a wave of plague at the end of the Roman period and these bones might also reveal traces left by boils, scurvy, mouth ulcers and a host of dental problems too painful to think about.'

'So something grisly to look forward to tomorrow?'

Alan frowned, but he didn't reply. He knew he'd already said more than enough.

Then the credits rolled.

# Twelve

Alan had a restless few hours' sleep, which ended in a nightmare in which the graveside collapsed and he crashed onto the skull, smashing it to pieces, while Harriet looked on in stern disapproval. Then, quite out of the blue, a fire engine, all bells and sirens at full blast, was hurtling towards them. At that his brain woke up. It was the phone. The bloody phone. Last night he'd been too tired to turn it off. He reached out and picked it up. His sleepy eyes wouldn't focus on the screen.

'Hello?'

'Alan,' the voice was half-familiar. 'It's Alan, here.'

Alan? For an instant his woolly brain thought he was going mad. Then sanity returned: it must be Dr Alan Scott, the soil micromorphologist in Cambridge.

'I finished with the soil samples last night, but thought you wouldn't welcome a call so late, as I know you've been quite busy these evenings.'

'Yes, it's been a bit frantic.'

'And last night's was good. We had it on in the lab. The

students cheered when the skull appeared. And that Tricia has won over the blokes, big time. You'd better watch it, Alan, or she'll up-stage you, unless you're careful.'

'I hope she does. I think she wants a career in TV, which is more than I do. But the samples?'

Small talk. He hated it.

'Oh, yes, the samples. Well, for once I think we took them from the right place and the sequence doesn't seem to have been disturbed too much by post-depositional effects.'

'Ah, that's good. So not a lot of drying out?'

'No. So I think we're deep enough down to be able to say some useful things.'

'Like?'

Alan's sleepy mind had now fully woken up. He wanted Dr Scott to get to the point.

'There's a clear cut-line in the lower part of the alluvium.'

For Alan, that was the big story. It confirmed what he had seen, but couldn't prove in the trench.

'Yes, we could see something very faintly, which lined up well with the edge of Grave 2. Is that what you spotted in thin-section?'

'It is, I'm certain of that. And the other thing that's very clear are the separate episodes of flooding, which form a series of quite distinct varves, about half a millimetre thick.'

This was more music to Alan's ears. He'd learnt about varves when studying the history of archaeology at Leicester. They were first identified in Scandinavian glacial lake-beds in the 19th century.

'I couldn't spot any obvious standstill or weathering horizons,' Dr Scott continued. 'So I must assume the flooding was a regular annual event. And you say the pottery dates the start of alluviation to the later third century?'

'That's right. Sometime shortly before AD300.'

'Well, in that case the grave-cut was made some fifteen centimetres, say three centuries of flooding episodes, later. I'd guess sometime between AD600 and 650 – certainly no later.'

'And presumably flooding continued?'

'Well, no. There's a standstill horizon almost immediately after the cutting of the graves.'

'Any idea how long that was?'

Dr Scott took a deep breath. 'That's difficult to say. Maybe two or three centuries? Then flooding recommenced, but worse than before. This time the varves are at least twice as thick.'

'Does that sound to you like they'd introduced flood-control measures? Maybe a cemetery wall, or else they did something to improve local drainage?'

'I'd go for the drainage,' Dr Scott replied. 'Walls tend to collapse, whereas drains were maintained.'

'Yes,' Alan was thinking aloud. 'That certainly fits with the archaeological evidence. And we know the early monastic communities were keen to drain. It gave the brothers something useful to do.'

That wasn't quite fair, but what the hell. Alan felt elated. That call was just what he had wanted to hear. It had given him the reliable, accurate dates that are so often lacking on early post-Roman sites. It had also allowed them to characterise and date the onset of flooding, which was somewhat later and initially slower than he had originally suspected. Then he thought back to Stan's notebook and those buried horizons just off the edges of Fursey island. Yes, he thought. All of that was now starting to look a lot more credible. Stan had been on to something, there was no doubt about that – and it gave Alan grim satisfaction. But why conceal it? Common sense would suggest it would boost Fursey as a visitor attraction. Or were they worried that it might affect the way they farmed? And what about the impact on land prices?

* * *

Alan decided to walk to Fursey for the final day of the 'live', because of Candice's 'small wrap party' in the catering tent afterwards, which he feared it wouldn't be that small. He was picking his way through the trees around the edges of the park to avoid the visitors who were already queuing along the drive, and was thinking, as he did every day, about Stan. He thought back to his wake. Things had seemed so straightforward back then: black and white; goodies and baddies. He had been quietly confident that he'd soon get to the bottom of it all: the strange curse; the river deaths and the loss of his friend. But that was almost four months ago and, since then, even Lane hadn't managed to unearth anything strange or unusual. And now the latest discoveries on the dig, together with the soil micromorph results, were strongly suggesting that prehistoric and ancient Fursey had been a very much more prosperous and populated place than anyone had hitherto supposed. He shook his head. He was in no doubt that his friend had started to glimpse this for himself. Stan would have been very excited, and he was like Alan: there was absolutely no chance that he would have killed himself once he'd found something important to chase. He wondered again about the notebook, and why Stan had hidden it so carefully. There was so much to think about.

Alan headed towards the fringes of the park and leant against a fallen tree trunk that had been dragged there many years ago. Its surface had been pecked away by generations of woodpeckers and boring insects. It felt soft – more like a chair than a log against his backside. It was also damp from the morning dew. Now what, he wondered, were the implications of these discoveries for the current generation of the Cripps family? First and foremost, they gave John and Candice solid reasons to be optimistic about the future: any heritage-sector asset based on such a rich and developing story must have a promising future, especially if the asset happened to lie so close to the tourist Mecca of Cambridge. But Alan also knew that Stan was discreet – cautious even. And he certainly wasn't the sort of person who shot his mouth off or bragged about his discoveries. However, it would be quite another thing to mention them to a fellow professional. Maybe he even sought advice. Alan could readily imagine he might have mentioned something about his research off the island edge to his new confidant, Peter Flower, who might have told Candice (and for what it was worth, Alan was becoming increasingly suspicious that Flower had his greedy little eyes on her 'assets', too). Then maybe together they hatched up the plan to re-introduce Stan to drink, as a means of getting him to tell them more? It was a nice idea, but somehow it lacked conviction – and it may not have worked.

On the other hand, Alan's earlier idea that it was all about Flower controlling Stan through the bottle, seemed to make even greater sense now. In fact, the more he thought about it, that bottle of 20-year-old Glen Hubris McTavish from

Fisher College hidden in Stan's 'cupboard' was the only firm, tangible new clue that Alan had so far been able to discover.

But there was another element to the case – and Alan was now 100 per cent convinced that it was indeed a 'case' in the police sense of the word – that had to be examined. For a moment he considered the curse myth. He smiled wryly, then pulled himself up short. These things shouldn't be dismissed out of hand. Yes, he thought, they do get exaggerated and overblown, but they can also highlight fundamentally important themes and tensions. And why had water for so long been important to the Cripps family? In the past drainage had unlocked untold wealth and had given them a competitive edge that was hugely resented by their less successful neighbours. But today, especially in the southern Fens, the picture had changed. The big money now lay in development, not in farming. And personally, he was sad about that and what it might mean for the social health of rural communities, where pushy and oblivious incomers were increasingly being resented.

He altered his position against the log and felt the warmth of sunlight on his face. Then he opened his eyes. An idea had struck him: Sebastian and John may not have been the closest of friends, but they were brothers and it mattered to both of them that the estate regained some of its former glories. So had John, or indeed Candice, hinted to Sebastian that Stan had revealed rich and extensive Roman and Iron Age remains, buried beneath his fields in the fen around Fursey? Because if they had, Sebastian, who was a local councillor after all, would instantly have realised that these deposits would have constituted a permanent and profound planning blight to any ideas he might have had to sell or, more importantly, develop the land. Even assuming that the remains weren't immediately given legal protection through scheduling, their excavation ahead of sale or any building work would have been cripplingly expensive.

Meanwhile, John would have been delighted at the new discoveries, as they would enhance Fursey – especially if they could be excavated in public. So there could have been very real tension between the two brothers – and indeed their wives, too. But tensions strong enough to cause a death? Well, why not? Livelihoods and reputations were at stake. Maybe even marriages too?

Then he had another idea. The wake hadn't quite worked out the way he'd expected. The scene-in-the-library that he'd anticipated, had turned out to be less straightforward and very opaque. And why? Because he hadn't pulled any strings; he had made no attempt to intervene and probe for information. He had just observed and he had discovered that the Cripps family were very good at thwarting observers. But now Candice had offered him another scene-in-the-library, only this time it would be a dinner, not a wake. And it would be his last chance. He *had* to do something active. Mere observation wasn't enough. Intervention was required.

# Thirteen

He went across to the new coffee stall that had been set up on Day 3 and ordered two large lattes to go. While these were being made, Frank joined him. He ordered an Americano with hot milk. The lattes were placed on the counter and Alan was about to pick them up, when Frank, who had noticed the two coffees, asked, 'Oh, has Harriet arrived?'

Alan had explained to Frank earlier about the need for a bones expert and his professional experience with Harriet. Alan hated his familiar tone. Alan glanced at his watch: it was 8.55.

'Not yet,' he replied. 'Dr Webb's always punctual. I've arranged to meet her at nine.'

'Oh, excellent. I'd love to meet her, too. I'll come along.'

Fuckin' Ada! Alan almost exploded at the man's cheek. Not so much as a 'perhaps I might join you?'. Then he paused. Maybe this was what their re-introduction needed. If a third party was there, then a degree of formality would be expected. Yes, on reflection, it wasn't such a bad idea, after all.

'Fine, Frank. Let's head to the staff car park.'

* * *

Alan instantly recognised the Mini Cooper as it drove its way gingerly over the bumpy temporary track that lead into the car park. It didn't look like it had been washed since that time he had given it a hose down, in a failed attempt to patch-up their collapsing relationship.

Alan had pictured this scene many times in his mind's eye, but never with a stranger looking on. He had seen her long legs in high-heeled shoes step out of the car, then the mid-length skirt slipping slowly over her elegant calves as she straightened up. In Alan's memory she always wore tall-heeled shoes, not high-heeled court shoes, but more sensible shoes for country wear. Wearing them, she was almost precisely as tall as him. Eye-to-eye; lip-to-lip. And those skirts: so very well-tailored and always elegant.

Today, however, she was wearing a pair of close, but not too close, fitting jeans and flat-soled shoes. She was dressed for digging. She didn't appear to have noticed Alan and Frank enter the car park, as she stretched and yawned. Then she pulled out her phone and started to text. Alan called out.

'Harry!' Then a second time. 'Harriet!'

She heard him the second time, and put the phone away.

'Harry, I'd like you to meet Frank Jones, he's directing the live shoot.'

For Alan, doing things this way was great as he didn't have to decide how to greet Harry: a kiss on the cheek, or a handshake. He did neither.

'I'm so pleased to meet you, Harriet. Alan has told me so much about you.'

It wasn't a deliberate *faux pas.* Harry gave Alan a look which spoke volumes.

He tried to explain. 'Well, not really. I mean not about us . . .'Alan paused, he was making things worse.

Harry turned away to hide the smile she couldn't suppress; Alan did discomfiture so ineptly.

He took a deep breath to steady his nerves. 'I told Frank all about your work with human bones.'

Frank was looking mystified, but for once he kept his mouth shut. Harriet was now smiling openly.

Alan's phone beeped and he grabbed it, grateful for the distraction.

He read it aloud: 'I've arrived.'

'Yes,' Harriet said quietly. 'I do believe I have.'

* * *

Alan gave Harriet a tour of the set-up and showed her where all the essentials were: the catering tent, the coffee booth, the staff toilets, the Fursey offices and the three archaeological Portakabins – the general office, where Alan had his desk, the tea shed and the finds shed, where they found Hen. She knew Hen of old and they greeted each other warmly. Then, after a quick walk through the abbey ruins, they entered the shelter over Trench 1.

Alan looked down with approval. They'd left things in a bit of a mess at the end of Day 5's filming and he'd asked Kaylee and Jon to do a rapid clean-up before Harriet arrived. And they'd done a great job. The trench looked spotless.

After they'd all been introduced, Harriet stepped down into the trench. Kaylee had finished exposing the skull and neck of the body in Grave 2 and the bones had been beautifully revealed.

'You've done this before, I see?'

'Sort of,' Kaylee replied. 'But it was a big urban dig and we all had to teach ourselves. I'd love to learn to do it properly. I really would.'

Harriet was clearly delighted at this. 'That's great to hear, Kaylee. I'd be happy to teach you.'

Jon had moved back to Grave 3 and was standing rather diffidently by its side. They looked down: the toe bone was still there, in splendid isolation. Jon gave an excuse that was familiar to both Alan and Harriet. 'I thought I'd get the rest of the grave filling down to the same level. I didn't want to dig rabbit holes.'

'Yes,' Harriet replied. 'You were quite right. And it all looks beautifully level, too. But would you mind dreadfully if I took over now? I think Alan here wants me to start excavating bones.'

Jon didn't try to conceal the look of relief that spread over his face.

* * *

Slightly to Alan's surprise, the coach-load of county and district councillors were shown over the abbey ruins by Peter Flower, who had also given them a brief guided tour of the historic landscape as they drove from Cambridge.

Before he handed over to Alan he confidentially explained, 'Terribly sorry, Alan, but I've got to dash back to Fisher. We've an important college council meeting at noon which I've absolutely *got* to attend.'

Alan didn't trust the man at all, but he knew he must appear friendly, if he was ever to discover anything.

'Sounds like you're in for a pay rise, Peter?'

It was meant to be jocular, but it sounded rather pointed. Shit, Alan thought, I blew that. But he hadn't.

Flower positively beamed. 'Young Cadbury, you must be a mind reader! I'll let you know later.'

Time to sound genuinely concerned. 'No, seriously Peter: I *do* hope it goes well.'

Flower turned to leave. 'Thanks, Alan.' This was half-mimed, as he headed out of the catering tent towards a waiting taxi in the staff car park.

Alan was glad to see him go. Somehow he was going to prove that Flower had encouraged Stan to drink again. It didn't have to be a big public exposure: he just wanted Flower to know that he couldn't get away with it. You couldn't treat people like dogs: jump, and I'll throw you a treat.

* * *

Were it not for the power of television, the 55 councillors would have treated Alan as the support act to the main attraction, the famous Dr Peter Flower. But not now. As he stepped forward, he got a round of applause. Slightly disappointed at himself, he found he was rather enjoying the attention. It was certainly much better than being ignored, or worse, patronised. He also thought he caught a few whispers of 'It's a grave'. But then he saw Harriet in the trench below, and in an unexpected attack of nerves found himself blurting out the obvious.

'Welcome to Trench 1. And as you can see in front of you: it's a grave.'

This earned another, prolonged, round of applause. While hands were enthusiastically clapping, Harriet looked up at him with a look of quiet exasperation. Alan immediately regretted being so flippant.

After their tours of the two trench shelters, the group gathered outside for the Q and A session that the council leader was keen to have. He had also asked Alan to give them a short summary of the area's archaeological potential. Alan discussed the superb preservation of the human remains and the fact that flood-clay had preserved whole landscapes virtually intact. He even hinted that the Roman presence there might be far more substantial than anyone had suspected – and he strongly advised them to watch Day 6 of the 'live' tonight, when the results of the Lidar survey would be revealed.

'What are you expecting, Alan?' the leader asked.

Alan smiled, in reality he didn't know. And he didn't want to know. Spontaneity isn't always easy to simulate on camera, and he knew he was a lousy actor.

'I honestly don't know. And that's the truth.'

'Oh, go on,' a councillor called out. 'You can tell us. We won't breathe a word . . .'

That got a laugh.

Then a young woman – Alan recognised her as the leader of the increasingly popular Green Party – asked, 'What's the hidden potential of these landscapes, Alan?'

'Do you mean under the flood-clay and peats?'

'Yes, I do.'

Suddenly Alan was aware this was potentially difficult. The Green lady seemed very friendly, but others had different, usually vested, interests, too. He could see Councillor Sebastian Cripps looking very serious, but giving nothing away.

'I think there's little doubt that the Roman occupation levels extend beyond the limits of the upland here at Fursey.'

'Yes, but for how far out into the surrounding fen?' It was Sebastian's voice.

For a moment Alan wished Stan had been there to answer him.

'We won't know that without further survey. But I'd be very surprised indeed if any Roman material will be found below about a metre above OD.'

Sebastian nodded sagely. Did he understand the implications for him? Alan couldn't decide.

Another councillor asked, 'OD? That's sea level, isn't it?'

'Yes,' Alan replied. 'And contrary to popular opinion, the Romans didn't do much actual fen drainage. They mostly took advantage of naturally drier conditions in the first and second centuries AD.'

'And what about the graves?' another councillor asked. 'You said you thought they may prove to be quite early. How does that leave Ely? High and dry?'

This got a laugh.

'There have been modern digs around the edges of the Isle, and they've proved that Ely had ancient beginnings, too. Maybe even earlier than Fursey. Modern archaeology is transforming our knowledge. These graves are just a small part of it. If you don't mind me saying so, local councillors of all parties around here should be aware that this is one of the most important archaeological regions in Europe.' He let this sink in, then finished with, 'And I mean that.'

Not exactly a memorable ending, but it earned him generous applause.

Alan paused as he headed back to his Portakabin to collect the context lists for the day's work. That had been fascinating, but he had been too general. If he was going to elicit anything from the people around the dinner table tomorrow, he must come up with something far more specific. Maybe a story/parable: something they must respond to.

Alan was lost in thought as he watched the councillors' coach head slowly down the drive.

* * *

After the lunch break, Alan and Jake realised they hadn't done their weekly run-through of the site Finds and Samples Register. Both trench daybooks looked pretty thin and the site diary was almost non-existent. As Alan had observed on previous televised digs, essential paperwork often takes a back seat if you let TV people take the upper hand. And Alan wasn't going to allow that: not on a site of this quality.

Half an hour later, he was back in the dig tent, but still deeply enmeshed within context sheets and sample lists, having just spotted a small but potentially awkward error in the spot-heights around Grave 3. If left uncorrected, such mistakes could lead to graves and other features being placed in the wrong phase. He was annoyed with himself: it was the sort of mistake that happened if you were constantly being interrupted. Then the tent flap was pulled back. Talk of the devil, he thought angrily. He was about to tell whoever it was to kindly sod off, when John Cripps entered. Alan bit back his words. He couldn't afford to be rude to *him*, of all people. He was even more glad he'd controlled himself, when the next person entered.

He was a man in his early forties, thinning on top, Alan noticed, as he dipped his head to pass through the gap; he wore a pair of baggy, but neatly pressed, blue jeans, which didn't altogether go with the shiny black shoes, white shirt, dog collar and dark suit-like jacket. The jeans were held up by a narrow, shiny leather belt that was probably bought to go with a pin-stripe suit. Presumably, Alan thought, the weird jeans were intended to show that he could identify with young people. He was 'hip to their vibe'. Then he winced at his own cruelty: no, I'm going too far. He's probably a very nice man.

'Alan,' John said. 'I'd like to introduce you to Jason. Jason Grimes.'

Alan had half expected Theobald, possibly even Julian, and both would have sounded good alongside Grimes. But never Jason. He smiled broadly, largely to conceal his surprise, as they shook hands.

'I'm the Fenland rural dean. It's a new appointment that replaces the old ADI.'

Jason could see this meant nothing to Alan.

'That's Archdeacon *Regiones Inundatae,* or Archdeacon of the flooded regions. The appointment came into existence during monastic times, before the widespread drainage of the seventeenth century, when Fenlanders had very specific social needs.'

'Yes, malaria had become a major problem and the Church grew and processed opium poppy seeds, for example, which it distributed among the poor and needy.'

Alan smiled. He had never thought of the Church as a drug-pusher. 'It's an interesting image,' he said.

'If not completely fair,' the dean broke in. 'Opium has

little strength when grown in our climate, it would have been used as an analgesic: an alternative to aspirin, today—'

It was Alan's turn to show off his knowledge. 'Made from willow bark, which of course was also plentiful in the Fens.'

The dean smiled broadly. 'Quite. And I'm sure you'll also be pleased to know that I'm already known as the Dyke Dean in certain quarters.'

Alan smiled and refrained from the obvious ribald comment.

It was John Cripps's turn to ask a question. 'You mentioned earlier that you had taken samples from directly above one of the graves which you hoped might throw light on their date. Has there been any news?'

'Yes. Dr Scott, the micromorphologist, phoned me first thing this morning,' Alan replied. 'And he's quite convinced they're very early. Of course it all depends on what you take as a starting date, but he is of the opinion they were cut in the first decades of the seventh century.'

'Good heavens!' This was clearly as close as the dean ever got to swearing. 'That *is* early. Very early indeed. In fact, it makes these graves pre-date the foundation of the cathedral!'

'Which was in 673, as I recall.' John Cripps was obviously keen to show off his knowledge. 'By St Etheldreda, following the death of her second husband, a prince of Northumbria, called Ecofrith.'

Alan listened earnestly, nodding his head, as if on camera. He was pleased: at last John had found a chance to air his erudition – even if he had got prince Ecgfrith's name a little wrong.

'Yes, yes . . .' The dean seemed to be in another world. 'Yes . . .' he resumed, almost visibly clambering out of his subconscious. 'Yes, that's right. The name has always puzzled me.'

'The prince, you mean?' Alan suggested.

'No, this place, here: Fursey. If these bones are as early as Dr Scott seems to think—'

'And that will need to be demonstrated by archaeology,' Alan added.

He deeply distrusted the attribution of known historic events to less precise archaeological data: all buildings that caught fire in the mid-first century AD were automatically assumed to have been burnt in the Boudiccan Revolt of AD60–1. According to some of his own colleagues, East Anglian bakeries and blacksmiths' shops never caught fire by accident in the mid-first century – it was always Boudicca's rebellious followers. He smiled, then the thought struck him: ancient events could be given new life in modern times by well-meaning people who had nothing to gain by inventing myths and legends.

'Of course.' The dean brushed Alan's remark aside. 'But if it does indeed date to the very first decades of the seventh century, then there's only one person who could have been involved.'

'Oh.' John Cripps was suddenly very excited. 'You mean—'

'St Fursey.' The dean said rapidly. He was not going to let John steal his thunder.

'Wasn't he a Celtic missionary?' Alan knew the name vaguely. 'Who came over from Ireland?'

'Yes, to East Anglia. And he founded a number of monastic sites, possibly including Binham Priory in Norfolk. But the other thing is, he often seems to have sited these places near existing Roman sites. And what have you revealed here?'

John rapidly supplied the answer. 'An important Roman settlement.'

'And when was St Fursey active?' Alan asked.

'Precisely when these graves were cut, in the 630s,' said the dean.

I never gave that date, Alan thought. But he decided to keep quiet; he couldn't face a long explanation.

'More importantly,' the dean continued, 'he is known to have died while continuing his missionary work on the continent around 650.'

'So well before the foundation of Ely.'

'Precisely,' the dean said firmly.

That effectively ended the discussion, and then the two visitors withdrew.

Alan's resumed trowelling the hard surface, of what was increasingly feeling like a path or track. But his heart had sunk. It was entirely understandable, but they had just erected an elaborate house of cards on a tiny shred of evidence. He could hear the excited discussion continue unabated, as John and the dean headed across to Trench 2.

* * *

The final, hour-long live session kicked off with some dramatic, if predictable, footage of the survey aircraft taking off and then doing its low-level pass along the Fursey Avenue. Next came shots of a smiling Alan climbing out of the plane with his heavy D300 camera slung round his neck; with the plane's door removed, he'd managed to get some dramatic shots. Then the screen was filled with the Lidar images. The main, sensational, discovery, which Craig Larsson was now describing with wild enthusiasm on the voice-over commentary, was the ditch and bank of a square Roman fort, with three right-angled corners and entranceways at the centre of three sides.

The graphics people had soon plotted the position of the trenches onto the Lidar plan. It turned out that Trench 1 had been positioned directly across the main internal road which ran in a straight line from the north to the south entranceways through the big ditch. Trench 2 lay a few metres north of the east-west roadway, very close to the centre of the fort; both Alan and Tricia reckoned the building with the large wooden posts was probably the command centre known as the *principium.*

It was just as well that the Lidar had produced such spectacular results, because the dig itself was rather routine, not that it mattered, as Weinstein had assembled an enlarged studio panel, which included no less than two Oxbridge professors. And Craig had been recalled to London to chair it. For his part Frank had prepared a scene where Tricia and Alan re-assessed all the finds in the light of the Lidar results.

With Craig away, Alan was now the effective presenter, addressing most of his remarks to Craig in London. They filmed an up-date of the graves in Trench 1 and the two skeletons, which were now almost half-revealed, and Harriet was able to suggest that one was probably a man in his forties, the other a young woman in her late teens or early twenties. Alan was delighted at what she had achieved: the bones were well-preserved and superbly excavated and looked fabulous on screen.

As Alan was finishing describing the second skeleton, he

heard the sound of rain on the shelter. He had thirty seconds to dash across to Trench 2 to shoot the very final scene of all.

The entrance flap was meant to have been left open, but some helpful person had re-tied the flap laces of the Trench 2 shelter. It was now windy and raining hard. Alan wrestled with the damp knots and managed to burst onto set with two seconds to spare. In the process, the wire to his earpiece got caught on something and pulled out. He stuffed it in a pocket as he ran towards the film crew. By now he was drenched and dishevelled. Tricia's smile broadened as he arrived at the trenchside.

'Alan, how nice of you to come.' Weinstein had told her to lighten the mood. 'Is it raining outside? We're lovely and snug in here.'

All three cameras had red lights on. They were live.

'Some idiot tied down the shelter flap and it's chucking it down!'

Weinstein was delighted at this. After the previous episode one or two viewers had tweeted that it was all 'a bit too good'. Some had even suggested it wasn't live at all. But they couldn't say that now.

The contrast between Alan and Tricia could not have been greater. She was looking demure and composed; he was hot, a bit wild, and flustered. Over her shoulder, Alan could see Grump busily fiddling with the wires and plugs at the back of the recorder. Then a boom mike appeared over their heads.

Alan wasn't too worried about losing his earpiece as they'd done quite a detailed run-through of this scene earlier. They had a short discussion of the day's finds – two more *lorica segmentata* bronze armour fragments – and then Alan took Tricia on a tour of the various pits and post holes, before finishing with the timber wall of the headquarters building, as they had agreed to call the possible *principium.*

But Alan realised there was something different this time, and it wasn't just that actual live filming is always more exciting and urgent than even the best run-through. No, there was more to it than that: Tricia was far closer, physically and emotionally, too. She seemed to be hanging on every word Alan said, as if they were special, precious. Despite feeling damp and dishevelled, her presence so close to him added energy and urgency to his words. Tricia responded to this wonderfully by egging him on, and smiling all the time. Discussions about Roman military finds can be so boring, but not this one. And for Alan, who was having a great time, it flashed by.

When they had finished filming, Grump quickly repaired Alan's earpiece.

'I think the boss wants a word with you, Alan,' he said, as he handed it back.

Alan replaced it in his ear.

It was Weinstein. 'That was superb, Alan. Absolutely brilliant. It was *far* better than the ending I'd expected. Real food for thought.'

'That's very kind of you, Lew.'

'And did you realise that your mike had gone down?'

'Really?'

Then Alan remembered seeing Grump produce the overhead boom. Suddenly it all made sense.

'Yes,' Weinstein continued. 'That's why Tricia was so close. Her chest mike was picking you up. I told her to get up close and personal. And it worked well: you were clear, but very slightly distant. Gave your words a strange authority, like they came from a lecture hall.'

As he listened, Tricia kissed him lightly on the cheek and stepped out of the trench. She mouthed 'Must fly!' then headed for the exit.

Weinstein's words had upset him. So was that last scene together just a means of getting her mike closer? Was there nothing else to it at all? No body language? He had to be honest with himself: he'd taken quite a shine to Tricia. And it wasn't just that she was beautiful and intelligent, there was a lightness to her which he found very attractive. She seemed to enjoy the surface of life – the moments that come and go – and she didn't want to dwell on the meaning of everything. But it was more than just easy come, easy go with her. She wasn't flippant, just pleasant and relaxed. Straightforward. Yes, Alan thought, that was the word. Straightforward. Then he imagined Harriet. Tricia never had the same relaxed facial expression that Harriet had. She was completely unpredictable. Certainly not straightforward. Never that.

His thoughts were interrupted by Tricia who called out from the far end of the shelter. She was standing next to the flap, which had now been tied back. Outside the shower had passed over, and a full moon was rising above the silhouetted trees along the avenue.

'Bye, everyone. Thanks for everything. It was lovely working with you all. Have got to dash. Byee!'

And with that she left. Alan felt slightly let down. He found he sort of wanted a door to close loudly, or for something to happen that marked her departure. But no: the flap slid silently shut, while all around him the crew continued to de-rig.

* * *

Over his four years with *Test Pit Challenge*, Alan had attended at least three of the end-of-season wrap parties. They were put on and paid for by production so there was plenty of drink and usually a good disco, whose sound system was massively boosted by Grump. The food was bought in, but was usually adequate to mop up the drink. And over the last three years, they had also hired a karaoke and everyone was expected to take part. Points were awarded, and once Alan had even managed to come runner-up. That was in 2008. To this day he couldn't remember exactly what he sang, except that it was a blues song by Muddy Waters.

Alan wasn't much of a party animal, but he usually enjoyed wrap parties. For a start, there was an unwritten understanding that whatever happened at the party remained firmly within the circle. Sometimes tensions would build up, especially after a long, wet season like 2008, and people would then go a bit over the top, as a release of accumulated tensions. The other total no-no was social media. In the past, the ban was implicit, but in 2006 two very cocky volunteers filmed Craig miming to the Stones' 'Little Red Rooster' while dressed as Alice in Wonderland. Of course it went viral. When the commissioning editor at T2 saw it, it nearly cost Craig his job, as they were then in the process of establishing him as a credible presenter. He had never so much as hinted it to Craig, but Alan had told Weinstein that he would also walk out if T2 sacked the presenter. Eventually it blew over, but since then, all non-TPC guests to the wrap party were warned there was a total ban on posting anything whatsoever on the Internet.

At the start of the party, Weinstein appeared on all the monitors. It was a rather blurry Skype image, but that didn't matter. He thanked everyone for their contributions and announced that initial viewing figures for the final episode had topped 9 million, with an all-important audience share of 27 per cent. This merited a round of applause and loud cheers. Then Charles Carnwath, now also back in London, said a few well-chosen words and reminded everyone that that they had still to film another two, conventional (i.e. non-live) one-hour episodes, to go out later that summer. Finally, Candice said a few words of thanks on behalf of Fursey and Alan fully expected John to appear and say a short prayer. But they were spared that.

The formalities over, the sound system came up and the lights went down. Alan headed over to the bar and grabbed a pint of real ale before the cask ran out and they were forced to drink not-so-chilled cans of the usual factory-produced English muck they had the nerve to call lager. He spotted Hen Clancy, who was dressed to the nines, with bows and glitter in strategic positions; she was queuing for food along with Jon and Kaylee. Alan asked her where Harriet was.

'Oh, didn't she tell you?' she said, slightly surprised. 'She's got a headache so has gone home. I must admit, she did look a bit low.'

Alan was devastated. He had really been looking forward to being with Harry at the wrap party. She was great on such occasions and always managed to make him feel good, too. And who knows, he thought, I might have been able to convince her that I'm not a complete waste of time?

'Had she been feeling bad all evening?' he asked Hen, as casually as he could manage.

'I don't know. I only saw her afterwards, as she was heading back to her car. And as I said, she looked all-in. She really did.'

'So you don't think she'll be coming to the party?'

'Oh, no chance,' she continued, oblivious to Alan's distress. 'She told me outright. She said, "Tonight it's a couple of aspirins and bed." Can't say I blame her. I get migraines myself.'

Alan knew Harry didn't suffer from migraines, but he said nothing. He moved away from the bar, leaving his full beer glass on the table behind him. He didn't know where he was heading, or who he was going to meet, but now he was dreading the long hours that lay ahead.

# Fourteen

Alan had a lousy night; he wasn't sure he'd had any sleep at all. He couldn't believe that Harriet had just walked out like that. He was sure it had to have been something he had done, but he couldn't think what. In fact, he'd done his best to build up the importance of the burials and what their careful study could reveal about Dark Age life and death in the Fens. He didn't normally like to use the term 'Dark Age', but it still had impact and Weinstein had stressed to him how important it was to carry their live audience forward to the two filmed docs in the summer. But deep inside he knew it wasn't something he had or hadn't said. It was something he'd done.

Shortly before they'd started last night's live, Tricia had explained to Alan that she and a producer at T2 had pitched an idea for a mini-series about the role of women in Roman Britain to the commissioning editor at 2-Much, T2's online and digital channel. They were all going to have a key meeting in the crew's hotel on the outskirts of Cambridge as soon as they could manage it, after the 'live'. And that was why she had left so early. By then, they should have all the provisional viewing figures and the commissioning editor could make a decision on the spot. Alan could see that Tricia was very excited by it all, but try as he could, he didn't share her enthusiasm for digital television: yes, you could float unusual ideas, but it lacked the disciplines and constraints that gave terrestrial stations their urgency and appeal. He wouldn't have admitted it, even to himself, but tiny audiences didn't get his juices flowing, either. He didn't really care, but he was becoming a bit of a television snob.

He had left his phone turned on all night on the tiny off-chance that Harriet might call. But of course she didn't. But then the phone rang, just as he was sitting down on the toilet. He kicked off his pyjama trousers and dashed back to the bedroom. Just in time.

'Oh, Alan, I'm so excited.' It was Tricia. 'And I wanted you to be the first to know: they've commissioned it.'

'Wow! That's fantastic. I'm so happy for you.'

He was, but he was also starting to realise that March mornings in the Fens could be cold, and his thighs and legs now felt very exposed.

'They've agreed to do a first series of twelve half-hour shows, where I show a guest around a different site and we discuss how Roman women would have lived there. We're even hoping that some episodes will be live.' She paused to gather breath. 'Don't you think that's great?'

Alan was astonished: a first series of *12*? When *Test Pit Challenge* began they did a pilot, followed by an initial series of just three programmes. It had taken two series to reach their current total of ten episodes. But even Alan realised that this was not the moment to raise such things. He must stay enthusiastic.

'That's really great, Tricia. And when do you start?'

'They're talking late June. But I'll tell you more tonight. Byee . . .'

She'd rung off.

For a moment Alan was confused: tonight? Why tonight?

Then he remembered: Candice's 'Thank You' dinner. And his heart sank. He wished he could get a headache too, but he couldn't. He needed to stick to his plan. And besides, he suspected he'd been asked there for a reason – and he wouldn't know what that was, if he didn't show up. The live filming had been fun, while it was actually happening, but now it was over, everything would rapidly return to abnormal. The Crippses would be up to their tricks and he had to keep an eye – both eyes – on them, constantly.

As he thought about the evening ahead, he found himself picturing tonight's dinner and the tale he had prepared to trigger their reactions. In his mind's eye, John and Sebastian were glaring at each other on opposite sides of the table while their wives dutifully handed round plates and dishes. Tricia was sitting beside him, but was talking animatedly to John Cripps on her other side. Opposite them both sat Stan with a tumbler of water, not wine, and a rather sad, all-at-sea look on his face. That brought Alan up short: with the sole exception of the moment yesterday morning when he leant against the dead tree, over the rest of the live week he hadn't given his old friend much thought. But Stan wasn't looking at him, his stare was at someone else. Then he snapped out of it and tried to recall who Stan had been watching. Was this his subconscious trying to tell him something?

* * *

Sundays are usually the busiest days of the week for most visitor attractions, and Fursey was no different, especially after six evenings of live coverage on national television. In fact, 'busy' hardly described it. 'Crawling' was the word Alan would have used as he carefully drove past the crowds walking along the drive. It was nine o'clock in the morning and they didn't open till ten – and by then the queue would be almost back to the village.

Alan was owed several days off, but he knew he'd have to stay on-site until the three graves had been emptied and fully recorded. Too many people were watching their every move; so nothing, absolutely nothing, must go wrong. Harriet appreciated this too and had also agreed to stay on-site until she could safely take the bones back to her lab in Cambridge. Alan thought she might resent this, but to his surprise, she seemed quite happy to do it. Was that her professionalism trumping personal feelings, or something else?

Candice had told Alan on Friday that a special board meeting had been scheduled for Fursey Heritage Developments that morning to discuss how to manage and make the most of the surge in visitor numbers. The frequent board meetings were making Alan increasingly suspicious. Cars were now assembling outside the FHD on-site office, rather than the hall, as, she said, Sebastian had suggested. She had cast her eyes to the ceiling at this. It was typical: he just couldn't grasp that they had to show their potential collaborators they were businesslike. They had to provide proper parking. Sometimes, she laughed, Sebastian seemed to think he was a Victorian squire, rather than a small-to-medium-sized farmer in an increasingly competitive world. Alan had to agree. In fact, he had more than a little sympathy for Sebastian – a country person in an increasingly urban world.

Alan thought back to his research into the Cripps family's history. He knew that Woolpit Farm, which Sebastian now ran, had about 400 acres, after the last payment of death duties. He had casually mentioned this to Candice earlier. He wanted to learn what she thought of Sebastian's farming enterprise. He knew she didn't think it made much money, but what did she think he should do to put matters right? Sell up? Expand the shoot massively? What?

'I'd be surprised if it was even as much as that,' she had told him. 'Sebastian's always selling-off building plots. He says he's going to invest the money in more land – far safer, he says, than stocks and shares. But so far we haven't seen any new fields. In fairness to him, I think the money gets used up in running the hall and setting up the shoot.'

As he headed towards the excavations he could see that one or two riggers were already working on removing some of last night's filming paraphernalia, but Alan had persuaded Weinstein to leave them the two trench shelters and he was keen to see that they didn't get taken away by mistake.

It was starting to drizzle when Alan pulled back the flap and entered the shelter. He almost bumped into Grump Edwards, who was unplugging wires and winding them into neat bundles. They exchanged a few words, but Grump didn't stop working. He had a lot to do. As Alan watched, he folded a couple of lighting stands and laid them on the ground by the flap. Harriet was on her hands and knees in the trench, busily excavating the bones in Grave 2. Alan was aware that she must have heard him and Grump talking, but she had chosen not to notice. Not a promising sign.

Grump unplugged the monitor by the side of the trench, then unfolded a black canvas carrying case and was about to lower the set into it, when Harriet looked up.

'Oh, thank you so much,' she said without the slightest hint of irony. 'Do please take that horrible thing away.'

This was so unexpected that even Grump was lost for words. But Alan wasn't. Oh shit, he thought to himself, so that was why she went home. She had seen Tricia and him on screen, close up in every sense of the word.

He knew it was almost certainly a big mistake, but he tried to explain what had happened.

'Harriet, you must understand,' he began. 'It wasn't like that—'

'Like what?' she broke in. She wasn't going to make this easy for him.

'Like it seemed . . . She wasn't—'

Again she cut in. This time more icily. 'Flaunting her boobs at you. And in front of millions of people. Still you seemed to be lapping it up. You weren't even slightly embarrassed. If anything you moved closer to her.'

Was that true? Did he? He had to admit to himself that there was an element of sexual chemistry in it all, but then that often happens when filming: people feed off each other's emotions. It doesn't mean the other person becomes an object of lust or physical desire. Life isn't as simple as that.

'I didn't know it,' Alan tried to explain. 'But my mike had gone down. So Lew told her through her earpiece to get closer, to catch what I said on her chest mike. That's all it was. And she did it quite well—'

'You think this is about some adolescent flirting, Alan?' Harriet said, cutting through his bluster. 'I couldn't care less.

This is about you betraying your talents and your professionalism. It's a grave? You looked like a performing monkey!'

She resumed trowelling, her head firmly down.

Alan turned to go. Grump was standing a few feet away, his mouth half open in astonishment.

'Sorry, mate,' he muttered under his breath as Alan passed. 'Didn't mean to drop you in it.'

'No, it's not your fault, Grump.'

But whose fault was it? Or was it unavoidable – whatever he did, however he behaved? For a brief moment Alan didn't care, which came as a short-lived relief. But it didn't last, and he felt wretched again as soon as he headed back out into the drizzle.

* * *

Abbey Farmhouse oozed history. It had been built in the 1650s, using surviving walls of the Benedictine abbey's guest house. This earlier building occupied half of the south range of the outer court of the monastery, and was positioned on the west side of the gatehouse, which, although not as large or well-preserved as many, was still part of the Fursey visitor attraction. Alan had done more research since that visit to the library in Cambridge back in November, and had discovered that after the Dissolution in 1538, the Abbey was leased by the Court of Augmentations to a man named John Cheney, who was, in effect, a dealer in defunct monastic estates. Cheney leased it to a local landowner who then sold off much of the building stone, most likely to help the then expanding colleges of Cambridge University. By the early 1600s the land was worth little, and in 1652 Colonel Crowson Cripps, who had enjoyed (if that is the right word) a highly successful Civil

War, bought the freehold of the entire monastic estate, by this time amounting to just 150 acres, for an undisclosed (but probably, Alan reckoned, tiny) sum.

Alan gasped when he entered the dining room. Many houses built on monastic estates after the Dissolution had been restored and enlarged in the late 19th century by well-meaning and often very insensitive architects. These people were usually employed by wealthy industrialists who were seeking somewhere romantic, where they could create wonderful gardens, replete with real gothic ruins, to wow their guests. In this process, the emphasis was on retaining the earlier, medieval parts of the houses. The post-Dissolution stuff was often removed or ignored. But this had never happened at Fursey, largely, Alan supposed, because the Cripps family had lacked the necessary cash. As a result, much of the seventeenth century interior of Abbey Farmhouse was still intact, including many of the wall surfaces, which had been painted in a dark, gravy-like red-ochre paint. The ceiling featured restrained plasterwork decoration, but all four stud-and-plaster walls still retained their ochre finish. As he paused inside the threshold to the dining-room, Alan was immediately transported back to that short visit to Mount Grace Priory with Harriet – less than a couple of years ago. The Mount Grace post-monastic house still had one red-painted wall like this, although nowhere near as well-preserved. Then he remembered the terrible phone call later that same afternoon. It had brought news of violent death. And suddenly the dark ochre became less warm and welcoming. More ominous. He paused then, and unable to help himself, he shuddered. Subconsciously he wondered: were these blood-red walls a warning to him now?

He sighed as he pondered this. It was strange; during the live week he had grown used to existing and thinking at the very edge of the future and the present. Everything had to be an instant response; there was no time for any reflection. So now he wasn't used to the process of contemplation and didn't trust his own feelings. Had he dredged that memory of Mount Grace from his subconscious deliberately, or was it a genuine warning: part of his survival instinct? His confidence was shaken. He knew he needed to talk to someone. In the past, he would have phoned Harriet, or confided to her at home. But that was no longer possible. Again he sighed, but this time he was aware that his feelings of sadness and regret were only too real.

* * *

Alan didn't know quite what to expect of the meal itself: servile service from cringing flunkeys, or something cheap and cheerful from local caterers – and of course he got it completely wrong. The large dining-room table had been set for nine guests and the food was excellent, as indeed it should have been, given Candice's long experience in the catering trade. The guests helped themselves from a big Jacobean oak side-board and Candice encouraged people to change places between courses – 'Let's all get to know each other', was how she put it.

There were five guests from the Cripps family: John and Candice, Sebastian and Sarah and, of course, Barty, whose relaxed presence gave the gathering a quiet dignity. There were three from the television side: Alan, Tricia and Frank. And then there was Peter Flower, neither one thing nor the other, was Alan's impression – yet Alan couldn't help but notice that Candice was treating Flower like the main guest of the evening. He'd arrived about ten minutes after everyone else, apologising profusely and blaming the traffic out of Cambridge. It would seem he had had to return to the university after that morning's board meeting of FHD, for some urgent business to do with wind turbines on the college estate in Suffolk. As he told everyone within earshot, 'At Fisher we care deeply about global warming.' And you're happy to trouser the huge index-linked feed-in Tariff, too, Alan thought to himself – having recently helped his brother Grahame install solar panels on the barn roof at Cruden's Farm.

As Alan had expected, quails' eggs featured prominently among the starters and he had helped himself to a dozen, plus a teaspoonful of celery salt. There was a large shed full of free-range quails at Fursey; as John and Candice had discovered many years ago, their eggs were hugely popular at Cambridge College halls on feast days, and with visiting students and academics for the rest of the year. Alan found himself sitting with Barty, who had made precisely the same choice, but with half the number of eggs. Alan learnt that it was Barty who had introduced quails to Fursey.

'And they have proved – how do people say it today? – a "nice little earner" ever since!' Barty smiled, as he dipped a freshly-shelled egg into celery salt.

'I imagine the Abbey Project has done quite well out of the current surge in visitor numbers, too?' Alan enquired. He was keen to steer the conversation discreetly around to that morning's board meeting if he could.

'Oh yes, we're all absolutely delighted. And it seems to have achieved what we've all been seeking for years: an end, at last, to the stupid rubbish about the Cripps family curse. I cannot for the life of me understand why such absurd, almost medieval, superstition should have persisted in the area for so very long. So I say: good riddance!'

Alan raised his glass.

'I'll drink to that, Barty. And I'm certain you're right. It's finished. It has to be.' He paused for a moment, then said, 'I've come across similar things elsewhere in archaeology. For example, strange legends often get attached to monuments such as barrows, that are associated with death. And more often than not, these stories and legends have nothing to do with prehistory at all. Anything can trigger them: big events such as the Civil War or Black Death, or smaller, local happenings – like a severe flood or a failed harvest.'

Alan tried to make this sound convincing, despite his personal doubts. Alan was convinced there was little supernatural about what had happened to Stan, nor to Hansworth.

Barty didn't answer directly. Instead he took the conversation in a different, and happier, direction.

'The crowds have been enormous.'

Alan nodded his agreement.

'Frankly, it's been very difficult indeed, and I wonder whether we would have coped at all, had John not brought in help from HPM—'

'They plainly know what they're doing, don't they?' Alan needed to confirm this.

'Yes, that's right. It's no secret that John and Candice – and of course Peter Flower – have long favoured much closer links with them.'

'So what's Peter Flower's involvement with them?'

This was something Alan had never fully understood.

'John has been on their board since shortly after leaving

Cambridge and one of the first things he did was get Peter appointed as their historical advisor. He seemed to have an unrivalled knowledge of small projects.'

'Like White Delphs?' Alan added.

'Precisely. And there were many others, too, which they took on and built up. But they've always been careful not to kill-off local character, at the expense of some greater corporate identity.'

Alan decided to go for it. 'I know there was a board meeting this morning and I'm keen to find out what happened. You must understand, Barty, this isn't just idle curiosity: I feel I've become an integral part of the Fursey set-up,' he was searching for the right word. 'No, it's more to me than that: I'm talking about the Fursey *family* – because that's how it feels.'

Barty placed his hand on Alan's arm. 'Thank you, Alan, that means a lot.' He paused briefly. 'Well, we decided to contract the day-to-day running of Fursey Abbey to HPM. To be honest, it wasn't a difficult decision at all, as they're effectively doing it already.'

'And I can see it makes lots of practical sense: together the Abbey and White Delphs would attract a very diverse set of visitors to the area.'

'I agree, in hindsight it does. But that wasn't how Sebastian and Sarah saw it. They thought it would somehow cheapen the abbey's rather up-market image. And I have to admit I shared their concerns. So together the three of us were able to block any moves towards closer integration.'

'That sounds unfortunate.'

'How do you mean?'

Alan lowered his voice. He was surrounded by Cripps

family members. 'Surely, family splits are never easy to live with, are they?'

'Oh no.' Barty smiled. 'It was never like that. We knew why John and Candice felt as they did, and they could see why we didn't want to join them. But we all knew we'd come to some arrangement in time. Sarah played an important part. She could see that HPM knew what they were doing and were highly experienced. She also appreciated that they could lay their hands on capital. And all of these things matter if you're to run a successful visitor attraction.'

Alan also detected Barty's calming hand at work here.

'So you all think that it's time to hand the day-to-day management of Fursey over to them?'

'We do. And Blake has proved a huge success with the staff and volunteers here at Fursey.'

Alan had met Blake Lonsdale, HPM's very successful and hands-on CEO, who took an active role in the management of White Delphs. He remembered his matching suit and Bentley and had been immediately impressed by his manner. He could see that he knew what he was doing and where the company should be heading. He was a businessman to his fingertips. Alan also knew from the notice board at White Delphs that HPM's head offices were in east London, and the man himself had the stage Cockney's bright, humorous directness. Alan, like everyone else at Fursey, had been completely won over by him.

'They've certainly introduced a lot of practical improvements.'

'Yes,' Barty replied. 'And more to the point they can lay their hands on the capital sums needed, too. You'll be amazed by the improvements we'll be seeing in the next few weeks here.'

* * *

Alan was returning to the table from the buffet carrying a plate of venison casserole, when Candice called across.

'Come over here and sit with us, Alan.'

It was an instruction, not a request.

She moved one chair to the left and Alan sat down between her, John and Sarah. A few moments later Peter Flower took a seat on her other side. They began the main course with a few words of praise for the food. Alan had never really enjoyed venison, which was usually either too rich or too gamey, but this was superb.

'It's muntjac,' John told him. Recently muntjac deer had reached his brother Grahame's farm in the Lincolnshire fens, where they had decimated his vegetable garden in one night. Alan had always thought of them merely as a pest, but now he felt rather differently. Out of politeness he was about to ask Candice about the sauce, but noticed she was deep in conversation with Peter Flower. So he started to discuss the decision to bring in HPM to handle the day-to-day management at Fursey.

Before he could say anything, though, Sarah spoke. 'Aren't they delicious?' she said, pointing at the venison steaks.

'Yes, they are.' Alan took another mouthful. He was about to discuss the taste of the meat, but then he remembered: you must be more proactive, less observational. Move the conversation to them: 'Do they come from the estate?'

It was hardly the Spanish Inquisition, but it was a start. And it worked. Sort of.

'I'm trying to persuade Sebastian to start farming them. But he isn't too keen. Wants to grow things – which would be fine if prices weren't so unstable. I think it's essential to diversify. A few hundred muntjac in a purpose-built barn could well be the way forward. It wouldn't prevent him from growing oilseed rape or wheat, now, would it?'

John, and now Candice, were listening. Alan could see their sympathies were with Sarah, not her husband.

'And how do you feel about diversification?' Alan asked John.

'Well, actually,' he replied, 'when it comes to tourism, as opposed to farming, I'm more in favour of integration than diversification. Our long-term goal is to integrate the Abbey and White Delphs. That's the only way we will ever persuade visitors to spend a full weekend out here, at Fursey.'

'So you're planning a hotel as well?' Alan enquired.

'Yes, we're currently thinking about building an extension onto the Cripps Arms, but so far planning aren't being very helpful. They seem to think it would be out of character in a rural village.'

Alan didn't have much time for bureaucrats either, but for once he was glad they were there.

'I suppose that's only to be expected, isn't it?'

'And dear brother Sebastian also isn't being particularly helpful.' He took a long drink and refilled his glass. He lowered his voice, then continued: 'He's a councillor, dammit. You'd have thought he could use a bit of influence to help out the family.' Alan could see the wine was going to his head. 'But, no, he told Candice that for once he agrees with the planners.' He took another drink. 'Can't understand him. Just can't.' He sighed loudly. 'Ah well, that's brothers for you.'

The rest of the 'conversation' with John was one-sided and hard work. Why was Sebastian being so seemingly uncooperative? Candice would know. So he tried to intervene, but she remained deep in conversation with Flower. After a bit, Alan gave up the unequal struggle and helped himself to some more wine. What the hell – and he didn't have to drive home. He looked across the table. Frank Jones was discussing something very earnestly with Barty, who was looking slightly shell-shocked; at the other end Tricia was listening politely to Sebastian, but Alan could see by her fixed smile that she was being bored stiff. Then for a brief, charged moment their eyes met. Immediately they both looked away.

Alan was about to make another attempt to converse with John, when his idle gaze was caught by the two bottles of very unusual vintage port that stood alongside the decanters that now held their contents. The small labels on the back bore the very distinctive coat-of-arms of Fisher College, Cambridge.

* * *

Tricia was standing by the sideboard helping herself to home-made mulberry flan and ice cream. She leant close to Alan and whispered under her breath, 'Your turn, Alan.'

'OK,' he sighed resignedly, spooning thick clotted cream onto his slice of flan.

Deftly, Tricia handed Sebastian over to Alan, then made her escape.

'Alan, I'm so glad we've managed to catch up. I thought Candice's musical chairs would mean we'd pass like ships in the night.'

Alan smiled: he always enjoyed a good mixed metaphor.

Maybe with a few sharp nudges Sebastian could be tempted to reveal rather more than his wife or Candice. Alan framed a leading question, but Sebastian got in before he had a chance to speak.

'When I came round with the councillors on Saturday, you told us that the Roman layers continued out into the fen. That intrigued me because, as you know, Stan had told me something similar. So are you more convinced now that he was right?'

'Well, we haven't discovered anything new, if that's what you mean?'

'What, not even with those exciting new Libor images.'

Alan smiled. Sebastian had a unique way with words.

'No, and sadly we can't manipulate them either.'

The weak topical joke was for his own benefit entirely and Alan immediately felt slightly ashamed of himself. But he needn't have worried, it had passed Sebastian by completely.

'Really? You can't even enhance them?'

'Oh yes,' Alan said. 'We can do that sort of thing, but we can't get them to show anything that isn't actually above the surface of the ground. You mustn't confuse Lidar with geophysics – although lots of people do.'

'So the – what did you call it? – Lidar only works down to the edge of the fen?'

'Sort of. That's where we stop discovering new things. Once the alluvium and fen deposits get too thick, everything buried beneath them remains hidden.'

'And that's still the situation?'

Alan hesitated, but decided not to tell him about geophysics. He wanted Sebastian to speak, not himself. 'That's right.'

Sebastian thought this over. Then his face brightened up. 'Now tell me about the bodies,' he asked eagerly. 'What happens next?'

* * *

After the meal, the ladies withdrew and the gentlemen drank port. Alan couldn't believe that such things still happened, but secretly he rather enjoyed being a part of it – and the port was to die for. After less than half an hour John suggested that they rejoin the ladies. Alan could see he wasn't entirely at home acting like a Victorian country gent. And by then Alan, too, was starting to feel a little uncomfortable: it was *so* anachronistic; he felt they ought to have been wearing starched white collars and tailcoats.

When they entered the drawing room they discovered Tricia, Candice and Sarah sitting on two sofas in front of the huge fireplace, complete with their own bottle of port, plus a box of dark chocolate peppermint creams from Charbonnel et Walker. Alan smiled to himself: had he really expected Haribo?

'Alan, come over here.' Candice summoned him to her, for the second time that evening. 'And bring over a chair.'

Alan did as he was bid, and sat down opposite Candice and Tricia, each of whom had reclined decoratively at either end of the large sofa. There would have been space for two Alans between them. Tricia proffered Alan her glass.

'Do be a dear, Alan, I'm positively parched.'

She gave him a wonderful smile and he topped her glass up, pouring himself one in the process.

'Tell me, Alan,' Candice asked. 'How long do we have to wait before we know more about the bodies?'

For a second Alan couldn't believe his ears. This was like the worst blockbuster thriller, the murderer brazenly challenging his – or in this case – her investigator. But then he realised, of course, what they were talking about. The bones from the dig. And Harriet. He hoped his expression had not given away his thoughts.

'I've worked with Dr Webb before, and I can tell you, she really knows what she's doing, and when she gets going she works quite fast. It's all about confidence—'

'Oh, so you know her?' Tricia broke in.

'Yes, we worked on the same project almost two years ago.'

Despite the conviviality, the warm fire and the three glasses of port, Alan couldn't help blushing. He turned away to top-up his almost-full glass. He was now furious with himself.

* * *

Alan slipped away from the post-dinner drinks and somehow found his way upstairs to the bedroom Candice had shown him to earlier that evening. He thought he would have no trouble sleeping, but although his body felt tired, his mind continued to work. That question of Sebastian's worried him: 'So the Lidar only works down to the edge of the fen?' Was Sebastian trying to tell him something? Or were his words a thinly disguised warning: stay off my land if you know what's good for you? Or again, was he interested in what actually lay below the ground, but was ashamed to admit it? And then there was Candice: as friendly as ever, but this evening she seemed to have eyes for one man only. And it wasn't her husband. No, Peter Flower seemed to have his feet very comfortably under the table.

He looked at his phone to set the wake-up call, but saw the

battery was very low. So he turned it off. Time for Mother Nature's daylight alarm. He took off his clothes, turned off the light and made his way over to the window, where he pulled back the heavy, lined curtains. He eased the sash window down an inch or two and felt the cool night air fall lightly into the room. Outside it was clear, with a near-full moon, whose pale light was reflected back off the frosty lawns. Across the gardens the abbey ruins looked serene and timeless. For a lingering moment, Alan was captured by the beauty of the scene before him. Then suddenly he heard something in the room behind him.

He turned round and stared in horror as the door handle slowly turned. Suddenly he realised he was very scared. Could the person who had killed Stan now want him out of the way too? He took a step into the shadows of the hanging curtain and watched. But the slim figure who slipped silently into the room was not intent on malice. The moonlight was on the floor and back wall and did not illuminate the bed, as she tiptoed across the carpet towards it. For a second she paused, then she slipped off her dressing gown.

Tricia was standing in the moonlight, wearing nothing at all. Alan had never seen such a perfect figure.

* * *

Mother Nature's alarm did the trick and Alan was wide awake just before seven. Tricia lay snuggled up alongside him, her hair spread across the pillow. Alan looked down at her. Even without the heavy make-up she wore during filming, her delicate face was still very beautiful, in fact, Alan thought, even more beautiful without it.

The curtains moved, as outside a light breeze got up. Alan

could hear the faint sound of a powerful diesel as a tractor began its new working week somewhere in the fen, out Chatteris way. And he had to return to work, too. Reality was returning, and with it a sense of guilt, or was it shame? He felt as if he had betrayed Harriet – and himself. Or had he? Wasn't it she who wanted things between them to be 'professional' from now on? He looked at Tricia beside him. She stirred. His gaze moved from her face: her hands were beautiful too and she still wore a sparkly evening watch. Then the guilt returned – and lingered, as he knew it would. The tiny hands of the watch showed five to seven. Time to get going.

Quietly Alan reached up onto the bedside table and fumbled for his phone. He didn't want to wake her. He pressed the on switch and waited while it searched for a signal. A new text message flashed up, and Alan quickly selected it, as the battery warning light was now flashing. DCI Richard Lane had sent it at 5.08 this morning.

Alan just had time to read: *Phone me ASAP. Thorey found in river at Denver.*

Then the screen went dead.

# Part 3

## Facing the Dead

# Fifteen

Alan loved Denver Sluice. Its massive green-painted steel gates and wide embanked artificial channels were the ultimate symbol of man's prolonged and continuing struggle to dominate nature. This was engineering that made a real difference to people's lives: without Denver, not only would large areas of eastern England flood, but east London's water supply would fail and of course supermarkets right across Britain would rapidly run out of salad greens and vegetables, which were grown in their tens of thousands of tons in the southern Fenlands.

Denver was the complex of water-courses and sluices that regulated the outfall of the rivers of the Great Ouse system into the shallow waters of The Wash. It was all about retaining river flood water in huge collection areas, also known as washes, and then releasing them out to sea when the tides were low enough. If the floods coincided with a period of unusually high tides, as happened in springtime, the results could be catastrophic: like in 1947, when 10,000 homes were damaged, and 1953, when over 300 people died.

In its strange, open, unearthly way, Alan had always found Denver just as moving and spiritually uplifting as Ely Cathedral, which would revert to a remote island abbey if the great gates at Denver failed, and he could never come here without emotion. This vast landscape was so fragile: disaster lay in the strength of a sluice; one of the towers at Ely Cathedral had collapsed because the footings gave way. Fortunes had been made and lost on the rise or fall of water levels and not just in times of flood, either. The waters below the ground were even more crucial, as poor Sebastian had learnt to his cost. The land he farmed would always be second best and he would never be able to grow a crop that was really profitable: no salads, no vegetables, no cut flowers. For a moment Alan found himself sympathising: it must be so frustrating – and with the good land around Isle Farm, which the family had once owned, within sight. But that was the Fens for you: one dyke was all it took to separate the best from the merely second-rate.

On this unexpected visit to Denver, his natural respect for the place and all that it stood for, was enhanced by a feeling of profound concern. As he had driven along the Great Ouse itself, and over the banks of the many tributaries, dykes, delphs and engine drains that fed into it, he pondered what he would find when he met Lane. The body itself would probably have been removed, but the cause of death? Accidental? Probably – or at least, he thought, that's what it would seem. But the reality: what would that prove to be? By now he had no doubts at all: Thorey's death was more than one too many. And as for the Curse of the Cripps? Barty was wrong, it was far from over. It was being used. Someone was deliberately manipulating the superstitions to fuel the family's bad reputation. He was 100 per cent certain of that.

* * *

The uniformed sergeant took Alan's details, and entered them into the Scene of Crime log. Then they stepped out of the mobile unit and walked along the bank to the small sluice that managed day-to-day river flows in quiet weather. DCI Lane was waiting for him.

Before his friend could speak, Alan had to ask, 'Don't tell me, Richard, it was an accident?'

'No, Alan.' He smiled. 'For once you're wrong. I'm afraid it was suicide.'

'You don't say.' Alan was genuinely astonished. 'But Thorey was a big, loud-mouthed . . .' Suddenly he realised they were talking about a dead person. Some respect at least was needed.

'Yob?' Lane suggested with a quizzical look.

'Well, perhaps that's a bit strong. The thing is, I first met him at Stan's wake and he was extraordinarily rude to Candice: very self-assertive. I just don't see him as the kind of person with the sensitivity to take his own life.'

Briefly Alan had a strong sense of déjà vu. They'd had almost exactly the same conversation beside the Mill Cut when Stan had died.

'So you're suggesting somebody else stuffed his jacket pockets full of bricks and pushed him into the water? And don't forget, he was a big man. Just over six foot two.'

'Yes,' Alan had to admit. 'And he was fit, too. Most keepers are.'

'Trouble is,' Lane continued, 'we've pretty well pinned

down his disappearance to the evening of the thirteenth of January.'

Alan nodded, he too couldn't forget that date.

'And as you know, it's been quite a wet late winter. Decomposition isn't as advanced as it would be in August, but I got a phone call from the lab, who are doing a priority autopsy for us, and they suspect, but they can't yet confirm, that he died by drowning.'

Yes, Alan thought, it had been a while. They'd started the car park dig, done two documentaries and of course the live show, since then. It felt like an age. He closed his eyes and did a rapid mental count. It was now 7 March.

'So that's almost eight weeks.'

'Yes, it's a long time.'

They both reflected on this. Alan couldn't help thinking about the condition of Thorey's corpse: how it would have looked after so long in the water. And his mind's eye kept returning to the last dead body he had seen. It had been in a gruesome state. That gave him an idea.

'I suppose it's too early to say if he'd been drugged?'

'Yes,' Lane nodded. 'That'll probably take longer – if indeed they can tell at this late date. But I've got some pictures here.'

Lane's car was parked a few paces away. His laptop was on the back seat. He opened it on the bonnet. Alan didn't know what to expect, but he knew it would be grim. And it was.

The first image was a general view, showing the body lying on the grass where it had been laid out by the workman who was operating the mechanical grab that was fixed to the screens across the sluice. The grab operator had had the presence of mind to empty the rest of the cage separately alongside the skip. In the background Alan could see this small heap of debris and driftwood was being searched by two officers in white scene-of-crime overalls.

'They'll be there most of the day, poor devils.' Lane smiled. 'It's a thankless task.'

'Any other clues?' Alan asked.

'Hard to say,' Lane replied, pointing to the second image. This was not a pretty sight: a close-up of the body, skin largely removed from the head and neck, but still wearing his keeper's tweed Norfolk jacket and knee breeches and above-calf, stout lace-up leather boots. 'As you can see, he'd zipped up the jacket and buttoned all the pockets; he'd even stuffed more brick pieces inside the jacke—'

'Or someone had,' Alan broke in.

'OK,' Lane continued patiently. 'His jacket and its pockets were stuffed with brick pieces and it had been securely buttoned and zipped closed. There was no way those bricks were going to fall out.'

Alan nodded; he wished he could cancel his hasty remarks about suicide.

'Any idea how much they weighed?'

'We'll discover that soon enough, but I suspect somewhere around ten to fiften kilos.'

Alan recalled the 20-kilo feed bags he had struggled with as a lad on the family farm. That was quite a weight.

'What were the bricks like?'

'Nothing special. SOCO reckoned they were modern, mass-produced. The sort of thing you'd find on a building site anywhere. But we'll be getting them analysed. My bet is they're London Brick Company, Peterborough or Bedford.'

Alan had learnt to respect the judgment and experience of scene of crime officers.

'And was it just bricks, or were there stones and other things there, too?'

'No,' Lane replied, clicking to the next image of five pieces of brick arranged on a folded disposable cover-all. 'That's what struck me at the time. It was just brickbats, nothing else. It all suggested cold-blooded preparation. The bricks had probably been broken with a lump-hammer and sharp bits had been knocked off. It's almost as if he'd done a dress rehearsal to get the maximum number in each pocket.'

Alan's mind immediately flashed back to Stan's death.

'Was he drunk?'

'He's been a long time in the water, so forensics were very dubious. But of course they'll check.'

'And what about the rest of the body?'

'Decay was quite advanced and there was a lot of obvious bruising and battering. The skin beneath his clothes wasn't as badly decayed and damaged as his face and neck. And he probably went through several sluices before fetching up here.' Lane paused while he selected another picture.

'But there was one injury that puzzled me,' Lane continued. The screen now showed a close-up of Thorey's tweed knee breeches and the pale, mangled flesh beneath. The fabric over one leg, Alan reckoned his right, had been torn in a jagged line just above the knee. 'You can see that whatever did this tore the fabric on both sides of the leg. And the flesh at that point was cut and damaged. Trouble is, it has also been nibbled by fish or eels. Anyhow, SOCO reckoned it was the sort of injury he'd seen previously when bodies got limbs stuck in those grilles that protect power stations or sewage outfalls – that sort of thing.'

'And do you agree?'

'I don't know. But it seems reasonable enough. We'll see what forensics think later.' His radio bleeped. Lane put a hand up to his earpiece. 'Sorry, Alan, I'm needed back at base.' He closed the laptop and put it away.

As he was about to drive off he asked, 'Fancy a quick pint later? I've found a great little pub in Ely. I worked through the weekend, so I'm off early today.'

Alan remembered it was Monday. Tricia had already returned to London for more meetings about her new TV series. Slightly to his own surprise he felt glad she was doing this: it was so obviously what she really wanted to do. But there was also a feeling of regret, if not pain. She had sent him a text saying 'Thanks for a fun night' and apparently that was it. She was so refreshingly straightforward, and Alan was aware that he was anything but. He caught a glimpse of his face in a pool by the river's edge. He was looking serious: we are drawn to our opposites.

Lane's voice broke into his thoughts. 'Is that a yes, Alan?'

Alan grinned. 'Sorry, Richard, I was away with the fairies. Yes, that's a great idea; I could murder a pint.'

He was in absolutely no rush to return to Fursey and face Harriet.

* * *

Alan headed back south, across a couple of miles of open flat fen, towards one of the low ridges that extend north from the much higher Isle of Ely. After a quarter of an hour he arrived in Ely. He didn't often find himself with time to kill, but now he decided to park the Fourtrak in one of the little medieval streets down by the river and take a stroll up the hill, through the Priors Gatehouse and into the old monastic precincts. The first view of the great Benedictine Abbey Church, which had dominated the small town around it for over a thousand years, never failed to move him. And this visit was no exception.

As he passed beneath the gatehouse and drew clear of the buildings, he deliberately didn't look up. Instead he walked over to the fence that bounded the rough pasture, which now covered many of the monastic buildings that were demolished after the Dissolution. He could hear the sound of sheep grazing close by and could detect their warm, lanolin presence, but he kept his eyes firmly to the ground. Then he looked up. As his focus lifted towards the park and its trees, some just coming into leaf, he found his gaze was following the edge of a patch of sunlight, which rapidly expanded to bathe the scene before him in a glow of spring brightness. Soon he felt the warmth on his own back: a hint of the season to come. The air was crystal clear and the great south tower of the massive cathedral stood out pale against the scudding clouds. It was a transcending experience. For a brief, wonderful moment, time itself seemed suspended. Then he noticed that the sky above the cathedral was identical to the opening sequences of *The Simpsons.* The magic vanished.

The pub was back down the hill by the river, and even though it was still very early in the year, people were sitting at tables outside. Alan went inside to order a couple of pints. Several people recognised him and there were a few calls of 'Itsagrave!' He hastened back outside with two glasses of Old

Slodger and had barely sat back down at his table, when he spotted Lane coming towards him.

If they'd been meeting in a Leicester pub three years ago, the chances were that one or two people would have recognised Lane. Alan had learnt to spot the one's Lane had nicked in the past: they smiled at him in a particularly subservient, ingratiating fashion and then acted the wronged criminal to their friends, but only behind his back. Here, however, he was still just a bloke in the crowd. Alan rather envied him this.

Alan handed Lane his pint, which he gratefully received.

'Well,' Lane said, as he placed his glass back on the table with a contented sigh. 'That wasn't unexpected, was it?'

'No.' Alan immediately knew he was referring to Thorey. 'Not after he'd vanished. But I'll be interested to see what happens next.'

'How d'you mean?'

'Whether it restarts all that bollocks about the Curse of the Cripps. Because if it does, I think this is deliberate. Using the rumours to build up bad feeling against the family.'

'Interesting you should say that. The desk sergeant at Ely has told me he's already received anonymous calls suggesting that we "look more closely", or some such.'

'I wish I could say I was surprised.'

'That's not all,' Lane continued. 'In fact, as I drove here, I got a call from a reporter from the *Enquirer*, who wondered if there was any truth in the "rumours" about a possible murder. Reports of his death have already been on local radio and will be on all the regional lunchtime TV bulletins.'

'So it's big news?'

Lane leant back and stretched. ‘I don’t know about that, Alan. Maybe locally. But it certainly won’t make the nationals.’

‘That’s a relief. I feel for the Cripps family. They’ve put a lot of time and effort into the project and it would be a shame if—’

‘Oh, don’t worry about that,’ Lane broke in. ‘It won’t make people stay away. Far from it. If anything, it’ll bring them in.’

But that wasn’t what Alan wanted to hear, either. It was bad enough having to deal with ‘Itsagrave’ and thinly disguised questions about death and decay, without introducing ancient curses. Before they knew it, they’d have vampires and werewolves to contend with.

Lane took a second long pull from his pint. Alan could see his friend was very tired.

‘So tell me, Alan,’ Lane’s voice came as welcome relief, ‘what’s been happening behind the scenes at Fursey?’

Alan told him about Heritage Projects Management, led by John Cripps, taking on the day-to-day running of Fursey – and how it made sense, which it undoubtedly did – to pool publicity budgets and run Fursey and White Delphs together. When he had finished, Lane thought over what he’d just been told.

‘That’s very interesting,’ Lane reflected. ‘I don’t know whether you ever knew, but when HPM took over at White Delphs there was a rumour that they were just a cover for a property developer based in London. They were known to have loads of spare cash and we all thought they’d buy acres of land and then apply for development rights. That way it would be win-win for them: they’d attract more visitors to the area and the attraction – and of course they’d make a killing on the property deal.’

Alan was puzzled. These stories had escaped him entirely. 'But did it happen?' He asked, still slightly astonished.

'No, it didn't. And that's the point. Instead, they invested heavily in the attraction and even put a largish sum into the new Community Centre. In fact, they're very popular locally.'

'Yes,' Alan said. 'And with their workforce, too. I took their digging team on as soon as the White Delphs dig ended, and none of them would hear a word said against HPM.'

'Really?' Lane continued, smiling now. 'It's not very often that I get to deal with paragons of virtue in my line of work. Who's the man behind it all?'

'I met him on my first visit to White Delphs. Drove a flash Bentley. We didn't have an in-depth conversation, but I got the strong impression he was no fool. Name's Blake Lonsdale. I gather he's a successful east London businessman. Certainly John Cripps thinks highly of him. Sarah Cripps, too, so far as I can tell.'

'Any idea of his "business"?'

'I don't know how he made his money originally, but now he manages Water World historical theme park near Hackney Marshes. It's getting really big now that the 2012 Olympic Park is gathering pace. They're just down the road.'

'But you still don't know how he earned it in the first place?'

Alan shook his head.

'Can't say I do. But Barty told me he was the biggest investor by far in HPM – which is unusual, seeing as how he runs them, too.'

Alan was intrigued: why was Lane so interested all of a sudden? He tried fishing. 'Why the questions about HPM? Do you suspect something's going on?'

'No, not really. It's just that I'm – how can I put it discreetly – interested in large sums, or potentially large sums, of investment money coming into the area.'

'Something to do with your new job with Fenland?'

'Yes, sort of. The thing is, as you know, Cambridge is the fastest-growing city in Britain and development land is very hard to come by. Prices are sky-rocketing. So far, most of the development has been to the south, east and west.'

'On the higher, drier land, presumably?'

'That's right. But recently there's been much talk of "Silicon Fen" and many developers are now looking around here. And some of them have got very big wallets – and backers – indeed.'

'So the police are worried about corruption?'

'Well, wouldn't you be?' Lane was now leaning forward, talking very softly. 'There's billions involved and local politicians could set themselves up for life with just a small backhander.'

'And do you have anything to go on yet?'

'I've got one or two likely looking cases starting to grow, but these are much closer to Cambridge. Part of my brief is to keep an eye on what's happening around here, too. The one thing a police authority doesn't want is to be taken off-guard. If I'm nosing around, however incompetently, they can tell their political bosses that everything's under control.'

'So will you be checking out HPM and Blake Lonsdale?'

'Oh, yes, don't worry. I've got an old friend who's a DC down in Hackney. If there's anything to turn up, he'll find it.'

'But do you smell any rats around Fursey?' Alan had to ask.

'So far I don't. In fact, it smells very clean—'

'*Too* clean?'

'No, Alan.' Lane laughed. 'I never said that, and you know it.'

* * *

Back in his house in Fursey, Alan poured himself a strong black coffee and opened a packet of chocolate digestives. He'd already started to work on Stan's hidden notebook, but hadn't made much actual progress with interpretation, although he had managed to disentangle some of the initial, upland layers and levels. But now he was far more interested in what lay around the fringes of the drowned prehistoric and medieval island. And that meant trying to make sense of the borehole logs.

A search on the Internet had produced location maps of all dykes maintained by the various Internal Drainage Boards of the Fens. Alan clicked on the Padnal Delph IDB, and stared closely at the map. The drains leading into the South Padnal Engine Drain formed a distinctive Y shape, with a long, curved dyke to the south, which skirted the edge of Fursey island and fed directly into the dead straight Engine Drain which headed north for a mile or so to Padnal Pumping Station Number Two. This was the pump that raised their water into the embanked Padnal Delph. It was a very distinctive drainage pattern and it precisely matched what Stan had sketched in the back of his notebook.

Alan's next job was to copy Stan's sketches onto the large sheet of graph paper he'd bought the week before the live shoot. He arranged them around a horizontal datum line, or TBM (temporary benchmark), precisely as Stan had done in the notebooks. He'd be able to level-in the benchmark, which was on a disused 1950s sluice gate, when he could find an hour or two to spare. Just glancing at the profiles, Alan reckoned that Stan had set his TBM somewhere around half a metre above sea level, or OD (Ordnance Datum), as the notebook had it.

By four o'clock he'd done about a dozen profiles and couldn't face another coffee. He needed fresh air. He knew he ought to have gone to the dig that afternoon, as it was the start of a crucial week, but he was certain that Stan's notebook held the clue to his death, and they were also becoming increasingly relevant to the latest discoveries at Fursey itself. But he had to admit they were an excuse not to visit the dig. He stared up at the ceiling, then took a deep breath, he was behaving like a gutless worm. Not turning up would only make matters between him and Harriet worse.

When he entered the shelter, he found Jake and Kaylee starting to clear up. Harriet wasn't there.

Alan asked after her: had she been there at all, today?

'Oh yes,' Jake replied. 'She was here all day. Said she had to get back promptly for a college commemoration feast or something.'

'Damn, I wanted to catch her before she left. Any news?'

'Not really. She said Grave 2 is almost exposed. She should start lifting tomorrow.'

Alan was impressed. He was also glad that Jake had been there. He felt he owed him a word of explanation for his absence.

'The thing is, I thought I was going to get down here first thing, as usual, but I got a text this morning and had to see someone at County Hall ASAP. I've only just got back.'

'Yes.' Jake smiled. 'She said you'd probably not show up. Candice had told her how much booze they were providing for the dinner. Apparently she had said it was the least they could do, after all you'd done.' By now Alan was frowning. 'I think Harry thought it a bit of a laugh,' he added, by way of explanation.

Alan tried a smile; he knew that wouldn't be the case. But his mind was still working overtime: did she really think that booze was the reason he hadn't turned up? Or did she guess that her words had hit a nerve? When they had last worked together, Alan had come to respect Harriet's powers of deduction – and even more her intuition.

* * *

Alan stayed on to help clear up, then made his way back to his cottage with a heavy heart. He was sure Harriet had guessed the truth about Tricia. He paused at the end of the Fursey drive to let a huge John Deere tractor pass, with lights flashing, rubber tracks and a vast Danish seed-drill behind. Somebody's getting their spring barley in early, he thought. As his eyes followed the tractor down the village street towards Littleport, he noticed the pub was open. That's what I need. A pint of Slodger – and to hell with women. Suddenly he felt less tired.

He was expecting to be greeted with cries of 'Itsagrave!', but it didn't happen. At the bar, the two Hibbs brothers, Davey and Sam, were having a quiet drink together. Alan joined them. The discovery of Joe Thorey's body was mentioned, but respectfully. Then they discussed other topics: the price of wheat, the weather, football, the impending Olympics – things that mattered. It was very relaxed and friendly. The beer was going down well, too.

Halfway through Alan's second pint Sam asked Davey. 'I thought your new job was meant to start today?'

Suddenly Alan felt concerned: Davey had been his machine driver and he was relying on him to do some more work.

'No, they had trouble with Cripps's agent: he wouldn't give them way leaves. But the office phoned this afternoon. It's all sorted.'

'So you start tomorrow?' Sam asked.

'A long contract?' Alan asked.

'It's with the IDB, so it'll probably last a couple of months.'

Alan always liked to keep an eye on the IDB's dyke maintenance. Freshly scraped dykeside were the only way to get a clear idea of what lay far beneath the surface, well beyond the reach of most geophysics.

'Do you know where you'll be working, Davey?'

'If I told you, you'd be down there like a shot. I know you archaeologist blokes. Too curious by far!'

This was said with a huge grin. Davey and Alan had worked very well together. It was one of those easy-going relationships where differences in education were irrelevant and where respect was earned, not assumed.

'I suppose you're right,' Alan replied. 'But seriously, d'you know where you'll be working?'

'Course I do. We'll be starting in the Padnal Engine Drain, by that big running silt we thought we'd fixed last year. Your mate Stan was always visiting.'

Alan knew precisely where he meant. The Lidar had showed the ridge of a large rodden crossing the fen quite close to the abandoned sluice gate, that Stan had used for his TBM (temporary benchmark) in the notebook. Roddens, or rodhams, were the remains of pre-Roman tidal creeks, many of which still ran with water in wet seasons. This water took the form of 'running silts' which could destabilise and undermine dykesides, often causing a landslip, or in severe cases, the blocking of the entire drain. Today, some IDBs held back running silts with porous geo-textiles; but the traditional way was to make bundles of hawthorn branches and pack these fascines into the dykesides, where they acted as pipes-cum-filters.

'What happened?' Alan was curious.

'Matt said they'd used the wrong grade of textile. Not porous enough. So this year it's back to bundles.'

Alan smiled. He'd met Matt Grimshaw, Padnal Delph IDB's chief engineer, before. He was hands-on and very conservative. Alan could imagine his delight when the new technique had failed.

'Can't think why they changed.'

'Money,' the two brothers said in almost perfect unison.

Then Davey added, 'The Board reckoned it was cheaper to try the modern way. But it didn't work.'

Alan had a thought. If he was going to follow up Stan's work, he'd need permission to visit and sample IDB dykes.

'Will Matt be there tomorrow?'

'Yes, at seven sharp. We've got to shift that old sluice gate. It's messing up the new profile.'

Suddenly Alan was galvanised. That sluice carried the TBM and without it, he would never understand the levels in Stan's notebooks. He had to level it into the Ordnance Survey benchmark at the pumping station. Put simply, if he didn't get an accurate level on the TBM, all the work Stan had done would be useless. Laying aside the question of the motive behind Stan's killing, Alan owed it to his old friend not to see all that work made irrelevant – because that's what would happen if they lost that TBM on the old wooden sluice gate. He decided not to have a third pint. He had to be on top form tomorrow.

* * *

The following morning Alan decided to drive round to the pumping station rather than trudge across the fields, especially given the rain of the night before. The portentously named Padnal Pumping Station Number Two looked remarkably like Padnal Pumping Station Number One, which Alan could see from off the Fursey-Chatteris road. The building had a cast concrete date stone with the legend 'PDIDB Padnal Pumping Station No. 2 1957'. Presumably, Alan thought, this was where the new electric pumps were installed, but like most IDBs, they had kept the older, 1930s diesel pumps as a back-up and they were housed in a slightly smaller building alongside. This building had a tell-tale massive exhaust pipe protruding from one side. Behind both buildings, and at a slightly lower level, were the mould-made bricks of the wall footings of the Victorian steam pumping house. He was about to start looking for traces of the original windmill scoop-pump, when someone called out his name.

It was Matt Grimshaw, chief engineer, complete with a folder of papers and an assistant who was carrying an expensive, state-of-the-art GPS total station down to the dykeside below the high Delph banks.

'Young Davey Hibbs phoned me last night. Said you might be here.'

Typical of Davey, Alan thought: always considerate. They shook hands.

'Been working out the sequence?' Matt asked.

Like many engineers in the Fens, he had a profound interest in the history of Fenland drainage. Alan was familiar with a couple of papers he had written for the 'Notes and News' section of the county archaeological journal. He knew his stuff.

'Yes.' Alan smiled. He pointed to the early wall footings. 'That, I presume, is the Victorian beam-engine house, but where were the earlier windmills?'

Matt stamped his foot. 'Beneath us. They demolished them in 1938 when the Delph bank was raised. I've got photos back at the office.'

They stepped to one side as the IDB's large Swedish Ackerman excavator tracked by, driven by Davey, who greeted them with a cheery wave. But he was concentrating hard, as the digger's wide bog-crawler tracks were protruding a foot or so over the edge of the gravel roadway beside the Engine Drain. The digger's bucket and long-reach dipper had been replaced with a heavy-duty hook and chain. Alan knew what that was for.

'Matt, I've got to check for a temporary benchmark on the sluice gate. It was put there over a year ago by my colleague Stan Beaton—'

'Oh yes,' Grimshaw broke in. 'That was sad news. Terrible, really.' He shook his head. Alan could see he was genuinely upset.

'Yes, dear old Stan. Everyone liked him. Didn't have an enemy anywhere.'

'No, not anywhere . . .' Alan agreed softly, with just the slightest hint of a question.

Again, Grimshaw shook his greying head. Alan waited.

Nothing. It was worth a try. Rapidly he resumed. 'When Stan was working down this dyke last summer, he drew up a series of dyke profiles and tied them all into a single TBM—'

'That's right, he told me, it's on the sluice gate – but didn't he level it in?' Matt sounded genuinely surprised.

'No,' Alan replied. 'I don't think so. At least it certainly didn't find its way into his notebook.' Suddenly a thought came to him. 'Why, did he ask where the OS datum point was?'

'Yes, he did.'

'So he intended to come back and level his TBM in?'

'Yes. But we had a better idea.'

'Really?' Alan was intrigued.

'That's because the old Ordnance Survey benchmark had gone when we repaired the foundations here three years ago. Early last year the OS people came down and surveyed in another one, but it's round the front, down there.'

As he spoke, Matt pointed down to an engineering brick stub wall, just above the double pump inlet sluice. Alan peered at it: he could just see a metal plaque with the distinctive arrow benchmark.

'Anyhow,' Matt continued, 'we used it to transfer a level to the sluice gate for him. We were working here, so it was no extra work to do it. And he was such a nice bloke. It was the least we could do.'

'Oh well,' Alan sighed. 'I'm afraid it doesn't seem to have survived.' He paused, deep in thought. If the crucial TBM had been levelled in, surely he would have found the information somewhere? It certainly wasn't something a professional like Stan would mislay. So had it been removed? And if so, by whom?

Matt broke into his thoughts. 'Well, don't worry.' Suddenly he was more businesslike. 'That's easily rectified.'

By now Matt's assistant, Dave, had set up the GPS. A few minutes later he looked up from the instrument, and called across the Engine Drain from almost a hundred yards away. 'Minus zero point four seven!'

'Blimey, that's high!'

Alan had expected a level at least half a metre below that. It meant that the archaeological levels around the edges of Fursey island would extend far further out into the surrounding fen than he'd originally expected. Stan would have been astonished too.

Matt shouted back. 'Please check that, Dave.'

There was a short pause while his assistant went back to the instrument. Then he looked up. 'Same result: zero point four seven. That's below OD,' he added to make himself clear.

'Thanks, Dave!' Alan shouted back, giving him a thumbs up.

Meanwhile Matt was helping Davey attach the chains to the steel framework of the old sluice.

'Hope that level's OK, Alan,' he called over his shoulder.

'A bit higher than I'd expected.'

Alan was gazing across the peaty fields surrounding them. He now knew there was far more archaeology beneath their surfaces than anyone could possibly have imagined, even five years ago. It was great news for archaeologists, but other people – farmers, landowners, developers, for example – would be less than delighted.

'Yes, I could see that from your face. But I'm sure it's accurate. Dave's very good on the GPS – and it wasn't a long traverse.' He paused briefly to check the final position of the chains. 'Right, Davey, my friend, time we got this old lady out of the way.'

He nodded at Davey who had returned to the excavator. He tweaked the throttle lever, to the right of the driver's seat. Alan expected to hear the revs roar, but there was only a small puff of smoke and a very slight noise as the huge machine effortlessly pulled the old sluice gate, still embedded in its concrete footings, bodily from the mud of the fen. It was almost too easy; an anticlimax. Alan glanced up. The sun was now well above the horizon and an old grey heron was surveying them quizzically from 50 yards away. At the far end of the field across the dyke, Alan could see a tractor with a set of rolls turn in through the gate. A Land Rover followed it. A large man got out and shut the gate. Then suddenly his attention was reclaimed by a loud splash and gurgle as the gate swung clear of the ground. Pieces of reed and lumps of peat dropped into the clear waters of the Engine Drain.

As he headed back to the pumping station, Alan couldn't help thinking that they'd nearly lost that TBM. No wonder Stan had been so excited when they'd last met. Those levels were very much higher than anyone could have supposed. Even the Royal Geographical Society's 1970 survey couldn't have predicted they'd find Roman occupation at just a gnat's above OD. He sighed heavily: it had been a close-run thing. For a few satisfying moments, he let relief take over. He felt better. Much calmer. More relaxed – even a bit complacent. But these were not emotions he was very familiar with. In fact, they were so strange, he began to wonder why his subconscious should regard something as relatively trivial as a lost benchmark so important?

Then he realised. It was all about credibility and authority.

Had the levels in Stan's notebooks been a bit hit-and-miss, they wouldn't be so significant. The fact was, they were tied in to an OS benchmark and the TBM had been on a known and fixed point in the open fen. So there could be no possible argument about it: those levels were absolutely accurate and could be validated by anyone. They proved beyond any possible doubt that there were extensive and superbly well-preserved, waterlogged ancient remains in the depths of this fen. More to the point, Alan reflected, their significance was not lost on someone. And that someone was worried. Scared even – but enough to commit murder? Quite possibly. But who – and why?

As he climbed into the Fourtrak, Alan was suddenly overtaken by a feeling of dread. He knew he wasn't on top of this case. He was aware that things were happening and that people out there were being driven by powerful motives. All his instincts told him, too, that the pace was about to hot up. But this time, he thought, I'll be ready and waiting.

# Sixteen

Alan was still thinking about those high benchmark levels, as he drove away from the pumping station and headed left back towards Fursey. As he came up onto the island, he noticed that the grass was starting to acquire that lush, early spring green and some trees, especially the older limes, were just coming into leaf. Then the sun came out. He found he was feeling very peckish so he wound down his window and eased the Fourtrak into a field entrance. Time for a mug of coffee and a bite of breakfast (a ham roll bought in the pub the previous evening). It was a fabulous early spring day. In the distance he thought he heard the bleating of young lambs, between, that is, the noise of passing cars on the road beside him. He glanced down at his watch: 8.50. Late-running commuters were hurtling through the village on their way to Ely and Cambridge. He took a long drink of coffee. Then his eye was caught by a familiar Mini Cooper, but unlike the others, it was heading into the village. Alan recognised it at once: it was Harriet. Guiltily he finished his coffee and wolfed down his roll.

As he drove up the avenue towards the abbey, his stomach started to gurgle. Of course he knew why Harriet's passing had made him gobble down his makeshift breakfast. And yes, he had to admit, he did feel guilty. He knew he'd been disloyal: disloyal to her and to himself, too. He still couldn't admit it, but he was slowly becoming aware of the depths of his own feelings for Harriet. And they put him in a weak, Subservient position – something he wasn't used to, and was finding hard to accept.

Deliberately, he drew up on the opposite side of the car park to the Mini Cooper. He went round to the back and took out his toolbox, camera case and waterproof. As he slammed the door shut and turned the key in the lock, he was being overtaken by a very different emotion – his mother would have called it 'your stubborn side, Alan'. Dammit, he thought, she's not my boss. It's the other way around. I'm the one supposed to be in charge around here.

He headed straight down to the dig. He knew that Harriet would be at the cafeteria. She couldn't function without an early coffee. And he was right. Jake and Kaylee had just arrived and were pulling the last plastic sheets off the trench surface. A few moments later, Harriet joined them, mug of coffee in hand.

'Morning, everyone,' she said as she lifted the shelter flap to one side. She was carrying several empty finds trays, all neatly labelled and ready to receive bones. She put them on the ground, then stepped down into the trench. While she was doing this, Alan picked up the trays and carried them across to Grave 2. As she approached, he handed her the coffee she had left in the top tray.

'Thanks, Alan,' she said as she took a sip. 'Ah, that's better. Very much better.'

By now Jake had joined them. 'Will you want me to be your clerical assistant, Dr Webb?'

Jake was smiling broadly as he spoke. He was also brandishing a Sharpie felt-tip pen and a roll of self-seal plastic bags.

'I think so, Jake,' she replied with joke formality. 'If you can remember what we did for Grave 1, we might as well repeat the procedure for Grave 2.'

'Right, ma'am.' Jake tugged his forelock, then up-ended a wheelbarrow and sat on it.

Alan looked on. He wished he could be a part of the scene before him. He'd give anything to be Harry's 'clerical assistant', right now. But it wasn't to be. And that wasn't just because he was dig director, either. Frankly, he didn't feel he was worthy to be sitting down there on that barrow.

'Must get on,' Alan said quietly, and slipped away.

But Jake and Harriet didn't notice; they clearly had other, far more important things to think about.

* * *

The following morning, as Alan arrived in the car park, a clean hire car (experience had taught Alan to recognise them a mile off), driven by Frank, the *Test Pit Challenge* director, drew up alongside him. Behind them was an unfamiliar crew van. Frank lowered the passenger window and leant across to speak to Alan.

'Sorry, Alan, didn't have time to tell you, but Lew wants us to spend a day on-site getting cut-aways and GVs for the main doc crew, who'll be coming here later. He was worried in case we missed the lifting of the bones. I hope Harriet hasn't finished, has she?'

Cut-aways and general views would be used either as illustrations, or to conceal edit cuts in longer sequences of the main film.

'No, she hasn't, but you'd better get a move on, I don't think there'll be many bones left in Grave 2 by the end of the day.' He paused. 'And then she's got to start exposing Grave 3.'

'OK, that's fine. We won't bother you and will try not to get in the way. Speed and Grump are on another job in Norway, I believe. So we've hired some local stringers.'

Alan went straight down to the dig. Better warn people there'd be a crew lurking around the place today. Jake raised his eyes to the roof, Kaylee smiled broadly and Harriet said nothing.

To Alan's immense relief, as deadlines were now starting to loom, Frank lived up to his word, and nobody was really aware of his, or the TV crew's, presence.

After morning tea break, the cameraman had finished his close-up filming of the lifting and was now at the back of the shelter getting GVs of the dig. Alan was becoming increasingly desperate to break through the layer of professionalism that seemed to cocoon Harriet from him, and seemingly from nobody else. It would be nice, he thought, if she could treat me like Jake, or even like Kaylee. It was as if Harriet had read his mind.

'Fancy a chance to redeem yourself, Alan?' she said with a smile. 'Jake's busy with context checks and finds' level and I need a man I can trust.'

Alan took the Sharpie and the plastic bags that she held out to him. A peace offering, of sorts.

Shortly before noon, Alan looked up from the list he was compiling as Harriet carefully removed some of the many bones of the left hand, one by one. It was a meticulous process and they were chatting quietly about what they were doing as they worked. He glanced at the cameraman who was standing by the shelter flap and noticed there was something odd. The normal lens for GVs in the shelter was quite short and fat – the equivalent of a 35mm on a SLR. But this time the camera was fitted with something much longer. Frank was leaning close to the cameraman, whispering in his ear, while clearly pointing down to Alan and Harriet. Suddenly Alan realised what was going on, and a sharp wave of anger overtook him.

'Frank,' he shouted. 'That's a close-up lens. Are you fucking filming us?'

Of course Frank protested his innocence and said they were only getting GVs, but they both knew he was lying through his teeth. He was up to his old US-style 'reality' tricks again. Immediately Alan phoned Weinstein, who promised to check through Frank's rushes as soon as they returned to London.

Alan was slightly mollified, but only slightly. Eventually Weinstein convinced him that no harm had been done. And at least he had been able to show Harriet that he wasn't completely buying into the media circus.

* * *

As always, it had taken rather longer to excavate the three skeletons and remove them from the ground than they had originally intended, but by the start of the third week in March Harriet had returned to her lab in Cambridge. Meanwhile, the team at Fursey had been augmented by three new diggers, who had just finished working for the university unit on the long-running Castle Hill excavations in Cambridge. They were making good progress, but there was no way they'd be finished in time for the opening ceremony of the new visitor centre and museum at Easter. So the temporary car park would continue to be in use, as before.

Alan had tried to phone Tricia a couple of times, but her phone was always turned off. Presumably, he thought, she must be filming. Eventually she did make contact by email and he was right: filming had started, as their executive producer had managed to raise money from a large foundation in the States. Excitedly she told him that it was going out live every day on 2-Much. Alan even caught an episode: the programme was terrible, although Tricia looked good – and very pretty. As he watched her on his cheap TV at home, Alan realised he was looking at her much as he would a gorgeous fashion model on the catwalk. She had become commoditised; she was now an item, not a person. Strangely, he found he accepted this, largely because she probably did, too. Of course, he couldn't be absolutely certain, but there was no hint of regret in her voice as she told him about their immediate plans. All he could detect was enthusiasm for the future, rather than regret for the past. They were about to head over to Ireland for three weeks filming in and around Dublin. So presumably, Alan thought, the programme's main theme had changed, as he wasn't aware there were many Roman women, let alone Romans, across the Irish Sea. They must have found yet another sponsor.

* * *

To Alan's surprise, the following day the Irish theme was repeated. It was the last Monday morning in March and Alan returned to the site after a rare weekend off for him and the other excavators. The visitors hadn't liked it, but the team had been getting very tired, as the split-shift system they'd been working hadn't proved a great success.

The two-day break, however, was a success and morale was high. People were returning to the trenches carrying their tools and equipment for the day, when they were stopped dead in their tracks by Kaylee's cry. She didn't so much call out as squeak.

Everyone stood still. Kaylee had lifted up the piece of plastic sheeting that covered the empty Grave 2. Beneath it was a wilted bunch of something that looked like clover, plus four red roses. A liquid had been poured over the flowers and it stained the grave floor beneath. Kaylee touched it, then sniffed her fingers.

'Smells like wine to me.'

There was a note tied to the bunch of wilted leaves. She read it out. '*Shamrock from Holy Ireland. Picked 17 March*'.

'Bloody Hell,' Alan said softly, 'That's St Patrick's Day. Looks like we've been visited by a bunch of religious nutters.'

'Makes a change from the New Agers,' Jake muttered, as he looked down.

Like Alan, he, too, had worked on henge sites where they'd arrive in on Monday mornings to find little gifts to the 'gods', and mini-shrines placed quite openly out in the trenches and on spoil heaps. But they only got truly annoyed by burnt offerings, as these could contaminate radiocarbon dates.

In general, Alan tended to be relaxed about such things.

OK, he thought they were stupid irritations, but at the same time they were fairly harmless. But this time, despite his dismissal of the hysteria surrounding the Cripps Curse, this felt more focused. The timing was more than coincidental and all his instincts told him it wasn't spontaneous. Someone was behind it.

* * *

Two days later, Alan found himself sitting on the monks' night stairs on the southern side of the church ruins. The cloister and most of the other monastic buildings had been completely robbed after the Dissolution, but this part of Fursey Abbey had survived quite well. It was a peaceful spot where Alan often came during his lunch break to enjoy the increasing warmth of the spring sunshine. As he munched on a homemade pork pie he'd bought at the village butcher's, he was startled to see Candice hurrying by carrying a full black bin liner. She saw Alan.

'Morning, Candice,' he called out. 'You're looking a bit flustered?'

She stopped. He could see she wanted to talk.

'It's these blinking offerings that people feel they must leave behind.'

She held the bag open and Alan peered in. There were several home-made palm-leaf and twig crosses, and many faded flowers, some with stems wrapped in tinfoil. At the top lay what Alan now recognised as a bunch of shamrock.

'Ah, shamrock . . .' He pulled it out. 'We had a bunch like this placed in a grave in Trench 2, on Monday. Must have been left there over the weekend, when we'd all left site.'

He'd almost said 'by a loony', but remembered that her husband John was a devout Christian.

'Oh, I'm sorry. We should have kept a closer watch—'

'No, don't worry about it. These things do happen. But the Irish thing's a bit odd, isn't it? I mean, it's not like we're near Dublin.'

'You're right. And the abbey was inspired by the Rule of St Benedict, not St Patrick.'

'So you've found more than one, have you?'

'Yes,' she paused. 'Yes, we have. Of course we've always had one or two offerings placed on the altar stone and sometimes people ask if they can do it. Often it's when a child dies. So we always say yes.' She shrugged. 'It's the least we can do, really.'

'But the shamrock, when did that start?'

'Very recently. In fact, the number of offerings has increased massively over the past month. And the shamrock started appearing at about the same time.'

'What, from the first week in March?'

'Yes.' She frowned, trying to recall. 'About then, but certainly no earlier. Everyone here has put it down to the increased visitor numbers and the television. I suppose you could see it as the downside of popularity.'

'It's better than bombs, I suppose.'

She laughed. 'Quite. But John reckons the shamrock is all about St Fursey.'

'Oh, that's right.' Alan had done a little research on Google, after John and the Fen dean had had their trench-side discussion. 'Fursey came from Ireland, didn't he?'

'Yes, and John tells me the three lobes of the shamrock leaf were used by St Patrick to symbolise the Holy Trinity.'

After she had left, Alan took out his newly-acquired iPad and checked out some of the local evangelical Christian websites. He was amazed: it was obviously a very active scene, with a number of one-off events planned in the lead-up to Easter. There was even a blog and chat room devoted to developing the links established by the Blessed St Fursey between East Anglia and Mother Ireland. Fursey featured prominently. And everything oozed gobbets of well-meaning love. Alan couldn't help it: he cringed as he hurriedly flipped the cover shut.

* * *

Later that afternoon, Alan was working in the Portakabin trying to update and check the correlation of the small finds and contexts registers when his computer beeped. Anything was better than what he was doing now, so he clicked across to the project's email account. There was one new message from a Dr Hilary Porter, of the Department of Geology, at Saltaire University. Alan glanced through it. He felt for her, as he'd been in the same boat many times in his life: it was near the end of the financial year and she had been checking through her invoices. The one she'd issued to Fursey had been sent to Stan last year, and it hadn't been paid. Her direct number was at the end of the email. Alan rang it.

Alan thought her name rang bells with him, and it did: she had been on the advisory panel for the first Forensic Archaeology course, way back in 1996. In those days she was more interested in pedogenesis and the decay of sedimentary rocks, but Alan learnt that after she'd had three children she had found something part-time to do that also paid her reasonable money.

'Unless,' Alan joked, 'you have clients like us.'

'I rather guessed Stan wasn't too keen on administration. I remember handing him my report, which included the invoice, in the pub at Fursey—'

'The Cripps Arms?'

'Yes, that's the one. Anyhow, he'd obviously had a few beers. He wasn't drunk, mind, but merry. I'd have said he was distinctly merry.'

It was like someone behind him had fired a shotgun. He snapped to attention. He'd never before heard anyone at Fursey mention Stan's drinking.

'When was that? Can you remember?'

'Yes, I've got the invoice here and I wrote it out before I left home that morning.' There was a brief pause. 'Let's see . . . Yes, here it is: 7 October.'

'Blimey . . .'

Alan was lost for words. That was the day before Lane recovered Stan's body from the river. For a moment he found himself wondering about the suicide theory. But no, that was ridiculous. A couple of beers aren't the same as half a bottle of whisky. He was brought back to reality by Dr Porter.

'Sorry, Alan, I missed that?'

Alan briefly explained about Stan's death. Dr Porter had already heard about it, and was suitably sympathetic. At the end of his account Alan had to ask the question that had been on his mind throughout their conversation.

'I don't want to sound callous, but did you manage to identify the source of the building stone used here at Fursey?'

'So my report got lost, as well as the invoice?'

'It would seem so, yes.'

'I'll print you off another one. But, yes. And it's what both

Stan and I had expected: it's most probably from one of the quarries at Barnack – near Stamford,' she added by way of explanation. Not that any was needed: the quarries were well known.

'So that would explain some of the masons' marks, which Stan mentions in his draft report.'

'Yes, he let me use them in my report. They're identical to ones found in Ely Cathedral. There must have been a thriving trade in good building stone across the medieval Fens.'

Then Alan had another thought. 'Did all the samples Stan sent you come from around the abbey?'

'Well, they must have done. That's all there is at Fursey. Or am I wrong?'

'He didn't happen to mention, for instance, if any came from lower-lying land?'

There was a pause, then she laughed. 'Oh, I'm sorry, I'm being so dense.' He could hear her shuffling through papers. 'Yes, you're right: he did mention that three samples came from a dyke . . .'

'The Engine Drain?' Alan suggested.

'Yes, that's right. It was the Engine Drain.'

Suddenly Alan could see light at the end of a long and very black tunnel. The high benchmark, the low-lying monastic stonework. It would seem Fursey Abbey was not as tightly confined to its island as was often supposed.

'Thank you so much, Hilary. And have no fear; I'll write you out a cheque here and now. And if you'll agree, I might ask you to identify some more samples, when, that is, we come across them in the future.'

* * *

Alan was never much good at organising set-piece revelations on his own. Those revelatory library scenes in Agatha Christie didn't just happen by magic. They had to be organised. Normally, he liked to have somebody else, preferably his brother Grahame to help him out. But now there was nobody he could turn to. And besides, as staged deceptions went, it was hardly a big one. Not exactly the run-up to D-Day.

He'd had the idea the day he'd spoken to Hilary Porter about the building stone IDs. He had been tidying up the clutter on his desk after his phone call when an email arrived from Candice. She wanted to arrange a quick meeting at the Abbey Farmhouse after work the following day with Alan, Barty, Sebastian and John Cripps. A guest at the meeting would be Dean Jason – the Fen dean. The ostensible purpose of the small gathering was to introduce everyone to the new visitor services manager, who had just been appointed by Historic Projects Management to oversee Fursey.

The email went on to explain that Candice also wanted to use the meeting to float a proposal that John and the Fen dean had hatched together. In a personal PS to Alan, she mentioned that visitor numbers were starting to tail off and she was keen to give them a boost over the Easter holiday, and this seemed just the scheme to do it. But she didn't mention what was being suggested. Alan could hazard a guess and he might even have considered skipping the meeting, but then his own idea had occurred to him. And this time he wouldn't screw up, like he had that night of the dinner. No, this time he'd be far better prepared. Which was why he now found himself driving the Fourtrak up the short drive to the Abbey Farmhouse.

As he got out and locked the door behind him he found

he was looking up at *that* bedroom window on the first floor. The memories did return, but now they were in monochrome, and his pulse barely quickened. Still, it had been a great night and Tricia was now doing what she had always wanted. He smiled: would that all his girlfriends were that straightforward – and forgiving.

As he approached the house, Candice was standing by the open front door. She greeted him with a kiss on both cheeks, and ushered him into the now familiar ochre-painted dining room, just off the front hall.

When she had handed Alan a cup of coffee, she sat down and began the meeting. Alan noted she was very much in charge, but he couldn't help noticing that she was also the person who served him with coffee. None of the men present could possibly have done it; this was still a very conventional family. Business was what men did in such circles. That set him thinking: so had that narrowed the field? Maybe it had. Alan allowed himself a moment of optimism.

Candice began by saying a few words about Joe Thorey's death. She then introduced Steve Grant, who would be starting work at Fursey from the first week of April. This would give him a three-week run-up to the events of Easter and the start of the main, summer tourism season. His CV looked impressive. He was 34 and had a good degree in Leisure and Tourism from Southport, followed by a short stint as a volunteer at the Tower of London, before moving to HPM and the Water World historical theme park. He started work there as a tour guide, but in just four years he was running the shop and, shortly after that, was put in charge of events planning. The founder and CEO of HPM, Blake Lonsdale, had provided a glowing testimonial.

Steve Grant was a good-looking, slim young man with neat short hair and a fashionable, but not, Alan noted, flashy, suit, which he wore without a tie. He had an easy-going manner and everybody in the room took to him instantly. Even Alan, who had a profound dislike of suits and the people who wore them, couldn't help being charmed by the warmth of his smile.

Candice began by mentioning that she had discussed the scheme she was about to propose with Steve, as she immediately called him, and he had given it his wholehearted approval. As if to back her up, Steve was smiling and nodding as she spoke.

She explained that the scheme had been 'dreamed up', as she put it, by her husband John and his good friend Dean Jason. Alan looked across the table. John and the dean were sitting next to each other wearing almost identical dark suits.

'And I should add,' the dean chipped in, 'that although it's not official, all my colleagues in the cathedral think it a splendid notion, as it appeals to a young demographic and has the enthusiastic support of both the Scouts and the Mothers' Union.'

Wow, Alan thought, they were just the organisations to get everyone's juices squirting. But his face was a rigid mask of polite interest.

She went on to outline how, after their visit to Fursey during the live shoot, Alan had told them about the early date for the foundation of Fursey and how it probably predated that of Ely by one or even two generations. Alan hated the glib way non-specialists merge history and archaeology. He still had big misgivings about the dating of this supposed 'event'.

'And I have important new information,' the Fen dean broke in for a second time, 'that was only confirmed two days ago, by no less an authority than Professor Jacob Hawkins of St Luke's College, Cambridge.' He paused for the names of the man and the college to drop. 'The idea was suggested to me by Dr Peter Flower and he agreed to run it past the great man, who was also very excited when it was suggested to him. So it would now seem highly probable – and these were the very words used by Professor Hawkins – that the name Fursey "is a Norse corruption of the much earlier Celtic saint's name, "Fursey".'

Alan almost brought up his lunch. He'd never heard anything so ridiculous: 'highly probable'? My arse. Wisely, he looked down at the table and said nothing.

While he was speaking, the dean pushed his chair back to give himself more room to be enthusiastic. It was then Alan caught a glimpse of his trousers. They were being held up by the same narrow shiny belt he'd worn with his jeans the last time they'd met. And then disaster struck. Suddenly it was as if Alan was wearing head phones. The lead singer of Half Man Half Biscuit, right now Alan's favourite band, was singing the chorus to 'We Built This Village On a Trad. Arr. Tune', the last track on the CD he'd just bought. The next verse started with his current favourite line in rock music: '*Yonder the Deacon in misguided trousers . . .*'

It was too much. He forced his face into a frown, stared down at the table, then rapidly left the room and headed across the hall to the small downstairs lavatory at the back, where his urge to giggle suddenly vanished. He flushed the toilet, feeling a bit of a fool.

Alan re-entered the dining room with a composed and

serious face. The dean was drawing to a conclusion. He nodded to Alan.

'Of course, Alan knows all this, so I won't repeat it for his benefit, but I think you'll all agree, our conclusions must be valid.'

He stopped, seemingly exhausted by the intensity of his announcement. Just to be safe, Alan kept his eyes off the decanal trousers.

The dean's news was greeted with an amazed silence. Alan said nothing. Mercifully nobody asked for his views on St Fursey at Fursey. Maybe, he thought, they detected his scepticism, or remembered it from that afternoon. He could never express his true opinion: that it was a classic example of how to mismatch archaeology and place-name studies. There were so many Viking place names in the area that ended in '-by', which simply meant farmstead. But nobody said a word. So he sat silently. Why make a fuss? What could that possibly achieve? And besides, he knew he had bigger and more dangerous fish to fry.

Alan had a shrewd suspicion that John and the dean's proposal – however misguided – might actually precipitate action. He also realised that things couldn't go on like this forever. The small community at Fursey seemed completely unaware of what was happening around them. Although Alan feared the consequences, he knew something was needed to bring everything out into the open. He had prepared a story. Somehow he had to use it, even if he was on his own, without his brother, Graham, to help him. Time to concentrate: look for an opening, then jump in. He leant forward, concentrating hard.

Candice resumed the discussion. 'So to put it in a nutshell,

St Fursey was a Celtic missionary from Ireland, who converted much of East Anglia to Christianity, then moved on to the Continent. He died around 650. Ely Cathedral itself wasn't founded until 673, by St Etheldreda – which makes us here at Fursey the senior foundation, yet our name never appears in any of the history books. It's always Ely, first, second and third.' She paused for a sip of water. 'Dean Jason and John thought it would be appropriate, in these days of devolution and the Big Society, for the great cathedral to be seen to be reaching out to make a loving and magnanimous gesture to its more ancient, but far smaller, neighbour. We also know that many small evangelical groups in the area have been very inspired by the recent revelations about St Fursey. They've even left small offerings of shamrock and flowers with us after their visits to the abbey and the dig. So our friends at the cathedral have agreed to help us organise an Easter pilgrimage, the Fursey Penance, where pilgrims will set out from Fursey, carrying pieces of rock from the collapsed walls of Fursey Abbey, which they then transport, via water, to Ely Cathedral, where a carefully tended heap, or cairn, will gradually accumulate.'

'And I should add here,' the dean said enthusiastically, 'that the cathedral's dean has given us permission to place the cairn in the transept – directly below the magnificent lantern, which should bathe it in light.'

Alan was astonished. Everything about this was wrong from a conservation point of view. But on the other hand, it might trigger something. So he bit back his indignation and asked in the pleasantest voice he could manage.

'Surely you're not telling us that this cairn will be permanent, are you?'

'No, no,' the dean replied, all smiles. 'That would be out of the question, and I'm sure the cathedral archaeologist wouldn't hear of it, either. English Heritage have also insisted that the stones be returned to the stockpile at Fursey on Tuesday. And a local contractor has already kindly agreed to do that for us, for free.'

Candice then finished. 'The cairn will be blessed by the bishop himself on Easter Monday. At the same time, a small plaque to the memory of St Fursey will be unveiled in the north aisle. That should provide a fitting, and permanent, memorial. Finally, I should add that local media are already showing great interest in the project, and the cathedral dean has kindly arranged for us to hold a press conference at his offices in the Close, next Monday, at 10am.'

At the end of the practical discussion, Candice asked if anyone had any further questions. Alan raised his hand.

'Yes, Alan,' Candice smiled. 'You haven't said much this evening.'

This was the opportunity he had been seeking. He had decided on a humble, diffident approach. But he was finding it hard to conceal his anger: were these unfortunate pilgrims about to carry lumps of rock to Ely, as penance for John Cripps's, or his family's role in Stan's, Hansworth's and now Thorey's deaths? Or was it a bare-faced attempt to lay the curse myth? Either way, Alan couldn't see it working.

'Well,' he began, 'I'm not a regular churchgoer, so I thought it would be inappropriate if I commented on this splendid scheme, which I'm sure will be a huge success, both for Fursey, the cathedral and, of course, for the pilgrims themselves.' He paused. That seemed to have gone down very well. Everyone was listening intently. 'But I thought you might be interested to know that I have just been informed by Dr Hilary Porter of Saltaire University that the building stone used at Fursey Abbey originated in the Barnack quarries, which of course provided the stone used in the cathedral.'

Alan was watching his audience closely as he released the news. Whoever had carefully chosen those mass-produced bricks to weigh-down Thorey's body must have been well aware that the limestone used at Fursey could have been identified. It was almost as good as a fingerprint – especially given that Thorey worked for the Cripps family. With the exception of Steve Grant, at least one person around the table once had a strong motive for stealing Dr Porter's original identification and then for killing both Stan and maybe Thorey too – for why else were his pockets exclusively filled with modern bricks? It was very odd for a suicidal person to be worried about such things. And would Thorey have understood? But now the secret was out, and their reactions were absolutely crucial.

Alan watched everyone intently, carefully noting every detail of their responses: John and Candice were wide-eyed with amazement. They seemed genuinely surprised – and pleased. The Fen dean was delighted, too – there was no disguising that. Young Steve Grant had just received a text and was looking down at his screen, so no surprise there. Then Sebastian yawned and rose to his feet to pour himself a cup of cold coffee. Not guilt so much as bored indifference. Alan was terribly disappointed: nobody was looking even slightly shifty, embarrassed, or guilty. It had certainly not been like a library scene in an Agatha Christie novel.

The dean was the first to speak. 'Alan, that is splendid news. In our outline of the pilgrimage route we included a stretch of the Padnal Delph to symbolise St Fursey's crossing of the Irish Sea. But your announcement now gives it added symbolism.'

'And we also know,' Alan found himself saying, 'that the stones were transported across the Fens by water, as hewn blocks of limestone were revealed on the bottom of Whittlesea Mere after its drainage in the nineteenth century. We assume these blocks were pushed overboard when the boats transporting them south, ran aground in the shallow lake. But what's interesting is that those blocks carried mason's marks that can be matched at Ely. It would now appear that by the time work started on the Norman Cathedral, cross-Fenland trade links had already been long-established.'

This was news to the Fen dean, whose previous appointment had been in Sunningdale. He was obviously astonished. Alan deduced that he had not come across such direct links with the remote past before.

'Thank you so much for that, Alan.' Candice was almost gushing. 'I'm so glad you were able to come this evening.' Suddenly she stopped. John was looking at her, slightly shocked. Then she resumed quietly, her eyes down. 'It would seem that our Penance is very timely indeed.'

But Alan wasn't quite so certain – about anything. Ruefully, he thought, I have to admit it: my cunning set-piece didn't work. But surely somebody at Fursey must have known about the Barnack stone and what it implied for any future development in the area. It was so frustrating.

Then he had second thoughts: or maybe someone in the room is a very good actor?

* * *

Alan was the first on-site the following morning. It was cold and there had been a sharp frost overnight. He needed a coffee. As if reading his mind, Candice called out from the back door of the temporary farm shop.

'Fancy a coffee, Alan? I've just made some.'

Anything was better than instant, and hers was always good. He was soon inside the steamy Portakabin, grasping a hot mug. They were sitting at the table where flowers were cut and prepared for sale. Even though it was now the last day of March, Alan could still detect quite a strong smell of daffodils.

'Alan, I do hope you didn't think we were springing the pilgrimage thing on you. As we talked I couldn't help thinking that you looked slightly overwhelmed by it all. And dear Dean Jason is *such* an enthusiast, isn't he?'

Alan smiled. This didn't need a reply.

'But I have to confess,' she continued, 'John and I do have an ulterior motive – if you can call it that. Of course, as you're no doubt aware, John is a devout believer, so his motives are – how can I put it? – more *Christian* than mine, but he agrees with me that this Thorey business is reviving that stupid curse myth.'

In other situations, Alan might have denied this, but there was a limit to how far he could push the truth, especially when talking to Candice, whom he knew to have closer relationships with local people than the other members of her family. And the truth was that every time he went to the village pub, somebody mentioned the curse – even if just in passing. But after the discovery of Thorey's body, it had once again become a hot topic.

'Still,' he said, as brightly as he could manage, 'don't you think it'll prove a flash in the pan?'

Alan had run out of clichés for ephemeral. And his own words sounded hollow to him.

'No, sadly, I don't – and nor does John. Because, don't forget, this comes on the heels of dear Stan's death and then, of course, there was poor James Hansworth's death in 2004. And it's not as if the background story is modern. It has genuine roots that extend way back in history.'

'Yes, I know.' Alan had to agree with her.

And yes, on reflection he could see they did have good grounds to be worried – especially as she and her husband depended for their living on a visitor attraction, which in turn relied heavily on local goodwill.

'John thought – and I have to say I agree with him – that the pilgrimage idea might cause local people to view the family in a new light. I mention all this to explain why we're so very keen that this Penance goes ahead smoothly. To be honest, I don't think it should affect the dig, but it's always good to know what's going on, isn't it?'

'I'll have a word with the team. They're all very professional, but sometimes on digs the language can get a bit fruity. Devout churchgoers might get upset – and of course we'll keep an eye out for more offerings.'

'No, don't worry. We've put up a sign asking religious people to show restraint when they arrive. We're also providing a special mini-altar for offerings in the abbey ruins. That should deal with the problem.'

The clinical way in which Candice outlined how they proposed to 'deal' with the 'problem', confirmed Alan's impression that, unlike her husband, she wasn't a believer. Not even an agnostic. But did that make him feel warmer towards her? It took a few moments to think this over, and then, rather to his surprise, he realised it didn't. Candice was someone who 'managed' situations, and it occurred to Alan, not for the first time, that perhaps she was managing him.

* * *

Alan unwrapped the fish and chips he had just bought from the travelling chippy, which came in a converted London Transport red Routemaster and parked round the back of the village shop on Friday afternoons. There was always a short queue there, but it was worth the wait. Greasy but gorgeous – and with a double portion of chips. He'd just wolfed down the fish and was about to start lingering over the second portion of chips, when his mobile rang. Reception wasn't too bad, so he didn't bother to run upstairs. It was Lane.

'Hi, Richard. Any news about Thorey?'

'Yes, that's why I'm ringing.'

'Changed your mind about the suicide?'

It was worth a try. For his part, and despite all the evidence against it, Alan increasingly suspected foul play. Why would a suicide want to conceal the source of the weights he used? More to the point, would Thorey have even known about the Barnack quarries – let alone their significance? And what about the link to Stan's death?

'No. Can't say we have. Trouble is, the pathologist, Dr Lindsay Harris, couldn't be as helpful as she, and we, had hoped. And she's one of the best.'

Alan had heard Lane talk of her with approval before.

'But why couldn't she be more certain?'

'Two things, really: the length of time since death and the fact that the body had been in water.'

'Could she tell if he'd been drowned?'

'No, decay was too far advanced for that. But it seems more than likely.'

'Could anything else have killed him?'

'Again, it was very difficult to say for certain. There were no major traumas to the skull, for instance, and they didn't find any shot in his body, either – which you might have expected, given that he was a gamekeeper.'

'So she didn't think he'd been killed in a struggle and then dumped in the water?'

'No, she didn't. But again, it was hard to be absolutely certain.'

'Presumably the weight of the bricks stopped his body from floating off?'

'That's an interesting point. A fit and healthy swimmer should just be able to carry that sort of weight if, that is, he was desperate to stay alive. But that's not the mindset of suicides, is it? And of course, if he'd been weakened in any way – even something like a nasty cold – he'd have gone fairly rapidly to the bottom.'

Alan was thinking hard. 'OK,' he said slowly. 'So what would have happened then? Presumably his body would start to decay and pretty soon the gasses would bring him to the surface?'

'That's right. But you've got to remember that river levels were high, so the body could have been moved while it was still submerged.'

'And drink? Any signs of that?'

'After that length of time, in or out of water, any ethanol in the corpse would have been a by-product of putrefaction.'

Then Alan had a thought. 'So the alcohol they found in Stan's body was probably real?'

'Yes, if by that you mean he'd drunk it. But then we don't reckon his body had been in the river more than twenty-four hours.'

'What about that deep mark just above Thorey's knee? That is a bit odd isn't it?'

'Yes, I agree, it is. Lindsay reckoned it had happened sometime around the time of death, but she couldn't be more precise than that. The body snagged on a sluice gate grille, or something similar, which held it below water and caused the damage to the leg. However, when she came to examine the surface of the femur—' The line went fuzzy for a few seconds. Then it returned.

'The bone itself?' Alan wanted to be quite clear.

'That's right. It had been scratched on one side. Even odder, there were two small, fresh cuts – scratches more like – into the surface of the bone, one a bit deeper than the other.'

'And when did that happen?'

'As before, she can't be certain. But it was around the time of death.'

'Any thoughts?'

'We discussed it in the station. There's a certain amount of river traffic, so it could be damage from a passing boat, and, of course, there's Smiley's Mill at Fursey, and a couple of even larger mills downstream, not to mention all the various pumps and sluices. If you counted all the puncture marks on your friend Stan Beaton's body, there were many more than just the two on Thorey. But none were so deep.'

Briefly Alan held the phone away from his ear. His mind was racing.

'Thanks, Richard. You've given me lots to think about.'

He rang off. He knew he'd been a bit abrupt, but he needed time to think. He dipped a near-cold chip into salt then ketchup and munched. He didn't taste anything. His brain wouldn't slow down. Carefully he went over everything they'd said. Line by line, word by word. And again, he had to agree with Lane: it all seemed plausible. Almost too plausible. And there was another thing that neither he nor Lane had mentioned, but which both of them knew: Stan and Thorey both worked outdoors doing physically demanding jobs. They were both fit, strong men. Even if they were taken by stealth or surprise they would not have gone down without quite a struggle. And that, surely, was the explanation for the deep cut on his thigh. Maybe he'd been hit by a fork-lift? Or a tractor? Something big, powerful and with sharp edges. That cut, he now realised, was the key to it all.

By the time he'd finished the last scrap of cold crunchy batter, he knew he could never accept a word of the official explanation of Thorey's death. He got up from the table, chucked the fish paper into the bin, and headed out for a beer.

Suicide? he mused, as he pushed the pub door open.

Like hell.

# Seventeen

One or two late daffodils were just coming into flower beneath the budding lime trees that lined the avenue leading up to what had once been Abbey Farm, but which Alan reckoned now looked more like a motorway services, what with the builders, their trucks and the morning delivery vans. It was the first Monday in April and Alan was keen to introduce Steve Grant, the new manager, to the digging team before the next round of filming. He arrived at the back door of the farm shop to scrounge his usual early morning mug of coffee, only to find Candice and Steve were already sitting there waiting for him. His mug had been freshly filled and sat steaming on the table.

They asked him how he thought things could have been improved over the past few weeks. Alan didn't want to sound negative, but he did mention that aspects of crowd control hadn't been too good, especially during the live filming. Steve listened intently. It was plain to Alan that he knew his stuff. He also knew where to hire or buy the necessary equipment. But they couldn't do anything without an efficient comms system around the farm shop, museum and abbey. Alan mentioned the one used by New Ideas Productions. Steve nodded; he knew all about it. Apparently it was fine if you needed something temporarily, but it was expensive and not always robust enough for day-to-day use. The system he had in mind was actually more powerful, a bit more economical, and the handsets were far lighter. All in all, Alan was impressed. Candice was smiling broadly, too: they had made the right decision when they called in HPM.

After Alan had introduced him to the archaeologists in Trenches 1 and 2, Steve said he had to make arrangements for the press conference for the Fursey Penance and headed back to the site office, which had recently moved out of the Portakabin and into new purpose-built facilities in one of the converted Victorian farm buildings. Alan had sneaked a view of them on Friday afternoon. They were very impressive: they even had an ante-room which was lined with stout coat hooks and fitted trays for wellies and muddy shoes. Alan had smiled: the 'new' Fursey was going to be something special. Then he had looked out of the brand-new double-glazed window at the old, long-abandoned pig sties, which were in the process of being demolished. Moss-covered bricks and old breeze blocks lay on the ground with pieces of angle iron and fragments of asbestos roofing. A depressing sight. He wondered how long it would all last. There was something panicky, almost desperate, about the whole pilgrimage/Penance business. It was done in such a hurry. Were they really *that* worried about a small dip in visitor numbers? Wouldn't it have given them a chance to improve facilities on-site in a controlled way? Deep down, he knew something wasn't right. And he was growing more convinced of that every day that passed.

Penance suggested guilt, somewhere deep within the Cripps family. There was no getting away from that. The question was: who was guilty?

* * *

The press conference was scheduled to start at 9.30, to give local TV and radio reporters time to get the story back for the midday and evening news bulletins. But Alan had decided to stay well clear of it, and had arranged to meet Clare Hughes so he didn't have to attend. He found the whole Fursey/Fursey thing more than a little strange and couldn't understand why seemingly sane, rational people were getting their knickers in such a twist about it.

The press release had stressed abstinence and effort. It read like a medieval monk's manual. 'Our aim is to achieve purity of mind through fasting and strenuous physical labour.' It was a simple vision, but one that seemed to appeal. Alan also slightly resented his and Stan's archaeological research being hijacked by a load of toffee-nosed Cambridge academics who should have known better. And, of course, it gave him yet another reason to dislike and distrust the ambitious Dr Peter Flower.

Alan glanced at his watch. It was 9.15 and the first reporters were starting to arrive, but he didn't particularly want to be recognised. If anyone asked him about 'Itsagrave' he'd probably thump them. He climbed into the Fourtrak and breathed heavily onto the windows, which soon misted up. An old trick if you want privacy. He had a few minutes to kill, so on impulse, he phoned Harriet. He'd been wanting to do this for days, but hadn't been able to think of a suitable excuse.

'Harry.' She still insisted he called her that.

'Oh, it's you, Alan. No more bodies, I trust?'

'No.' He brushed that aside. 'I just wondered whether you'd met, or knew anything about, Professor Jacob Hawkins?'

'That crashing old bore? I can't imagine him getting off his backside to visit anywhere, let alone Fursey. Why, has he been over?'

Alan was surprised. It was not like Harriet to be quite so indiscreet.

'No, he hasn't. It's just that his name came up recently when people were discussing an Easter pilgrimage that the Fen dean and John Cripps have come up with. It's all about ancient connections between Fursey and Ely. Frankly, I think it has to be a PR stunt to whip up interest and visitor numbers over Easter.'

'Oh really. And how can I help?'

'It's just that Flower apparently cited Hawkins as a leading authority on place names. Is he?'

'He was, but that was back in the '60s. His book for CUP on *-ingas* names and the spread of the Pagan Saxons through southern Britain had a huge effect. I had to wade through it when I was starting my doc research. Of course, it's been completely out-dated by archaeology and now by DNA. But it earned him the last-ever Life Fellowship at St Luke's, the lucky devil.'

'So he hasn't done much since?'

'Nothing at all – other than get immensely fat at the college's expense. He's such a reactionary old pig.' Alan could hear she was getting angry. 'Did you know, one or two of the younger fellows have been trying to get a baby-changing room attached to the toilets below hall? And he objected! In the end he scraped around and found enough reactionary old farts to get the idea rejected. None of us suspected that he was capable of organising *anything*, let alone any*one* in college. But he did. Damn him. He did . . .'

Alan didn't say anything for a moment to let her cool off.

'So I shouldn't take his thoughts very seriously, then?'

She laughed out loud. 'Anything else, Alan? I'm in a seminar.'

He could picture the wide-eyed students.

'Whoops, so sorry to have interrupted. And thanks for that.'

Hmm, Alan thought as he hung up. A bit abrupt. Business-like, certainly, but not hostile. He sighed. There was a long way to go. Still, she had confirmed what he'd suspected about Hawkins – and, come to that, Flower. But why hadn't Peter Flower done anything to challenge the Fursey myth? Did he say nothing because it suited his own academic profile? Alan knew he was a man who would favour self-promotion over the truth. He'd known that fourteen years ago, and nothing had changed. The question was, what else would he do in order to further his own ambitions?

* * *

Clare wasn't in the sweetest of moods when she arrived on-site – and Alan couldn't blame her. The previous week, the County Council had announced its end-of-year spending review and her department was to be cut to the bone. Essentially it would now consist of just her and a computer which held the Sites and Monuments Record (she refused to call it the more PC 'Historic Environment Record').

Like Alan, she was more interested in the post holes in Trench 2, than the three graves in Trench 1, which had clearly been cut through the gravel surface of the principal north-south road of the Roman fort. Everything, in other words, was fairly straightforward. But those post holes in Trench 2 were altogether different. They appeared to be post-Roman, but even that was far from certain, as there was so much residual R–B pottery knocking about the place. But to both Clare and Alan they did look later. And very substantial, too. Indeed, they both agreed, their close spacing was more reminiscent of a hall, than a barn – and a big hall at that.

They'd been examining them for several minutes, when Clare turned to Alan. 'It's no good, Alan, we can't leave things as they are. I don't suppose for one moment that my councillors will like it – especially not the Tory ones – but you'll have to extend Trench 2.'

Alan could have hugged her. It was precisely what he wanted to hear.

'I couldn't agree more, Clare. It's obviously one hell of a building, as those posts are going down deep. And the trench is too narrow to pick up any floor levels. So what do you suggest?'

'Ten by ten?'

Alan nodded. 'Yes, at least that. Maybe more. I think we should meet again in a couple of weeks. What do you think?'

'I think you're a brick, Alan.'

As soon as they'd left the shelter, she leant forward and kissed him on the cheek. Her eyes were bright now.

'Thanks, Alan, that was just what I wanted to hear – you can't imagine what it's like at County Hall these days. The atmosphere's sheer poison. Horrible. D'you know, there are times I'd like to chuck it in and go back to fieldwork, I really would.'

* * *

The following morning Alan arrived early on-site. It was one of those cold, still, almost airless spring days, where the fog hangs around and even the voices of the dawn chorus seem a bit restrained. He was supping a hot coffee from his favourite Nikon lens mug, when the low-loader drew up on the edge of the car park. Davey Hibbs was in a small, battered white van behind it. He parked and walked across to Alan while the lorry driver got the trailer ready for Davey to unload the digger.

'Morning, Alan.' Davey greeted him with a warm smile. 'I've just had Matt Grimshaw phone me from the IDB office. He hopes you won't be using the machine for too long as he wants to get on and finish the Engine Drain.'

'Tell him I'd be very surprised if it'll even take us all day today. It's quite a small trench, but we'll need to go very steady.'

'OK. That's great. Matt'll be pleased. I'll have a quick word with Reg, here.'

Davey arranged with Reg for the low-loader to return the following morning, then he tracked the machine down to Trench 2, with Alan, in hard-hat and hi-vis, leading the way on foot. As they were nearing the trench, Alan's eye was caught by movement in the car park behind them. A car and a van had just arrived. The car was driven by Frank Jones, who gave a cheery wave. The van had tinted windows, but Alan recognised it as Speed Talbot's and he correctly guessed that Grump Edwards, would also be sitting in front.

The previous evening, when Alan had told Frank Jones about the trench extension, Frank had pleaded with him not to start without the crew. But Alan knew from past experience they could be delayed. London was a long way away, and he had to get the digger off-site soon. So he wasn't going to say yes to that – although he agreed it would be good if they could catch the first scoops of the big ditching blade.

Behind him, he could see Trudy, doing what PAs always did at a new location: pouring coffee from two big flasks. Frank, the crew and Terri Griffiths were standing around joking – without a care in the world. Suddenly, Alan thought he would have some fun.

He jumped onto the machine and briefed Davey. Davey grinned. He liked a laugh, especially at the expense of smart Londoners.

As the digger approached Trench 2, Davey rapidly increased the revs. Everyone in the car park turned round. By now Alan was standing at the spot where he wanted the extension to begin. He made various hand signals to Davey, who returned them with a thumbs up. Then, as planned, they 'discovered' that the digger wasn't quite level, so Davey tracked back a few metres and gave the surface a couple of light scrapes. From the car park it must have looked like the digging had started.

Up until now, Alan had wanted to appear as if he was completely absorbed in what he was doing. But when the digger started to level the ground he allowed himself a glance up. Quickly he looked down. He didn't want any of them to see his grin. Frank was stumbling across the uneven ground as fast as his legs could carry him, while somehow managing to carry a monitor set and spare tripod. Trudy was frantically rooting through papers and clipboards on the damp ground. Behind Frank hobbled Terri, still wearing her London shoes. Speed had grabbed a camera and tripod and was leaving the van at a brisk walk – he was going as fast as Alan had ever seen him move. And Grump Edwards? He was finishing his coffee. Around him on the ground lay steaming mugs. He raised his cup to Alan. Alan smiled: good old Grump.

It took a little longer to get set up, thanks to Alan's little prank, but he and Davey both had flasks of coffee, which they drank while the crew scurried about. Alan had positioned the machine about five metres away from the line of post holes, which they would probably get to in a couple of hours' time. He never liked 'wall chasing' and preferred to work on a broad front. That way, it was easier to keep features in some sort of context. So he wasn't expecting to find much in the first couple of hours.

After the first half-dozen or so scoops had removed topsoil and alluvium, Alan signalled to Davey to slow down and shave, rather than dig, the exposed surface. The first pull-back of the 2-metre wide ditching blade revealed the clear, dark, outline of a rectangular pit. At the end of the draw-back, Davey stopped the bucket. He pointed down at the ground, but Alan was already there, trowelling at the fringes of the exposed feature. The edges were sharp and seemed to be going down vertically. There could be no doubt what it was. In retrospect he could have kicked himself for what he called back to Davey, but it did at least have the merit of genuine spontaneity.

'Blimey, Davey: it's a grave!'

Of course, Frank could have hugged him.

While Speed was filming the new find from every conceivable angle, Alan was looking at the fresh surface left by the machine. There was something strange about the pattern of silt and small pebbles at either end of the grave. Somehow, it just didn't look natural. So he started trowelling. Realising that Alan might be on to a new feature, Frank tapped Speed lightly on the shoulder and whispered in his ear. The camera panned right, and at the precise time that Alan's trowel revealed the dark outline of a large post hole, Speed tilted up to catch Alan's delighted smile. Then the process was repeated at the eastern end of the grave. Another, slightly smaller, post hole.

'This grave was important, Davey,' a smiling Alan called out. 'It's marked at either end. That's very unusual.'

By the end of the day they had revealed another five graves, all aligned roughly east-west. The line of post holes that they'd originally intended to investigate could clearly be seen to have been part of a wall, which ran for about 7 metres on the same alignment as the graves, then there was a sharp corner, followed by a semi-circular curve to the north. Alan was no expert on early churches, but even he could spot a likely apse. It was the right sort of curve, it faced east and it was at the east end of a substantial timber building. He was elated.

Alan was aware that the Frank was pleased, too. He had filmed some great exchanges between Alan and Davey as the new features had appeared. This time they had tried a new technique and it had worked: Frank himself had become a temporary cameraman and had filmed Davey on the smaller webcam, leaving Speed to concentrate on Alan and any cut-aways of emerging features or new finds – which were few and far between. This new way of working was far less disruptive for the archaeologists, but it also gave a more natural feel to the film.

As the morning progressed, Alan had found himself thinking more and more about the Fursey Penance, John Cripps and the Fen dean. His heart sank. They would certainly name the early apsidal church they were now revealing 'St Fursey's', as soon as the news got out. He could picture the headlines already.

Quite suddenly, Alan had been gripped by a surge of anger. Why did he have to involve these people? What the hell right did they have to tell him what he was doing? Then he paused and reflected: but what right did *he*, an incomer, have to hold forth in this way? This was their land, their place – they had a right to their own stories. For a moment he recalled walking across the car park of Blackfen Prison and the feelings of righteous indignation about a young man's innocence. But that was just over two years ago. He had been on a personal crusade – and it had all blown up in his face. No, he reflected, it was too easy to think you were right. It was better, if so much harder, to seek the truth first. Anger – even indignation – could always happen later. He began to feel a little calmer: it wasn't just revenge that was best enjoyed cold.

* * *

The next morning was fresh and clear. Alan stood in the car park and watched as the low-loader, followed by Davey in the little white van, headed back down the avenue. Next stop for him, the Engine Drain, Alan thought, as he turned round and looked out across the open fen towards the Padnal Delph pumping station in the distance.

A text message arrived. 'Next job fallen thru. Any chance we cd discuss Fursey pollen today? Bob'

Alan glanced at his watch: 7.45. No time like the present. And besides, he liked Dr Bob Timpson. He pressed dial.

Bob was one of those rare archaeological scientists who had made a living as a freelance. His wife loved horses and kept three Exmoor ponies on a smallholding in the Wolds, about five miles outside Lincoln. Bob had converted an upstairs room into a study and he also rented lab space in Nettlesham College. Alan suspected the rent was very cheap and was mostly paid for by the informal botanical talks he gave agricultural students. In the cut-throat world of modern academia, such handy arrangements were becoming far less common. Being a freelance himself, Alan liked to steer work Bob's way, whenever he could.

Alan had been thinking that they needed an up-to-date local pollen survey quite urgently. They now understood much more about the ancient soils, but very little about the trees, the crops and the wet-loving plants of the fen, that would have been growing on them. The Fenland Survey of the 1970s had provided some useful sequences, but they mostly covered the fen to the south and west. Far less was known about the Fursey area. Alan was particularly interested in the Iron Age to Roman transition. Stan's discoveries at an unexpectedly low level OD suggested that conditions weren't as hostile in the early first century AD as had previously been believed.

* * *

Alan called in at the tool-shed and collected a shovel and wheelbarrow, which he took down to the Trench 2 extension.

He wanted some time on his own to think about the implications of the new discoveries, and he knew from experience that the best way to come to grips with something like this was complete immersion. Some people could contemplate from afar, but not Alan. His brain worked best when his body was also fully engaged.

So he set about doing a quick 'shovel clean' of the new extension. Essentially this involved removing all clods, stones and patches of loose earth. Once that had been done, he, Jake, Jon and Kaylee would get down on their knees and trowel the entire surface at least once, and if needs be, twice. It was a part of the excavation process that some people hated, but not Alan. He loved it and enjoyed trying to 'read' or interpret the freshly-trowelled surface. In Alan's mind, that was when archaeology became art, not science. Often the brightest people were hopeless at it: they were too clever, too analytical. Alan's approach had more in common with Zen Buddhism, than soil science: he would stare at the ground for long periods, either continuously, or at close intervals, watching for changes as the various soils dried out at different rates. The clever dicks lacked the patience, or indeed the imagination, to do this.

* * *

Dr Bob Timpson arrived during the mid-morning tea break. Archaeology is still quite a small world and he more or less knew everyone on-site, so the atmosphere was relaxed.

Alan had decided not to cover the trench extension with a shelter, partly because it was expensive, but also because it cut down on the light he needed to spot new features. They could always erect temporary shelters over the graves once they started to dig them. Earlier that morning, and with the shelter not there, Alan had watched Davey's digger track along the Engine Drain to the stones of the partially collapsed monastic precinct wall that skirted the park towards the edge of the island, about 200 yards from where they were excavating.

Alan called across to Bob, and together they set out for the Engine Drain, carrying Bob's auger and sampling tins between them. They headed down the slope, through the park from the abbey excavations, down to the roofed lychgate through the stone wall that surrounded the abbey land at the edge of the fen. Beyond the wall was a 20- to 30-yard-wide screen of wet-loving shrubs that prevented the wall suffering any agricultural damage; it also provided much-needed ground cover for breeding pheasants and partridges. Alan recognised alder buckthorn, guelder rose, dogwood, and in the drier spots, blackthorn and hawthorn. But it was quite unlike a game-cover on drier land. Alan noticed that Bob, a good botanist, was enjoying it, too.

Back out in the open fen they paused to catch breath. It had turned out to be a gorgeous day, with a light spring breeze and occasional fluffy clouds. Even from this distance they could see that Davey was a superb operator, and had already smoothly cleaned and recut one side of the Engine Drain for a distance of almost 50 yards. Alan looked towards the western horizon where the breeze was coming from: no sign of any showers and more summer-like weather. He could just see the south tower of Ely Cathedral through the trees of the park, whose buds were starting to open. Nearer to home, a small cluster of seagulls was following a double-wheeled tractor that was rolling spring barley, which had just begun to germinate. A tranquil, rural scene. Or so it seemed.

Alan recognised the tractor as being one of Sebastian's, and he knew why he was rolling the barley: it had been very dry for the past two weeks, and the light ridged rollers would slightly compress the soil to consolidate the growing roots and draw moisture up from beneath. It was an important job and he'd done it many times for his father and for his brother Grahame.

Alan pointed out the machine-cleaned dykeside to Bob.

'Alan,' he replied, 'that's absolutely perfect. I can see the peats from here. It looks ideal.'

They took it in turns to carry the heavy canvas bag that held the auger and the sample tins, which they both knew would be very much heavier when they'd finished.

Bob decided to take samples from about a metre behind the edge of the Engine Drain, and soon they had begun the familiar task of turning the auger for a few screws, then together pulling the head from the ground, removing the peat, and going down further. Across the field, the tractor was getting closer, and a few seagulls diverted to see if Alan and Bob were going to offer them any food. They circled briefly, but soon gave up.

At the end of the day, there were three small heaps of sample tins, all bagged and carefully labelled. For a moment Alan paused, trying to decide what to do next. The tractor was getting closer, but it would stop at the track along the Engine Drain. Alan decided the heavy sample tins could stay there quite safely overnight, and he'd collect them with the Fourtrak the following morning.

* * *

There were only nine days to go before Easter and the joint opening ceremony of the new visitor complex, and with it the

Stan Beaton Archaeology Centre. This was where Alan and his team would henceforth be based. Candice and Steve Grant had decided it would be far too complicated to have the opening ceremony on Good Friday, when the Fursey Penance was to be launched, so it was scheduled for the previous day. That way, they could start Easter with good publicity, which they could then build on. Steve had done some local soundings with the press and TV, who all agreed with this decision.

Alan watched Harriet's Mini Cooper pull into the car park from where he was standing in Trench 2. He couldn't decide whether he should be there to greet her. He didn't want to seem too keen, but he also didn't want her to think he was indifferent. He hated such decisions. In fact, as a planner of amorous campaigns, Alan was a complete disaster. His overall strategy was always wrong and the tactical implementation was invariably even worse.

She had driven to Fursey with Toby Cox, a bright young PhD student she was currently supervising. Alan had met Toby previously and, to his surprise, had been quite impressed: he wasn't one of the typical, impractical, theory-obsessed Cambridge graduates he had expected. In fact, he was quite self-effacing and soon became a member of what had become a very close-knit team. The archaeologists had remained the same, even though television crews had come and gone with extraordinary speed and efficiency. But Harriet still remained slightly remote. And of course, Jake and the others all knew why. Word travels fast in what was left of the old 'digging circuit'.

When eventually they did arrive in Trench 2, Alan had his phone to his ear. It was Clare Hughes, who needed someone to listen while she sounded-off about a further round of council budget cuts. By the time Clare had finished talking, Harriet and Toby had started work, and Alan hadn't even had an opportunity to offer her so much as a welcoming handshake, let alone a kiss. As reunions went, it had fallen pretty flat.

* * *

It was Thursday morning, and just a week to go till the opening. Tension was building, both in and out of the trenches. Clare Hughes had said she'd be on-site around tea break. But she didn't arrive. Eventually, Alan and the Trench 2 team returned to work. For some reason there were more visitors than usual. Maybe it had been the initial publicity for the Fursey Penance, but whatever had brought them, the crowds had been growing steadily since first thing that morning. Around noon, Alan decided he'd better send Clare a quick text: it wasn't like her to miss an appointment and he was a little worried that something unfortunate might have happened. Or was that being ridiculous? He paused. Ridiculous? Was it?

The more he thought about it, the more his anxiety grew. Thanks to the recent cuts, she was now the sole person in planning who could make crucial decisions about key developments – many of them probably worth millions. And her knowledge and experience were an essential part of the decision-making process: no computer on earth would be capable of making the varied value-judgements she had to make every hour of every working day. No, he decided, I won't text, I'll give her a call. He stood up and walked over to the spoil heap, which he started to climb to get a better mobile signal. Suddenly he froze. Somebody was calling for him.

Alan looked behind him. He didn't spot her at first, but it was Clare. She was standing close to a group of visitors who were being given a guided tour. Normally, she would have stood out from them, wearing the regulation digger blue jeans and practical top, but not now. Instead she was wearing a short, lilac pleated dress, worn over a pair of tight pale-green leggings with pink flowers. It was an unusual colour combination, but strangely, it worked. Alan hadn't seen her in civvies before and she looked good – no, he thought, very good – in it.

He hurried across to her and she moved away from the visitors, who were now staring at them both. The guide was starting to look annoyed so they stepped out of sight, behind the shelter.

'I'm so sorry, Alan,' she said, 'but it's been a very busy morning. There's been one hell of a row in the council chamber about the effect of the cuts. It's now official that Cambridge is the fastest-growing city in Britain with more development than anywhere else, except London. And yet they want to cut the District Planning Department. It doesn't make any sense.'

'No,' Alan agreed. 'That's what I thought when you told me on Tuesday. But then politicians, even local ones, live in a remote world of their own, don't they?'

'Well, in this instance, reality is starting to strike home. We've already had to defer three crucial expansion decisions and even the Tories are starting to realise that you can't make cuts without consequences.'

'So what's going to happen?'

'They've convened an all-party planning review panel and it's having its first meeting this afternoon, at two.'

'And you're going to be a witness?'

'Yes,' she continued, still wide-eyed with the excitement. 'I'm on second. After the CPO.'

Alan looked puzzled.

'Chief planning officer,' she added.

'Ah.' Alan smiled slightly mischievously. 'So that explains the frock and shoes.'

'Well, sometimes it pays to dress up. I've got to make a good impression. Apparently for us women, charm and a bit of flirtation are still our best weapons.' Clare said this with a barely concealed distaste. Then she shrugged. 'So, much as I'd like to, forgive me if I don't get down on my knees in the trench.'

Alan had to smile at this.

By now they had walked round to the trench and were talking in hushed voices, so as not to disturb the tour.

'So how's it all going?' she asked, as they surveyed the trench from the south side.

'Well, that post-built wall is looking increasingly church-like, as we expected.'

'And the graves?'

'I think there were five when you were here last?'

She nodded.

'Well,' Alan continued, 'there are eight now. In fact, we had to do three trowel-cleans before we could spot them all.'

She looked very pleased. 'And when did you start on the graves?'

'Harriet returned the day before yesterday and brought a graduate student with her. They're working on the two graves closest to the post-wall. We thought we'd get them cleared before we started on the church itself.'

Somehow Harriet seemed to sense she was being discussed.

She looked up and waved. Very friendly. Almost too friendly, Alan thought. Clare waved back. Just as enthusiastically.

'Yes,' Clare replied. 'That makes lots of sense.' She paused for a moment – as she took in the scene before her. 'I bet you're feeling happy, aren't you?'

'My head's happy,' he said with a grin, 'but my knuckles are still smarting.'

'Poor lad. So I don't imagine you're planning to enlarge the trench immediately?'

Alan shook his head.

'No, I'm not, but depending on what Harriet reveals in the graves nearer the post holes, we might want to look at those two in the south-east corner there.' He pointed out two graves at the far end of the trench.

'Yes,' she nodded. 'You'll have to do a small extension, if that's what we decide. But there's absolutely no rush. Give me a ring nearer the time.'

'If you've still got a job.'

'Oh, I'll have a job all right. And who knows, I might even have some staff by then.'

'That's good – I think the way you're being treated is disgraceful. I honestly do.'

They started to walk back to her car. Alan could feel the rising indignation. Everyone acknowledged that Clare was one of the best county archaeologists in the country.

'Well,' she said with a smile. 'I owe a lot to you, Alan.'

Alan was genuinely puzzled at this. 'What, to me? How come?'

'Alan, don't be so dense.' She was laughing now. A light breeze got up and ruffled her skirts and her long hair blew around her face. She brushed it away with the back of her hand. 'Your TV programmes showed the whole country how rich the Fens are in archaeology. Some councillors, who should have known better, had even been trying that old "flat and boring grain plain, not worth preserving" rubbish. But they soon shut up when you started finding things. In fact, my boss is keen to meet you. He asked me to find out if you'll be at the opening ceremony here next week.'

Alan groaned. 'Yes, I will. Can't say I'm looking forward to it much, though.'

'Well you should, Alan,' she said with smiley irony. 'It will offer you an opportunity to network. And that's what life is all about these days.'

Alan cast his eyes to the heavens.

'Anyhow.' She turned to leave. 'It's time I was going. Can't afford to be late for this one.' She paused, then added, 'Wish me luck,' as she leant forward and offered a powdered cheek for a farewell kiss.

Alan watched as she walked away. He had long had a soft spot for Clare. She was a nice, uncomplicated person who took people at face value. That's why she and Stan had got on so well together. They hadn't had a chance to speak at the time, but he well remembered watching her weep quite freely at Stan's wake.

Then suddenly he stopped in his tracks. What was it she had said, exactly? 'Charm and a bit of flirtation are still our best weapons.' He thought about that concealed bottle in Stan's 'cupboard'. OK, it came from Fisher College, but it didn't have to be given by Flower. The more he thought about it, the less likely that seemed. Whoever had persuaded Stan back on the booze must have used charm. It would have taken quite some persuasion, if not flirtation – Alan was convinced of that. But he also knew that Flower lacked charm and besides, Stan would have been in some awe of him, a senior academic figure. It was far more likely that Stan would pretend he was still teetotal than risk jeopardising his professional reputation in front of him.

Alan didn't suppose for one moment that Clare had done it, because she had told Alan on the Cambridge Antiquarians' visit to Fursey last year, that she was so proud of the way Stan had kicked the drink. And besides, she wouldn't have had ready access to the cellars of Fisher College.

So that left just one other woman. And she had enough – more than enough – charm.

And a motive?

Alan pondered this for a moment. Oh yes, he thought, she had plenty of that, too.

# Eighteen

Alan had arranged to meet Davey Hibbs and Jake Williamson in the Cripps Arms at eight o'clock. He got there around 8.15, having fallen asleep in the bath. He'd been there for about 45 minutes, before the rapidly chilling water woke him up. His fingers and toes were stiff, white and wrinkly. He needed a pint badly.

In the pub Davey and Jake were with a group of young men – farm and estate workers mostly – who lived and worked in the village. They were all regulars and Cyril treated them like gold dust.

As he headed towards the bar to buy another round of lager and Old Slodger, a man proclaimed, in a loud and very middle-class voice, 'I say, there's that archaeologist chappie.'

Alan turned his head, but continued to make his way to the bar. Davey, Jake and the others fell silent. As one, they looked at the man. He seemed oblivious and continued louder than before.

'Are you ever going to finish that damned dig? Some of us around here would like our weekends back. You can't move in the village on Sundays. If we wanted crowds, we'd have bought homes in town. This village is meant to be rural, you know.'

Before Alan could say a word, a young woman in a pale silk scarf and fashionable Barbour jacket, loudly declared to the world and her near-identical friend loudly, 'Well said, Jeremy! This place is being ruined by all the visitors. Quite destroying its character. Something should be done about it.'

At that, one or two people said, 'Hear, hear,' but not very loudly. Alan caught Cyril's gaze as he handed him a beer. Both men raised their eyes to heaven. The pub was packed. The last thing Cyril wanted was for second-homers to stop coming.

When Alan returned to his friends, he knew what their response would be to the loud-mouthed incomer. All of them, and their families, needed the extra work and business the visitors to Fursey brought in. They knew, too, that the numbers would eventually settle down and that Fursey would never become another tourists' Jorvik, nor indeed an Ely.

But if tension was increasing between incomers and residents who worked in the village, the older generation were not exactly relaxed, either. Alan had detected quite a strong feeling that there was indeed 'something' behind the Curse of the Cripps. Of course they were too polite to raise the subject with him, a close friend of one of the victims, but he was detecting references to it on a daily basis, if not more often. People of a particular age would suddenly stop talking, or would exaggeratedly change the subject, whenever he approached. But he knew what they had been discussing, nonetheless. And he also detected a certain look behind the eyes. He couldn't be certain, of course, but he was pretty sure he was right.

But Davey, Jake and the lads around them weren't bothered by stupid curses. They were a genial, straightforward bunch who liked nothing better than a good laugh and plenty of beer. Alan glanced up at the clock over the fireplace. Half past nine. Suddenly he felt his phone vibrate in his shirt pocket. He pulled it out. It was Richard Lane who at once detected he was in the pub – and having a good time.

'Alan, I've been doing a bit of background research on some of the people you mentioned when we last met.'

'Oh, yes?' Suddenly Alan wished his head wasn't fuzzy after three pints of Slodger.

'But I can't discuss it over the phone – even if you hadn't enjoyed a skinful of Old Slodger. So I was wondering whether you'd care to have lunch with us in Whittlesey tomorrow?'

* * *

Sunday morning was fresh, bright and breezy: a fabulous spring day, and just the time, Alan thought, for a drive across the Fens. He opened the Fourtrak's window to let in a blast of cool air. That felt better. It eased the nagging headache that invariably followed a hard night on the Slodger.

On a whim, he decided to point the Fourtrak in the direction of Ramsey, rather than straight north, which would be a shorter route to Lane's house in Whittlesey. It had been a while since he'd driven across the bed of the old Whittlesey Mere. And besides, he thought, I've loads of time.

As he drew closer to the old mere, the roads got increasingly uneven as the deep peats beneath them shifted and shrank. An engineer friend had said it was like building a causeway across blancmange, or custard. As he passed the mere, just south of Peterborough, Alan could see the East Coast mainline that Stevenson had floated on bundles of brushwood in the mid-19th century, just as the Romans had done with their roads, two millennia previously.

Alan drove out of Ramsey Heights, one of the lowest-lying settlements in Britain, and was heading due north in a dead straight line. He loved that name. So very Fenny. The story went that two old boys were leaning on a gate surveying the grass in a meadow when a passing young surveyor for the first edition of the Ordnance Survey 1-inch map, asked, 'I say, can one of you good men tell me the name of this village?'

The nearest turned round, pushed the cap to the back of his head and slowly replied, 'It be Ramsey Eyots.'

He then turned back to his companion and the meadow and the surveyor departed.

Eyots, pronounced 'eights' is the old word for island, but the surveyor mistook it for 'heights'. And it stuck, immortalised by the map. Alan smiled, mistakes with place names can easily become fossilised forever, and they do matter, because they're not just dots on maps. Towns and villages are where people live; their names are part of their sense of place and have the power to create passionate loyalties – and not just for football clubs.

This turned Alan's thoughts to the Penance, which was starting in just four days' time. He was sure that it was all based on an error, but would it prove to be harmless, like Ramsey Heights? He wasn't so sure. And as time passed he found he was feeling less and less certain. He didn't like the word Penance – too melodramatic; it went with Curse and

Retribution – but there was no other way he could describe it. No, the more he thought about it, the more he had a sense of foreboding. Religious people liked penance. It let them do what they wanted, and then they asked God to wipe the slate clean.

Halfway across the bed of the Mere, Alan turned left and headed towards the uplands of old Huntingdonshire. It was a vast and largely open landscape. On the edges of the deep black dykes were heaps of old tree trunks, the so-called 'bog oaks' that were dragged up by the plough every autumn. It was a sign, of course, that the surface of this fen was still shrinking, as drainage ate away at the layers of peat. In his father's day the bog oaks were Roman or Iron Age, today they were more likely a millennium earlier. Whittlesey Mere had been the largest body of freshwater in England before its drainage around 1850, and had partly survived because it was used as fishing, wildfowl and game reserves for great landed families, particularly the Rothschilds. He had seen photographs of their huge fishing and shooting parties. He smiled at the thought: that was how very influential people networked in the 19th century. It was strange to think that this bleak open fen with its huge and very wild birch wood had once been such an important social centre for the banking elite.

For a moment, Alan thought again of the great stone blocks with the mason's marks that were pushed out of barges when they grounded while on their way to Ely from the quarries at Barnack. Those marks were the medieval equivalents of brands; they were in effect 'Keep Off' signs. They proclaimed ownership and authority. Nobody in their right mind would have chipped or damaged them deliberately. It would have risked the wrath of God. Such fears can be very long-lived – especially in people of Faith. Maybe, Alan wondered, that was another reason why the man – or just as possibly, the men – who filled Thorey's pockets, chose to use bricks alone?

He was now in a hurry to get out of the deepest Black Fen. It was magnificent, yes, but it could also get him down. It was so black, so flat and sometimes, too, so oppressive. He reached the crossing over the East Coast Main Line, which was closed. Then he remembered. It was Sunday. Engineering work. He'd been stuck here previously, for ages, on a Sunday. So he did a U-turn and headed back the way he had come. Twenty minutes later, he turned off the main road towards Lane's house.

* * *

Alan eased the Fourtrak into Straw Bear Close and parked on the gravel in front of number 6. Good roast dinner smells wafted through the air. Mary liked to spoil Alan. Sometimes he thought it was because she was trying to tame him by example: find a nice woman like me and you could eat food like this whenever you chose. But other times he thought differently: maybe she was always like this and wasn't trying to be clever at all. Maybe she just liked to cook well. Maybe life wasn't that complicated. Sod it. He rang the bell.

Mary answered the door. She was wearing an apron, and Alan could smell beef cooking in the kitchen. She kissed him on the cheek.

'Come in, Alan. I'm just basting the joint. Lunch will be ready in about half an hour. Richard's in the front room. He's looking something up. Told me to welcome you.'

'And that was convenient?'

'Yes.' She raised her eyes to the sky. 'Just what I needed when trying to start a Yorkshire pudding.'

Gingerly Alan opened the door to the sitting room. Richard Lane was in front of his computer. He waved Alan to a seat and after about a minute turned off the screen and joined him. He poured a glass of beer.

'Sorry about that, Alan, but I've been following up a few leads about your friend John Cripps. I was intrigued by what you told me about the religious stuff—'

'You mean him and Dean Jason?'

'Yes, the Fen dean. He's causing a bit of a ripple – waves even – with this Penance. I don't think we've seen the dear old C of E generate quite so much local interest in years. And I was surprised that John Cripps was a part of it.'

'Yes, and a key part too, from what I can see. The thing is, he's quite an expert on tourism. And what's a pilgrimage involving probably dozens of people—'

'No, Alan,' Lane interrupted. 'According to our sources there are likely to be hundreds, maybe even up into the low thousands, of pilgrims.'

'Blimey!' Alan paused as the implications of this sank in. It was going to be a rerun of the live shoot. 'But as I was saying: what's a pilgrimage if it isn't a form of tourism? People travel and then spend money. It worked very effectively in the Middle Ages and the Church certainly exploited it economically – indeed everyone did – and I bet it'll work *just* as well today. And of course John Cripps is a consultant who understands these things. He'd have been involved, even if he was an atheist.'

Lane was sitting back nodding in agreement while Alan was speaking. He took a sip from his beer.

'Well, anyhow,' Lane eventually said. 'After our chat last month about the estate, Historic Projects Management and the new manager, I thought I'd do a little quiet research into our religious friend John Cripps.'

'Yes, John has always struck me as a bit contradictory. I don't know much about him, but he got a good history degree at Cambridge—'

'That's right,' Lane broke in, 'A 2:1, "a workaday upper second" as one old man described it to me.'

Alan was aware that even given ten years of study, he could never hope to achieve a Cambridge 2:1.

'So he's very bright. D'you think he had intended to get a first?'

'What, and become an academic?' Lane asked rhetorically. He took a sip from his glass. 'Possibly – I don't know. But he would certainly have had to abandon any such thoughts after his third year, when he fell in with a crowd of rich young men who spent most of their time at Newmarket.'

'But presumably he didn't have the money?'

'Precisely. By the mid-1980s Barty had done a lot to raise the fortunes of the estate, but we also know he was heavily indebted to the bank and there would have been very little cash floating around. Both John and Sebastian's school and university costs had been met by a private trust fund established by the second baronet when he rationalised the estate after the war.'

'So in other words,' Alan continued, 'he had the background, but not the cash.' It was his turn to take a sip of beer. 'So what happened next?'

'I can't discover anything about the two years after he graduated. That's something we'd have to learn from a close family member – and I'm certain it's not worth it, as it would alert everyone.'

'Yes, I agree.' Alan nodded.

'The next thing we know for sure, is that he was part of a trading partnership set up in 1989 to manage a series of small, mostly amateur, visitor attractions in east London. At the time, money to fund tourism projects was becoming much more freely available and several local volunteer groups were restoring and repairing the Napoleonic and later defences on the shores of the Thames, on the eastern approaches to London.'

'Yes,' Alan said. 'I was reading about one in an archaeological magazine. They're still very popular.'

'With the volunteers, yes. But they never seem to generate many actual fee-paying visitors. None of them are in the same league as Jorvik, for example.'

Alan wasn't sure where this was all leading. 'OK, so he formed a partnership. What happened then?'

'One of the partners was Blake Lonsdale – and I have been able to find out a bit more about him. By all accounts, he's a very bright bloke, but completely unqualified. In his early twenties he got involved with drug dealing and illicit gambling and served two short terms inside. During his second spell in prison he "found Jesus", as he puts it.'

'Ah, just like his colleague—'

'And now, it would seem, his close friend: John Cripps.'

'I must admit,' Alan said. 'I didn't know that Lonsdale was religious too?'

'Yes,' Lane replied. 'They both are. And it goes back a long way, too. One of the older volunteers at Fort Marlborough, just outside Tilbury, told me that Lonsdale persuaded a local vicar to hold a short service of blessing in one of the casemates. That was back in 1990, before any work had started, and he clearly remembered that both Cripps and Lonsdale attended.'

'But when did HPM begin?'

'That was also in 1990.'

'So the partnership was very short-lived?'

'Yes. The two other partners left—'

'Or were they pushed?'

'That's hard to say, Alan. Put it this way: they're both still actively involved in business – and the businesses are entirely legit, so far as the local force is aware. One runs two greengrocers, the other's an insurance broker.'

'So they dissolved the partnership to set up HPM?'

'Yes, that's how it seems. HPM is a management company. It doesn't have charitable status itself, but the visitor attractions that it services all do.'

'Right . . .' Suddenly the jigsaw was starting to fit together. 'It's all starting to make sense now. I know about Fursey and White Delphs, and the last time we spoke, I remember mentioning another one that Barty had just told me about – something to do with water – in east London. Can you remember it?'

'Oh yes, I wrote it down then and there. And since then I've started checking up on it. It's the Water World historical theme park on the edges of Hackney Marshes. According to their accounts lodged at Companies House, it's been a great and growing success – and for some time too. Thousands of school children visit every week of the winter season, and in summer the place is packed, too. I spoke to a senior exec in the leisure industry and she sang their praises. It's the wintertime when visitor numbers always collapse at historical attractions, but not at Water World.'

'No, nor at White Delphs or Fursey, either,' Alan added. 'HPM obviously know what they're doing.'

'Yes, you're right, they do. My source also said they were incredibly well-financed and capitalised. That's how they could afford to build all the winter walkways and observation platforms. She told me that visitor-flow management is a key part of their "offer".'

And that continuing supply of money, Alan wondered, has got to come from somewhere. Now, however, he was feeling far less frustrated. Once more, a discussion with Richard Lane had clarified his mind. He realised he had become too concerned with Sebastian. Sure, he was no angel, but he wasn't the brightest of people, either. The more he considered John's early career, the more he wondered how far the younger brother was pulling the elder brother's strings. And then there was Candice. Alan was becoming increasingly convinced it was she who had got Stan back on the booze. She could be so charmingly persuasive. Now he realised she may not have been acting alone: together with her husband they made a mean team. Effectively, they now controlled everything: Sebastian, the estate and probably Barty, too.

Alan leant back in his chair, his eyes closed. Lane looked on. He knew he mustn't interrupt while Alan was having one of his thinking blitzes.

OK, Alan thought, I don't know all the details; I don't even understand the means or the mechanisms likely to have been employed, but he now knew when, and possibly even why, it had all started. Families, especially declining high-class families, can do the strangest things in their desperation to avoid humiliation. And once you had grasped the history, the truth often followed close behind. Suddenly his thoughts had become grim: and as for the perpetrators and their motives, they would all come out – in The Wash? He hoped not literally, but feared the worst. Suddenly his imagination flashed up images of Stan in the river and Thorey at the sluice.

Mary called from the kitchen door. She, too, had been observing Alan.

'Come on, Alan, time to eat. You can't put the world to rights on an empty stomach.'

Her words rang bells. Alan remembered John's enthusiasm for the physical side of the Penance, as he'd expressed it in the press release: 'Our aim is to achieve purity of mind through fasting and strenuous physical labour.' Maybe that would be the catalyst that would force things out into the open? For the second time that Sunday, Alan was gripped by a strong sense of foreboding.

* * *

The rain had started overnight on Tuesday, and by Thursday it was well set in. It wasn't so much stormy and dramatic, as springtime weather can often be, but dark, gloomy and persistent. It was the sort of weather that reminded Alan of backstreets in some big city: no sky, nor skyline, just enfolding pavements, tall walls and low cloud ceiling; not like being outdoors at all.

Before the bad weather started, Alan had been dreading the opening ceremony – and it wasn't just the little speech of appreciation of Stan's achievements that he'd agreed to give at the unveiling of the plaque in the Stan Beaton Archaeology Centre – and anyhow, he quite liked public speaking. No, it was the forced smiles and endless networking which went with it – that was what he found hard work. It would be an event where everyone involved with the Fursey project would be present. Yet another Agatha Christie all-in-the-library moment. His heart sank. Despite his depression he had become increasingly convinced that behind-the-scenes pressures were starting to reach a point where something had to give. Maybe the heightened emotions leading up to a big public event might provide the trigger, or the tipping-point? Whatever happened, Alan knew he had to be ready for it. And he determined to keep a close eye on John Cripps and Peter Flower. They were the men to watch.

For Alan, the impending opening ceremony was horribly reminiscent of Stan's wake, a bare five months earlier. Such a long time ago, but the days, the hours, seemed to be passing so much faster. And it wasn't just time; other things were different, too: at last he had solid facts to work with.

* * *

Alan didn't possess a suit, but he did have a fairly respectable jacket and just one pair of smartish, dark-blue trousers. His black Oxford shoes weren't exactly shiny, but at least they were clean. He'd done his best to look formal.

He arrived at the ceremony promptly, as requested, and walked up to Candice and Peter Flower who were welcoming the arriving guests. He waited while they greeted a middle-aged man in a dark suit and his wife who was wearing a smart, doubtless designer, creation, that was slightly too tight for her. As they moved towards the tea table, Candice looked up and saw Alan. She kissed him on both cheeks.

'Thanks for arriving so promptly, Alan. Have you got your speech prepared?'

'Don't worry. It's here,' he tapped his breast pocket. He could see she thought he'd learnt it by heart.

'We'll unveil the plaque in about half an hour, when everyone's assembled.'

'Are Stan's parents here?'

'Oh, didn't you hear? His dad had a stroke last week. He's in Addenbrooke's. His mum's staying with him, poor woman.'

Alan was deeply shocked.

'I imagine, it was the stress . . .' he began, but trailed off. There was nothing to say. He felt bad: he should have kept in closer touch.

'And in case you're wondering why I'm here—' Peter Flower's voice broke into Alan's thoughts. Alan suppressed the urge to reply that he didn't give a damn why he was here – or anywhere else, come to that. 'It's because John is preparing for tomorrow's pilgrimage—'

'No, it's a *Penance*, Peter,' Candice corrected him.

It was plain to Alan that neither of them took tomorrow's big event even slightly seriously.

'Oh, sorry, yes. He's preparing for the Penance. With the dean and a group of disadvantaged youngsters from Stratford-upon-Avon—'

Candice was smiling as she cast her eyes to the ceiling and made a show of correcting him yet again. 'No, Peter, it's *Stratford*. Don't you remember: east London, not the west Midlands?'

'Well, anyhow,' Flower continued, undaunted. 'He can't be here. He's on his knees in some church hall somewhere, doubtless fasting.'

Alan was surprised that Candice allowed this: it was her husband he was caricaturing so unkindly. Stranger still, she was smiling, broadly.

* * *

The greetings were taking place in a temporary porch-like tent erected outside the old double doors of the converted 17th-century reed barn, which had probably been built to house dry reeds for thatching; or it may have got its name from its large reed-thatched roof, which had been beautifully restored with reeds cut on the farm. It also featured two sets of double doors, which appeared, so Alan reckoned, to be contemporary with the original build – which suggested to him that the barn may have served a dual purpose: for storing reeds and for processing crops such as wheat and barley, where a through-draft, provided by the two double doors, would have been essential. But Alan was impressed: they had done a splendid restoration – the brickwork had been cleaned and repointed where necessary, and even the floor had been surfaced with modern woven rush matting, which gave the space a more homely atmosphere.

Alan was looking up at the roof trusses, many of which were oak and original, when somebody called his name. He glanced down: it was Clare, who was walking rapidly towards him from a small group of people standing in the corner of the barn.

'Alan.' She beamed. 'Come and meet my boss, the CPO. He's dying to meet you.' She kissed him on both cheeks. Then lightly she whispered in his ear, 'He's a huge fan of yours.'

David Harper was the chief planning officer and as they

walked towards the group of three in the corner, Alan recognised him and his wife as the people ahead of him in the welcoming queue. The other person was Sebastian Cripps who was talking very earnestly to the CPO.

After the introductions, Harper asked Alan about the Fursey/Fursey connection.

'Tell me quite frankly: do you accept it?'

Alan paused. This was going to be tricky with Sebastian alongside them.

As if reading his mind, Sebastian said, 'Don't worry about me, Alan. I'm far from convinced. It all seems a bit contrived: almost too good to be true. And why on earth would they then found another, much greater, abbey such a short distance away?'

'That's a good point,' Alan replied. 'But it was well over a thousand years ago and they didn't apply the same rules as we do today. Take the Witham Valley, just outside Lincoln. There are abbeys and priories next to one another, like the rungs of a ladder: they reach right down the river valley and into the fen. And they're far closer to each other than Ely and Fursey.'

'But the place-name business.' Harper was looking very sceptical. 'That does seem a bit – how can I put it? – a bit convenient, if not, as Sebastian says, contrived?'

Alan sighed. 'I must confess, I'm an archaeologist, not a place-names person and it's fair to say that you could make such assertions fifty years ago and get away with it. Back then, people assumed that if a town or village had, say, a Saxon or Viking place name, then it was a new foundation. They chose to disregard the fact that people were perfectly capable of renaming existing settlements.'

'Like old New York was once New Amsterdam?' Harper's

wife added, as if miming to the song. They were all still waiting for tea, but somehow she had managed to find a glass of white wine.

'Exactly.' Alan nodded. He could not have put it better himself.

'But do you accept the Fursey/Fursey connection?' Harper asked.

'It's as good an idea as any, but no better than the original one.'

'Which was?'

'It was a bit complicated, but as I recall it was something to do with the Viking word for a "rump-shaped island"—'

'Which describes Fursey to a T.' Harper's wife broke in. She turned to Sebastian. 'So the Crippses own a rump-shaped island!'

She thought this very amusing – unlike Sebastian whose smile was distinctly strained.

'It's the same old Scandinavian word as Furness, as in Barrow-in-Furness,' Alan continued. At least Harper was listening – and intently. 'I think the actual word was *futh*, however you pronounce it.'

'So that doesn't exactly sound a like a clear link, does it?' Harper asked.

'No,' Alan replied. 'I agree, it doesn't. In some ways Fursey is just as plausible.'

'But you're not happy about either?'

Alan smiled. At last, somebody understood. Sebastian looked blank.

* * *

Alan rose to his feet. His sheet of notes was still folded inside his breast pocket. Somehow he didn't think he would need to refer to them. He knew damn well what he was expected to say, but he had just followed the CPO's tipsy wife and had discovered where the wine was kept. It wasn't hard to mime to a hired Latvian waitress that he needed two glasses of red for some aged relatives. Then rapidly he drank both of them – one to Stan's memory, the other to his absent parents. He had, of course, already seen the plaque:

To the Memory of Stanley Gilbert Beaton, Archaeologist.
17 January, 1972 – 8 October, 2009

The precision of those dates had really struck home. That was Stan's time on this planet, among us. Now he was gone and would never be coming back. Alan found the unforgiving finality horrible. But it had been made ten times worse by the now almost certain knowledge that his death was no accident, nor had it happened on some mad impulse. Everything was pointing to a well-conceived plan. There was no way this was manslaughter. No, it was murder, pure and simple. Manslaughter cannot be intentional.

Around him the room had grown quiet. All eyes were on him. Normally he would have looked away – to the curtained plaque behind him or to his notes – anything to avoid those eyes. But not now. He surveyed the crowd slowly and deliberately. At least one person out there had killed his friend and this was another chance to get them to reveal themselves. So far he had tried subtlety: gently probing, discreet questions, that 'set-piece' fiasco, to tempt them out. But none of them had worked.

Now it was time to be more brutal. He rapidly pulled the notes from his pocket, glanced down at them, and began.

'I first knew Stan Beaton when we were students at Leicester in the early 1990s. We went on many digs together and we became close friends. Very close friends.' He paused. There was a huge lump in his throat. Alan was angry with himself: this was not what he had intended. He swallowed hard. He took a sip of red wine from a stranger's glass and his resolve returned.

'Stan's speciality was the later Iron Age and Roman period, so when I heard he had started work here I was delighted. The area was known to be rich in archaeology, and if anyone could crack open its secrets, it was Stan. In fact, I visited him several times and we were in close, almost daily touch.' Alan took another sip from the borrowed glass, his eyes scrutinising the audience closely as he spoke. 'Not many people realise, even now, what he had discovered in and around Fursey and I'd like to use this opportunity to briefly describe his extraordinary achievement here.'

He wanted these words to sink in. While still observing the faces around him, he pretended to look at his notes. Then he put them away for good.

'Stan Beaton's revelations were extraordinary and I only hope the recent ill-judged staff reductions in the County and District Planning Offices will be able to protect the wealth of new sites that he discovered and that are still being revealed almost daily.' Again he paused. There were murmurs towards the back of the room. Several press camera bulbs flashed. 'Thanks to his research, we now know that the shore around Ely and the fringes of the pre-drainage islands, such as Fursey, were once dry, fertile plains. About the time of Christ, many of the pilgrims who will be taking part in tomorrow's Penance would have been walking through fields of wheat and lush grazing, rather than wet fen.' It was a slight exaggeration, but what the hell; he needed to make a point.

'Stan's work revealed that dozens, perhaps even hundreds, of previously unknown sites still lie around the edges of the higher ground. And make no mistake . . .' Again he scrutinised the faces around him. 'These aren't ordinary sites. They haven't been damaged by the plough, nor have they dried out in the two millennia since their burial. No, they are perfectly preserved. Everything will be, there: clothes, shoes, baskets, wooden boats, food, leaves, wool.' He paused for effect. 'Even human hair.'

As he turned slowly towards the plaque, he could see reporters scribbling frantically. What was it about human hair? It never failed to get people going.

He waited for almost a minute until the audience had quietened down.

'Thank you, Stan, for all that you have given us.'

This was said quietly – a trick he had learnt from a schoolteacher. It worked. He examined the audience. Every face looked sad, reflective. John's head was bent in prayer. Sebastian stood at the back, cleaning his nails with a penknife. The entire room was as still as a grave.

Then he pulled the cord.

* * *

After his short speech, Alan had everyone raise their glasses to wish Stan's father a rapid recovery. Then Candice announced that food was available and suddenly the mood of the place lightened.

Alan headed straight for the buffet where he found all the archaeologists already piling their plates, while the other guests continued to mingle and network politely behind them. Even Harriet, who was normally a better networker than any of his colleagues, was there. Normally she would have been talking to friends and relations of the clients. She wasn't a great fan of what was left of the archaeological 'circuit' – 'circus' she called it – and preferred to spend her time talking to 'real' people. It was a side of her that Alan didn't really understand. He liked the world of archaeology and felt comfortably at home within it. He also wasn't a party animal, whereas she loved meeting new people and delving into their lives. Before their earlier relationship had gone pear-shaped, he used to look forward to hearing what she had discovered after they'd been to a party together. He'd rarely have learnt anything new, whereas she always unearthed the most amazing stories. And yet, Alan thought to himself, I'm the one who spends my life unravelling mysteries.

But now here Harriet was, chatting amiably to Clare. He was seriously debating whether to join them or not when he felt a tap on his shoulder. He turned round. It was Lew Weinstein.

'I somehow thought I'd find you here, Alan.'

Alan swallowed back his irritation. Stan was his friend. Where else would he be? This was a matter of paying tribute, not a networking opportunity.

'So how's it going, the filming I mean?'

'That's what I want to talk about, Alan. There have been some big developments. Can we have a quiet word? It won't take long.'

* * *

They sat down on two dry, but paint-spattered, folding chairs in an adjoining room that was still being decorated. The window was open a crack, which let in some welcome cool air. Alan saw the silent white of a barn owl as it swooped past in the gathering twilight.

'As you know, Alan, the "live" was a huge success, and the big news is that T2 are keen to run a second live series before the summer gets underway.'

'Blimey, that's a bit sudden, isn't it?'

'Not really. We've known for some time that focus groups have been telling us that the eighteen to thirty-five demographic wants to see more—'

Alan had had a bellyful of hearing about that particular 'demographic'. He cut in.

'And they can. But next year. It doesn't have to be now, this minute, does it?'

'I'm afraid it does – at least so far as that particular age group is concerned. As Charles Carnwath told me last week: if we don't offer them something now, we stand a good chance of losing them next year – maybe forever.'

Alan sighed. He could do without it. He wanted to get on and be an archaeologist – to do some archaeology without the whole world watching his every move.

'I suppose so.'

'And then when Peter Flower phoned me last week with news of the Fursey Penance, I knew we'd found the right vehicle—'

'For heaven's sake, Lew.' Alan had to interrupt. 'You can't possibly launch a full-blown "live" by tomorrow, because that's when it all starts.'

'We're not planning a "full-blown live" for the Penance.

We plan to use that as a come-on for the main show, which will start on Easter Monday. But earlier than the last series. We want to catch younger people before they go out. Saturday's show will finish by half past six. The channel are very keen indeed, but do you think you'll be ready?' He was looking imploringly at Alan. '*Please* say yes.'

'I don't see why not . . .' Alan trailed off doubtfully. Then another thought struck him. 'But will it be possible to organise the production at such notice?'

The thought of another series of live shows was daunting, to say the least. What with the weather and the ceaseless stream of visitors, it had been a hard season so far. In fact, he was looking forward to a short break – not more intensive work – over the Easter holiday. But then there was another side to it, too. He thought about the speech he'd just given. Somehow he had to get the Cripps family to show their hand – to make a mistake. So far they had played everything superbly – whether by accident or design – but it couldn't go on forever.

Alan never considered that he might be completely mistaken about the Crippses. Those days were long behind him and besides, Richard Lane was now backing him – clearly he had his suspicions too: hence his probing of Blake Lonsdale's murky past. So maybe, he thought, I could use the second live series to stir things up. He knew only too well that there's nothing like massive public scrutiny to increase tensions. His mind was made up; this time he was certain that something *had* to give.

'It would be a shame,' Alan continued, 'if we don't have familiar cameramen, for example. And there are practical things, too. New people would have to be trained not to walk all over the trenches.'

But Weinstein had answers for everything.

'We're nearly there already. All the familiar faces will be back. Speed's joining us on Easter Day and Frank will be here soon. But you're forgetting, we've had three days to work on it and so far we've managed to get almost identical crews and technicians to the first "live". So more or less everyone knows precisely what they'll be doing. It won't be anything like as bad as starting from scratch.'

'So what are you planning for the pilgrimage stuff?'

'It's tailor-made for the web and digital. So it'll be featured big-time on 2-Much and on our website. In fact, it'll start with edited clips of this party. It'll provide a nice contrast with the fasting of the pilgrims.'

'Fasting?' Alan still didn't know the precise details.

'Yes,' Weinstein replied. 'The really devout ones are going to go without food for the entire weekend. Some have even started this evening. It's all about a sincere penance for the corruption of modern life.'

'Hmm, I doubt if many of them are bankers.'

'But that's not the point, Alan, and you know it.' He took a bite from the buttered roll he'd picked up from the buffet table. 'No,' he continued when he'd swallowed. 'It'll finish the season with a bang, not a whimper.'

This surprised Alan. 'A whimper? Why? Did ratings fall-off after the "live"?'

'Yes, they did. Sadly, *Slow-Cook Countdown* wasn't the success the high-ups at T2 had hoped. It lacked the immediacy of a celebrity bake-off. Whatever else you might say about them, the Beeb still do food shows better than anyone.'

Alan smiled. He had visions of Lord Reith turning in his gravy. Then he had a disconcerting thought.

'And will Tricia be joining us again?'

'Sadly we can't persuade her. The people she's signed up with won't hear of it. They want her face to be identified with them, and them alone. It's not uncommon in television, especially with up-and-coming talent. The old phrase was "for contractual reasons".'

Alan was relieved to hear this. 'So who else are you planning to get?'

'Well, that's one of the things I wanted to discuss with you, Alan. Obviously we'll have Peter Flower, and of course Michael Smiley is still available. I thought he did a very good job before, but was rather wasted chairing the studio panel on the last "live". So we've asked him to present a series of five-minute films on *Fursey in History*, which will be based around the new museum display.'

'So do you plan to drop the studio panel altogether?'

'Oh, no. It's far too important, as a link. And we also need somewhere to put the new finds in context. So it's staying, but now it'll be chaired by Peter Flower. And he's such a pro, he'll have no trouble combining chairing with being a panellist, too.'

No, he'll relish it, Alan thought. But he said nothing.

'But with regards to who else we'll have, I need your input. Who does the archaeology suggest to you? I gather there are more graves?'

'Yes, right now the score's eight. They're currently being dug and studied by Harriet Webb and a graduate student of hers. I know Harriet's done some television, but I don't know how much. In fact, she's here at the opening – at that corner table out there.' He nodded in the direction of the door.

'Do you think she could cope with a big role? I'm not saying we'll get her to present, or anything like that, but we do need a robust foil for you. And you must admit, Tricia did that very well.'

'Yes, I'm quite certain Harriet *could* do it, but . . .'

'But you're not sure she'd *want* to; is that what you're saying?'

It wasn't, but what the hell. Alan sighed heavily. 'Put it like this, Lew, there might be reasons why she wouldn't want to work with me. And it's got nothing to do with TPC. It's my problem entirely.' Alan decided he'd said enough.

Weinstein frowned. He knew that much was riding on Harriet's response.

'Well, we'll ask her now.' He rose from his chair, then turned to Alan. 'But please let me do most of the talking. OK?'

Alan nodded. They started walking.

'And are Kaylee and Jake still with you?'

'Yes they are.'

'Excellent.' Weinstein smiled broadly. 'That'll help with continuity. And they both acquired quite a following on our website during the "live". I gather Kaylee's now got a growing presence on Twitter.'

Alan smiled. She'd kept that one to herself.

* * *

Alan and Weinstein walked over to the group of archaeologists sitting at the corner table, eating voraciously and saying little. Clare had left them and returned to the CPO and Sebastian, who was now joined by his wife Sarah, and by Peter

Flower. Even from the other side of the hall, Alan could see their discussion was intense. And their body language was interesting, too: Sarah and Sebastian seemed somehow more husband-and-wife than they normally did. Clare was looking on, slightly out of it. She glanced up, caught Alan's gaze, and smiled.

Harriet hadn't piled her plate as high as the others and had finished eating by the time Alan and Weinstein arrived.

'Ah, Harriet, I'm Lew Weinstein. You might have heard Alan mention my name.'

'Indeed, he talks about you all the time.'

'Politely, I hope.'

'Of course.'

She was smiling as she stood up. Weinstein was about to shake her hand, when she leant forward and kissed him on the cheek. Alan could see the older man greatly preferred that.

After they had found a quieter spot, away from the others, Weinstein told Harriet about their plans for TPC Live 2. He explained how the format would follow the success of Live 1 and would start on Easter Monday and run for six days, with the last episode early on Saturday evening. He went on to explain that there had been some minor changes in the line-up and he was hoping she would agree to 'quite a prominent role'. Alan was expecting that she would be anxious about this – and not just because of their past personal problem. He was also conscious that she didn't always feel completely happy about television work – which was strange, given that she had a natural, dignified, screen presence. Maybe it reflected her family's quiet, upper middle class respectability: her father had been a successful solicitor in

Grantham and had lived in a beautiful Georgian manor house on the edge of Dawyck Fen. It wasn't the sort of upbringing that necessarily welcomed the harsh lights of television.

In the event, she showed no reticence at all when Weinstein described her new role. Quite the opposite, in fact.

'Gosh, Lew,' she replied. 'That sounds wonderful. I must admit to being quite a fan of *Test Pit Challenge*, although when it was announced I did have misgivings. But the format really works. And best of all, it has produced some real surprises. I need hardly add that the first Fursey live shows were amazing. Candice Cripps tells me they surprised the family as much as the participants.'

And yes, Alan thought, that's *just* what we need to repeat – only more so.

Harriet was looking genuinely delighted. Then she turned to Alan. 'And I'm sure we could manage it together – don't you, Alan?'

'Er, absolutely. Yes, we could – we can.'

Blimey. He took a large gulp of wine. Suddenly his world had turned upside down. What did it all mean? Was it good? Bad? He had no idea. But it was certainly very different.

Alan thought he had concealed his confusion. But he hadn't. Weinstein and Harriet were standing together, smiling at him. Suddenly Weinstein looked very serious.

'Alan?' He said this slowly. Portentously.

'Yes, Lew?'

There was a short pause. Perfect timing.

'You're the worst bloody actor, I've ever seen!

# Nineteen

Directly after the opening ceremony, Harriet returned to Cambridge. Alan, Jake and Kaylee had spent the evening in the Cripps Arms. Davey Hibbs had been there, plus one or two locals, who also enjoyed a couple of pints. In fact, Alan thought, as he popped two aspirins, we had a cracking good night. Drank rather more Slodger than was good for us; but he didn't care – inside his head he felt more relaxed than at any other time during his stay at Fursey.

He rolled over and turned on the bedside light. It was eight o'clock on Good Friday morning. No need to leap out of bed, as Jake was supervising the dig today. Then he remembered: last night he'd agreed to give Weinstein, Frank Jones and Michael Smiley a quick tour of the site and the new museum.

Alan lay back on the pillows. He had arranged to meet his small tour party at 9.30, so there was no rush. Then his phone rang. It was his brother Grahame. He told Alan to turn on BBC1 who were covering the Fursey Penance all morning on their regional news programme, *Face East.* Alan jumped out of bed and ran through to the kitchen and turned on the TV. He had high hopes: maybe a real sinner will be attempting to atone.

He didn't have to wait long. The five-minute clip showed some of the pilgrims filing out of a Victorian chapel, where they were individually blessed by the Fen dean. Then they formed into informal groups and made their way down to the river, where a flotilla of narrowboats was waiting to take them to Fursey for the start of the Penance proper. John Cripps was one of the last to leave the chapel. Like everyone else, he had just been given a white rucksack with a prominent red cross of St George. To Alan's eye, John already looked tired and the prominent red cross looked odd and made him seem more like an England football fan, than a humble penitent. Despite Alan's many misgivings, the Penance seemed to have gone down well with the crowds, which were growing all the time, despite the persistent rain.

* * *

Alan drew up in the car park alongside a nondescript Ford Focus estate, and as he climbed out he heard the Ford's front door open and close. It was Michael Smiley. What a surprise: Alan had expected him to have driven a Bentley, or a Jag at the very least.

They shook hands.

'Alan, it's a great pleasure to meet you. I've been such a fan of your Fenland work. That survey of the dykes around Thorney was a real eye-opener. I had no idea the old Abbey Estate concealed such a well-preserved set of prehistoric sites. They were astonishing. Are they going to Schedule any of them?'

This was not at all what Alan had expected from the retired TV quiz show presenter.

'Yes, I think they're planning to. But first we've got to do a follow-up survey with a more detailed look into local conditions and conservation. There's no point in protecting sites that are already drying out.'

Smiley was clearly fascinated. 'No, that makes lots of sense. But how do you plan to raise water levels? That must be by far your biggest problem?'

Blimey, Alan thought, this is like a post-doctoral research seminar. Then, to his relief, another car pulled up alongside them.

Weinstein and Frank Jones got out. Alan noted a slight change in Frank's demeanour since the first TPC 'live'. He seemed a little less cocky and over-confident. Who knows, maybe he'd learnt from his mistakes? Maybe. Alan decided to be kinder, but not to let his guard drop.

Alan had hoped they might have a leisurely cup of coffee before heading for the museum, but Weinstein explained that that he and Frank would have to drive back to London sooner than expected. As Alan had suspected, organising such a big operation as a multi-camera 'live', at very short notice, was not proving simple. He also suggested that Frank and Alan should have a detailed discussion on Easter Sunday morning, as Charles Carnwath needed to see shooting script outlines for the first three episodes. Alan smiled when he heard this. Even Carnwath knew that trenches were never predictable. But he, in his turn, had to keep the top brass at T2 happy.

Alan had been busy with the trench extension for the previous two weeks, so hadn't been able to see how the new museum displays were coming along. He'd written and checked all the labels for the earlier finds, but everything after the Norman Conquest was being handled by Peter Flower and a colleague in the history department at Cambridge. Being a good archaeologist, Alan decided to start his tour at the beginning of the story, with geology and drainage, but he had barely got started, when Weinstein's phone beeped. It was a text. He sighed in exasperation as he read it.

'I'm so sorry, Alan, half our technicians and the mixing truck are needed for a football match in Burnley. We'll have to look around for a replacement for Day 1. Could you get us back to the car in fifteen minutes?'

'That depends on what you want to see?'

'Well, we're looking for material to illustrate the short films that Michael here will be presenting.'

'OK. So what periods do you plan to cover?'

'Probably three on the Victorians and one on modern drainage problems. That should help make the place seem more exciting.'

'And something on the Civil War, too,' Frank added.

Alan looked at Frank closely. Had he heard something about the Curse of the Cripps? He hoped not, because it would be on TV screens nationally if he had. And that would undo everyone at Fursey's efforts to improve the place's local image.

' . . . And then finish with the Middle Ages.' Weinstein was drawing to a close. 'And of course we'll need to cover the foundation of Ely Cathedral.'

'And St Fursey?'

'Naturally, Alan. We can't do without our friend from

Ireland.' There was more than a hint of irony in Weinstein's voice.

* * *

So, for fifteen intensive minutes, Alan led them round to the start of the gallery, which opened with a wonderful 3-D panorama of a woodland scene, complete with life-like trees and animals, and echoing birdsong in the background. The display was all about game and shooting culture in the Victorian upper middle classes. It featured three keepers, all wearing authentic tweed suits with Norfolk jackets from the storeroom at Fursey Hall, which also produced their green woollen socks and stout lace-up boots. He'd seen Joe Thorey wearing an identical outfit – and it had suited his arrogant manner. Each plastic man carried a 12-bore shotgun. Beside them were two realistic mannequins of country gentlemen, this time wearing authentic-looking, but 'recreated' clothes. Arranged discretely around them were stuffed pheasants, woodcock, snipe and English partridges. A water bailiff and his young assistant stood in the background, holding rods and keeping nets, plus four glistening salmon and sea trout dangling by the gills from a pole. In the foreground was an arrangement of carefully labelled traps and snares, ranging from the very large to matchbox-sized. There were also three reproduction Victorian 'Wanted' posters for well-known local poachers, plus a couple of photocopies of newspaper cuttings describing in graphic details the heartbreaking scenes in court when convicted felons were sentenced to transportation.

Alan immediately recognised all the labelled objects, which had been part of what had become a rather moth-eaten display in the old Fursey restaurant. When they closed, just before Christmas, all the items on display had been professionally cleaned and carefully restored by a firm of conservators in Cambridge. They were not returned until a couple of weeks ago. Each trap and snare was clearly marked in white ink with one of the estate's display collection accession numbers, which were first assigned when Barty set up the shop and tea rooms, in the late 1970s.

The rest of the new museum was more informative, but it was also something of an anticlimax: mostly maps and objects. Alan realised that Candice, who had masterminded the new displays, had decided to spend the bulk of their budget on that eye-catching initial tableau. It was intended to hook visitors – and he had to admit, it did work. But the more he looked at it, the more Alan could see the hand of Candice behind it all. It was *so* carefully calculated. And it was projecting an image; there was no attempt to portray the social reality of the times. The wealthy squires were benign and didn't dominate the display. And there were no women, either. No, Alan thought, that splendid display has been made to impress the rest of the family. It's saying: you must all trust me. I'm on your side. Alan realised with a chill that she had taken control of far more than just the display budget. Alan was smiling as he turned away. Deep inside his head a voice whispered: Thank you for that, Candice. Her motives were as clear as the display they had created.

* * *

After about a 20-minute tour and hasty farewells, Weinstein and Frank scurried out into the rain and their car, and drove rapidly away. Alan and Michael Smiley strolled to the restaurant for a leisurely coffee.

The big room still smelled slightly of fresh paint and was largely empty as the first batch of the day's visitors were still out on-site. Alan thought Smiley was going to discuss water levels again. But he didn't. His first question took Alan completely by surprise.

'I would imagine you've heard local tales about the Curse of the Cripps?'

'Yes, but I can't say I attach much importance to them.'

'You're probably right, Alan.' Smiley was not living up to his name. He looked serious. 'But this Thorey business, coming hard on the heels of your friend's sad death isn't helping.' He paused to take a drink, then continued, slightly ominously. 'And of course the disappearance of the banker, Hansworth, hasn't been forgotten either. Us old boys remember that one very clearly.'

Alan wasn't surprised. Hansworth's death had only been six years ago, and it had made a big impact locally and regionally.

'Oh really?' Alan didn't ask a direct question. He didn't want to steer him in any direction: he knew that was the way to deflect fresh information.

'Yes. And the searches for Thorey and Hansworth's bodies were both so protracted, weren't they? I can remember somebody saying that was the best way to wash off any clues.'

Alan was genuinely surprised at this. 'So local people didn't believe they were accidental deaths?'

Smiley finished his coffee, then sat back. 'I'm accusing nobody. And of course tongues will wag. But you must admit the parallels are quite striking.'

'Yes, they are.'

And you haven't mentioned either, Alan thought to

himself, that both Hansworth and Thorey had very close contacts with the Cripps family.

'Anyhow,' Smiley continued, 'The rumour-mongers are gossiping as much as ever.' He paused. 'Worse, if anything.'

'What, you've heard rumours over in Newmarket?'

'Only among old fen fogeys like me. As I said, we all remember Hansworth. And then, of course, there's all that stuff about the early days of drainage. And even after the war, the Crippses behaved in – how shall I put it? – in a very hard-nosed fashion. They showed little consideration for others. My great-uncle, for instance, paid an arm and a leg for the mill.'

Smiley signalled for two more coffees.

'But I gained the impression it was left to him in a will?'

Alan knew from his research in the library that it had been sold, but he needed more information.

Smiley shook his head. 'Good heavens, no! Far from it. He paid a small fortune for it and even when he'd bought it outright, we discovered later that the Crippses had retained all the riparian rights.'

Alan looked puzzled.

'They're the rights to access and fish along the river banks. It sounds ludicrous, but my cousin Derek, who after all manages the place, can't even fish along his own Mill Cut without permission from Sebastian Cripps.'

'And has he allowed him?'

'Of course he has. He's not unreasonable. But he's never mentioned granting him the legal rights. He's stayed well clear of that. Oh no, they remain firmly with the Crippses.'

'That's ridiculous . . .' Alan shook his head.

'And Derek is such a hard worker and a very kind man,

too. I like him a lot.' He paused before saying, 'We're all aware that those Crippses have patronised us Smileys for hundreds of years. We were always the people-of-trade; "mere" millers. I'm sure that's why they didn't part with the mill until they absolutely had to. The lump-sum Granddad paid went a big way towards paying off their death duty debts.' He took a sip from his steaming mug of coffee. 'But did they ever express any gratitude, any thanks?' He shook his head in frustration.

'But what about Barty?' Alan asked. 'He's always struck me as a very reasonable sort of man?'

'Yes, I think he is. But you won't find him ever doing anything that goes against the family interest. As a younger man, he had a reputation for always being very close to his land agent. In my experience, those people tend to put business before charity.'

'So do you think the current television and PR campaign is going to get rid of the myth?'

'Maybe. To be honest, I don't altogether care. If it kills the stories for the current generation, then that's as much as we can expect – or hope.'

'If you don't mind me asking, Michael, why are you taking part? You're happily retired and you don't need the work, surely?'

'No, I don't. Although I do quite miss the TV world. I like the people, especially the ones behind the cameras. But no, you're right; I don't really need the work.' He paused briefly to collect his thoughts. 'If you must know, I plan to approach Sebastian and Barty at the end of the shoot and ask them outright to give cousin Derek the permanent legal right to fish along his own river. It irritates him enormously having to ask permission every year. And it's not as if he actually speaks to Sebastian; it's all done through their bloody agent!'

Alan could see the elderly man was getting upset.

'Really? Every *year*?' Alan was amazed.

'Yes. Just after Christmas he's visited by the man from Sackwells' Ely office, who brings along the form letter, together with a bottle of vintage port, which he gives Derek as soon as he's signed.'

'But surely there must be easier ways of doing it?'

'I think subconsciously it's Sebastian's – or just as likely his wife, Sarah's – way of maintaining rank and distance. The fact is, the mill's doing very well these days, and I'd be surprised if Derek isn't actually better off than Sebastian and Sarah. You'd be amazed how the cakes and flour fly off the shelves in the two baking boutiques they've opened in King's Parade and Trinity Street.'

'So they own *them*, do they?'

Alan had bought Danish pastries in both shops when visiting Cambridge in the past. And they were delicious, if rather pricey.

'So when I've finished filming, and the programme is a success – as I'm sure you'll make it, Alan' – he said this with a big grin – 'I'm going straight up to the hall and I'm going to ask Sebastian and Barty outright to give the Smileys the right to fish their own waters.'

Alan was fascinated. Smiley was an intelligent, educated man, who'd made a huge mark on the world, yet he was getting terribly het up over something as trivial as fishing rights for his relative. It was extraordinary: like listening to a conversation in a Trollope novel. But as the older man was speaking, he began to realise that such seemingly little things really mattered because they weren't little at all. They were about deeply held resentments and long-running social inequalities. Ultimately, like so much else in life, they were about power, prestige and dynastic influence.

It came to Alan that logic, truth and justice were all irrelevant here. Even sense and reason took a back seat, when such feelings were involved. The trouble was, such profound motives could influence the least likely suspects. Short-term ambitions were far easier to read. Alan sighed: no member of the Cripps family could now be ruled out. Not even benign Barty.

Once they'd finished their coffee, Alan returned to his car and slowly eased out into the drive, while his mind continued to whirl. Was there more than just a superficial resemblance between the Hansworth and Thorey killings? There was, after all, the Cripps family connection. But there was something so similar about the MO, as Lane would have put it, the *modus operandi*, of both deaths. But then the victims were so different, too: a rich banker and a gamekeeper. The similarity of the MOs suggested the same murderer, but the contrasting victims implied different motives. So were the two events necessarily connected?

Then Alan had another idea. Maybe Hansworth and Stan's deaths were somehow linked together? And what was the extent of Thorey's involvement with Hansworth's death? He knew he had picked up and cleaned the fishing tackle. But what else had he done?

The more Alan thought about it, the more it made sense. But it also followed that a double killer was perfectly capable of killing again, especially if he or she believed they were under threat.

* * *

It rained steadily throughout Good Friday. After the morning's tour of the museum, Alan decided to stay at home and do some more work on Stan's notes and drawings. It was now quite clear that the Iron Age occupation levels extended much further into the surrounding fen than anyone had suspected previously. Although stonework only occurred for a couple of hundred metres beyond the fringes of Fursey island, Alan reckoned that Romano–British fields and droveways continued beyond that for a very long way: maybe up to half a mile. And of course it had been prime grazing land; some of the best in Britain. Alan realised that the publication of Stan's report would cause a huge sensation locally and in the wider archaeological world. Stan's reputation would be assured forever. That made him feel a bit better. But only a bit. The way he had been treated was beyond cruel and inhumane. It was disgusting and Alan was still grimly determined to get to the truth.

All afternoon the television in the corner of the room had shown the pilgrims arriving at Fursey for the start of the Penance. Many were looking wet and bedraggled. As he worked, Alan could hear the man on the TV announce that earlier in the day two youngsters had dropped out. He walked through to the front room and looked out: there was still a steady stream of visitors turning into the Fursey Abbey drive. The Penance was proving a big draw.

Then the TV cut to a different scene. Now pilgrims were loading their white rucksacks from the pile of old building stone in the yard behind the abbey. People with clipboards were recording the number of stones taken by each person.

Alan smiled, Clare had told him that English Heritage had insisted that this be done to minimise loss.

On the other side of the yard, some old farm sack-scales had been set up to weigh each filled rucksack. A qualified nurse then assessed if the weight was appropriate to the person carrying it. If she deemed it too heavy, they'd have to return to the heap and empty some stones out. Again, Alan was amused. Candice had told him that the nurse had been a condition set by the event's insurers.

Having filled their rucksacks, the penitents formed a queue at the old pigsty gate, where another man with a clip-board, standing beneath a broad umbrella emblazoned with the name of the event's sponsor (a big manufacturer of unpleasant lager), took down people's names and the weight of their rucksacks, before recording the precise time of their departure. Then it was up to them to reach Ely without using wheeled transport of any sort. And that route had to be half on dry land and half on water. And, of course, nobody had reckoned on so much rain. Poor buggers, Alan thought, it really is going to be a penance for them. But what would they actually achieve, other than a couple of days' self-delusion followed by smug satisfaction. Deep down, he felt emerging anger. So he turned back to his desk, frowning with concentration. Did he have any sympathy for them or what they were trying to achieve? Absolutely none.

* * *

Around midnight Alan walked rather unsteadily home through the rain from the Cripps Arms. It had been another good night and Davey Hibbs had been on particularly fine form. He was a natural clown and his mimicking of the pilgrims filling their rucksacks – he did it with packets of peanuts and crisps – got a huge laugh from everyone in the bar, including the lady vicar, who locals agreed was a big improvement on the previous dry old stick.

As he stood by the back door trying to discover which of the many pockets in his waterproof jacket held his keys, his phone began to vibrate. He looked at the screen. It was Lane. Suddenly Alan's blood ran cold.

He pressed the answer button and waited for the news.

'Alan, I'm at Smiley's Mill. There's been a terrible accident. John Cripps has drowned.'

Immediately Alan's head cleared.

'I'll be with you in a couple of minutes.'

Rapidly Lane's voice returned. Now he sounded like a policeman. 'Not so fast, Alan. Have you gone to bed?'

'No. Why d'you ask?'

'You been to the pub?'

'Yes, I've just got back.'

'Well, you're not bloody driving. Do you understand? I'll be with you tomorrow morning, bright and early.' He rang off.

Alan unclenched his left fist. It was tightly cramped. The Fourtrak keys had been in his grip all the time. He relaxed his hand – and now it hurt: the keys had bruised his palm. Stigmata.

Sod it, he thought, as rain started to trickle down the back of his neck: I'll never forget this Good Friday midnight.

And he was right: it would stay with him forever.

# Twenty

The next day started dry, but clouds out to the west threatened yet more rain. Alan felt terrible: dry mouth and sore head. As they drove through the village, then turned left into Mill Drove, DCI Lane gave him a succinct summary of the events leading up to John Cripps's death.

'He was one of the last pilgrims to leave Fursey Abbey. According to their timekeeper he left the yard there at 4.32 and was carrying a rucksack that weighed 27 kilos. He then made his way to Smiley's Mill, where his wife, Candice, had rented a holiday cruiser, which sleeps two people. When he arrived at the cruiser, which was moored in the Mill Cut, downstream of the mill—'

'So quite close to where you found Stan's body?'

'Yes, on the same side, but about a hundred yards upstream. Anyhow, when he arrived at the boat, his wife was shocked at his appearance. He was completely exhausted and, to use her words, "not making a lot of sense". It would seem he hadn't eaten anything for over 24 hours. So she insisted that he must have rest and sleep. That would do more good for him than any amount of food, which he told her repeatedly he wouldn't eat. He was determined to "do the Penance properly"'. She said he did sleep for several hours. When he woke up he had a bad headache, which she reckoned, correctly, I'd guess, was caused by dehydration. So he drank a lot of water and in about half an hour felt much better. Sometime shortly before midnight, he declared he was fit and ready to go. So she helped him put on the rucksack and they went out on deck.'

'I just don't understand these people, Richard. They're educated – just like us. It's not as if ignorance and superstition dominate their lives. I can't imagine any religion forcing me to do such weird things, can you?'

His friend thought for a moment before he replied. 'Yes, I think I can. Take away the religion and imagine you're part of a team, because that's how the penitents thought of themselves. They had come together before the service in the chapel where they'd been blessed by the dean. Then they travelled in a group to Fursey. All afternoon, they had helped each other fill their sacks. Candice said that John kept repeating that he couldn't let the others down: he must arrive in Ely before the bishop blessed the cairn.'

Alan understood teamwork profoundly. As with all fieldworkers, it was his life.

'And when is the blessing?'

'Tomorrow, before Evensong. Around five – that's if it still goes ahead, which I now doubt.'

'Yes, I suppose that's understandable.'

'The rules of the Penance clearly stated that all pilgrims had to make their way to Ely under their own power, so they had arranged to borrow a two-man canoe from Littleport Grammar School's Boat Club. John would occupy one seat, his knapsack the other. That, at least, was the plan. But when she came to collect the boat in Sebastian's Land Rover, it turned out that the school had taken all its two- and three-man canoes on an expedition to the Lake District in the Easter holidays. So Candice decided to take a single-seater.'

'And that's confirmed by the school?'

'Yes, it was the first thing I checked. The party had left for Kendall on Friday. Well, it would seem that neither John nor Candice had any practical experience of boats or boating. So John strapped on his rucksack and clambered into the canoe, which Candice was holding steady. But almost as soon as he pushed away from the cruiser he turned turtle. Candice said she jumped in and tried to turn him upright, but she didn't have the strength. And I don't suppose her task was made any simpler by the higher than usual river flow after all the recent rain. She certainly wouldn't have been able to touch the bottom at that point, because the pool downstream of the mill is actually quite deep.'

'Yes,' Alan said, remembering his recent conversation with Michael Smiley. 'Presumably that's why it's so good for fishing.'

The expression on Lane's face showed it wasn't the reply he had expected.

Lane drew to a halt in the mill car park. They got out, crossed the wooden bridge and walked a few yards along the towpath, to a small hired river cruiser that was being guarded by a bored WPC. Lane turned to Alan. 'So as things stand, I think we've been presented with a tragic accident.'

'Hmm,' Alan agreed. 'Yet another one. But there'll be absolutely no way anyone will be able to stop tongues wagging now.'

Alan was about to go aboard, when the WPC stopped him.

'I'm sorry, sir, forensics haven't checked it out yet. I've been told not to allow anyone aboard until they give me the go-ahead.'

'Don't worry, that's fine,' Lane said as he showed his warrant card. 'We just want to get an overall impression of the situation. I assume the boat's still where it was originally moored?'

'Yes, it is, sir. Nothing's been touched.'

'And Mrs Cripps, where's she?'

'Her brother-in-law came and collected her. She was in a terrible state, poor woman.'

Alan had taken a short walk downstream of the boat. He looked at the pollarded willows that fringed the water's edge and noted four steel mooring posts and a floating wooden walkway. Candice's cruiser had been tied to the trunks of two willow trees, upstream and downstream. Then he spotted something that looked like an old washing-line pole. Alan had noted several as they walked along the bank.

Lane answered his unspoken question. 'They're used by boat residents when they moor up for the winter. There are temporary washing lines all the way along this stretch of river in January and February.'

Alan went to take hold of the pole, when the WPC stopped him again. 'Best not touch that, sir. Forensics might well want to check it out.'

As they walked back to the car, Lane's radio crackled. A disembodied voice told them that the Fursey Penance had just been cancelled. Then it started to rain and soon it was heavier than ever.

* * *

The following morning was Easter Sunday and Alan felt terrible. He had thought he was starting to get a handle on what was going on, but suddenly he was back in the dark again. Had Candice killed her husband? At present that seemed the only option, as she was the only person present when he died. But there were problems. For a start, Alan had reckoned that John was the brains behind the Cripps family. Certainly Sebastian or Sarah weren't. And yet John was the one who had just died. It made no sense whatsoever, unless of course Candice wanted him out of the way. Could it have been an accident? He hated to admit it, but all the facts suggested it might have been. In fact, had there not been three other deaths that's what he'd have opted for. But a fourth death – and involving the river, too? Every nerve in his brain told him that was crazy. It was *so* frustrating: he hated the feeling that others were managing events, and he'd had a lousy night's sleep, as a result.

After a strong cup of coffee and a slice of cold pizza, he decided to phone his brother Grahame. As he had hoped, he asked Alan over for Sunday lunch. It was just what he needed.

Sometime during the early morning, a warm front had swept in from the south, bringing a much-needed spell of dry weather. And of course it was warmer. As he drove through the flat, treeless landscape, the dark peaty fields slowly merged into paler, silty ground. Gangs of Eastern European workers were cutting cauliflowers, broccoli and spring cabbages. A mile or two outside Spalding, the vegetables gave way to great expanses of daffodils. His father had grown them on the farm in the 1980s and he had loved their scent, as a child. He wound down the windows and dropped his speed as he passed fields of daffs on either side. He breathed in deeply.

Bliss! Nothing was more evocative than that perfume. And for a few moments he was back in his dad's cab, untangling packets of rubber bands for the pickers, as the tractor inched forward. 'Keep your eye on the job, son, and don't let your attention wander. Those pickers depend on you and you mustn't let them down.'

He was woken from his reverie by the loud horn of a BMW whose driver had been held up behind him. But Alan was unmoved. Those few moments of peace had done the trick. I bet she watches *Road Rage*, was his only reaction as the young, dyed-blonde driver accelerated angrily past the muddy Fourtrak.

Lunch at Cruden's Farm was a relaxed affair, and the food was delicious – Liz was a superb cook – and Graham and Liz's two children were also there. Alan was very fond of his niece and nephew who were now almost ready to leave home. Claire was finishing at Spalding Grammar and Dan had left the Grammar School and, like his father before him, was now at Nettlesham Agricultural College. So many of his contemporaries were unkind about young people, but these two, he thought, as they bustled about the kitchen helping their mother to clear up the lunch things, led their lives simply and with quiet competence. They had been very well brought up.

Grahame and Alan took their coffees through to the sitting room, where the embers of a log fire were still glowing in the fireplace.

In traditional English manner they began by discussing the weather.

'Soon be letting this go out,' Grahame said, as he dropped another log on the fire. 'Weather's warming up at last. Crops need it. The winter barley's well behind and we haven't finished drilling the spuds yet. Far too wet.'

'I know. I've never seen the rivers so high.'

'Yes. And wasn't it terrible about that John Cripps? And those earlier deaths in the river? Fursey's all over the news, you know.'

Alan smiled. Yes, he thought, I am aware of that. But in a part of his brother's subconscious, Alan still led a migrant digger's life, moving from one remote and cheerless dig to another, far beyond the normal world of newspapers and television.

'John Cripps is – or rather was – one of my employers. It's his family that owns Fursey Abbey.'

'Oh really?' Grahame paused for a moment, while this sunk in. 'This morning the T2 news was followed by a trail for another series of live shows from Fursey. I think I even saw your face flash by.' He took a sip from his coffee. 'So was that planned before the accident?'

'Yes it was. But only by a few days.'

'And do you think all those deaths are accidental? It's a bit odd, you must admit.'

Alan was going to reply that he had no views on the subject, as he was only an archaeologist. But he knew his brother would never accept it.

'Well, that's the conventional wisdom.'

'OK, Alan, but what do you really think, deep down, in your heart of hearts?'

It was Alan's turn to take a long drink of coffee. 'Well, it's difficult. The thing is, I've got a bit wary of following my instincts. I got things so wrong the year before last.'

Grahame wasn't having any of that. 'Oh, that's ridiculous,

Alan. Sure, the end results weren't what anyone expected, but if it hadn't been for your sometimes bloody-minded persistence, some very nasty people would still be at large. Nobody's perfect, but you have a real talent for smelling rats. Always did, come to think of it.'

Grahame laughed quietly. They both remembered a time when Alan detected whiffs of a nasty smell in the straw barn, which did indeed turn out to be a large nest of dead rats.

'The thing is, all the deaths have been put down to either accident or suicide, but it's not difficult to find reasons why certain people would like to have seen them out of the way. There are hints of clues, too, but they're only hints. So far there's been nothing concrete for Richard Lane to work on.'

'So what does Richard think? Have you discussed it with him?'

'Good heavens, yes. We're in close touch. I think he shares my doubts. But as he says, we can't do a damn thing without a firm clue.'

'And do you see it all as one single conspiracy, somehow united by the waters of the river?'

'That's the way the press and media are starting to go—'

'But do you agree?'

Alan thought for a few moments. His brother, as ever, had posed the key question.

'It would certainly make a better story if it was all about a Mr Big. But again, that's what I suspected last year. But the reality turned out to be more complex, more nuanced, than that.'

'So why the river?' Grahame asked.

'Why not the river is my gut feeling. The thing is, rivers are everywhere down there. Far more than up here. The land is lower-lying too. More liable to floods. If I was a farmer down there I'd eat, drink and sleep rivers—'

'So you reckon it's just coincidence, then?'

Alan reflected for a moment. 'No, I wouldn't say that. But I think it's something that's being used. I also wonder whether the various deaths haven't inspired others. It's not hard to fake accidental death in water. It's not like pushing someone off a tall building or under an approaching train, is it?'

* * *

It was early evening when Alan eventually headed back to Fursey. By now the gangs had long left the fields, and the vegetables they had picked had gone to the packing stations where they had been loaded into chiller lorries, which were now heading down to London and to supermarket distribution centres right across the country – at a closely governed 42mph. So far he had been stuck behind a series of them, and it was proving a very slow journey.

But Alan was in no hurry; he needed time to think. Despite all the events of the past weeks, one of the few hard and fast clues he still had to go on was that bottle of whisky in Stan's little 'cupboard', which had originated in Peter Flower's Cambridge college. Much as he disliked Flower, the simple link between the Cambridge don, his college and Stan's drinking wasn't the only one. Maybe it was now irrelevant. If, and only if, Candice had indeed killed her husband, then she would have been perfectly capable of reintroducing Stan to the bottle, too. Maybe Flower encouraged this? It would certainly fit with his agenda: if, that is, Alan was right in his supposition that Flower wanted to control Stan if he were to gain academic credit for his discoveries, which would happen when his name appeared on Stan's report – and even more prominently if that report was posthumous. Then he remembered what Harriet had told him, that Flower had recently been appointed bursar of Fisher. And what do bursars do? They look after the college's wealth.

He recalled his research last autumn in the Haddon library. He'd learnt that Fisher had substantial holdings of land around Fursey and Littleport. This was ideally positioned for the second wave of 'Silicon Fen' Cambridge expansion. Was Flower somehow trying to get his hands on Cripps land? And if so, how? Perhaps he just wanted closer co-operation, and maybe John, who had a limited stake in the main estate, wasn't so keen. This would surely explain why Flower and Candice would *together* want John out of the way.

Alan was now leaving the silt land and the fields were growing blacker as he headed south. He gave an involuntary shudder. Somehow their blackness matched his mood only too well. He thought back to his recent conversation with Grahame about 'declining high-class families' and a close link to a renowned Cambridge college would certainly shift attention away from the curse and raise their status, locally – if not nationally.

* * *

As the powers that be at T2 had anticipated, their frequent trails and many press releases had done the trick. The dig was more popular than ever, and Alan was forced to abandon any idea of driving to Fursey on Easter Monday morning. Even by nine o'clock the place was heaving and they didn't open to the public till ten. So he pulled his hood up and walked through the trees around the edge of the park. Eventually he managed to make his way to the trenches, unrecognised.

Soon he was joined by Jake, Jon and Kaylee who were working in the extended Trench 1. Harriet's graduate student, Toby Cox, was also there, having spent the night at Jake's place because Harriet couldn't be on-site until around teatime as she had agreed to take an elderly relative out for lunch. For a moment Alan was surprised: on a Monday? Then he remembered it was Easter – and he hadn't so much as seen an egg or a smelled a piece of chocolate.

At morning tea break Candice appeared at the door of the site tea shed – a small Portakabin with a self-contained loo. Considering what had happened to her, this would normally have been quite unexpected, but Alan was far from surprised, given what he now strongly suspected. She was carrying a gift-wrapped box, which she handed to Alan.

'This is something,' she said bravely, 'that John and I arranged last week, when we heard they were planning a second week of live programmes. We both feel . . .' She hesitated, then gathered strength. 'We both felt that the people who were doing all the hard work didn't get enough credit. So this is our little way . . .' She was losing the battle with her tears. Kaylee stood up and put a consoling arm round her shoulder. ' . . . Our way of saying thank you.'

Then she left. There was a stunned hush. People were genuinely moved. Alan was very impressed by her acting, but he was also intrigued by the parcel. Could it be chocolate? Suddenly he realised he could kill for chocolate. With the most serious face he could achieve, he undid the glittery ribbon and opened the box. Everyone gasped as he lifted the lid: it was a chocolate sponge cake, decorated to resemble a dig scene, complete with trenches, a Portakabin and a spoil heap. Chocolate archaeologists were barrowing crème Easter eggs. It must have cost a fortune. Alan lifted an egg off the miniature spoil heap and tasted it. Superb.

Sometime ago, he remembered, he'd enjoyed sharing a similar, if much smaller, cake and chocolate treat when visiting Cambridge with Harriet. She'd bought it from the classy pastry shop in Trinity Street – the one he now knew was owned by Smiley's Mill. He wasn't suggesting a direct link with the shop, that would be ridiculous, but he bet Candice had arranged a substantial discount. Could the cake be a tiny clue that a link existed between Candice and the Smileys? Maybe even Candice, Flower and the Smileys? That would be quite an alliance. Yes, Alan thought, together, they'd be more than a match for the Crippses. Then he pulled himself up short: that surely was going too far. He must beware of castles in the air. But even so . . .

* * *

Harriet hadn't arrived on-site by the time the afternoon tea break ended, and everyone assembled in the trenches for the first evening run-through and rehearsal. Alan wasn't panicking, as she wasn't his problem, but Frank was getting very agitated.

Then, at four o'clock precisely, she appeared on set. She was dressed in jeans and digging clothes, but she was wearing them with flair. To Alan's eye the jeans were just a touch closer-fitting than normal and her bright top, while not revealing, left little to an active imagination. Her hair, too, was fresh and lively and gave her movements just a hint of ballet.

'So sorry I'm a bit late, Frank: traffic was terrible through Grantham.' She smiled at Alan and the others in the trench. Everyone admired her cool in the circumstances. She looked back at Frank Jones, who was staring at her, almost open-mouthed. 'Be a dear, Frank. Tell me what you want me to do.'

Alan and the others had to look away. Kaylee's shoulders were already twitching. Even Grump Edwards, as laconic as ever, was smiling broadly.

Unobtrusively, Trudy, the young production assistant, handed Harriet a script.

There was a short pause while Frank Jones assembled his thoughts. He unfolded and consulted his own script. Then he announced. 'Right, everyone. I'll be Craig Larsson. I'll read his lines: This is *Test Pit Challenge.* Welcome to the second series of six live episodes from Fursey Abbey, in the shades of the awe-inspiring Ely Cathedral, here in the heart of the Cambridgeshire Fens. In the first series we discovered three completely unexpected graves and the remains of what appeared to be a massive timber wall . . .'

Sadly, Frank Jones lacked Larsson's charisma and Alan soon found his attention wandering. Soon he knew the adrenalin would begin to pump, but not yet. Might as well relax and observe the scene. Enjoy it.

At the rear of No. 1 film crew, two gaffers were erecting new lighting stands. Alan was impressed: they looked bigger and better than before. A young technician was positioning a flat-screen monitor on the edge of the trench, just behind Grump's feet, which he nudged. Grump glanced down, irritated. Alan smiled: all was well. Without thinking, he looked across the trench to Harriet, who was watching Frank, with her eyebrows slightly raised. She was so gorgeous. Quickly, he averted his gaze. But not before he'd caught her smile.

But what did that smile convey? It could have been warmth, but Alan found his confidence had slipped. Maybe it was. Or just mockery – even amusement?

* * *

As always, the real thing was much more exciting than the run-through. And it wasn't just that they now had the real Craig Larsson with them and he was pumped up and in fine form. Previously Alan had got the slight impression that Craig and Tricia hadn't exactly seen eye to eye. Maybe he viewed her as competition, since she clearly had no real intention of becoming a full-time archaeology professional and saw television as a much better career option – as she would have put it. Harriet, on the other hand, was already a respected figure in her own world and he immediately found she was easy to work with. In fact, Alan thought as he watched, the two of them hit it off remarkably well. And then she broke all the rules of live TV by making Craig laugh when he wasn't expecting it. It happened directly after his opening piece-to-camera when a large insect landed on his head and she told him to 'Hold still, you naughty boy' as she carefully picked it up and placed it in the grass beside the trench, revealing as she did so her perfectly shaped behind. And then, with seemingly all the time in the world, she stood up, smiled at the astonished Larsson, and to the delight of 6 million viewers, asked in a matter-of-fact voice. 'Now, what were you saying?'

She said this with a huge smile that the close-up camera captured superbly. Craig, ever the professional, managed not to corpse completely. He turned to the camera, wiping an eye.

'And for everyone at home, this is Dr Harriet Webb. She's my minder and is also our resident expert on human remains. You may remember seeing her in our last series, when things were running rather more smoothly than they are now . . .'

Alan couldn't remember precisely what came next, but he recalled Weinstein's delighted voice bubbling away in his earpiece. Everyone knew it had been television gold and it came right at the top of the first show. From that moment on, viewing figures and audience share could only climb.

The first two scenes were finished, and it was time to roll Michael Smiley's five-minute history film. Alan could hear the countdown in his earpiece then the monitor beside the trench flickered and came to life.

Viewers at home might well have expected a rather dumbed-down, jokey series of short films, given their presenter's quiz show past. But as Alan had recently discovered, the real Michael Smiley was thoughtful and intelligent and it was that persona who came across in the documentaries. The first was about the Fursey Estate as it was today. Sebastian made a fleeting, and very wooden, appearance but most of the interview was with his wife Sarah. As he watched, Alan was impressed: yes she did have a Sloaney accent and said 'Yah' rather too often, but that went with her role as the squire's wife. An intelligent, amusing and business-savvy woman lay behind the thin upper-crust exterior.

Smiley asked her about the history of the house.

'It's been in the family for some 400 years, although the building you now see was built in Georgian times. The earlier house was timber and not as grand as this one, which reflects our family's growing prosperity in the later eighteenth century.'

She spoke with fluency and charm and Alan enjoyed the way she used the word 'our' to describe the family she had married into. She clearly identified with the Crippses and was completely at ease with their class and status. In fact, Alan thought, as he watched her finish, she positively enjoyed being a member of the county set. Again, he recalled Grahame's 'declining families' remark. She certainly wouldn't welcome it.

The first half of the film was a rapid tour of Fursey Hall and Park. There were cut-away shots of the river and the mill, taken the previous year, when the trees were in full autumn colour. Then the film moved on to the large panorama case in the new museum. To guide the viewer through the various traps, guns and gadgets Smiley had brought in a gamekeeper from a large estate in the West Midlands. Alf Kammidge was also very knowledgeable about game and shooting history and made regular appearances on the BBC's hugely popular *Wax Jacket Show.* Alan had seen him before and although he slightly suspected the intensity of his rustic accent, he couldn't deny the depth of his knowledge. But it had been an exhausting two days, and as he watched the screen, he felt his eyes beginning to droop.

Then suddenly he was wide awake. Kammidge was walking towards the large mantrap that stood with the other traps and snares at the front of the case.

'That looks like a vicious thing, Alf.'

'Yes, they were, Michael. Absolutely vicious. When those jaws shut there was no escape. The springs were far too strong. Most of the poachers they caught soon passed out through loss of blood.'

'And presumably,' Smiley said, 'their legs were broken, too?'

'Surprisingly not. Especially with these very large ones that closed above the knee. The femur bone is very tough. It was the smaller traps that bit on or below the knee that did the most lasting damage. Thinner bones got shattered. Many transported criminals in Australia were said to have walked with "mantrap limps".'

'And those horrible teeth: they seem rather unnecessary?' Smiley couldn't conceal the horror on his face.

'The main point of these traps was to deter organised gangs. Quite often the head keeper would put word out in the local pub on the night they set them. They weren't after village lads out to shoot the odd rabbit for the pot. So they nearly always set several traps and placed them at the main entranceways into the wood.'

'Presumably,' Smiley suggested, 'local chaps would have their own, private, ways into the woods.'

'Precisely. And anyhow, the keepers weren't after them. They wanted to get the big boys up from Smithfield and the large London markets. The problem got even worse when the railways came, and gangs could get their poached birds and deer to any local station.'

Alan looked up from the monitor. Suddenly it all became clear to him. He had been so dense! They were there all the time – the two clues he had been seeking for so long. And it wasn't just the nature of the injury these traps inflicted: it was the setting of the traps themselves. And that took expertise, experience and knowledge.

# Twenty-One

As soon as the filming was over, Alan left the trench and phoned the pathologist, Dr Lindsay Harris. He told her he had important new information about Thorey's death. She agreed to come over tomorrow morning, first thing.

Then he returned to the set. Coffee was being taken around by Trudy Hills on a large two-handled wooden tray borrowed from the Fursey kitchens. Alan helped himself to a mug, then started to approach Harriet and Craig, who were talking animatedly to one side of the main gathering. After a few steps he had second thoughts. Was this wise? They were so deep in conversation. He dropped back and faced the other way.

Soon he became aware that Frank was talking to him.

'Lew wanted to have a few words with you, Alan.'

'Why, is there a problem?'

'No, none. He's delighted, that's all. Really loved your pieces with Harriet. Thought they came across very well indeed.'

'And what did he think of that opening exchange between her and Craig?' He couldn't resist asking.

'Oh, what they're already calling the Insect Incident on Twitter?' Frank was smiling broadly now. 'He loved it. It seems viewers at home loved it too. It was so spontaneous – and fresh.'

Yes, Alan thought, as he started to head back home: it was certainly that. Very fresh.

* * *

Normally at most visitor attractions crowds thin out fast after Easter, but not this time, Alan thought as he eased the Fourtrak gingerly down the drive, trying to avoid the gathering throng. Lindsay Harris was waiting for him in the museum.

'I'm afraid I'll have to make it short and sweet, Alan, as I'm a witness in Ely Coroner's Court, in about an hour's time. So what have you got to tell me?'

'Well, it's more show than tell. Come over here.'

He led her over to the large panorama and pointed down at the jaws of the mantrap.

'Do you think metal teeth like those could have nicked Thorey's femur?'

She said nothing, but leant forward to examine the trap more closely. Then she stood back and produced a clear plastic folder from her briefcase. It contained photos taken during the post-mortem.

'Well, what d'you think, Alan, you've had to match a few axes to cut-marks and woodchips?'

Alan was surprised. She must be referring to a paper he'd published on Neolithic carpentry in the *Journal of Applied Archaeology* four years ago. He thought it had vanished without trace. But apparently not.

Alan was quiet as he compared the trap with the damage to Thorey's thigh bone.

He straightened up. 'I'd have said they were dead ringers. Could even be the same trap, except I know it couldn't be, as this one has been on permanent display for years.'

'Presumably they were made by village blacksmiths to a pattern?'

'I honestly don't know,' Alan replied. 'But I imagine, yes, they were.'

'Which might suggest there were others around, closely similar to this.'

Alan nodded his agreement, but he had one further question. 'Be honest, Lindsay, do you think it's conclusive, as it stands?'

'That's difficult. If the coroner were to ask me if such damage could only be produced by a mantrap I'd have to say that it was very probable, but not beyond any doubt. To be absolutely certain, we'd have to be able to find the actual trap that did this. Then match the teeth to the scars microscopically.' She pointed to the photo in Alan's hand. 'And presumably that would still have traces of flesh, blood—'

'Or fabric, sticking to it, yes.'

She stood back again and took a photo of the trap with her phone.

'That's one hell of a spring, Alan, isn't it?' She took another picture, then looked up. 'You'd have to be massively strong to set such a big trap, wouldn't you?'

Alan could remember setting gin traps in the barn for rats with his father. His dad always used two steel rods to lever the jaws apart. And there were two notches on the trap's jaws, which made this simpler. Alan showed them to her.

'It's about skill, not brute force,' Alan explained. 'You never let your hands anywhere near a jaw-trap. Dad even used a pair of tongs to place the bait on the footplate. But a man-trap wouldn't need any bait. They were concealed – usually along a footpath or walkway.'

'And the victim just stepped in.' She said it slowly and grimaced. There was a short pause while they pictured the scene. Then she looked down at her watch.

'I'm so sorry, Alan, but I must get going.'

As soon as she'd left, Alan took out his own phone and took a couple of quick snaps of the trap's teeth.

As he dropped the phone back in his pocket, he could hear Sebastian and Sarah's voices out in the gallery. They were showing a small group of friends around the new displays.

He opened one of the double doors and held it open. Sarah, who was wearing a black dress out of respect for her brother-in-law, gave him a restrained smile. It seemed genuine, but he wasn't sure he trusted anyone anymore – especially not someone who was proud to be a Cripps.

Once back in the yard he called Richard Lane, then he headed down to the dig.

* * *

Alan met Lane two hours later in the pub in Ely. It was a fine day, so again they took a table outside. The policeman had to appear in court later that afternoon, so was drinking orange juice and soda. Alan took a sip from his pint of Slodger and got straight to the point.

'I think I've found evidence that might show that Thorey was murdered.'

Lane sat back, expressionless. 'I thought as much. Tell me about it,' he said.

Alan explained about Lindsay and the mantrap and showed him his pictures of the teeth.

'And what did Lindsay think of it?'

'She was as convinced as me. But it's still circumstantial evidence, unless we can find the actual trap that had caught Thorey's thigh. Even if it's been cleaned, we'll be able to use micro-wear to match the teeth with the scratch in the bone, and if it hasn't been cleaned, it should have DNA traces, too. Either way, we'll get a match that'll stand up in court.'

'And you're absolutely convinced it can't have been the trap in the new display. Could our murderer perhaps have "borrowed" it for one night?'

Alan shook his head.

'No, that's out of the question. I checked: all the items on display in the new galleries had been conserved by a firm in Cambridge. Candice gave me their number and they confirmed that everything from Fursey was held in secure conditions.'

Lane frowned and pulled out his diary.

'They haven't yet fixed a date for Thorey's inquest, but I'd have expected it to be announced quite soon. I'll have a word with the coroner's people. I'll mention we have some leads and would like a bit more time.'

Then he looked at Alan, who was nodding in agreement.

'Tell me frankly, Alan,' Lane continued. 'Do you think we are ever likely to find the actual trap?'

'To do that, we need to find the man who set it.'

'Of course. Any ideas?'

'It's still only a guess, of course.' He paused, collecting his thoughts. 'But yes. I think there might be someone.'

Alan could see Lane was about to make a suggestion. But he changed his mind.

'Go on . . .'

'When I was a boy,' Alan began. 'I'd seen my dad set gin traps . . .' He took a pull from his beer. 'But as I was describing all this to Lindsay, I think I said something about it being "about skill, not brute force". As I said it, I got a clear picture in my mind of the ex-head keeper Bert Hickson.'

'And he was the man,' Lane said, 'who found Stan's body.'

'And don't you always say, that's the most likely suspect?'

'OK, so he may well have the skills, but what about the motive?'

'I'm afraid he has that in spades. Again, I've been able to check on this in the village, but he was quite roughly pushed aside by the family – but mostly, I suspect, by Sarah, who saw him as too old-fashioned for a more commercial modern-style shoot – in favour of Joe Thorey who was then in his mid-thirties, young, active and dynamic. I suspect Thorey wasn't too careful about putting pressure on Bert to go, either.'

The frown on Lane's face grew as he listened to what Alan was saying.

'Anyhow,' Alan continued, 'Thorey was made head keeper in 2005 and Bert Hickson "retired". He even had to move out of Keepers Cottage into one of the estate's few remaining terraced houses in the village. He told me he couldn't face kicking up a fuss and I also suspect that Barty made sure he was financially OK – in fact, he even went so far as to get him a rowing machine.'

'Which was actually very intelligent of him. "Healthy mind, healthy body" and all that.'

'And that's the next thing,' Alan continued. 'Bert Hickson had served in the army, and before joining up he was an assistant keeper to his dad. So he'd always been a fit man. It was just his mind that was affected by what he'd seen in Northern Ireland.'

'So you're saying that he knew how to do it, and was physically capable of setting a mantrap?'

'Yes. And of course he had the biggest motive of all: revenge.'

Lane dropped his voice. 'But I don't think we can bring him in yet. It's almost like we're arresting him for being a gamekeeper. We need more to go on, especially if we're going to find that trap. You mustn't forget: he's an ex-keeper and would know how and, more importantly, *where* to conceal it out there in the woods. And we'd never find it. Not in a million years.'

Alan hadn't thought of that. He'd been about to suggest a full-on raid of all the Fursey barns and out-buildings.

'No, you're right, Richard. We do need more to go on.'

'I think I've got enough people to keep an eye on him for a week or two, if not longer. I'll see what can be done.'

* * *

The clouds that had threatened yet more rain that morning, had largely cleared, and it was turning out to be a warm, pleasant afternoon, when Alan arrived back at Fursey. There was a long queue of visitors and he was astonished at the amount of interest the second live series had generated.

There could be little doubt that a proportion of viewers had turned on because of Fursey's increasing notoriety.

Alan was walking across the car park towards the dig, when a woman called his name. Clare Hughes hurried towards him.

'I'm so glad I've managed to catch you, Alan. I was just passing by.'

Alan waited, while she caught her breath.

'But I thought I ought to tell you. I had a phone call from our new inspector at English Heritage . . .' She trailed off, trying to recall the name.

'Shelley Walters?' Alan suggested.

'That's right. And she'd just been speaking to Cameron Roberts.' She paused. Everyone in archaeology paused after they mentioned the name of the EH chief archaeologist. He had a fearsome reputation.

'Oh, really? And what did he want?'

Alan had a shrewd suspicion, but he kept quiet. In fact, he was surprised they'd heard nothing from Cameron after the first series of 'lives'.

'He's seriously thinking about scheduling this site. Maybe even on an emergency order. It was that apsidal end that did it.'

Alan frowned at this news. Scheduling could be a mixed blessing, especially if you were actually digging. Often it meant being prevented from examining the most interesting deposits, as they were usually the most vulnerable.

By now they had reached the trench, where Kaylee and Jon had started trowelling half-sections through two of the beam-slots between the wall posts. The line of the apse was looking particularly clear.

'Well,' Alan said. 'It's looking very striking now, isn't it?'

'Yes, it is. And there can be absolutely no doubt that semi-circular curve is deliberate and well-executed. It *has* to be an apse, don't you think?'

'I agree. It's aligned correctly and is part of a very substantial building. And this morning Kaylee found two sherds in the beam slot.'

Kaylee, overhearing their conversation, stood up, holding the finds tray, which she offered to Clare.

'And they were broken in antiquity?' Clare asked.

'Of course,' Kaylee replied.

They both grinned: as if Kaylee would be so careless as to break potsherds when trowelling. But the fitting edges were dirty and would need a good soak if they were to be glued together. This meant, of course, that the sherds had broken in antiquity and had then been discarded. Two conjoining sherds are not likely to be earlier, or residual, to use the jargon. Together, they would date the context where they were found quite securely.

Clare handed them to Alan. They were dark grey, quite hard and with a distinctive sandy feel. At first glance their finish resembled some of the early wheel-thrown pottery made around Thetford. If that was the case, they would post-date 800 or 850. But these were subtly different. Alan knew that Harriet's PhD research had involved the Early and Middle Saxon periods and she had a good working knowledge of the pottery.

'Harry, can I see girth grooves on these sherds?'

She leant back from the bones she was excavating. 'Yes, you can. I'm certain they're Ipswich Ware. Couldn't be anything else.'

'That's what I thought. Fantastic! A real result.' Alan was

delighted. Ipswich Ware was made on a freely revolving turntable, rather than a pedal-powered wheel, which the potter turned with the side of his thumbs on the vessel he was forming. These little pushes left the distinctive shallow marks known as girth grooves. But most important of all, Ipswich Ware was Middle Saxon and could be dated to the years 650–850. It was indeed a result: this church was one of the earliest ever found in Britain. By now Alan didn't really care that this news would re-energise the happy clappies of the Fursey Fan Club.

Alan and Clare turned to go back to the car park. Harriet's quiet, but urgent, voice was unexpected. 'But there's something else, Clare.'

They both stopped and turned. Uncharacteristically, Alan was annoyed Harriet had addressed Clare, and not him. She was a county official whereas he was director of the dig. But he said nothing. They both crouched down by the graveside. Harriet tapped with her fine plasterer's leaf on a ridge of bone roughly level with the skeleton's ribcage, but about six inches to one side of it.

'I think it's a shoulder of mutton. Certainly an ovicaprid scapula with fused ends. So mutton, rather than lamb.'

Clare was looking puzzled. She didn't get the significance.

Alan explained. 'Early Christian burials were sometimes accompanied by food. It's generally thought that these newly converted ex-pagans were hedging their bets. If the promised Afterlife of Christianity didn't materialise when they reached the other side, then at least they'd be prepared for whatever the Pagan gods had in mind for them—'

'And they'd have something nutritious with them to eat,' Clare finished Alan's sentence.

Harriet had picked up her trowel. Her final remark was by way of dismissal. 'I think we'll have to tell the television people that the pottery was found earlier, but I plan to "discover" the meat bone on the "live". I told Frank that's what I'm doing and he seemed very excited.'

Blimey, Alan thought: that's one way to treat a director. 'Yes,' Alan replied in astonishment. 'I bet he's over the moon.'

# Twenty-Two

The first five days' live filming had gone very well indeed and Weinstein was delighted. The previous evening Alan had received a call from the London publisher who normally handled T2 programmes' tie-in books. Alan was about to say politely that he didn't write such stuff – and then the man mentioned the advance sum. It was vast – quite beyond anything he had ever been offered before. It didn't take much persuading before he agreed. If nothing else, he thought, it would more than pay for a holiday. And, boy, did he need a break.

It was early Saturday morning and Alan was heading out of the village on the Cambridge Road. He was going to meet Bob Timpson in his lab to discuss pollen analysis and details of the research budget for the coming financial year. As the road came off the island and headed into the open fen, it ran parallel to the Engine Drain, about 400 metres to the south. Alan slowed down and looked across the field, over the dyke and towards the band of game-cover in front of the monastic wall. Beyond was the park, then their excavations and the ruins of the abbey church, in the middle distance. It was one of his favourite views and it was looking superb on this crisp, clear morning. He wished he'd brought his camera. It would have made a good opening photograph for the final report.

The fine weather came as a welcome relief after four days of heavy and near-continuous rain. The production company had even been forced to erect a large, and very expensive, single-span temporary shelter over the trench extension. It was bright yellow and stood out clearly in the low morning sunlight. He could see from here that the Engine Drain was full and as he lowered the window, he could hear the throb of pumps running in the pumping station two large fields away to the west. The winter wheat before him was quite well advanced, but there were also large areas of water down towards the dyke. Alan realised that they'd soon be doing lasting damage to the growing crop.

He was about to accelerate away, when he noticed that a large low-loader was coming down the road towards him. So he stopped, engaged four-wheel drive and reversed the Fourtrak onto the verge. Then he sat and waited for it to pass.

But instead of passing, it appeared to slow down, then indicated left and drew into a field gateway about 50 yards ahead. A mud-spattered Land Rover behind it overtook and immediately pulled over, too. The driver got out. It was Sebastian Cripps. The low-loader belonged to an agricultural implement hire company in Aldreth and it was carrying one of the new, powerful, rubber-tracked Caterpillar tractors. Behind it was a two-tined pan-buster. Normally such equipment is deployed as part of seed-bed preparation in autumn, but certainly not in the spring, when crops are growing. Alan had just seen the two large puddles – small lakes would be a better description – and he realised that desperate measures were called for.

His window was still open as he eased the Fourtrak towards the low-loader, which was occupying half the width of the road. Clearly the driver didn't dare pull over any further onto the soft verges. Sebastian recognised him. The big man stepped forward. He was smiling. Alan was the first to speak.

'Blimey, it looks like Lake Windermere out there!'

'I know. It's bloody awful. But look out there, beyond the Engine Drain. The land around Isle Farm is dry. Not so much as a puddle. Makes you sick, doesn't it?'

Alan looked across. And yes, he could see why Sebastian regretted the sale of that farm so much. But even from a distance, Alan noticed that the trees and hedges around it were poorly tended and overgrown with brambles and hawthorn scrub. The Cripps family wouldn't have let that happen when they still owned it. Alan acknowledged that Sebastian may have many faults, but he did understand how to maintain the look of a rural estate.

'Anyhow,' Sebastian continued, 'the contractors drilled too late. I thought it was a bit wet at the time. And it must have been, for such a pan to have formed.'

Alan sympathised. 'And I'm sure all the drains are running. At least they were when we were down there earlier.'

'Yes, they are. Checked them again last week.'

'I suppose it's all the flood-clay in the subsoil.' Alan added. 'The peat wouldn't pan like that, would it?'

'No, not round here it doesn't. How many layers of clay are there, do you reckon?'

Alan thought back to Stan's notebook. 'Must be six or seven, depending on where you are. And come to think of it, those two patches of water are directly over where the clays are thickest. In fact, there's very little peat in one spot out there; it's nearly all clay.'

There was a roar as the tractor's big diesel engine fired up. Sebastian had to shout. 'And how's the filming going? Tonight's the last night, isn't it?'

'It's gone well. Very well, in fact. It's the wrap party this evening. Starts at nine.' Then without thinking he added, 'You coming?'

Sebastian shook his head. 'No, sadly, I can't. It wouldn't be right, considering John . . .'

'Oh, I'm sorry, Sebastian. You must think me an idiot . . .'

'Don't worry, Alan.' He sighed deeply. 'If you must know, I'm having a lot of trouble getting to grips with it myself.'

There was something about the way he said it that made Alan believe Sebastian couldn't have been his brother's killer. His regret was genuine, unfeigned.

* * *

Alan got back to the dig early in the afternoon. By now it was starting to cloud over, but the forecast rain would probably hold off until the end of the shoot. That would also give Sebastian time to finish pan-busting the field alongside the Engine Drain. Alan couldn't help but sympathise with Sebastian. In the old days, before low-cost contractors appeared on the scene, his dad would decide precisely when to do the various jobs of the farming year. As a result, problems like panning arose less often. But today, everything could be sorted out with a bigger, extra-powerful tractor, or a more potent spray. Despite what agronomists would have you believe, much of the subtlety was going out of farming. There were times when Alan was glad that his brother Grahame, and not he, had taken on the family farm.

By now Harriet and her student Toby had excavated four graves, another one of which contained a joint of meat – beef this time. The church wall was progressing well and the paved surface and foundation layers of the main north-south roadway of the Roman fort, the *Via Principalis*, had been lifted to reveal what appeared to be an intact late Iron Age occupation horizon beneath. This had been the big discovery of Day 5.

By four o'clock the archaeologists and film crews were on stand-by for the run-through. Then Alan's phone rang. Everyone in the trench looked across at him. Harriet and Craig were smiling broadly. Harriet even wagged a reproving finger at him, while pointing accusingly at his ringing phone. He ought to have turned it off by now. He glanced down at the screen: it was Sebastian. Alan frowned. He knew he would only ring if it was something important. Had there been yet another death? For Alan, the curse was starting to become an uncontrolled, grisly nightmare.

'Hello, Sebastian. About to start rehearsing. Can't talk for long. Anything important?'

'Yes, very. We've just hit a stone wall. Bloody great thing. Bent both the tines. Can you get down here?'

'Not this minute, no. We're about to do a run-through. But when we're finished filming I can.'

'When's that?'

'About half six.'

'OK. I'll wait. We're right by the dyke, about halfway along. I'll put the machine off-hire. See you then.'

Halfway along? Alan was very surprised. He'd have expected to find walls much closer to the island edge, but certainly not *that* far out in the fen. It must be a very early one: maybe even Roman or Iron Age. Despite the recent horrors, Alan realised the adrenalin was starting to flow. An early wall? Wow, that really was something! He turned off the phone and looked up. Back to reality: Craig was talking earnestly to Frank. Grump was fiddling with the monitor and Speed was helping the gaffer to adjust one of the lighting gantries. Harriet was looking towards him, worried. He gave her what he hoped was a reassuring smile, but she didn't respond.

* * *

The final lead-up to a live shoot is always tense, and this was no exception. Everyone was at their starting positions, and the five-minute countdown had begun. Trudy Hills had just been around with flasks of coffee and milk, which she set on the edge of the trench, alongside the monitor screen. Harriet and Craig were laughing over something at the far end of the trench. They were to do the opening sequence together. Harriet had found time to change and was looking gorgeous, now in lime-green jeans and a silvery top. On Frank's advice she had started to wear a little eyeliner, 'just for the cameras', and Alan had to admit, it did work. Yes, he thought wistfully, it worked very well indeed. Then a loud voice announced, 'Four minutes!' and everyone looked up. Alan was miles away, remembering happier times. Then he realised Harriet was looking at him. She had caught him staring at her again and he was intensely embarrassed.

The final shoot went like clockwork. Craig began with an exciting intro where he summarised the reasons why this was such an amazing excavation: the unknown Roman fort, the early church, and the first Christian burials. And now they had solid evidence of an intact Iron Age settlement below the lowest levels of the Roman fort. It was an extraordinary layer-cake of superbly preserved buried remains, and of course it now extended well out into the fen, where, in addition, everything would be waterlogged, with wood and timber perfectly preserved. Archaeological sites – no, Alan thought, *landscapes* was the word – just didn't get any better than this.

Harriet and Toby had carefully arranged the bones of one body against a black cloth on a trestle table by the edge of the trench. Then, and as they'd rehearsed, Craig made an excited move to pick up one of the femurs, whereupon Harriet laid a restraining hand on his arm.

'No, Craig,' she said in a reproving voice. 'We don't just pick up human bones willy-nilly. These were Christians, just like us, and like bodies of all dead people, of whatever faith, they must be treated with respect.'

Yuk! Alan had felt nauseous when they'd rehearsed this saccharine scene earlier but, if anything, the real thing was even worse. He remembered a dig he'd been on in the 1980s when on an open day they'd dressed the skulls up with dark glasses and red chilli pepper noses. Most people had laughed. Only one or two staid elderly folk seemed to get a bit upset. Then, just as she'd done on the first day, Harriet broke all the rules.

She called across to Alan. 'Alan, would you come over here and show this man how to handle human parts?'

She said it absolutely straight-faced, without even a hint of innuendo. Alan swallowed hard. Very hard. He was having great trouble controlling a fit of giggles. In his earpiece he heard Weinstein's incredulous 'What's going on?'

'What's the problem, Harry?' It was the first time he had used her familiar name on-screen.

'After all these years, friend Craig here doesn't know how to handle human bones. You're the dig director, Alan, you'd better show him.'

Both Craig and Alan were staring at her open-mouthed. There was a look of quiet amusement, almost of satisfaction, in her gaze – which Speed was capturing in extreme close-up.

Alan then handed Craig a pair of blue nitrile gloves, while Harriet gave a brief running commentary. 'We wear the gloves to prevent any acids on our hands—'

In his ear, Alan could hear Weinstein laughing, almost out of control. 'Priceless, bloody priceless.'

Alan's own prearranged scene had gone quite well. Good old Kaylee had found a worn bronze coin in the Iron Age occupation layer. Alan wasn't much of a numismatist, but he could clearly discern the three capital letters CAM, which told the world it had been minted in Camulodonum, modern Colchester – the tribal capital of the Catuvellauni. As he announced the news to an astonished Craig he could imagine the ratings clock ticking ever higher, and Weinstein's delighted face in the London mixing studio.

But now it was all over. Alan was sipping yet another coffee from his Nikon mug. Craig and Frank had had to dash back to London for a late-night chat show on BBC2 about the current crop of live documentaries. Harriet was standing at the back of the shelter, talking anxiously into her mobile phone. She glanced hurriedly across at Alan, then turned round, still deep in conversation. Grump had plugged his iPod into a speaker which was playing one of his many Ian Dury tracks: 'Sweet Gene Vincent'. The wistful melancholy of the song suited Alan's mood. He glanced down at his watch: 6.45. It'd be getting dark soon. He mustn't keep Sebastian waiting.

He stood up, collected his knapsack from the side of the trench and dropped his mug into it. Then he checked inside: a roll of sample bags, his tough little on-site camera, a trowel, two hand-tapes and a 30cm black-and-white photographic scale bar. All present and correct. He zipped it up and slung it over one shoulder. As he did so, Harriet approached. She was smiling. And that wasn't something he'd seen much over the past few days.

'I thought that went very well, didn't you, Alan?'

'Yes, I did. It was less dramatic than the first "live", but I gather from Lew it's done, if anything, rather better.'

'That's brilliant, I think we should celebrate.' She put her hand on his arm, to lead him away. 'Let's go to the farmhouse. Candice has a secret supply of Champagne. It's long gone six. Come on, I'm parched. I think we've both earned a glass.'

Alan could have used a drink, but he shook his head. 'Sadly I can't. That was Sebastian who phoned before the final run-through—'

'Yes – you naughty boy! Caught you with your phone on.'

'I know. But this sounds exciting. Says he's found a wall.'

'Is that all? It's probably something to do with the abbey, some outbuilding. Surely it can wait till tomorrow? I'd give Sebastian a ring. I'm sure he won't mind.'

Alan shook his head. 'No, that's not the point. It wasn't at *this* end, near the island and the abbey. It was halfway across the fen, towards the pumping station. So God knows what age it might be. It can't possibly be medieval. It has to be Iron Age, or even earlier, in which case it probably isn't a wall at all – maybe a rampart or a cairn, even. Whatever it is, it's got to be unique. And waterlogged. And anyhow, I won't be long: it's going to be too dark to see anything, if I don't get going, soon. And don't fret, I'll be back *long* before the wrap party – in plenty of time to join you for a drink.'

By now she was looking very anxious.

'Oh, Alan, are you absolutely sure? Do you think you're going to make any sense of it, whatever it turns out to be, in your current state? You're absolutely exhausted.'

He hesitated. Was she right? Was he being pig-headed? Then another thought crossed his mind: she needs to keep control of me. She wants to have her cake and eat it too. Their body language together had left Alan in little doubt that Harriet and Craig had struck up a close relationship. Of course he knew only too well that he had had his chance earlier and had blown it. So he shouldn't be feeling so jealous: after all, it was in the past. Over and done with. But he did. And it was getting worse. If he didn't get away, he'd do or say something he'd regret. Even if Sebastian hadn't found a wall, it wouldn't matter. He had to get out, to get away and let off steam. And now he found he was dreading the wrap party. Maybe he'd cut it? What the hell, he had to escape.

Ignoring her pleading looks, he pulled on his waterproof jacket, picked up his rucksack and headed out of the shelter, and into the rain, which they could just hear on the tent roof during the final scenes of the 'live'.

* * *

Alan was angry. Harriet was doing exactly what she'd accused him of after the ill-advised 'it's a grave' moment. She wasn't taking professional responsibility. He had begun to rationalise his emotional reaction: couldn't she see that a stone structure, built at or just below sea level, had to be of major importance? Everything, but everything, would survive: all timbers would be intact, as would ropes, twine, cordage, fabrics, wattlework, basketry even. It would even make the timbers of the Haddenham long barrow look ordinary. Forget about mere log coffins or stray bog bodies: here, *everything* – the entire monument, from top to bottom – would be waterlogged. Bloody hell, he thought, why can't she see it? It's unbelievably important! By now the new find was something real and tangible: something that had to be seen, and it couldn't wait.

Alan strode briskly through the tall trees of the park, feeling increasingly excited and invigorated by what he was about to see. He didn't notice the rain, which continued to fall relentlessly. He had reached the abbey's boundary and passed through the roofed lychgate, which gave onto an outer footpath around the abbey walls. This was popular with dog walkers in winter. But there was no one here now. He crossed it into a narrower, less formal opening through the shrubs of the game-belt. This was the route down to the Engine Drain. Some of the dogwoods were already in leaf and they felt clammy, cold and damp, as they brushed against his face. He paused, wiped some wet hair from his eyes and pulled up his hood, yanking the laces tight. Then he hunched his shoulders, lowered his head and started along the narrow path, down to the dykeside.

He was about to come out of the shrubs and could just see the water in the Engine Drain glinting in the evening sun, when everything went dark.

It was the last thing he remembered.

# Twenty-Three

Distant, echoing voices were calling his name. Fish were slapping against the side of his face and the ground shook, rolling him over onto his side. His head throbbed and he became aware of pain somewhere inside his skull. Everything was hot, then cold. His eyes wouldn't open and his brain was about to explode. Then the fish returned, but harder, more insistent than before. Slowly the fish became wet hands. Then his eyes opened, but wouldn't focus. He could see grass and reed stalks and beyond that, the edge of the dyke. Then his lids came down. Blackness. Gently two sets of hands rolled him onto his back. Another person supported his head. He lay there, still and helpless, while the pain inside his head slowly intensified. Then the light returned. He was looking up into Harriet's face. Her eyeliner had run down her cheeks and she was crying. Her silvery top was torn and smeared with mud.

'Drink this, Alan.' She held a bottle to his lips and he took a few sips. 'You must drink.'

He lay back. The pain was still there, but not growing. He motioned for more water and drank again. Her hands were gently massaging the back of his neck. That felt good. Very good.

The next voice was familiar, too. 'Glad to have you back, Alan.' It was Richard Lane. 'You had us worried for a moment.'

'What happened? I fell over?'

'No, you were hit. From behind. By Sebastian Cripps.'

Alan groaned. He'd been duped. 'Have you got him?'

'Yes, he put up a struggle. But we've got him – entirely thanks to your friend, Harriet, here.'

'Yes, Alan, I put some rocks in my handbag and whacked him over the head.'

Alan's befuddled brain had a vision of a drowning Thorey. Harriet grasped his face gently in both her hands, and moved closer to him.

'No, Alan, I didn't. I was being silly. All I did was film him on my phone. But we captured everything. Every last detail.'

Alan looked up at her. She was smiling through the tears. Slowly, her eyes came nearer to him. He could feel the warmth of her breath as she leant forward, closer, closer. Lightly, she kissed him. Then quietly the lights went out; only this time it was sleep, not oblivion.

* * *

Alan woke up in his own bed. He was wearing pyjamas. The duvet cover had been changed and the pillows smelled clean and fresh. A temporary curtain had been rigged over the window. There was a jar of daffodils on the wardrobe. He could hear feet on the narrow stairs leading up to the attic bedroom. The door opened. It was Harriet. She was carrying a tray with a teapot, mug and little jug of milk. She put the tray on the bedside table and filled the mug.

'I'm taking you to the outpatients in Ely,' she said, as she put down the tray. 'You're to see the cranial impact specialist at ten. Richard Lane insisted that I make the appointment.'

He glanced at his watch. It was 8.30.

'So tell me, Harry, what happened after I left the shelter? Presumably you followed me down?'

'Yes, I did, but not before I'd phoned Richard Lane – and you saw me doing that, didn't you?'

'Yes, but I'd no idea who you were talking to. But what made you suspicious?'

'It was partly the timing, which seemed so contrived. And Sebastian must have known that everyone would be busy de-rigging the set, or getting ready for the wrap party. And besides, I'd never really liked Sebastian. He has a huge chip on his shoulder. Feels he ought to have been a big aristo. He has the house, but lacks the estate to support it. In many ways I felt quite sorry for his wife, Sarah. At least she was trying to do something to raise money.'

'The shoot and the fishing, you mean?'

'Yes, that and the social side that went with it. I think she very much admired what Candice and John were doing here: the farm shop, the restaurant and more recently the archaeological venture. It all made sense, and she approved of John's plans to go in with the White Delphs people – although she didn't dare to support him at board meetings. Sebastian would never have allowed that.'

'So do you think he was behind Thorey's death? I'd always thought it was the old head keeper, Bert Hickson. He had no reason to like Thorey, either.'

'I don't know. Anyhow, I've never trusted Sebastian further than I could spit.' Despite the seriousness of the moment Alan smiled at the unlikely image of a gobbing Harriet. 'Besides,' she continued, 'Lane tells me there's going to be a thorough investigation, so that's something, at least.'

Alan had his doubts: Hickson was a very wily old boy. But then something brought him up short: why had she, Harriet, spotted the real villain, and not him? After all, he was meant to be the dig director, the man who could follow up clues. He believed passionately in deduction: move from the specific to the general. Look for clues. Build up a case, point-by-point. And for the past four months he had been doing just that. Almost obsessively.

Then he remembered the set-piece he'd organised a month ago. He'd observed everyone in the room closely. Yet nobody betrayed anything. He might just as well not have bothered. And now it had come to this: he had been bashed over the head by a man he should have suspected from the outset. It was Harriet who'd had the confidence to ring up Richard Lane and call in reinforcements – and at the critical moment. So was all that based on her 'female intuition': her suspicion and dislike of Sebastian's character? He lay back, his mind reeling. Somehow, he thought, I need to redeem myself. I've got to find out what it was that drove Sebastian to act the way he did. And was it just Sebastian on his own? What about Hickson? What about Flower? What, come to that, about Candice?

Suddenly he realised that Harriet had resumed speaking.

'So I knew where you were heading and I told Lane about it. He was great and swung into action immediately. He said he'd be there in fifteen minutes, and with support. They parked in the road and took the path along the wall to the lychgate.' She took a sip from Alan's tea. 'I was following about a dozen paces behind you when Sebastian ambushed you.'

This was too much.

'By then Richard Lane had arrived with a couple of constables dressed for the part. They each stood astride, like in the films, and pointed their Tasers at him, two-handed. Then Lane shouted at him to stop what he was doing.' She frowned as she remembered the scene. 'But he had some cool. He looked up, all smiles of relief. All innocence. He said he'd managed to stop you from committing suicide. But I caught it all on my phone. Turns out that Frank's "reality show filming technique" has its uses after all.'

'Caught what, exactly?'

'Plenty of time for that, later.' She took another sip from Alan's mug. 'Richard asked me to hand the phone over as important evidence. I gave it to one of the PCs, who sealed it in a bag, which I signed with the time and date.'

Alan was looking at her with admiration and amazement. Putting the tea down, she became the efficient nurse once again.

'Come on, Alan, up you get. There's just time for a quick slice of toast. Then we must get going. Can't keep the specialist waiting.'

She gathered up the tray and headed downstairs.

Alan rolled over and picked up his phone. He had to speak to Richard Lane. Urgently.

'Richard. You must search the outbuildings at Fursey Hall. The thing is, they rarely made those traps as one-offs. They were normally set in groups as part of a bigger plan to beat poachers. So there's got to be another one somewhere. I'm sure it'll have clues to Thorey. And to Sebastian.'

He had tried to keep his voice down, but failed. He could hear Harriet's feet on the stairs. The bedroom door opened. She strode briskly across to the bed, picked up his phone and pocketed it.

'I'm having that, if you don't mind, Alan. You're meant to be recovering. Phone calls can wait till we get the all-clear from the doctor.'

* * *

The visit to the outpatients lasted a couple of hours and ended with an MRI scan. The specialist looked at the results for some time, then concluded that he could see no immediate problems, although Alan was to contact them at once if there was a return of the headaches. Harriet, who was driving them home, wasn't a great one for talking when at the wheel.

He still couldn't accept that he had missed so many clues. It had almost become a matter of self-esteem – it worried him so much and was now something of an obsession with him. It was like that time two years ago, when he couldn't spot the clue in the lists of samples from Flax Hole in the museum basement in Leicester. That too had become an obsession. Then, purely by chance, he realised that he was looking in entirely the wrong place. Instead, he needed to think outside the box, to use a cliché he detested. In other words, he had to look beyond the intricacies of the moment, to what might have appealed to, or motivated, a criminal. And as it turned out, that had nothing whatsoever to do with what was preoccupying him at the time.

He began to rethink the reactions to his set-piece at the end of that first meeting about the Fursey Penance in the ochre-painted dining room of Abbey Farmhouse. He had been expecting people to show their emotions, but the more he thought about it, the more naive that now seemed. Then he recalled how the day before, at the run-through, Harriet had seen him staring at her, and how he had got up and taken his Nikon mug to the flask of coffee at the other end of the trench.

He well remembered pressing down on the flask's lever, and the sound of the now-tepid liquid filling his mug. Meanwhile he didn't have to act a role. The muscles of his face had relaxed naturally; they knew what to do. He didn't have to act when he concentrated on pouring coffee. That way he covered his confusion. A simple trick, but effective.

He ran the events of his 'set-piece' through his mind again, more slowly. He had a clear picture of precisely what had happened – he had been concentrating with such intensity. For the hundredth time he was back in the red-walled dining room and he had just announced that the building stone used at Fursey had been hewn from the medieval quarries at Barnack, near Stamford. That meant the stone had effectively acquired a unique identity. The modern equivalent might be fine Italian marble; buildings made from it were extremely important, especially so far away from the quarries. John and Candice were amazed at the news; the Fen dean was predictably delighted; Sebastian yawned and went to pour himself a cup coffee; and the new Fursey manager, Steve Grant, never looked up, he was too intent on his mobile phone. Nobody at the table looked even slightly guilty.

The first two reactions were natural and genuine – he was

sure of that. But then it came to Sebastian and Steve Grant. Steve was a new appointment, so could immediately be discounted. But what about Sebastian? Then another thought struck him. The dean's 'misguided' trousers. That song and his own rapid exit for the toilet. It was all about covering up, concealing and diverting attention. At long last, he'd got it. The action of rising to get coffee signalled that Sebastian knew about Barnack and everything in Stan's hidden notebook on the day he was murdered.

And now Alan had no doubt: it was murder.

Then Alan thought about Joe Thorey's death: his pockets had been stuffed with pieces of brick. And only brick. Sebastian must have known that he couldn't have used stone from the abbey, if he didn't want the body traced to the Fursey Estate – which would immediately have implicated him. Then Alan had a second thought: the complete absence of any limestone and the careful selection of mass-produced bricks revealed paranoia and guilt. There was no way Thorey's death could possibly have been suicide. Whatever else he may have been, Thorey was not a thinking man. He'd have simply stuffed his pockets with whatever came to hand and probably wouldn't have even bothered to button them up.

* * *

On their way back home, Harriet had diverted to a giant Waitrose store on the outskirts of Ely. She led Alan round to the coffee shop, where she bought him a large latte and a curly Danish pastry. Then she selected a copy of the *Independent* from the rack and led him to a comfy chair.

'Stay there, Alan, and don't move till I come back. Understand?'

He nodded. It was like being 12 all over again: warm, loved and safe.

She took a deep breath and pulled out a long list. Then she headed towards the shelves.

An hour and a half later they arrived back home. Harriet took Alan through to the sitting room, and turned on the heater. Then she poured him a beer and went to make lunch. While she was in the kitchen, there was a knock on the front door. She answered it. A constable had returned her phone, 'with Detective Chief Inspector Lane's compliments'. Smiling, she handed Alan's phone back to him.

After lunch Alan asked if he could view the footage on her phone. He'd not been able to think of anything else since the constable had returned it. He needed to know exactly what had happened, and yet part of him was also terrified. She sat on the arm of his chair and looked over his shoulder.

At first the image was very shaky, but then it steadied as the camera closed in on Sebastian who was carrying a pick-handle and staring intently ahead.

Alan shook his head. 'I'm amazed he didn't spot you. How close were you?'

'I don't know, I wasn't measuring, but I was standing on the edge of those shrubs behind him and he was completely focused on you. I don't think for one moment he thought anyone else would be there. So he wasn't looking.'

But they were. Slowly Sebastian raised the pick handle. Harriet grabbed Alan's shoulder and buried her head in his sleeve.

'This next bit's horrible.' Her voice was muffled by his clothes.

And it was. With all his strength Sebastian brought the pick handle down on Alan's head, but at the last minute he must have heard something, or just decided to move, because instead of catching him square-on, it was a glancing blow to the side the head and his right shoulder, which was still very sore. Alan rubbed his right shoulder. It was still very sore.

Now the camera moved very slowly towards Sebastian's rear. Harriet had raised her head and whispered in Alan's ear, 'I didn't want him to spot me, and I thought I'd heard some branches breaking in the distance. I hoped and prayed it was the police.'

And what if it hadn't been, Alan thought, what then? He was so impressed by her bravery and composure. He put his left arm around her shoulder and she snuggled in closer.

'I thought he was going to finish you off there and then,' she continued. 'But he had other plans. While he'd been waiting for you he'd gathered up a pile of stones, presumably originally from the wall.'

Alan nodded: there was a lot of loose stonework at the foot of the monastic boundary.

Then the image cut.

Alan paused the film, while she explained. 'I turned the phone off briefly, as I knew I was running out of time. I could also hear Richard Lane and his men approaching, although Sebastian was so intent on what he was doing that he heard nothing. Then I turned it on again.'

Alan did the same.

'I was less worried about being seen, as I was now sure help was at hand. So I dared to get a bit closer.'

And she did. Alan was astonished by the clarity and steadiness of the image. That took some self-control.

On screen, they could clearly see Sebastian taking rocks

from the small pile and cramming them into Alan's rucksack. Alan shook his head as he watched Sebastian. He was really jamming them in. He meant business all right. That rucksack must have weighed a ton. Then suddenly, Sebastian looked up: his face was horrified. His mouth sagged open. Rapidly he looked around him, then dropped his head. He was surrounded.

Briefly the image shook, then the screen went blank.

# Twenty-Four

By the next day, Alan was beginning to feel much better – both mentally and physically. Harriet was still keeping a close eye on him, but she, too, felt less worried now.

Alan had come to realise that his old feelings for her had never gone away and he was kicking himself for being so slow to have recognised it. But he had had other things to think about – or at least that was what he told himself until, for a second time, he brought himself up sharply. What else was there to think about that mattered? In the greater scheme of things, the Crippses and their curse could all go to hell. He should think more about his own life, which was the only one he would ever live – and he knew enough about himself to realise that he couldn't do that on his own. So was Harry just a means to an end? Was he being his old selfish self again? The doubts flooded in on him.

Shortly after lunch, Lane paid a visit. Alan was sitting at the kitchen table with a cup of tea. Lane asked after his health. Harriet replied that they had just had the follow-up review of the MRI scan, which hadn't revealed any major problems. So barring disasters, they were probably in the clear. She then went back to the washing up.

Lane pulled up a chair and Alan outlined his suspicions of Sebastian as regards both Stan and Thorey. Lane took detailed notes.

As he was drawing to a close, Alan asked, 'And have you managed to search the out-buildings at the hall?'

Lane smiled. 'I went there myself. And now I know what it's like to make a big discovery.'

Harriet had rejoined them. She just caught Lane's last remark.

'Really, Richard, you sound like an archaeologist,' she said with a smile.

'I got the team to do a methodical finger-tip search starting with the buildings closest to the yard, and working back.'

'But you decided to take a quick peek where you suspected it might actually be. Am I right?'

'Yes, Alan, you are.' Lane was grinning; he was enjoying this. 'I decided to check out an old log-store, round the back. It was accessed by an overgrown block-paved yard track and had double doors, which looked in fairly good nick. It even had an electric light with a cracked Bakelite switch. But it worked. Inside were all manner of antique-looking things: an old beet-chopper, several hand-pumps with long curved handles, two sack-scales, plus weights, and several wheelbarrows, not to mention a couple of dozen hand tools, any one of which would have fetched £200 in Cambridge. But round the back I came across what we were looking for.'

'And what was that?' Harriet rapidly cut in.

'A mantrap,' Lane replied. 'And I reckon it had been moved there quite recently, too – but we'll be able to check that out. So I immediately sealed the door and called in forensics.' He took a sip from the fresh cup of tea that Harriet had given him when she had re-entered.

'Anyhow, I got a phone call this morning from Dr Lindsay Harris.'

Alan could see the name meant nothing to Harriet. 'She was the pathologist who examined Joe Thorey's body,' he explained.

'I had told her to check the trap's teeth, as we'd both discussed.'

Alan nodded.

'She's still got more photos and scans to do before her evidence will stand up in court, but she says she's already 98 per cent certain that she has a good match. Apparently the scars are very distinctive.'

'So we're starting to build up a case against him, aren't we?' Alan's question was rhetorical.

'And there's another thing. The scene of crime people reckon it had been moved quite recently, although there were no tyre marks on the paved roadway. They also reckon it had been thoroughly cleaned, almost certainly with agricultural diesel. It certainly stank enough. But when they turned it over they found green man-made fibres snagged in a couple of places where the rough steel hadn't been smoothed-out. I was at Fursey when the news came through, so I went and checked Sebastian's Land Rover and the estate car—'

Alan had to break in. 'That's the one Sarah drives. And don't tell me: it had a green carpet.'

Lane was smiling. 'Correct. And they soon confirmed the two sets of fibres were identical.'

'So surely you've got him?' Harriet asked.

'Yes. But there's also another way we could look at it.'

He was sounding mysterious. Alan and Harriet didn't get it.

'You said it yourself, Alan, just then: it was the car Sarah drives. So I'm going to suggest to him that his wife was closely involved, too.'

Harriet suddenly looked up. She was outraged. 'But, Richard, you can't do that! Her husband's a massive great thug. She couldn't possibly have lifted or set that heavy trap. And surely the car was owned jointly? You know it's not right – and it isn't fair, either.'

Lane was taken aback. He raised a calming hand, which Alan could see was having the opposite effect.

'Harriet,' Lane said in an attempt at soothing tones. 'I'm well aware of that. And I wouldn't dream of suggesting she was even slightly implicated in the crime – and certainly not in a court. But we need something to make Sebastian confess. Don't forget: there's more than one death that needs explaining, here. I agree, he's plainly not a very nice man at all, but he's also quite old-fashioned. Has old-world values. And if I were to suggest to him that he had implicated his wife in his crimes, I feel quite confident that he'd confess to everything.'

Harriet looked suitably contrite. Lane got up and started to head for the door. Then he paused. He turned to Alan. 'Oh yes, there was one other thing. Dr Harris mentioned that when she saw you at the museum last Tuesday she bumped into Sebastian in the entrance hall on her way out.'

Alan thought back. Given that so much had happened of late, he couldn't be absolutely certain. But yes, he thought, she might well have done. He vaguely remembered hearing Sebastian and Sarah's voice. Then he recalled leaving the museum building quite hurriedly. So, yes, Lindsay Harris was indeed right: Sebastian must have been there.

'Sorry, Richard, my brain's still a bit creaky, but I think he was there on that day.'

'Well, Lindsay said Sebastian wanted to know if she'd been talking to you. Seemed quite insistent. She said she told him the truth: that she had. But later it struck her as a bit odd.'

'Yes,' Alan replied. 'I don't think friend Sebastian is quite as thick as he would like us to believe.' Alan remembered Sebastian's non-response when he told the visiting councillors about the buried archaeology beneath his land. It was as if he didn't realise the implications. Now Alan realised that was an act. 'So,' he continued, 'I suspect he thought I was on to him.'

'Well, weren't you, Alan?' Harriet asked, seemingly in all innocence.

She had recovered her composure and was smiling at his discomfort. She had always enjoyed teasing him.

'You know damn well I wasn't.'

He tried to make his reply sound light. Throwaway, even. But he knew he'd failed abysmally.

* * *

By Wednesday morning Alan was pretty well back to normal. The swelling had largely vanished and had been replaced by a dark bruise, which looked far worse than it felt. First thing on Monday morning, Peter Flower had called an emergency meeting of Fursey Heritage Development, which was scheduled to take place today at 9am. It was to be attended by Candice, Barty and Steve Grant. Alan was also asked to attend, as an observer, along with their English Heritage inspector,

Shelley Walters. The only other FHD director who wasn't dead or in police custody was Sarah Cripps, who had fled to stay with some cousins in rural Northamptonshire as soon as her husband had been arrested. She could only be reached through expensive lawyers in London.

The atmosphere in the red dining room at Abbey Farmhouse was subdued. Barty looked terrible. Alan reckoned he'd aged five years in as many days. Candice sat tight-lipped, and as far away from Peter Flower as possible. Their body language was hostile verging on hatred. Steve Grant was remarkably calm, given his lack of experience. But to Alan's surprise, Peter Flower seemed to have risen to the occasion. He, at least, was prepared to make uncomfortable decisions. He began the meeting by asking Shelley Walters if she could outline English Heritage's position.

She replied that she had been in touch with the chief archaeologist who was keen to see that the excavation was brought to a 'sensible' conclusion, without leaving any waterlogged deposits exposed to desiccation. The site should then be back-filled and turfed over, pending a review of the existing Scheduled Monument's curtilage.

Steve Grant looked puzzled at this, so Alan whispered 'boundary' in his ear. That earned him a thumbs up.

Shelley went on to say that money was being set aside for post-excavation research and publication. Alan was relieved to hear it – at least he would have work for the next few months. Steve Grant reported that his managers at Heritage Projects Management sent their sympathy and offered to do everything possible to aid the site's orderly winding down, even if this cost them money. Reading between the lines, Alan reckoned that they were worried stiff about the affair turning into an even bigger PR disaster and were desperately keen to ensure that the good name of their 'brand' wasn't damaged too badly. And if that cost money, then so be it.

After the meeting, which didn't last for more than about 45 minutes, Peter Flower drew Alan to one side.

'As you may have noticed, Alan, a certain distance has developed between myself and Candice. I'd rather not discuss why this happened, but it did and I must confess that I'm not altogether sorry.'

Alan could see Flower wasn't finding this easy. It was now quite clear to him that Flower had played no part in the Fursey crimes whatsoever. But strangely, he didn't feel any sense of victory and he had to admit, too, that his own prejudice against the man had clouded his judgement. He thought back to his own PhD. Was prejudice – this time suspicion of him, a fieldworker, by Flower, an academic – what lay behind Flower's critique of his thesis? Quite probably. Alan had the sense to realise that it was now time to put away these grudges. For good. But there were things he still needed to discover. The mystery was not completely solved.

'Can I ask, Peter, was there growing tension between the commercial side of the operation and the archaeological research? Was that part of the problem?'

'No, strange as it might seem, there was no tension there at all. John, whose background was in the world of leisure and tourism, was always very keen that the research must go ahead. Even Candice, who understood rather less about our work, was sympathetic. My disagreement with her was about something else, entirely.'

Alan then remembered what he had been meaning to ask Flower for some time.

'I know this might sound a bit odd after all that has happened, but are you aware that you ever told Sebastian that Stan had had a drink problem?'

They were walking towards the car park. Flower stopped.

'Do you know, Alan, I think you might be right. I remember now: Sebastian, John, Candice and I interviewed him. And, yes, I did feel I ought to tell them about his drinking habits. It would have been remiss of me not to.'

'No, I agree, I'd have done the same, if I'd been in your shoes.'

Flower smiled. 'That's a relief. But what's all this in aid of?'

'Sometime in mid-January I found myself in the old farm shop and offices building.'

'In those terrible converted pig sheds?'

'Yes, in them. Well, while I looking around I came across a small room that Candice tells me was known as Stan's "cupboard". In it I found a notebook and a half-empty bottle of twenty-year-old malt whisky with Fisher College on the back label.'

'That would be the Glen Hubris McTavish – a wonderful whisky.'

'I know the college supplied John Cripps with wine – he is after all a graduate – but do you know: did they also supply Sebastian?'

'Yes, they did. The family had long ties with the college and in such cases we sometimes make exceptions to the rules. And besides, if we didn't supply him direct, he could always have bought it from his brother.'

It was what Alan had expected, and it was good to know for certain.

'Thank you, Peter, that is very helpful.'

'Why?' Flower asked. 'Do you think Sebastian was encouraging him to drink?'

'Yes I do.'

'But why on earth should he want to do that? It doesn't make any sense, does it?'

'I'm not sure. But I'm fairly certain it was deliberate. Maybe even part of a larger plan.'

* * *

The next day began badly. Alan called all the supervisors and diggers into the site Portakabin and told them that the project only had enough money to pay them for a couple of weeks. After that they'd have to find work elsewhere. But he was also aware that most of the few commercial digs that were currently underway were all fully staffed. In fact, archaeological employers were laying off employees right and left. It made him angry: the recent financial crash and the greed of fat-cat London bankers had hit working archaeologists hard.

He was heading rather forlornly back to his desk to draw up a list of jobs that had to be completed before everyone left site, when his mobile rang. It was Lane. Quickly he opened his office door, shut it behind him and collapsed into his chair, as he answered the call.

Lane, as always, got straight to the point. 'I think Sebastian is ready to confess. I mentioned those green fibres from his wife's car.'

'And it worked?'

'Yes, it did. And I didn't need to push him. The prison had done our job for us.'

'So he's in Blackfen, is he?' Alan had spent long enough

there, lecturing to members of The Lifers' Club to know exactly what he meant.

'Yes, he is. His lawyer knew he'd never get bail. I'm sure he wants to come clean, but he's still reluctant to speak to the police—'

'Don't tell me, without a lawyer present?'

Lane's reply came as a bolt from the blue. 'No.' He paused. 'It's far stranger than that. The words he used were: "I want Alan Cadbury to be there. I need to apologise, face-to-face."'

'But he tried to kill me. In cold blood. And now he wants to say he's sorry?'

'So you won't come?' Lane sighed. 'Can't say I blame you.'

'But does this often happen?' Alan still couldn't believe what he'd heard. 'How can anyone be so violent, then act like that? It's . . .' He was lost for words. 'It's bonkers. Sorry, but that's the only word. Bonkers.'

'No, I agree, Alan, this is an extreme case, but I've seen it with other violent men. You see it with Jihadis – one minute they're praying, the next they're cutting people's throats. Certain people compartmentalise their minds and their lives. So when they come out of a particular compartment and look back, they then regret what they did. Anyhow, not only does he want to apologise, but it seems you're the only one he trusts.'

'It almost sounds like a split personality. Schizophrenia. That sort of thing?'

'Yes, that's one of the things we're concerned about, too. I've requested that a couple of prison psychiatrists listen in and observe the interview while it's taking place. But don't worry, they'll be well hidden.'

Alan took a deep breath. I must be bonkers myself, he thought, as he heard his own reply.

'OK, Richard, I'll be right over. See you shortly.'

* * *

Alan headed north out of Fursey and turned east towards the central Fens on the March and Walbeach Road. After he had agreed to be present at Sebastian's interview with Lane at Blackfen, he had begun to have misgivings. But they were irrational. There was nothing about the forthcoming meeting to cause him any real alarm at all: Sebastian was unlikely to be violent, and anyhow, there would be officers present. And besides, he had asked Lane to attend; so he was unlikely to get unpleasant. But still, his doubts were increasing.

A few miles south of March he picked up the first signs to HMP Blackfen. They had an instant effect. In fact, he felt so bad that he pulled into a lay-by. His hands were visibly shaking as he took out his phone and called Harriet.

When she answered he could tell she was preoccupied, but as soon as he explained where he was heading, and why, her voice changed entirely.

'Oh, Alan, why didn't you come and see me before you left?'

'It was those signs to HMP Blackfen that did it, Harry. Made me come over all weird. Shaky and strange. If there was a bottle in the Fourtrak I'd have a slug of whisky and to hell with the law. But there isn't.'

'So you'll have to make do with me.'

But she said this kindly, without a hint of sarcasm. It was clear she meant it.

'So Richard Lane asked you to go?'

Alan then gave her all the details of the morning's call. As they talked, he realised he was starting to calm down. It felt like he was receiving professional therapy. But there was one question that still worried him.

'I can't understand why Sebastian seems to trust me. Why *me*, of all people?'

'Oh, I can understand that, Alan.' She was laughing now. The mood had lightened. 'Don't forget, he was married to a posh woman who had big plans for the estate. Then she ran away as soon as he was arrested. And I don't think Candice has been much help, either – and besides, I don't think they ever saw eye to eye. And then there's Barty, poor old Barty. He's had to watch while his entire world has disintegrated around his head. I feel really sorry for him, but he won't receive any visitors.'

Although Alan wasn't a fan of the Cripps family, their collapse had been terrible, nonetheless. Then Harriet asked the obvious question. 'So when it comes to Sebastian, who else can he turn to?'

But Alan still wasn't completely satisfied. After all, the man had tried to kill him.

He thought for a few moments before he replied, 'Yes, I suppose that all makes sense, but it's not as if I've been a part of his life for very long, have I?'

'In a strange way, Alan, I think you have.' She was speaking slowly, choosing her words carefully. 'You've said yourself that Sebastian was a countryman and liked nothing better than being out in the fields on a tractor. And he was always talking to you about drainage and the difficult soils he had to plough and cultivate. He knew you came from a farming background and had the same basic values. And he told me once that he'd always admired the way you worked. You were hands-on. You weren't like he'd imagined an archaeologist might be: slightly airy-fairy and remote; more interested in museum cases than a muddy field.'

They were both quiet for a while. Eventually Alan sighed heavily, then replied, 'Thanks for that, Harry. I feel much better. The wobbly fit has finished.'

He was about to ring-off, when her voice came through again. She sounded deeply concerned.

'Dear Alan, please take things steady. I'm not at all surprised that Blackfen gives you the willies. It would me if I'd gone through even half what you had to face a couple of years ago. So take it easy. Act the calm witness: don't get involved. But above all else, be guided by Richard Lane. He'll see that you're OK.' She paused briefly, and when she resumed Alan got the impression that she was smiling. 'And he must know by now that if he lets any harm come to you, he'll have to answer to me.'

Alan could tell she meant it.

* * *

The Blackfen visitors' car park looked horribly familiar, with the same small groups of wives and girlfriends standing around the visitors' entrance, all smoking as if their lives depended on it. But there had been a change since his last visit. The old high security doors with their intercom and dead letterbox had been replaced by a bright new lobby, complete with a check-in desk. It was an improvement.

He gave his name and was asked to sit on the right-hand side of the lobby, on one of the seats reserved for 'witnesses'. Alan smiled as he sat down; doubtless this was to make people like him feel at ease. But it hadn't worked. The foreboding was starting to return. Mercifully, a policeman soon arrived accompanied by a prison officer. Then it was back into those interminable featureless corridors that he remembered so well. They even smelled the same. Several times they had to stop and open locked doors, only to enter another long corridor. Eventually they reached their destination.

The interview room had no windows to the outside, but there was a large sheet of one-way, reflecting glass, behind which, Alan assumed, sat the psychiatrists, pencils and notebooks in hand. Otherwise it was drab, non-descript and the sparse furniture was plain and functional. One of the overhead strip lights was a bit flickery and there was a slight, lingering odour of disinfectant.

'Ah, Alan.' Richard Lane rose to greet him. 'So glad you could come. This is Mr Alwyn who is representing Mr Cripps.'

The young lawyer shook Alan's hand. Alan wondered whether this was his first case – he seemed so shy.

Lane set the tape running and gingerly inserted an earpiece into his left ear. It put Alan in mind of the 'live'. But before anyone had a chance to speak, Sebastian, who was sitting beside a uniformed prison officer on the far side of the table, leant across to Alan.

Alan smiled at his one-time assassin. What else could he do? Strangely he found he was sympathising with him.

'So why did you do it?' Lane broke in, perhaps rather too forcefully. For a moment Alan thought Sebastian was going to tell Lane to get lost. But he didn't, instead he took a deep breath and answered the question. His words were directed straight at Alan.

'You'd understand, Alan. The television, the tourist stuff,

even the shooting, were all taking us away from our roots. We're farmers and land-owners. We're not bloody entrepreneurs and showmen. I've got a diploma in agriculture, not computing and management studies. All I have ever wanted was to lead a countryman's life. And preferably on good land. Is that too much to ask?'

His voice trailed off, as he hid his face in his hands. Lane glanced towards the reflecting glass and cupped a hand over the earpiece, which he clearly hadn't grown accustomed to. He nodded towards the glass. Alan supposed the shrinks were telling him to give Sebastian time to recover.

Everyone waited. Eventually Lane was given leave to restart questioning.

'First tell me about Hansworth: was it an accident?'

Sebastian paused to think about this. His reply was quiet and considered.

'Yes, it was.'

Sebastian was staring down at the table, avoiding eye contact with his interviewers. Alan's heart sank. This was not what he had expected. So he wasn't going to come clean after all, despite his earlier promise to Lane. Then he looked up. His eyes were now on Alan:

'It was the last day of the spring coarse fishing and I was having a discussion with Hansworth about money for the next season. He reckoned he was paying enough already, but my agent had told me we could ask for more if we wanted.'

Then Alan had a thought. 'And what did Sarah think of that?'

'She wasn't as keen as me. I know she felt we were taking plenty off him already, what with the rent and other things we were charging him for. She was always saying that his help with the garden was worth hundreds of pounds.' He paused. He obviously wasn't used to discussing family affairs in such a public fashion. 'But the way I saw it, we were providing him with the opportunity to do some gardening. It was another service to him. If he'd been a stockman who wanted to run a couple of calves along with our bullocks, I'd have made him pay. So what's so different about gardening?'

That all made good sense, to Alan, who nodded and said, 'Thank you, Sebastian.'

Alan was aware that Lane was looking at him, his face inscrutable, but he detected a 'so what was that all about?' look in his eyes.

Lane turned towards Sebastian. 'Please continue, Mr Cripps.'

'Well,' Sebastian resumed. 'We were standing close by the river. I had just started to speak to him, when the little bell at the end of his rod jingled. He'd had a bite so he sat down and grabbed the rod, as if I wasn't there. He just bloody ignored me. I was furious. I'm not used to being treated like that by one of the tenants. So I tapped him on the shoulder. I didn't think I was being aggressive, but instantly he swung his arm back sharply and caught his elbow here,' he tapped his belly. 'It was a hell of a whack and it winded me. I couldn't breathe at all and staggered around gasping for air. That was when Joe Thorey appeared—'

Lane broke in. 'And was that something you had arranged in advance?'

'No, it wasn't. He was doing his morning patrol, checking on licenses and permissions.' He paused briefly while he re-assembled his thoughts. 'He immediately jumped forward and kicked the rod out of his hands and followed up with a hard punch in the gut – just as Hansworth had done to me. And it winded him, too.' Again he paused. Alan could see he was reliving the situation. 'But instead of letting him gasp for air, as I was still doing, he caught him with a massive upper-cut to the jaw which sent him over backward into the river, where he was caught by the stream. As he floated away I saw him convulse a couple of times, face down in the water. Then the body seemed to go still, but it was floating away rapidly by then.'

Lane poured him out a glass of water, which he half emptied in one gulp. Alan was intrigued by his hands. For such a large man, and a working farmer, they were surprisingly small and delicate.

'Continue in your own time, Mr Cripps.'

Sebastian nodded, then resumed. 'Joe followed him downstream, as I couldn't move. The body floated past Short Acre Wood and when I joined him about ten minutes later he'd managed to snag him with a long branch and had pulled him to the bank. But by then we could both see he was very dead.'

'And was that when you planned the deception?' Lane's question had a hard edge to it.

'No. I was all for coming clean. After all, it was Hansworth who had started the violence, not me. And you could say that Joe was just doing his job: protecting his employer. But Joe reckoned that no court in the land would ever believe us – and now I think he was right. Everyone would assume that I, his landlord, had arranged it. I remember Joe mentioned a recent case over in Norfolk, where the keeper was caught with the carcasses of two dozen hen harriers and the jury found the owner of the estate guilty too. And it didn't matter that he protested his innocence. Nobody believed him.' He shook his head. 'It's all about class, not justice.'

Alan had read about the case and he still agreed with the jury's verdict. But he said nothing.

'So what happened next?'

Lane's question was deliberately vague. He didn't want the lawyer sitting with them to intervene and break Sebastian's chain of thought.

'Well, it was Joe's idea. He said we must make it look like an accident. So I left him to it. The next day Joe had already booked a few days' leave, as it was the end of the fishing season.'

Lane was frowning, shuffling through his notes. But Alan knew what the next question should be.

'What happened then, between you and Joe Thorey?'

Briefly the young lawyer looked anxiously at his client, who seemed unfazed. So he sat back and said nothing.

'Well,' Sebastian slowly began, 'Thorey replaced Hickson as head keeper.'

Alan noted that Sebastian was now using their surnames, as would befit their employer in such a hierarchical set-up.

'And Bert Hickson took early retirement,' Lane added helpfully.

Sebastian was starting to flag. He needed encouragement as there was still a long way to go.

'Yes, and Thorey moved into Keeper's Cottage.'

'And was Thorey still friendly?' Alan decided to risk another nudge.

'No. That was when things began to change between us. The shoot did well and credit where credit's due, much of that was down to Thorey. But he became very over-confident. Liked to shoot his mouth off. I'd have told him to shut up several times—'

'But you were in a difficult situation,' Lane cut in.

A little more encouragement. Lane glanced at the lawyer, who was sitting, motionless.

'And then he started the blackmail.' At this Alan looked at Lane, who was having trouble concealing his excitement. 'At first it was small things: extra leave, an end-of-year bonus, a new Land Rover. But soon he became greedy. And I didn't have the money. I told him so. He said he didn't care, that he'd ask Sarah – because he knew she did.'

'And did Sarah know about the "arrangement" you'd both come to over Hansworth's death?'

'Of course not.' Sebastian was indignant. 'I didn't want to implicate her in any way at all. But now I realised that was precisely what Thorey wanted me to do. And I was damned if I would.'

At this, even the young lawyer was leaning forward. He fully expected Lane to ask the obvious leading question: Did you kill him? But he didn't.

'So what did you do?'

'I decided he had to go. You can't give in to blackmailers. They're the lowest form of life. So I decided to set a mantrap for him. I knew there was one in an out-house on the farm and I'd been shown how to set one by Bert Hickson when I was a boy. I concealed it near some cages where we were raising pheasant chicks. I knew Thorey fed them twice a day.'

To Alan's eyes, Sebastian seemed much calmer now. He took a sip of water, then continued.

'The pens were in the woods down by the river. Anyhow, I set the trap one wet afternoon and went back there the following morning. And it wasn't a nice sight at all. He'd lost a lot of blood and had passed out.'

'But was still alive?' Lane asked.

'Yes, I could feel his pulse. But it was very weak.' He took a deep breath. 'I prised open the jaws and pulled him out. Then I filled his pockets with stones—'

'Actually you used broken bricks,' Alan broke in. 'Was there any reason why you didn't use stones?'

Sebastian shrugged.

'No, none. They were lying around, that's all.'

It was the reply Alan had expected. Brick rubble had been used to build up and consolidate the towpath after the catastrophic floods of 1947. Stone was confined to the area of the medieval abbey, some distance from the river.

'Well, anyhow,' Sebastian continued, 'I filled his pockets and dragged him to the river. Chucked a few extra bricks on top of him for good measure.' He paused. They could all see he had no regrets. Then he added, as an after-thought. 'And good riddance to him.'

'And Stan?' asked Alan, leaning forward. It was the question he had wanted to ask from the beginning of the interview.

'He was a good man,' said Sebastian. 'He didn't deserve what happened to him.'

This time it was not the reply that Alan expected.

Then Sebastian sat back and closed his eyes. Something inside him seemed to have closed down, as if he could not contemplate any more horror. Alan made to speak, but Lane placed a restraining hand on his arm.

'All in good time,' said Lane.

Alan almost exploded in frustration. But one glance into Lane's face was enough. His gaze was rigid. Alan knew when to shut up.

# Twenty-Five

It was early morning. Only just light outside. Harriet rolled over, reached down to the floor and flicked the switch on the electric kettle. She prodded Alan, who was still half asleep beside her. He grunted.

'D'you still want to do it, Alan?' she asked, as the kettle started to emit pre-bubbling sounds.

Despite drinking too much wine with last night's spaghetti, he knew exactly what she was talking about. The previous evening he had asked whether she would do him a big favour. He was having trouble laying Stan's memory to rest. He kept returning to that evening by the Mill Cut, when Lane had showed him the scene where they had just discovered Stan's body. He hadn't been there, but in the intervening months he'd recreated the scene many, many times and now was having trouble disentangling his memories from his imaginings. The more he thought about it, the more he knew that Stan's death had been no accident. And everything now pointed in Sebastian's direction. But why did he do it? What was his motive for taking so much trouble to kill such small-fry as Stan? The more Alan tried to reason it out, the less progress he made. Then on Thursday, just after he'd finished Lane's phone call about Sebastian's confession, it came to him: he knew what to do. Somehow he must exploit Harriet's emotional perception. If anyone could, she would discover what had driven Sebastian to kill.

* * *

Alan decided not to drive to the mill. He didn't want his distinctive muddy Fourtrak to draw people's attention – and being a Saturday morning the dog walkers would be out in force. So they took the footpath that ran diagonally across the low-lying fields that led down to the mill pool. When they got there, Alan talked her through everything Lane had told him: starting with the police in the car park, and what Lane had said about Stan's smart new bike. Stan loved that bike. He would never, ever leave it anywhere unlocked. But this time he had. Was it the drink? Was he intending to come back? But whatever he was contemplating, Alan didn't think it was suicide.

'Or am I wrong? Maybe it was,' he said to Harriet.

Harriet frowned as she thought this over.

'No,' she replied. 'It wasn't. He'd have locked the bike up if he was thinking of killing himself. That's what I'd have done. It shows the world that you are still in control. It's more dignified. And whatever Stan's other problems, he never lacked dignity.'

Harriet had got to know Stan a few years earlier on a Saxon cemetery site in Suffolk.

'Yes, that's it. You're right!'

He could have kissed her. Should have done. But didn't.

'So why did he come down here, do you think?' Harriet asked.

'I honestly don't know,' Alan replied. 'But we do know he'd been drinking. The official version is that in a drunken state he fell into the river, where he got carried through the mill wheel because the protecting grille over there' – he pointed across the mill pond – 'had recently been broken by a collapsing tree.'

'And did that happen? Had a tree collapsed?'

'Yes it had. Lane saw the damage with his own eyes.'

'And then?'

'I don't know how or why he fell into the water, but I'm fairly sure it wasn't an accident, and now I strongly suspect that Sebastian might have been involved.'

She paused to think about what he'd just said. 'So presumably he got bashed about when he passed through the mill wheel?'

'Yes. Lane said the injuries were terrible. In fact, that was almost certainly what killed him.'

'And then what?'

'He floated downstream and got snagged on barbed wire over by those trees in the distance, there. On Cripps land. His body was found by Bert Hickson, their ex-head keeper.'

'The man you thought might have killed Joe Thorey?'

'That's right. But I was wrong. I realise that now.' He was going to say more, but decided not to: he could see she was lost in thought.

'Can you throw any light on why he came down here, presumably after dark – or else he'd have been seen by dog walkers – in the first place? And drunk?' she added as an afterthought.

'As you can imagine, I've thought about that a lot. And I can only assume that Sebastian had arranged to meet him.'

'But why?'

'And this is where I'm having problems. I'm reasonably certain that Sebastian knew that Stan had discovered there were Iron Age occupation deposits that extended out into his land all the way around Fursey island.'

'How do you know that?'

'Because I'm also absolutely certain he knew that the stone used at Fursey came from Barnack quarries. He'd put that information in his daybook and he dated the entry 8 October, the day he died. And I've confirmed the IDs with Hilary Porter at Saltaire, who did them. I'm in no doubt at all that the combination of waterlogged Iron Age settlements and high-status medieval buildings built of Barnack stone would have blighted the family's land's development potential. He couldn't sell anything. He could never move: he was stuck. And it was all down to me – and Stan.'

'So presumably that notebook also had information about the levels and the earlier deposits in the dyke?'

'Yes, and I'm fairly certain that Sebastian must have known about them. And, looking back on it all, I can remember times when I think he was checking my movements. He once remarked that there was peaty mud on the Fourtrak and I'm fairly certain he was observing me when I went down to the Engine Drain to take pollen samples with Bob Timpson, and also when I met the engineer from the IDB, who gave me an accurate fix on the TBM in Stan's notebook. And those are just two occasions. There may well have been others.'

'So why was he so interested? Was it just the value of his land?'

'I don't know; that's what's been bothering me for weeks.'

'Well, let's think about Sebastian – as a person. What does he care most about? What motivates him?'

'I don't think it's his wife. Certainly he cares about her reputation in the eyes of other people, but that's not the same as loving her, is it?'

'No.' She looked rueful. 'Sadly, it isn't. And she left for Northamptonshire so rapidly when everything blew up. That's hardly the action of a person who cares. So there must be something else.'

'What, another woman?'

'No, Alan.' She was smiling now. 'Some men are motivated by things other than sex.' She thought for a moment. 'He was a councillor and a farmer. Which do you think he preferred?'

Alan was in no doubt. 'Oh, he told me once that he hated the local government work, but he needed the money it generated. The trouble was, he only owned four hundred acres—'

'Sounds quite a lot to me,' Harriet broke in.

'Not if the land's poor quality and badly drained. His grandfather, the second baronet, had sold off the good land to pay death duties back in the 1950s. You can't quite see it from here, but it's that farm to the north of the pumping station.'

'What? The picture postcard house, surrounded by trees and the apple orchard?'

'Yes, that's the one. Isle Farm, it's called.'

'Ah,' she said slowly. 'I think we might be on to something.' She paused, thinking this through.

'You mean he was planning to sell up and use the money to buy Isle Farm?'

'Or somewhere similar, yes, I do,' she replied.

'And of course development land is always worth far more than agricultural land.'

'But not if it's concealing huge Iron Age, Roman and medieval deposits. Developers would run a mile. Can you imagine the cost of digging the wet bits around Fursey?'

Alan shook his head. What a dig that would have been. He would have loved the job.

'Hundreds of thousands. Millions, even.'

'So that was why he had to silence Stan – and later, of course, you. You both had the knowledge he feared.'

Alan reflected on this. It all made sense. But there was one other small, but important, point.

'So how did he get Stan to come here?'

'Oh, that's simple,' she replied. 'I can see it all now.'

'But why down here at the mill, of all places? That's what I don't understand.'

'As I said, Alan, it's simple. He could give your friend something that meant more to him then than any treasure on earth. He'd climb up a volcano to get it. And it was their secret. Nobody else knew about it. If they did, Stan would lose his job and finish his career.'

Put like that, Alan understood, too. 'It was whisky, wasn't it?'

'Yes, as you told me, the very best malt. Maybe he drank half a bottle? I don't know. But then it was a simple matter to push him in the river, and who knows, even steer him into the mill.'

Suddenly, and without any warning, Alan wheeled round and dashed towards the river. Where he was violently sick.

* * *

The next day was Sunday. Alan was peeling potatoes, while Harriet prepared the joint of beef. The kitchen was warming up, so he opened a window. When the wind was from the right direction, they could just hear the morning cascade of the bells of Ely Cathedral.

Yesterday afternoon Alan had heard that Richard Lane's wife, Mary, would be spending Sunday with her father, who had been taken to hospital for observation after a minor stroke. So Alan had asked Lane to join them for Sunday lunch.

As Harriet carved the beef, she mentioned to Lane that she and Alan had revisited the mill the day before and had come up with a slightly different version of Stan's death. She then explained about Stan and the buried archaeology and the fact that Sebastian had undoubtedly seen Stan's notebooks and almost certainly understood about the low-lying levels.

'But why would that worry him so much?' Lane had to ask.

'Oh, that's simple, Richard.' Alan took over while Harriet placed thin slices of pink meat on their plates. 'He realised that the presence of so much buried archaeology would completely destroy the value of his land to developers. It would cost a fortune to excavate – and of course there was always the strong probability that someone at English Heritage might decide to have it Scheduled – as indeed they have now. And if that happened, it would be game over.'

'Yes.' Harriet smiled as she handed Lane a steaming plateful. 'And he would then be left with a small farm of not very good, poorly-draining land—'

'In a world of falling commodity prices,' Lane added.

'So does that make sense to you, Richard?' Alan asked.

The answer to this question was crucially important. They both waited anxiously, while the policeman wiped his mouth with his napkin.

'Yes. I agree with you both. It makes excellent sense.'

As one, Harriet and Alan raised their glasses to their lips.

'And will you be able to nail him for more than just Thorey's murder?' Alan asked.

'Well, that's a different matter. But we've earned ourselves some time with his confession. So rather than go for him bit by bit, I'd rather we arrested him for all three killings.'

'And what about his brother, John?'

'To be honest, Alan, I can't see that he was involved. And he has a watertight alibi.'

'Really, where?'

'He was at a big college dinner in Cambridge. Then he and his wife stayed the night at the University Arms. And it all checks out. He's in the clear.'

'Then I suggest we forget about it for a few days.' Alan said this confidently. He was trying to allow his instinctive side to guide him. 'I've got a feeling something's going to happen. I don't know what – or when – but I doubt if John Cripps's death will be a mystery for very much longer.'

Harriet was giving him a warm, but slightly quizzical look. This was not the Alan Cadbury of old. Alan took a drink. There was just one other point that worried him.

'So we think we know about Hansworth's death. In theory, it was manslaughter by Thorey – if, that is, we accept Sebastian's confession. But I wonder whether it was accidental at all? I find it hard to accept that somebody who was capable of killing two people – Stan and Thorey – didn't also do in the banker? I know it's just a gut feeling but . . .' He trailed off and sat back in his chair, looking worried.

Lane frowned, but Harriet leant forward.

'I can think of something else that might have motivated Sebastian to kill Hansworth.'

'And what was that?' Alan asked eagerly.

'When did they get married?'

'Sarah and Sebastian? I'm pretty sure it was in 1998.'

'So he and his young wife had spent six years living in the second-best apartment in his family's ancestral home.'

'But Sarah and Hansworth got on quite well: they both loved gardening.' Alan was looking puzzled.

'Well that proves it,' Harriet replied. 'She had to form a friendly relationship with him, otherwise tongues would have wagged. Everyone would have accused her of jealousy or ambition.'

'Yes,' Lane added. 'That makes sense.'

'And she's not particularly keen on gardening now.' Alan said this to himself. He was about to speculate on their pillow talk, when Lane added: 'And to make matters worse, Hansworth was gay and lived at the hall with his male partner. And, again, that's not exactly a reason to be calm and content – not if you've got a Victorian mindset, is it?'

There was a pause, while they all got stuck into their roast.

Then Harriet turned to Lane. 'I wonder whether Hansworth's death didn't give Sebastian the original idea of using the river, not just to kill, but also to dispose of any clues. Alan told me that Hansworth died in the river, but it wasn't clear whether it was passed off as suicide. Was it?'

'No,' Lane replied. 'It wasn't. I was working with the Fenland Force back then, and although I wasn't closely involved, nobody suggested it was anything more than a fishing accident.'

'And what about his fellow bankers?' Alan asked. 'How did they react?'

'Well,' Lane replied, 'it didn't help that he had vanished shortly before the end of the financial year when bankers traditionally did moonlight flits to places like Luxembourg and Switzerland.'

Harriet was curious. 'And did anyone uncover any wrong-doing at the bank?'

'No. None whatsoever. Apparently his accounts were bang up to date and in good order. And so far as we can tell, it doesn't seem like he was ever up to any funny business.'

'They found his body sometime in May, didn't they?' Alan asked.

'Yes, I think it was mid-May – around the fifteenth. Most of it was found snagged against an old landing stage, about half a mile upstream of Denver Sluice. But by then it was terribly decayed and several toes and fingers had gone missing.'

'Knowing what we know now, do you think he'd been weighed-down?'

'It's perfectly possible.'

It was. But something else was troubling Alan. Something wasn't ringing true. Sebastian was indeed old-fashioned, but he had never shown any signs of homophobia. And as for the big apartment at the grand house? Again, it didn't fit with the Sebastian Alan had come to know over the past few months. He was a farmer, first and foremost; he drove around in a muddy Land Rover. Whatever else Sebastian might be, Alan knew he had never been posey – unlike his wife, of course. She was happy to act the Lady of the Manor to yuppie bankers. And she did it very well. But not Sebastian: that wasn't his style at all. So what had motivated him to kill Hansworth?

Lane leant back in his chair. He had emptied his plate.

'That was delicious, Harriet.' He wiped his mouth and threw the napkin onto the table. 'And I think I've got enough to go on now. I'll nip back to Blackfen and have a word with our friend about Stan – and Hansworth, too. He's confessed once and I'm sure we can get him to do it again.'

Harriet was about to agree with Lane, but something in Alan's face made her hold back.

'Richard,' Alan began, 'you said yourself that the confession has bought us time.'

'Er . . . yes?' Lane wasn't sure where Alan was heading.

'I don't think we've yet got his true motive for killing Hansworth. Everything we've suggested is plausible, but too general, and if you'll forgive me for saying so, just a little bit predictable.'

'OK, Alan, I can wait – if you're quite sure. A few days won't hurt.'

'Thanks, Richard. You won't regret it. I don't often say this, but something doesn't feel right. And if we're going to get him to confess we'll need to be far more specific. Anyhow, if you'll give me the time, I've got an idea I would like to try.'

* * *

The last days of a normal, happy dig can be exhausting or exciting – and are often both. But a dig that has effectively been shut down is altogether different. Morale collapses and tempers quickly fray. It's then that a director really earns his, or her, money. Happily for him, Alan was ably supported by Harriet, who ensured that the remaining skeletons were dug to exemplary standards. Jake Williamson did his best to keep spirits up, too, but even he began to flag towards the end of the week, when redundancy was staring him in the face.

On Monday, Harriet had received a letter telling her that she would be interviewed for a full college fellowship at St Luke's the following Saturday morning. The Board of Fellows considered her publication record to be 'of the highest standard' and the interview would be an assessment of her 'communication skills in a face-to-face student situation'. Rubbishy jargon was even starting to penetrate the hallowed halls of Cambridge collegiate life. Alan agreed she should return to college on Friday evening. It would mean she would miss the end-of-dig party, but they both knew that wasn't likely to be a joyous occasion. In reality, Alan would far rather have joined her in college.

* * *

Sometime before John's death, Candice had invited the archaeologists to the farmhouse for a glass of wine and some nibbles. It was her way of saying thank you for all they had done. In the past, they would have had a proper meal, but now that the farm shop and restaurant had closed down it was nibbles or nothing.

As he walked up the drive, Alan could already detect signs of neglect. The grass hadn't been cut and rubbish, which had escaped from the wheelie bin a couple of days ago, still lay on the ground. He bent down and looked at it more closely. A cheap take-away hamburger bag proclaimed: 'I'm chewin' it!' Who was eating such stuff? he thought. Surely not Candice? He prodded it with his foot but decided not to pick it up.

Once inside the farmhouse, Alan could hear voices in the

kitchen. He went through and was offered one of the cold beers they had bought earlier in the village shop by Jake, who said nothing. But his look spoke volumes. Alan joined the small group standing around the kitchen table. He was deeply shocked by Candice's appearance. She appeared to have lost a couple of stone and her face had aged ten years. There were big bags under her eyes and for the first time he could see she had started to dye her hair. She was smoking, too, and had an e-cigarette on the go throughout the 45 minutes they were with her. She also drank a lot, but didn't seem to get any pleasure from it.

Her parting remark, as they bid her goodnight at the front door, typified the evening so far.

'Do you realise, today's Friday the thirteenth? They say it's lucky for some, don't they?'

And with that she closed the door.

Although Alan and Jake had bought some beers and a few bottles of wine, nobody felt much like drinking them. Somehow the grimy interior of the last remaining Portakabin didn't seem a particularly enticing venue, either. So they headed down to the pub. That was the place to escape Candice's haunted face and to drown their sorrows.

* * *

And it was. As ever, Davey Hibbs was on fine form, but even he didn't attempt to mimic Candice. Some things are too cruel, and she was still quite well-liked in the village. So they drank lots of Slodger. Alan knew that the landlord would turf them all out around one in the morning.

At eleven o'clock Harriet texted him. *How's things going?*

He replied, *In the pub.*

*Xoxox missing you. Sleep well. See you tomorrow afternoon. Keep your fingers crossed 4 me. Xoxox*

*I will. xoxoxox.*

Not exactly original. But it showed he cared – which he did. In fact, he suddenly realised, he wasn't enjoying himself. Not even slightly. He'd much rather be with Harriet in St Luke's. The evening was turning out to be a real bummer – as he'd have said in his student days.

After ten more minutes he made his apologies and left. Said he felt queasy – that the beer wasn't agreeing with him.

He started to head towards home, but stopped. He couldn't get Candice off his mind. And it wasn't just that she was looking so terrible. There was something else. But he couldn't think clearly. Old Slodger was having an effect. Then it came to him: her final, pathetic statement about Friday the 13th. And it wasn't the date, so much as the day. Friday. That was when John had died: midnight on Good Friday. He glanced down at his watch: it was almost 11.30. He might just make it.

He retraced his steps back towards the pub, then turned left and climbed the stile leading onto the diagonal footpath through the meadows down to the mill pool – just as he had recently done with Harriet. As he walked, it started to rain. Soon it got much heavier. He wasn't wearing a jacket. But what the hell, a little rain never hurt anyone. He lowered his head and strode as fast as he could, but didn't dare break into a run. He'd probably stumble and fall. Slodger was known to have strange effects on your legs.

He arrived in the unlit mill car park and spotted it immediately. It was the only vehicle there: Candice's distinctive blue Ford Ka. He clambered up the wet, slippery steps of the wooden bridge. He knew exactly where she would be. The rain stopped and the moon came out from behind a cloud. He could see her 50 yards ahead of him. She was clipping on a knapsack. He called out her name and started to run. But it was too late. She glanced back. And jumped.

Then the clouds returned, the moonlight vanished, and the rain resumed.

He knew there was nothing he could do. He wasn't a very strong swimmer and the Mill Cut was in spate. And besides, he couldn't judge from down the towpath precisely where she'd jumped in. And he also knew it was very deep there. Yes, he thought, and she knew that – only too well.

He stared at the flowing water, hoping that somehow she'd float to the surface. But of course she didn't. Eventually he phoned Lane. There was nothing else to do.

It was so sad: she didn't even wave goodbye.

# Twenty-Six

Lane accompanied Alan to the police station to take a witness statement about Candice's suicide. As they headed towards Ely through the low mists of morning, Lane told Alan that Sebastian had, at last, confessed to Stan's killing.

'He gave him whisky, didn't he?'

'Yes,' Lane replied. 'Just upstream of the mill.'

That was all Alan needed to know. They drove in silence while Alan thought about his friend's sad end. And it was so sad. He felt numb and wanted desperately to return home to Harriet. But it would have to wait.

The rush-hour traffic was building up, and there were interminable road works on the Downham Road, just outside town, but eventually they arrived at the police station. While they were waiting for Alan's statement to be typed up they went to the canteen for a cup of coffee from the machine. It was hot and wet, and that was all Alan wanted at this point. Lane asked him if he'd phoned Harriet yet, and Alan explained that she had a very important interview that day and he didn't want to upset her. Then he had a thought.

'Richard, you've got an office here, haven't you?'

'Yes?' He answered, uncertain. He couldn't think what might be coming next.

'And a computer linked to the Internet?'

'Of course.'

'Well, I want to go on one of those property search websites – the ones that give you the sales history of particular houses?'

'OK. Come with me.'

His office was on the second floor, down the end of a grey-carpeted, windowless corridor, which vaguely reminded Alan of his visit to Blackfen Prison, eight days ago. They entered the room. Lane sat down behind the desk and logged on. He chose a website he was familiar with from his own search for the house he now owned in Whittlesey.

'And what's the address?'

'Isle Farm, Fursey.'

Lane looked at him, puzzled. But he typed it in. The website came back with a post code. It looked plausible.

'Let's go with that, Richard.' Alan was looking at the screen over his shoulder. 'Now press Enter.'

Immediately the sales history for Isle Farm flashed up. The first recorded transaction was in October 2003, when the farm initially came on the market for £2,590,000. But it failed to sell. Thereafter the vendors had leased it to various clients for steadily increasing sums, first in 2004, next in 2005, and finally in 2007. Then the screen suddenly flashed up: '*This Property is Again Available for Lease! Offers in the region of £2,150 a month.*'

Blimey, Alan thought, that's steep, even for the Cambridge area.

Alan explained to Lane that Sebastian had always wanted to restore Isle Farm to the family. It had superb-quality land. He described how Sebastian had confided to him that he wanted, above everything else in life, to be a farmer. He would happily sell Fursey Hall and all the land he currently controlled just to buy Isle Farm. Alan reckoned that his first attempt to buy it was back in late 2003, when it originally came on the market. He couldn't prove it, but he probably approached Hansworth, the banker, for a loan. Hansworth might well have agreed, but he was conscientious and would have done a due diligence check, which presumably revealed that he wasn't credit-worthy. But meanwhile he'd raised Sebastian's hopes, which were then bitterly smashed. And that crushing disappointment was the motive that drove him to have the row on the riverbank – which led to his death.

Lane was very impressed. And he had to agree: it all made perfect sense.

'I'll see how he reacts.'

'And can you offer him any sweetener, like, say a reduced sentence?'

'I doubt it,' Lane replied, slowly. 'Not with three deaths to account for. But I'll probably suggest to him that a plea of guilty usually leads to a shorter sentence. That way we might get a full confession.'

'And will that reduce his sentence?'

'What, after three pleas of guilty to murder? I very much doubt it. No, I don't think he'll ever be seen outside a jail again. He'll get a whole-life sentence, without any doubt. As my old sergeant used to say, "They'll lock him up and throw away the key."'

* * *

A week later, Alan got a phone call from Richard Lane. Mary's father was now out of hospital and back at home, being looked after by his very capable wife – herself an ex-nurse. But Mary was exhausted, physically and emotionally. So Lane had hired a fully equipped narrowboat for a gentle four-day cruise along the navigable rivers of the central Fens. They planned to spend the following weekend travelling along the Old River Nene and had booked moorings on the western approaches to March. The place he had in mind was handy for a fine old pub that kept an excellent pint of Slodger. And there was a superb fish and chip shop about 50 yards in the other direction.

'Sounds like heaven on earth. Is that an invitation?'

It was. He and Harriet were invited for lunch the following Sunday at noon.

It was a gorgeous early summer's day. The sunlight was fresh, the air was clean and the diseased chestnut trees still had clean green leaves. Alan had brought an enamel bucket that held a gallon, but was more safely filled with six pints, of foaming Slodger. Meanwhile Lane bought four portions of cod and chips, plus mushy peas, which they enjoyed on the stern deck and wheelhouse.

After five minutes of concentrated batter-crunching, Alan looked up from the food.

'Richard, I'm fairly convinced that Candice did in fact push John over. I don't think it was an accident at all: most likely a stupid impulse, born of frustration.'

But it was the event itself that was worrying him now. In his mind he was there, in the chill of the evening, not like was now, in the cramped boat, but watching while a wife helped her husband into a rucksack filled with rocks.

He sighed heavily. 'The thing is, John was half-starved and feeling groggy. I don't suppose for one moment he was thinking clearly. And somebody must have helped him into that heavy rucksack. As soon as he had put it on, Candice must have realised he was dangerously top-heavy. Any normal person would have taken it off him. But she didn't. Instead she lowered him into the canoe and shoved him out into the stream. But I'm also certain that she soon regretted it bitterly and never forgave herself for what she'd done. That's why she went downhill so fast.'

Lane was still chewing, but he nodded. Eventually he wiped his mouth with the back of his hand.

'I agree, Alan. It's all very odd. And the boat was moored in such a deep spot. Was that intentional? I mean, she could have chosen a proper mooring with a floating wooden stage, like we've got here. There was one just a few yards away. But no, instead she secured the boat to two willows.'

'Yes, I noticed that. There was also a long pole nearby – the boat-people use it as a washing line support in winter. But it was also very convenient, if you wanted to test the depth of the water.'

'Or maybe push somebody back under, should they float to the surface,' Lane added grimly.

Harriet looked up. 'Are you sure about that?' she asked. 'Sounds a bit of a wild accusation, don't you think? A pole is just that: a pole. It doesn't have to be used as a weapon, as you suggest.'

'No, you're probably right,' Lane agreed. 'But it was odd the way she hadn't used the proper moorings. She must have known who owned them. And I doubt if they'd have charged much, if anything, at that time of year. I think Alan's right: the water at the moorings is much shallower. He might even have been able to stand up.'

They continued eating for a few minutes, while a couple of

afternoon strollers passed by along the towpath. For a moment, Alan wondered if they had any idea that the relaxed group of people eating fish and chips were discussing something as dark as a man's death and a woman's suicide. Then a thought struck him. He waited till the walkers were out of earshot.

'But what lay behind it all, Richard?' He was frowning: they were still missing something; there must have been more to it. 'What else do we know about John's life?'

Alan remembered a conversation with Candice, shortly before they began the car park excavation. John's consultancy was looking after the affairs of two large betting franchises. So he kept in touch with that world, even after he had supposedly given up gambling himself. Mary had been listening closely. Candice and John had long fascinated her.

'So is personal betting quite common behind the scenes in the gambling world?' she asked.

'Yes,' her husband replied. 'But as with drinking in the pub sector, people learn to keep it under control. Or else they get out, which is what John Cripps did. He then used the experience he had gained in the racing world to move into the management of visitor attractions. It wasn't a big step.' He munched on a chip. 'Anyhow, at some point he met up with Blake Lonsdale.'

'The man behind White Delphs,' Alan added for Mary's benefit.

She smiled at him in thanks.

'That's right,' Lane continued. 'He and John formed the HPM partnership in 1990. And they've been remarkably successful.'

'Yes,' Alan added, 'Jake told me that they were never short of funds at White Delphs, and my brief experience at Fursey showed them to be efficient. Money was always there if you needed it. I certainly had no complaints.'

'Well that doesn't surprise me,' Lane resumed the story. 'My sources at the Met now reckon their Water World historical theme park near Hackney Marshes is largely used to launder gambling money acquired through a number of shady partners abroad. They're watching them closely.'

'Which might explain how and why John and Blake got together in the first place,' Alan suggested.

Harriet hadn't said much so far. Alan got the impression she was having trouble coping with all the changes around her. She liked stability, even though right now it was in short supply. But like Mary, she had been fascinated by John and Candice – and one question still puzzled her.

'So presumably, John's conversion to evangelical religion had something to do with his gambling?'

'Yes, it did,' Lane replied. 'In fact, I was able to check on that myself. His conversion happened September 1985 when an American evangelist visited Ely. You might remember, he pitched a circus-style big-top on the outskirts of town and attracted thousands of people to his gatherings. I understand they were very emotional affairs. But the rejection of drink and gambling were a big part of his mission. And in John's case, the cure seemed to have worked. But then last year rumours began to spread that he had returned to his old habits.'

'But he didn't drop the religion?' Alan asked.

'No, he didn't. If anything, he became more mainstream – and hence his friendship with the Fen dean. And I don't think that was unusual: I can think of many alcoholics who are devout Christians.'

Harriet stood up and stretched. She had eaten too much.

'So do you think, Richard,' she asked, 'that Candice was aware John had resumed gambling?'

'Yes. I don't see how he could have hidden it from her. She was bound to have found out sooner or later, because he was in it in a big way – or that's what local bookies have been telling us.'

'So his gambling,' Mary said quietly, 'would have given her a reason for pushing him overboard. How very sad.'

It was a sorry tale. They were all silent for a moment.

'And what did she do then?' Alan asked.

Nobody made any suggestions. So he answered his own question. 'I think she made eyes at Peter Flower.'

Harriet was pouring herself a small beer. 'Oh yes,' she said under her breath. 'She certainly did that.'

'And I think it makes sense,' Alan continued. 'I mean, look at it this way: he was now bursar of a famous Cambridge college. He had strong links with a well-established television series and he wasn't a habitual gambler. And make no mistake, she was attractive, too – for her age.'

Alan realised that hadn't been the most tactful thing he could have said – and Harriet shot him a reproving look. He decided to press on, to cover his confusion.

'It would also have made business sense for Peter to have closer relations with the Cripps family, given the college's large land holdings in the area. So all in all, I don't understand why Flower didn't respond.'

'But Alan,' Harriet broke in, 'we don't know for a fact that Flower didn't respond, do we?'

'I suppose not.' Alan was frowning.

'He was – is – a very successful man,' Harriet resumed, 'and he continued to act very responsibly after things had collapsed at Fursey, You've said so yourself, Alan.'

'Well, it's true, he did.'

'So don't you think,' Harriet continued, 'that Flower could have acted kindly to her, as everything had gone so horribly wrong. He wasn't the sort of person who'd kick someone when they were already down.' She paused, then looked up. 'And I know you've good reasons not to like him, but he's quite well-liked in college. He wouldn't have been made Bursar, otherwise.'

'So you think she misread Flower's kindness to her?' Lane asked. 'Thought he was making a pass at her?'

'Well, why not?' Harriet replied. 'Put yourself in her position: she was desperate. Her husband was an obsessive gambler. The family business was in tatters and then along comes this attractive and highly successful, intelligent man – who was being kind and considerate to her. I can see how it could have happened. I honestly can.'

'And you think that was strong enough motive to kill her husband?' Lane asked.

'Added to everything else – the gambling and so on – yes, I think it was.'

'But then the truth dawned?' Alan asked, more to himself than anyone else.

'Yes,' Lane replied, 'and very quickly, too. But by then she could see there was only one way out.'

Then Alan muttered, almost under his breath: 'And I saw her take it, poor woman.'

Harriet wiped her eyes.

# Epilogue

They drove back to Fursey the pretty route to avoid Sunday drivers on the main roads. Alan knew the road well from when he had worked on a follow-up survey of fen dykes in the landscapes south and east of Peterborough in the late 1990s. It was during the original survey of the early 1980s that the now famous site of Flag Fen had been discovered. Alan frowned. He'd recently been helping Steve Grant establish closer links with them, and it had all been looking very promising. Now everything had been cancelled. What a waste.

As they approached Fursey from the west, they could just see the ruined tower of the abbey church protruding above the high, and dead straight, banks of the Padnal Delph. The road swung round a right-angled corner by a row of a dozen gnarled and pollarded willows. Beyond was a sign: *Private Road to Padnal Delph IDB Pumping Station.* Alan indicated left. Harriet looked at him, surprised.

'You're turning off?'

He smiled, and placed a hand reassuringly on her knee. 'Wait and see.'

Beyond the pumping station, where Alan had met the chief engineer a few weeks ago, the road suddenly deteriorated and the Fourtrak pitched its way through ridges and flooded pot holes. Then the land around rose perceptibly and suddenly they were driving past ash trees and shrubs. The road surface had improved, too. They were now on the Isle. On their right another sign read: *Isle Farm, 300 Yards Ahead* and just beyond was a 'For Let' notice on behalf of a large local estate agent.

They drew to a halt in front of a substantial, wisteria-clad Italianate farmhouse, probably built around 1850.

Harriet turned to Alan. 'Are you mad, Alan, we couldn't possibly afford such a place. It must cost thousands a month.'

'I know,' he replied. 'I just wanted to see the place that had motivated a man to kill. It must be pretty special.'

Lane knew the nice lady at the estate agents and had persuaded her that Alan could be trusted to look around on his own. When she gave him the keys she included a bit of paper with the burglar alarm code. Alan opened the back door and turned it off. From there they passed through to the large kitchen, equipped, of course, with a deep-red four-oven Aga. There was a fashionable island worktop in the centre of the room on which Alan placed a shopping bag.

'Wow,' Harriet's face was alight. 'What a fabulous kitchen!'

They explored the house from top to bottom, including the four bedrooms, three fitted with en-suite showers or bathrooms. But compared with Fursey Hall it was quite a modest house, really. The views from the ground floor were limited to the south-west by the banks of the Delph, but from upstairs they were absolutely superb, with the ruins of Fursey Abbey in the middle distance, and further away, but nonetheless dominating everything, the vast mass of Ely Cathedral and its single slender tower. Although they both knew it was an illusion, the view seemed to change from every window.

He found they were holding hands in the master bedroom, standing in front of the large Venetian window.

'Do you know what,' Alan said softly. 'That really is a view to die for.'

It wasn't meant to be humorous and she didn't take it as such. There were tears in her eyes as she said, 'How sad. How very, very sad.'

* * *

Back in the kitchen, Alan lifted a flask from the shopping bag and poured coffee into their insulated site mugs: hers in pink shiny plastic and his Nikon lens lookalike.

Harriet smiled as she asked, 'Do you like that mug?'

'Yes. It's my favourite. I take it everywhere. And I've got the lens it's modelled on.'

'Yes, I know you do.'

Her eyes were staring deep into his.

It was like an electric shock. How could he have been so stupid? The mug had arrived last Christmas by post. Anonymously. He had split up with Harriet acrimoniously a year earlier. It had never occurred to him that *she* had sent it.

He put the mug down, took her in his arms and held her for what seemed like a very long time. Eventually they drew apart.

'Isn't the world strange, Alan. This place has led to the death of three people, yet the man who killed them is still alive and the woman who may have helped her gambling husband to die, is no longer with us. Is that justice?'

Alan took a long sip from his mug of surprisingly warm coffee. He looked out of the window, where a red sun was approaching the top of the Delph bank. He thought for some time.

'I'd have agreed with you a few days ago, Harry, but I'm

not so sure now. I don't see how she could ever have lived with herself, because I'm convinced that deep down she loved John. She must have done, to have put up with his bad habits for so long. Her suicide laid that ghost to rest.'

He paused to screw the lid on his emptied mug. His gaze was on the slowly fading light that bathed the tall lime trees beyond the orchard, but his mind was in the exposed, wet fields around Fursey.

'But Sebastian,' he continued slowly, 'will never achieve any sort of peace or resolution. Every day of his life will be torture. And he will be his own tormentor – and believe me, they're the worst. They know all your fears and weaknesses and how to exploit them in the cruellest ways imaginable.'

He shuddered. It was a horrible thought.

They shut the back door. Harriet was wiping her eyes. Alan was grim-faced. Together they had glimpsed heaven and hell. And all in one Fenland farmhouse.

# Acknowledgements

It's an open secret that I have always rather disliked what the Roman Empire stood for. Maybe this was a way of rationalising my horror at the complexity of the period's archaeology and history. And of all its many aspects, the army in the province of Britannia is surely the most difficult, especially to the uninitiated. So I have relied heavily on my old friend Guy de la Bédoyère's very reader-friendly introduction: *Eagles Over Britannia: The Roman Army in Britain* (Tempus Books, Stroud, 2001).

Very special thanks are due to two other leading experts in their fields:

Professor Simon James of Leicester University, who has advised me on matters pertaining to cohorts *equites*, and other facets of Roman Britain, with his characteristic good humour, wit and clarity. I am led to believe that it was when he was one of Simon's undergraduate students that Alan learnt the phrase the 'Bloomsbury Lubyanka'.

The other expert is, of course, somebody no crime writer can ever do without: an authority who knows and understands forensics at a very profound level. And here I have the great pleasure to acknowledge Dr Chris J. Rogers of Glyndwr University, Wrexham. I suspect it's only a rumour, but Chris might have been an external advisor to the forensic archaeology course at Saltaire, which Alan attended in the late '90s.

As with *The Lifers' Club* before it, the writing and production of this book would have been impossible without the constant advice, help and encouragement of my editor, Elizabeth Garner. The detailed work of copyediting was done by Gillian Holmes, with great care and consideration. She was assisted by Annabel Wright and Molly Powell. The staff at Unbound have been their normal, helpful selves and I owe a huge debt of gratitude to Justin Pollard who first suggested that I should try crowdfunding. It has been hard work, but the greatest fun.

# Supporters

Unbound is a new kind of publishing house. Our books are funded directly by readers. This was a very popular idea during the late eighteenth and early nineteenth centuries. Now we have revived it for the internet age. It allows authors to write the books they really want to write and readers to support the books they would most like to see published.

The names listed below are of readers who have pledged their support and made this book happen. If you'd like to join them, visit www.unbound.com.

Roy Ackerman
Rob Adams
Carol Ainley
Patrick Alexander
Richard Alexander
Leigh Allen
Mark Allen
Nyree Ambarchian
Rita Arafa
Rita Arafa
Sandra Armor
Roberta Ashton
Tim Atkinson
Graeme Attwood
Alan Austin
Geoff Bailey
Lyn Baines
Aidan Baker
Rita Baker
Nick Balaam
Peter Baldwin
Mel Bale
Jason Ballinger
Michael Bamforth
Colin Barks
Tara Barnacle
Mark Barnes
Richard Barnwell
Joan Barrett
Huw Barton
Kaye Batchelor
Richard Bavin
Mary & Ian Baxter
Steve Baxter
Alex Bayliss
Josh Beadon
James Beatty
Bob Beaupré
Anne Beer
Martin Bell
Charles Bennett
Cindy & James Bennett
Stephen Benson
Catherine Berger
Tessa Beukelaar - van Gulik
Robert and Jill Bewley
Frank Blair
Roger Bland
Queen-Ruby Blessing
Mathias Blobel
Gill Bolton
Kate Boulton
Martijn Bouterse
Corrina Bower
Roger Braithwaite
Janey Brant-Beswick
Richard W H Bray
Mark Brennand
Andrew Brewster
Jonathan Bridgland
M. Bridgman
Michael Bridgman
Mick Bridgman
Chris Briggs
David Britchfield
Mason Broadwell
Sharon Brown
Fiona Bruce
Lesley Bruce
Emma Brunning
PJ Bryant
Richard Bunting
Betty Burgess
Gilbert Burleigh
Paul Burman
Jenni Butterworth
Alan Cadbury
Grahame Cadbury
Ian Campbell
Dawn Cansfield
Rachel Carey
John Carr
Spencer Carter
David Catley
Claire Charles
Charles and Katie

John Cherry
Sue Christensen
Karen Christley
Lauren Churchill
Meagan Cihlar
Helen Clark
Colin Clarke
Gloria Clarke
Philip Clarke
Ian Clarkson
Robin Claxton
Leisa Clements
Robert Clements
Guy Clifton
Ivan Clowsley
Jane Cohn
Marion Cole
Robert Cole
Stevyn Colgan
David Collison
Brian Condron
Lesley Cookman
Hilary and Georgia Corrick
Kerrie County
Catherine Cowan
Charlotte Cox
Wendy Crammond
David Cranstone
Mike Craven-Todd
Anthea Crawford
Terry Croft
Bes Croscombe
Simon Paul Crutchley
Paul Cumming
Nicola Curtis
Sue Daniels
Elizabeth Davey
Christopher Davies
Jonathan Davison
Tim Daw
Sue Day
John Dent
Sven Dettmer
Ian Devlin
Dave Dewey
John Dexter
Rissa Dickey
Boyd Dixon
Philip Dixon
Lydia Dockray
Steve Dockray
Jenny Doughty
Peter Dunne
Vivienne Dunstan
Robert Eardley
Frinton Earnshaw
Ann Eason and Jane Meadows
Mark Edmonds
John Edwards
Keith Edwards
Lynn Edwards
Ingrid Eglese
Elizabeth Eisenhauer
Jeannette Elrick
Kerry Ely
Dom Escott
Eton College School Library
Barbara Evans-Rees
Vanessa Farr
Peter Faulkner
Will Fletcher
David Foister
Isa Forde
Clare Fowler
Katharine Francis
Paula J. Francisco
Ian Frank
Peter Franklin & Lucy Ryder
Sarah Freck
Alex Fryer
Simon Fuller
Antonia Galloway
Dan Garner
Kasia Gdaniec
Julie Gibbon
Don Gibson
Jo Gibson
Matthew Giesbrecht
Chris Gingell
Peter Glass
Lisa Gledhill
David Gordon
Denise Gorse
Bebe Granger
Martin Green
Martin Green
Lenore Greensides
Jane Greenwood
Frederick Grounds
Trygve Guntvedt
Kate Haddock
Jim & Jackie Haile
Dorothy Halfhide
Rachael Hall
Teresa Hall
Mandy Halsall
Paul Halstead
Elizabeth Hammett
Christine Hancock
Elspeth Hardie
Phil Harding
Sandra Harling
Luke Harmer
Wendy Harper
Richard Harris
Neil Hart
Jacqueline Hartnett
Colin Haselgrove
Deborah Hastings
Mark Haworth
Iain Hazlewood
Andy Hazzard
Am Heath
Gill Hey
Mike Heyworth
Nicholas Higham
Anne Hill
John Hillam
Catherine Hills
Beth Hiscock
Peter Michael Hobbins
Michael Holdsworth
Michele Holland
Mandy Holloway
Jack Hughes
Sarah Hughes
Alice Hutchinson
James F Hutchinson
Martyn Ingram
Linda Ireson
Sarah Ives
Jordan Jacobs
Edward James
Simon James
Philip Jeffrey
Amanda Lloyd Jennings

Gregory Jennings
The John Peck Society
Colin Johnson
Richard Johnson
Tanya Johnson
Pat Johnston
Rhona Johnstone
Sue Joiner
Colin Jones
Phyl Jones
Tim Lund Jørgensen
Cordelia Karpenko
Leon Kaye
Bekz Kelleher-Walton
Paul Kenton
Dan Kieran
Nicola King
Iain Kitching
John Kjellberg
Julianne Knowles
Susan Knowles
Martin Kurzik
Susan Kyle
Beatrix Labeck
Anne Lamb
Anne Lamb
Tom Lane
Catherine Langham
Lars Larsen
Jane Lawrence
Nick Lawson
Jimmy Leach
Alex Lee
Eugene Lefeuvre
Helene Levenson
Carenza Lewis
Alice Limming
Claire Lindsay-McGrath
Suzannah Lipscomb
Frances Lynch Llewellyn
Joyce Lomas
Dr. Nick Low
Ann Lowe
Karl Ludvigsen
Sara Lunt
Ian MacInnes
Catherine Makin
Caroline Malone
John Manchip
John Manley
Eileen Marshall
Andrew Martin
Mary Masson
Richard Masters
Nigel Maule
Iain McCulloch
Chris J. McMillan
Peter Melkowski
Stephen Melville
Susan Memmott
Ute Methner
Paul Middleton
Viorel Mihalcea
Mark Miller
Martin Millett
Richard Mills
Jennifer Mirdamadi
David Mitchell
John Mitchinson
Joanna More
Anthony Morgan
Elizabeth Morgan
Mel Morpeth
Jane Morris
Martin Moucheron
Nicky Moxey
Karen-Babette Müller
Carlo Navato
Michael Nevell
Kate Nicholls
Sylvia Pryor Nicol
Martyn Notman
Anders Nyman & Görel Sundström
Julian O'Donovan
Hannah O'Toole
Keith O'Toole
Niamh O'Toole
Rosie O'Toole
Katherine Oakley
Jan Oldham
Marianne Olson
Jennifer Marie Osborne
Christopher Page
Rog Palmer
Edward and Clara Pank
Ian Panter
Rebecca Parr
Nicholas Parsons
Simon Parsons
Sarah Patmore
Lucy Payne
Mike Parker Pearson
Elizabeth Peers
Karl Pesch-Konopka
Eugéne and Carla Pesch-Stassen
Mary Peterson
Catherine Pickersgill
Caroline Pierson
Sally Pointer
Justin Pollard
Eike Wolf Postler
Dominic Powlesland
Zina Preston
Janet Pretty
Dirk Preusterink
Mark Lloyd Price
Roger Pritchard
Zoe Propper
Dorothy Prosser
Cressida Pryor
Jean Pryor
Jo Purvis
Jennie Pyatt
Huan Quayle
Sue Raikes
Kate Ramsell
Andy Randle
Helen Randle
Hans Rasmussen
Rachel Rawlins
Sharon Rea
Colette Reap
S Redlich
Graham Redman
Helen Reid
Val Reid
Ellen Richardson
Jamie Richardson
Henry Richardson and Daughters: E, S & H
Garner Roberts
Doug Robison
Doug Rocks-Macqueen
Angela Roden
Kenn W Roessler
Margaret Rogers
Andrew Rogerson
Deborah Roots

Alice Rose
David Rose
Keith Rose
Sam Ross
Peter Rowley-Conwy
Susan Royce
Zuzu Ruggiero
Susan E Russell
ML Ruwoldt
Sally Ryder
Peter Samaan
Bernie Sammon
Emma Samuel
Ruth Saunders
Carol Sayles
Rob Scaife
Kate Scarratt
Tim Schadla-Hall
Sebastian Schleussner
Suzanne Scott
Pamela Scrayfield
Dick Selwood
Moira Senior
Ruth Seymour, Oregon, USA
Rosie Shannon
Nicola J. Sharp
Nicola J. Sharp
David Shaw
Clare Shepherd
Nicholas Shepherd
Mandy Shuttlewood
Rebecca Sickinger
Eileen Silcocks
Glen Simmers
Lee Sinclair
Andrew Sinclair, Alice, Beth and Helen
Paul Skinner
Pauline Skippins
Alice Smith
Kath & Stuart Marston Smith
Lucy Smith
Nigel Smith
Samantha Smith
Steve Smith
A.M. Solomon
Carole Souter
Richard & Victoria Sowerby
William Sowerby
Martin Spencer-Whitton
Paul Spoerry
Paul Springford
Teresa Squires
Kim Stanford
Lawrence Howard Steel
Jason Stevens
Kathryn Stevenson
Marianne Stewart
Martin Stoermer
Peter Storck
Linda Stormonth
Kerry Swinnerton
Matthew Symonds
Nulani t'Acraya
Jennifer Taylor
Maisie Taylor
Adrian Teal
Gill Tebbutt
Andrew Tees
Robin Thain
Jools Thatcher
Roger Thomas
Brewer Thompson
William Thompson
Paul Tompsett
Katherine Toms
Richard Tracey
Christopher Trent
Caroline Turner
Oliver Twinch
Clive Upton
Louis van Dompselaar
Mark Vent
Kellie Vernon
Martijn Verschoor
Matthew Vincent
Manon Vraets
Laurence Vulliamy
Bill Wadsworth
Erica Wagner
Geoffrey Wainwright
Stephen Wainwright
Philip Walker
Sue Walker
Teddy Walker
Joerg Walther
Annie Warwick
Marion Washbrook
Peter Wass
Robert Waterhouse
Stan C Waterman
Caroline Watson
Chloe Watson
Frauke Watson
Harriet Webb
Chris Webster
Dee Weightman
Lorraine Welch
Nicola Wellband
Ian Wells
James West
Katy Whitaker
Richard Whitaker
Hazel Whitefoot
Steve Whitehead
David Whitehouse
Lindsay Whitehurst
Caroline Wickham-Jones
Fern Wilcox
Richard Wilde
Ian J. Williams
Derek Williamson
Justin Williamson
Tony Wilmott
Denise Wilton
Thom Winterburn
Gretchen Woelfle
Hayley Wojcikowski
Peter Wood
Emily Woodburn
Stephen Woods
Daniel Worsley
Richard Wray
Ian Wright
Rachel Wright
Linda Youdelis
Katharine Younger